AMERICAN TRIANGLE

An Historical Novel

NELDA HIRSH

Also by Nelda Hirsh

JULIA DU VAL

A BOHEMIAN LIFE: M. EVELYN McCORMICK
(1862-1948) AMERICAN IMPRESSIONIST

THE ROYAL HUGUENOT
HENRY OF NAVARRE 1553-1610

AMERICAN TRIANGLE

NELDA HIRSH

PUBLISHED BY GREEN ROCK BOOKS
270 Green Rock Drive
Boulder, CO 80302

Visit our website: www.greenrockbooks.us

Printed in U.S.A.
First edition, 2018

Green Rock Books / Boulder, Colorado

Designed by Nick Pirog

Cover art: *Monticello, home of Thomas Jefferson*
© Joe Sohm

For Anna, Joshua, Henry, & Junot,
who, I hope, will be mindful of the
brilliant words of Thomas Jefferson

CONTENTS

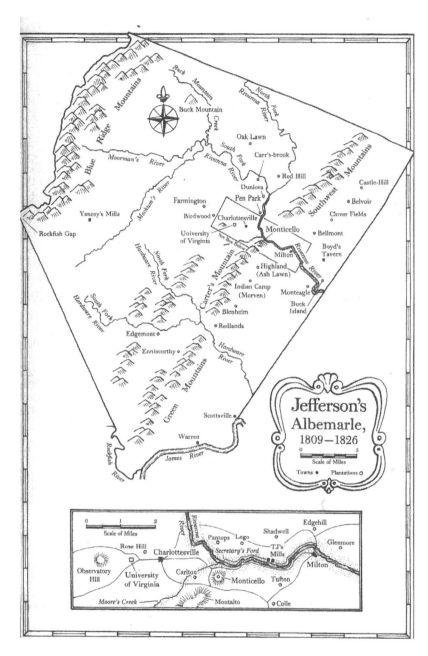

The Papers of Thomas Jefferson, Retirement Series, ed. Looney,
J. Jefferson, Volumes 1-3, Princeton University Press, 2014

Jefferson/Hemings Family Tree

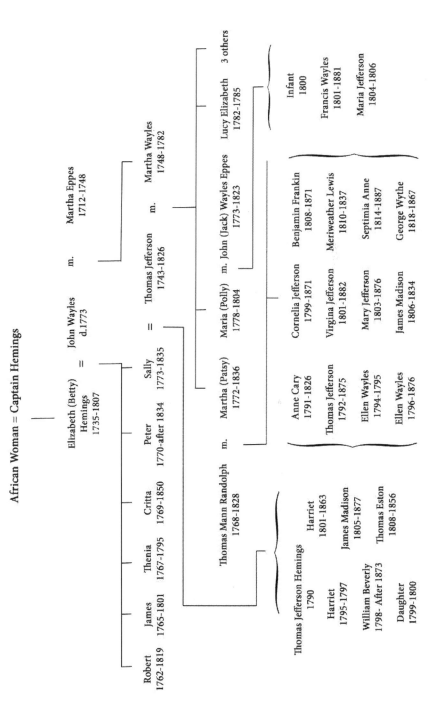

MONTICELLO, VIRGINIA

WIDOWER

1782

Richmond, Sep: 20. 1782.

Mrs Jefferson has at last shaken off her tormenting pains by yielding to them, and has left our friend inconsolable. I ever thought him to rank domestic happiness in the first class of the chief good; but I scarcely supposed, that his grief would be so violent, as to justify the circulating report, of his swooning away, whenever he sees his children.

Extract from Edmund Randolph letter to James Madison, RC
(<u>DLC</u>: James Madison Papers).

Martha "Patsy" Jefferson

Miniature portrait of Thomas Jefferson's daughter Martha at the age of 17 by Joseph Boze. An inscription on paper mounted under glass on the reverse reads: "Mlle Martha Jefferson fille de Monsieur Thomas Jefferson Ministre Americain à Paris MDCCLXXXIX." One historian theorizes it was made as a gift for some French friends. Courtesy, Jefferson Foundation.

PATSY

1782-1783

PATSY REGARDED HER FATHER with growing alarm. His head rested on his arms as he bent over his desk and his shoulders shook. His sobs were muffled in his jacket sleeves, but he did not attempt to hide his overwhelming grief from his daughter, seated on the floor behind him.

At first he would not even leave his room and had ignored her when she knocked upon his door. Now, at least, he would occasionally move to his study and allow her to join him. She rose from the carpet, where she had remained most of the morning, hoping her presence might allay his sadness. Her father's collapse frightened her even more than the death of her mother. How could a man who, in her eyes, stood as tall and strong as the red cedars that grew in Albemarle County, collapse so entirely? Patsy had watched her father help nurse his weak wife and then witnessed his pacing in his room for three weeks after Patty succumbed to her illness. So far, Patsy had tried, to no avail, to coax him out into Virginia's golden September sunshine.

Moving closer to her father's inconsolable figure, Patsy placed her small hand on the back of his head. Her reddish hair and hazel eyes echoed his, and indeed, many remarked on her resemblance to him. Thomas raised his thin, stricken face to her and placed his hand on her cheek before pulling her into an embrace. She needed comfort too and clung to him, trying not to cry again.

"Come, Papa." Patsy took his hand to pull him out of the chair, through the French doors, and onto a walkway leading away from the house. He allowed her to guide him further into the garden and held her hand tightly in his long fingers, following her lead like a blind man. Normally, she knew he smiled with pleasure over the brilliant fall foliage, but today he appeared unaware of the world around him. How could she make him see again?

Patsy had overheard Betty tell one of the other servants that Thomas Jefferson had sworn to his wife he would never wed again. Having witnessed these words at her mother's bedside too, she thought she understood why. She recalled hearing her mother say several times before her death, "Thomas, I was raised by a stepmother, and I don't ever want this fate to befall my own children." At the time Patsy was always glad, for she thought this indicated how much her mother loved them. Patty had even once told her that she hadn't known her mother, and her stepmothers had been unkind.

Patsy always believed what Betty said because Betty Hemings had special status among the slaves at Monticello. And Patsy had figured out the "why" for that also. The first clue was that the Hemingses were called servants instead of slaves. Then she heard the gossip at the big house that Betty had been the mistress of Patsy's own grandfather, John Wayles. When Wayles died in 1773, shortly after Patsy's birth, he had bequeathed his slaves, along with other properties, to his daughter Patty, Patsy's mother. Betty had borne six children with Wayles — Robert, James, Thenia, Critta, Peter, and Sally — who all now lived and served the Jeffersons at Monticello. Betty Hemings and Patty Jefferson had been pregnant at the same time with Sally and Patsy, and Patsy thought of Sally as her best friend. Sally's older sister, Critta, was asked quite frequently since Patty's death to help with Patsy and her sister Polly, and so often, it was two Jeffersons and two Hemingses playing together at the mansion, with Critta as the nominal babysitter.

"Perhaps we can ride tomorrow morning," Patsy hopefully suggested to her father. "I think the horses need exercise," she added to bolster her argument. She had often heard him say this.

"Perhaps, my dearest," he agreed. "But only if you promise me you will let me alert the doctor for a visit. I want to have you and your sister inoculated against smallpox. I cannot risk having another member of my family fall ill." He had been inoculated in 1766 in Philadelphia, having always kept his ear to the ground about the latest development in medicine.

"Of course, Papa," she consented readily, overjoyed that perhaps she had finally untethered him from his paralyzing melancholy.

Patsy would be ten in just a few weeks and was a fine rider for her age. She was determined not to allow her youth to get in the way of watching over her father in his demented state. Though he often headed for the least frequented roads, or through the woods, she stuck with him. She was his loyal companion and a solitary witness to many an outburst of grief. She no longer had a mother to forbid her from these dangerous outings, and in any event, she considered it her duty. She did not think it good for him to ride past her mother's tombstone every day, but he did and would stand there for some time.

Nay if even in the House of Hades the Dead
Forget their Dead, Yet will I Even There
Be Mindful of my Dear Comrade

To the Memory of Martha Jefferson
Daughter of John Wayles;
Born October 19th, 1748, O.S.
Intermarried with Thomas Jefferson January 1st, 1772
—Torn From Him By Death September 6th, 1782
This Monument of His Love Is Inscribed.

Patsy basked in her father's company as morning horseback rides with him became the daily schedule all through October. He talked to her more like an adult than a child, and she strove to live up to his expectations. She ardently wanted him to be proud of her, and her natural curiosity kept her locked on all he had to tell her.

Patsy missed her mother — in fact, she was shocked every day to see the empty space at the family table. Patty Jefferson had been graceful and ladylike as well as an accomplished musician, and Patsy also had admired her skills as a housekeeper, which made Monticello buzz with industry and contentment. Yet, Patsy thought, if she'd lost her father instead of her mother, she wouldn't be able to stand it. She had grown accustomed to his being away for long periods — for instance when he went to Philadelphia to attend the Continental Congress sessions — but now she became agitated if he left the plantation for one minute.

She didn't tell anyone, but one unhappy contretemps with her mother kept returning to her mind, as it had ever since it happened. Patsy recalled how her mother had chastised her for some misbehavior — she honestly wasn't sure now what she had done wrong. Perhaps it was during one of their sewing lessons. The part that stung was that later, whenever Patty was displeased with her, she would remind her daughter of this unhappy, fault-worthy incident. Patsy always felt humiliated at the painful reminder. But then one day, her father rose to her defense and said to his wife, "My dear, a fault in so young a child once punished should be forgotten." He had championed HER. How grateful she still was for his protection.

How she loved these times with her Papa! He would explain to her about things he thought she might need to know one day about running the plantation — scientific farming schemes and how to keep track of the expenses and income. She found it all fascinating and her young mind soaked it up. She wished these happy times could go on forever. When she wasn't with her Papa, she would mostly play with Sally and both girls would look to Betty for mothering. She now remembered how Sally would turn to Patty when Betty was too busy working. They both had been lucky to have two mothers, she thought.

In November it was time for the dreaded smallpox inoculations, and Dr. Gilmer arrived at Monticello. Jefferson was particularly worried now because of soldiers and escaped slaves returning from the Revolutionary War who carried the infection. He knew from his own experience that there were serious side effects from the treatment, but he believed that was better than the disease. Patsy and her sister were quarantined from the rest of the Monticello population and spent two weeks recuperating — with fever, nausea, vomiting, and even some pustules. Thomas himself did some of the nursing because he knew he was immune to the dreaded illness from his earlier inoculation. And he could see how frightened the girls were during the ordeal.

By the middle of the month, they were well enough for him to feel free to accept the appointment of Minister for the United States at the Revolutionary War peace negotiations in Paris. Before, because of Patty's frailty, he had refused. But this time, about three months after her death, he was free to accept. Indeed, he hoped a change of scenery would help his despairing frame of mind.

Thomas broke the news to Patsy on their first chilly morning ride after the girls' recovery. Patsy understood he needed to be away from home to serve his country and that he took great pride in his contribution by writing the Declaration of Independence in Philadelphia. Indeed, she was proud too. But this seemed like more than she could bear at the moment, and she hung her head to hide her quick tears. Immediately sensing his daughter's distress, Thomas spoke quickly, "No, no, my dear one, you misunderstand. I have made the proper arrangements for Polly and little sister Lucy to stay at Eppington Plantation with your mother's younger sister, Aunt Elizabeth, and Uncle Francis Eppes. Sally will go to Eppington with the girls to help. They all will be well cared for there, but you, my dear girl, will accompany me to Paris."

"Oh, Papa! Papa!" She raised her head and sat up straight in the saddle again. "I will be very good. You will not be sorry." She was special to him after all, and he wanted her with him!

"I'm sure of it, dearest one. We will continue your education together — in *France*." He had read about the extravagant beauty of Paris in his schoolbooks, the symmetry of the design, the gentle river flowing through, and the wide welcoming boulevards. "We will love it there," he assured her.

MONTICELLO, VIRGINIA

FATHER, AND MEMBER,
THE VIRGINIA HOUSE OF BURGESSES

1772-74

The legitimate powers of government extend to such acts only as are injurious to others. But it does me no injury for my neighbor to say there are twenty gods, or no god. It neither picks my pocket nor breaks my leg.

Notes on the State of Virginia
Query XVII, January 1, 1782 to December 31, 1782

Thomas Jefferson

Miniature portrait of Jefferson by John Trumbull; Oil on wood, 1788. The portrait supposedly depicts Jefferson at age 33, but it was painted when he was 45.

Thomas

1772-1774

THOMAS JEFFERSON PACED OFF the acreage at Monticello in the foothills of the Blue Ridge Mountains of Virginia — his six-foot-two, lean, loose frame resembling one of the scarecrows on his property. From afar his gamboling gait and his light red hair, having broken from its tie and blowing wild in the September Virginia breeze, confirmed the image. Originally, the land had been part of Shadwell, his parents' plantation. Thomas had inherited the property and 150 slaves from his father and his father-in-law, and he depended on these people to work his land. This Virginia territory, with its rolling verdant landscape, was in his blood, and he vowed to make it a productive farm and comfortable home. Densely wooded, undulating hills could be viewed from every vantage point of the house and served as a reminder of nature's beauty and bounty.

Awaiting the birth of his first child, Thomas nervously wandered among the oaks, laurels, and lindens crowding the forest and encroaching upon his lawn. He stopped for a moment to breathe in the sweet-smelling honeysuckle overrunning his path. Tightly packed trees became a seamless green carpet across the horizon with an often-changing sky above, and he reverently gazed upon this sight, which always lifted his perspective. He needed that solace now, for Patty had become the most important part of his world. At this tense moment, he recognized his gratitude for the way she could soothe him when his intense nature made him restless, or when his extreme sensitivity brought him low. Looking toward the house, he prayed with all his heart that she and the baby would survive the delivery. So many women did not. He claimed not to be religious but thanked God that Dr. Gilmer, their physician and neighbor, was with her for her first labor.

Thomas had met Patty, née Martha Wayles, only a year earlier while doing legal work for her father, who hailed from Lancaster, England, and who now lived at a plantation called Poplar Forest. Thomas always enjoyed seeing the handsome English furniture John Wayles had imported for his home and Mr. Wayles was a most agreeable companion. But there was a greater attraction at Poplar Forest than the furniture or Wayles's company.

Immediately, all Thomas's former loves had faded in comparison. Patty's blue eyes and auburn hair seized his heart and imagination, and he brought all his energy and talents to wooing her. He found her enchanting. Her gentle nature and emotional maturity beyond her years especially attracted him, and he couldn't look at her beautiful figure without longing to slip his arm around her slim waist. She had married for the first time at age eighteen, borne a son a year later, and then lost both husband and son in the following three years. She had returned to her father's home, to grieve and to heal. Thomas was awed by what she had so bravely endured.

Patty was five and a half years younger than Thomas, but he believed she surpassed him in her abilities to cope with life. He was so carried away by her beauty, he knew he couldn't be rational, but he heartily agreed with a friend who spoke of her good sense and good nature. He lingered long after every meeting with Mr. Wayles and spun away the hours talking with his daughter about literature. She especially enjoyed Defoe's *Moll Flanders,* but they both admitted a love for Shakespeare. Thomas confided to her that he had lost his own father when he was just fourteen, but the worst blow had been the death of his favorite sister Jane a few years prior.

The discovery that they both enjoyed music and books, and their mutual delight at gazing into one another's eyes while seated at the piano, propelled the relationship along at a dizzying pace. He quickly dubbed Martha, "Patty," a name meant just for him to use. She laughed with the delightful musical tones that enchanted him when he proposed. "Of course, my darling, Thomas. You knew I would say yes!" He gladly paid the marriage license fee of forty shillings, and they married on New Year's Day 1772, when he was twenty-eight and she twenty-three.

They had only been married nine months plus twenty-six days, and he already was to be a father. Patty, though she had proven fertile, was not having an easy time with labor, and his agitation wouldn't allow him to remain in the house, listening to her cries. She seemed so fragile, with her petite stature and fair complexion. He stopped to inspect one of the new peach tree varieties and was happy to find a few pieces of fruit still attached for him to take inside to Patty. His dogs yapped at his heels and he leaned down to ruffle the fur at their necks. Enough of his escape to the outdoors — he had better go inside and see how the delivery was proceeding.

As Thomas headed back to his wife's bedside, his friend presented him with a healthy baby girl. He felt weak with relief. Patty looked a bit pale but was smiling with victory. Always emotional, Thomas couldn't suppress tears of joy, gazing down on the infant's face. "Let us call her after you and your mother, my love. She shall be Martha Jefferson, but we should call her Patsy."

"Thank you, dear Thomas. That is exactly what I wished. Do you see how much she resembles you?" Patty asked, drawing the soft blanket back from the baby girl's face.

"No, I hadn't noticed. But that's a shame. I would wish her to look like my beautiful wife."

Patty laughed. "I'm just relieved she's safely here."

Patty failed to produce milk and so the couple called upon one of the housekeeping slaves to nurse the child. With so many young slave mothers on the plantation, it wasn't difficult to find a wet nurse. Patty wanted Ursula, who had borne many children over a twenty-year period, but Ursula sadly admitted she was too old now and hadn't borne a baby that year. Ursula's family received special treatment in the Jefferson household; in fact, he had purchased her husband George so that the family could remain together. The family fondly called them King and Queen, a joke on King George III. Their son Jupiter usually served as Thomas's closest personal servant. Indeed, Jupiter had grown up at the Jeffersons' Shadwell plantation, and he and Thomas had played together as children.

Thomas felt clumsy with the babe and kept passing her off to one of the slave women. He preferred just to stay by Patty's bedside and congratulate her. The cries of the infant sounded like music to him. And Patty was right — the baby did resemble the face that looked back at him in the mirror every morning.

First and foremost, Thomas worshiped Patty, but he was more than pleased at the way Patty brought her housekeeping skills to Monticello, as well as her ability to manage the house slaves. Of course, that was what she had been brought up to do, and she did it so well! He also depended more and more on her social skills to mask his quieter and more reserved manner. In fact it constantly amazed him that she had chosen him to be her husband. Of course, they both loved music and he often accompanied her on the pianoforte with his violin. She teased him about his singing when he walked about or performed any physical task.

Although especially known for his writing and intellect, Thomas liked gadgets, architecture, agriculture, and furniture, and he might be found any day experimenting with artisanal projects as well as working at his desk. He had spent his young years with private tutors at, or near, his parents' Shadwell plantation before being sent to the College of William and Mary in Williamsburg, the capital of the state. Always a serious student, he applied himself to Greek, Latin, literature, and law. At the age of twenty-five, he had been elected to sit in the Virginia legislature, called the House of Burgesses, representing Albemarle County. He had conscientiously built a reputation as a bright young man who could write well, and he tried to hide the fact that he hated public speaking — primarily because he had such a soft, unimposing voice.

Only a few months after Patsy's birth, Patty's father, John Wayles died. He bequeathed to his daughter 11,000 acres from her childhood home, the plantation they called "Forest," and 135 slaves. Among these was Elizabeth (Betty) Hemings, who had been John Wayles's concubine. This inheritance made Thomas and Patty one of the largest landholders and slave owners in the state, where half of the population was Negro.

Betty Hemings had secured a special place in the Wayleses' household, like Ursula with the Jeffersons, and she would continue that position at Monticello under Patty. When John Wayles's wife Martha had died in childbirth and two other wives subsequently passed away, he had turned to the mulatto woman, Betty Hemings, then age twenty-six, for his sexual demands. As his concubine[1], she would bear him six children, who came with her to Monticello after Wayles's death. In the world of Virginia's slave society, Thomas accepted this situation without shock or complaint. Race mixing between planters and their female slaves generally occurred, but was never talked about. The more decent landowners at least attempted to keep slave families together.

In his original design of Monticello, overlooking the majestic vista of the Blue Ridge Mountains, Thomas had purposefully placed the family home on top of the mountain — away from the fields that supplied their sustenance, and away from the slave quarters that housed the labor. This separation helped keep the issue of slavery at some remove, but he always

---

1 At this time, concubine simply meant substitute for a wife and had no derogatory connotation.

intentionally treated those who served in the big house much as family members.

In 1769, during his first year in the House of Burgesses, Thomas had made an effort to legislate permission for the emancipation of slaves by individual landowners. He believed every slave owner should have unilateral authority to free a slave. He strongly felt this would be much better than the present system, which stipulated that only the governor and council of Virginia could decide on requests for emancipation. He'd argued his case, stating: *Everyone comes into the world with a right to his own person using it at his own will . . . This is what is called personal liberty, and is given him by the author of nature, because it is necessary for his own sustenance.* When he lost the case, he didn't worry too much, assuming emancipation would happen eventually.

Despite the blow of the death of her father and the difficulties of childbirth, Thomas was relieved to see Patty regain her strength fairly quickly. Soon she was back to managing the mansion, which continued to be a construction site. She laughed at some of Thomas's outlandish ideas, enjoying her creative husband as she watched him hurry to erect the house of his dreams for his family.

Thomas had leveled and cleared his mountaintop for Monticello in 1768, and the next year his slave crew had begun laying the russet Virginia bricks. He didn't want an ostentatious house and admired the Venetian architect Andrea Palladio. He believed his handsome elegant design with porticos and pediments echoed the Palladian ideal, although the staircase, which was only two feet wide, appeared overly modest to many visitors. He had moved into the first-completed south pavilion in 1770, and as soon as he met the beautiful Martha Wayles, he had rushed to finish the rest of the house.

Knowing her husband enjoyed vibrant conversation, Patty often invited fellow landowners to their home to dine and listen to music. She especially liked entertaining but could also don other hats, being an expert in teaching and supervising the slaves how to make beer and soap. He also marveled at the way she never hesitated to tie back her hair and roll up her sleeves to better direct the process of slaughtering the hogs. But it seemed her primary goal was to make him happy.

The next year brought extreme trials for the Jefferson family. January of 1774 began with an earthquake, the first ever in Virginia's memory. The slaves were horribly frightened, falling on their knees in the fields, beseeching God to save them. What was this terrible trembling of the earth? Would it open up and suck them to its fiery center? Patty was crying with terror, hardly setting a calm example for Betty and the house slaves. Thomas tried to assume an unruffled stance to relieve the growing agitation around him as the earth shook and some of the less-secured, new construction crashed to the ground. But he, too, cried with relief when the noise and tremors ceased. A cataclysm such as this evoked existential fear.

Then spring snow and frost destroyed the Jeffersons' crops — wheat, corn, rye, and tobacco. Much of their fruit was damaged too. The new trees had been like children that Thomas coaxed along, and he found the loss devastating. Yet, the backdrop of the Blue Ridge Mountains of Virginia soothed and cheered his spirits without fail. So, when Patty went into labor again, eighteen months after Patsy's birth, he rushed outdoors to walk and calm himself. He tossed a stick for his new puppy, pacing anxiously along the dormant flowerbeds. He must harness his fears and go inside to find out how the birth was progressing.

Once again Dr. Gilmer placed a baby girl in his arms and the couple agreed to call her Jane, after Thomas's sister and mother. And as before, Patty had trouble with breastfeeding. Ever the reader, Thomas discovered an invention called "breast pipes," made of glass, that were designed to help with the problem of inverted nipples, and purchased them for his wife. He had built their house on a mountain, hoping to dodge all the diseases of the swampy, humid Virginia climate — malaria, typhus, and cholera — but he couldn't avoid the complications of childbirth, the principle problem that plagued his fragile wife.

Soon after baby Jane's arrival, Thomas decided he must leave Patty and the children with the household slaves and return to the House of Burgesses in Williamsburg. Relations with Britain had been deteriorating over the past several years, and a number of serious problems particularly needed attention. Thomas knew many in the Virginia population still felt a strong kinship with their original home country and identified with the king more than with the government of their state.

Thomas entered Patty's charming little sitting room, where she was struggling to nurse baby Jane. Thanks be to God for Ursula's wise presence, he thought. Kneeling down to reach their level, he offered the little girl his finger to grasp. "Patty, my dear, I must leave for Williamsburg tomorrow." She gazed at him in shock and he hurried to explain.

"It will be difficult to bring our countrymen along in standing up to colonial rule. Yet I am becoming more and more angry over the unreasonable demands being placed on the colonies."

"But Thomas," she argued, "Britain needs to raise revenue for its growing empire."

He stood up and began to pace. He always seemed too big for the room. "This may be true, but many of the colonists, including ourselves, carry heavy personal debt." He tried to explain. "On a big plantation, so many mouths to feed and bodies to clothe are proving to be a deep drain on our finances. As time goes on, the presence of British troops, the growing tax burden, and onerous trade regulations, have irritated the entire New World population. Also, I believe we should be the ones to decide about home matters — such as taxation, how to deal with the Indians, and how to legislate western land grants. You must face the facts, dearest — whether from Virginia, Boston, Philadelphia, or Baltimore, the colonials are beginning to think and talk about separation from the mother country."

She stared at him. Her luminous eyes, sometimes blue, sometimes green, depending on the light, and usually kind and bright, now darkened. "Oh, Thomas! What does this mean? What will you do?"

"I want you to understand," he said softly. "I've just received notification that the English Parliament has announced what they call the Boston Port Act. They have closed Boston's port until the city pays London for its losses in the Boston Tea Party last December."

Patty's eyes now widened with alarm as he recounted what was happening in their northern sister city.

"They even claim our people are responsible for the damages to the East India Company. I believe we must stand unequivocally with Massachusetts in resisting this demand. That is what we must discuss in Williamsburg. The word 'revolution' has not yet been uttered, but I fear it is in everyone's mind."

Patty clutched baby Jane closer to her breast. "You can not be serious, Thomas! We are all civilized people, and surely an agreement can be reached."

"I am beginning to have my doubts because the English will not give up on their demands. And we will not pay! We are *not* their servants, and we have our loyalties to our own country now."

Patty heard the intensity of his tone and noted his stubborn stance. He was not a man who gave in easily, she knew, for she had heard him argue philosophical matters with their friends and his colleagues. Seeing her concern, he attempted to console her. He hated leaving but firmly believed he had no choice.

"You will certainly be safe here," he said, cupping his hand upon her cheek. "You have Ursula, Betty, and others to care for you and the children. I will, of course, take Jupiter with me." Jupiter was a formidable, bulky man with a large head, and Thomas believed most people would think twice about assaulting them.

"But when will you be back?" she inquired with a shaky voice. He stood up, towering over her with his tall frame. He always had an erect posture, as straight and strong as one of Monticello's columns.

"That I cannot say, but I doubt it will be before too long."

Jefferson's visit to Williamsburg extended to six weeks, and when he came back, he happily turned his thoughts to cherry picking rather than impending revolution. He gloried in the comforts of Monticello and Patty's warm body next to him at night. In the early mornings, he propped himself on his elbow, delighted to gaze at her soft curls and beloved sweet face.

But only three days after his arrival, harsh reality intervened like a scythe cutting through his wheat field when he met with the landholders of Albemarle County. All agreed they must adopt a resolution calling for a ban on British imports, and they even went so far as to set a date fifteen months hence for an end to exports unless Britain addressed American grievances. The group also scheduled an earlier meeting of the national Continental Congress, to be held in three months' time, on September 5, 1774, in Philadelphia. Events were quickly disintegrating. Thomas hesitated to share with his wife the seriousness of the situation. He wouldn't worry her just yet.

Instead, he was inspired to sit down at his desk and write his first state paper, which he entitled *Of the Rights of British America*. He thought about these issues much of the time, and it helped quiet his mind if he set it down on paper. He wrote to remind King George III:

> *. . . that our ancestors, before their emigration to America, were the free inhabitants of the British dominions in Europe, and possessed a right which nature has given to all men, of departing from the country in which chance, not choice, has placed them . . . That their Saxon ancestors had, under this universal law, in like manner left their native wilds and woods in the North of Europe, had possessed themselves of the island of Britain, then less charged with inhabitants, and had established there that system of laws which has so long been the glory and protection of that country.*

Thomas looked up from his writing to study his wife and children. Little Patsy was just beginning to walk, and she held on to her mother's chair for balance, occasionally poking at her baby sister. His ideas were so clear when putting them on the page, yet the thought of the danger he might be inviting for his family was appalling. But what choice did he have if he were to be true to himself and his country? He continued his theme:

> *It is neither our wish nor our interest to separate from Great Britain. . . . Still less let it be proposed that our properties within our own territories shall be taxed or regulated by any power on earth but our own. The God who gave us life gave us liberty at the same time; the hand of force may destroy, but cannot disjoin them.*

Thomas decided he must deliver the document to Williamsburg himself and rushed to tell Patty what he planned to do. His wife looked too confused to offer any objection as he commanded Jupiter to saddle their horses right away. They had not journeyed far, however, before Thomas was struck with dysentery. He ordered Jupiter to hurry on to the capital with two copies, one for Patrick Henry, a Virginia attorney, who had made a name for himself as an orator, and one for Peyton Randolph, Speaker of the Virginia House of Burgesses. He knew he could depend on Jupiter to accomplish his mission.

Immediately upon receiving it, these men were able to hand-publish the piece to send to all the colonies, to King George III, and to Thomas Paine for dissemination among general audiences in London. Who should present it to the king, Thomas wondered? He would let Peyton Randolph, now president of the Continental Congress, decide that. He was pleased when he heard from Jupiter upon his return that George Washington was calling it, "Mr. Jefferson's Bill of Rights." He was developing a reputation as a fine and persuasive writer, although many found his ideas too radical.

Patty was not so sanguine either and spoke to her husband in some distress, "Thomas, I do believe you should perhaps take a more prudent and less hasty position!" Her cheeks became red as she continued. "I cannot believe you want to lead us toward war. And your fellow citizens might not share your passion. Indeed, you should not make yourself so visible to the British. I am worried for your safety." She looked as if she were going to cry.

It troubled him to see her so agitated, but he said, "I hope and fear they will come to understand that we have no choice."

DELEGATE TO THE CONTINENTAL CONGRESS

PHILADELPHIA

1774-1778

Whenever any form of government becomes destructive of these ends [life, liberty, and the pursuit of happiness] it is the right of the people to alter or abolish it, and to institute new government . . .

Thomas Jefferson, The Declaration of Independence
July 4, 1776

THOMAS

1774-1778

THE FIRST CONTINENTAL CONGRESS of the Thirteen Colonies met during September and October of 1774 in Philadelphia at Carpenters' Hall, with the threat of war looming heavily over the colonies throughout the remainder of the year. Thomas worried if he would have the courage to join the struggle since he had not yet experienced war. He journeyed back and forth between Philadelphia, Williamsburg, and Monticello, finding the challenge of being a statesman and a family man nigh impossible. Patty continued to plead with him to think more about cooperating with the British. But Thomas understood the differences between the countries had only intensified, and a Second Continental Congress was called for the early spring of 1775 to take place again in Philadelphia. At this meeting, the colonies reluctantly agreed that they must openly confront the English forces, and shortly thereafter, on April 19, 1775, American colonists and British soldiers exchanged fire at Lexington and Concord, Massachusetts.

It now appeared to Thomas that the entire populace of Virginia was at loggerheads. He clearly identified himself with the radicals, including John Adams and Samuel Adams from Massachusetts, who all believed the moderates were foolishly denying the inevitable. Arguments flew back and forth in the House of Burgesses, as well as in the Continental Congress, regarding the wisdom of engaging in battle. Slave violence in several locales — near Albemarle, Williamsburg, and the Northumberland Counties — alarmed him. The unrest worried many white elite landowners, who realized these uprisings would reveal to the English occupiers how slaves might become their hidden weapon. Thomas then witnessed the tide turn toward the radicals like himself among the local population when Lord Dunmore, a Scottish peer and colonial governor in the American colonies, outwardly declared he would free the slaves if they deserted to the British. In response, the threatened, angry colonists finally were inspired to rebel and prepare for war. Any hope for a peaceful resolution sifted away like sand in an hourglass, as everyone fearfully watched the slow but futile negotiations. Everybody easily recalled the recent, shocking musket shots at Concord.

The colonies' leaders, seeing no way back, united to appoint George Washington of Virginia to be commanding general of the Continental armed forces. And just in time — for the Battle of Bunker Hill broke out only two days later, on June 15, 1775. Still in Williamsburg, Thomas became frantic he couldn't be with his family to calm them at this terrible news. He sent Jupiter to hurry with a letter to Patty, begging her to have courage and to set an example of strength for the entire slave population at Monticello. He knew the nearest neighbors were several miles away, and so unfortunately, her only real protection would be the slaves on the plantation.

The colonies had learned from their spies that the British intended to send troops from the city of Boston in order to fortify the unoccupied hills surrounding the city. This would give them control of Boston Harbor. In response, 1,200 colonial troops, under the command of William Prescott, stealthily occupied Bunker Hill and nearby Breed's Hill. During the night, the rebels constructed a strong fortification on Breed's Hill, and their advance planning paid off. A cheer went up from their tiny brigade as they succeeded in repelling the enemy, giving the colonies a huge boost of morale.

Fears about what revolution would mean for his family constantly troubled Thomas, but he took some comfort that the center of violence appeared to be Boston and not Virginia. At least, for now, he could picture his loved ones in the Italianate house he had built for them on the hill, seemingly far away. He knew Patty was brave, but she wasn't physically strong, and now there were two little children to take care of, as well as managing the servants.

Hating the separation from Patty and his daughters, Thomas wrote to her often, and depended on Jupiter to carry their letters back and forth. He informed her about the men he was meeting in the Congress, and noted he was especially impressed with John Adams, from Braintree, Massachusetts. Adams had earned a degree at Harvard, was eight years older than Thomas, and had made his mark in Boston as a distinguished lawyer. They had already enjoyed exchanging philosophical and political ideas in the Congress and at a tavern nearby after hours. The representatives of the colonies were beginning to rely on one another as family as they crowded into the best rooming houses Philadelphia had to offer. Thomas longed to be back in Virginia, helping to draft the state's new constitution, but agreed with Adams, that he needed to be in Philadelphia for the time being.

Finally, in early September 1775, the Congress took a break, and Thomas hurried back to Monticello to be with Patty and the little girls. The visit turned suddenly and horrifically tragic when Jane, only a year and a half old, unexpectedly died. He judged Patty to be in shock, yet he felt helpless to console her. She clung to him in desperation when he announced he must leave again on September 25 for the Congress resuming in Philadelphia.

"You mustn't leave us now. You've only been home a few weeks. We need you here, with us," she begged.

"Believe me. I realize that, my love, and I don't want to leave you. But we must do this for our country." He held his wife tightly. How could he make her understand that he must do this? He had to steel himself against giving in to her pleas and plowed for the door without looking back. He wondered for a moment if he were using this predicament to escape the tragedy that had just descended on his little family. No, the country was in crisis. He must go.

Little Patsy grabbed him around the legs when he finally stood at the front door, ready to go to his carriage. "I will come back as soon as I can, my precious," he whispered in her ear. "Help take care of your Mama."

This turned out to be auspicious advice because in only a week, he learned that Patty was very ill. Overcome with anxiety and dread, he wrote to his brother-in-law: *I have never received the script of a pen from any mortal in Virginia since I left it, nor been able by any enquiries I could make to hear of my family. The suspense under which I am is too terrible to be endured. If anything has happened, for God's sake let me know it.*

When it seemed he could bear no more bad news, he heard that the British navy had targeted Virginia and was attempting to land at the port of Norfolk, only about 165 miles distant from Monticello. Peril appeared imminent. Then Congress received the news that Lord Dunmore had sent the order from his ship to white Virginians that any slave or indentured servant who took up arms against the American Revolutionaries would be granted their freedom. Thomas exulted when this maneuver backfired, as it drove any hesitant colonists to the side of the rebels. They all now clearly understood the British to be a threat to their way of life, especially the loss of their slaves.

Thomas chafed to leave the Congress, so concerned was he about his family. He immediately wrote Patty about his ideas for her escape and of his plan to join her in the event that the danger became too great. He totally depended on the household slaves to protect her and to execute his wishes, and prayed this would prove sufficient. She responded that everyone at Monticello was traumatized by the growing menace of war. Meanwhile, he urgently applied himself to the duties at hand: supplying the Continental armies, gathering intelligence, securing the defenses of forts, and strategizing offensive tactics.

Thomas had not even been able to get away for Christmas, but finally left Philadelphia on December 28. When he finally rode his horse Caractacus up the side of his mountain in early January, he luxuriously breathed in the healthy, brisk, country air. He delighted in the amber, green, and rose light filtering through the forest, dappling the ground like colorful confetti, and the crunch of dry leaves under Caractacus's hooves seemed a serenade to his ears. To his profound relief, word of his approach had traveled via the slave rumor mill, and he found everyone on the front portico, alive and well, assembled to greet him. The absence of baby Jane, however, felt like a fresh physical wound. Tears came so easily to him, and he wept with uncontrolled emotion.

A heavy mist hung over the Blue Ridge Mountains on an early February morning in 1776, casting eerie shadows on Thomas's morning view. From his 600-foot mountaintop, it appeared they were living close to a white heaven. He was busy making a census of the "number of souls in his family," in which he included his wife and daughter, sixteen free men (overseers and hired workmen with their wives and children), and eighty-three slaves. In his mind, they were all his family.

The morning mail cheered his outlook considerably. He opened a copy of Thomas Paine's *Common Sense*, where he read the line: *The cause of America is, in a great measure, the cause of all mankind.* He was elated to learn that more and more people were joining the movement supporting a break from England. What a great relief it was to know that others were now taking part in the effort to spread the ideas of the revolution!

Three months after he came home, a slave from Shadwell rode over to inform him that his mother Jane Randolph Jefferson had suffered a stroke at age fifty-five and died. Thomas ordered his slaves to bring her body to Monticello from Shadwell for burial. He wanted her to be near him and his family always, and so he decided to lay her to rest next to the granddaughter who had borne her name.

Jane Randolph had been a formidable personage in many ways, and although she could be prickly at times, her death left him feeling strangely disoriented, like a bird fallen from its nest. He was stricken with a violent migraine headache that felt as though it would rip his senses from his skull. He staggered around the house for a day, but the constant pain rendered him depleted and helpless, forcing him to remain in a darkened room for days. This wasn't the first time he had endured one of these attacks. How he hated this weakness in himself!

After a week of grieving and convalescence, he managed to pull himself together and left Monticello for the capital on May 7, again leaving Patty behind with Patsy. This time Patty appeared to recognize he must do his duty and bore it with at least, outward fortitude. However, he fully understood that the death of their child was a continuing shock for them all.

The trip took him a week. Events were moving rapidly when he reached Philadelphia. After mounting the few steps to the handsome red brick Pennsylvania State House, he rarely left it, as there were so many important decisions to make. The weather was pleasant — as though nature was snubbing her nose at the follies of man — and sometimes the delegates would take their arguments outside where they could stand around on the grassy mall and look back at the simple but charming white cupola crowning the building. Later, the cupola would become a symbol for them of this tumultuous time. After days of debate, a fellow Virginian, Richard Henry Lee, made a motion that the United Colonies were "absolved from all allegiance to the British Crown, and that all political connection between them and the state of Great Britain is, and ought to be, totally dissolved." The moment for action finally was upon them.

Thomas perceived that his political philosophy truly converged with his passion for his country, and he dedicated himself to expressing his convictions in a document that would carry the weight of reason and emotion. John Adams, who had experienced firsthand the tyranny of the British troops in Boston, supported Jefferson as the man to write the treatise.

At his friend's insistence, Thomas sat down at a small folding desk in the home of a bricklayer, Jacob Graff, where he slept in one room and wrote in a private parlor across the hall. As he began to gather his thoughts, he knew he still must convince some states that were not ready to declare independence — New York, Pennsylvania, and New Jersey among them. He worked on his draft from June 11 until the 28th, writing in his clear and emphatic style:

> When in the course of human events it becomes necessary for one people to dissolve the political bands which have connected them with another, and to assume among the powers of the earth the separate and equal station to which the laws of nature and of nature's God entitle them, a decent respect to the opinions of mankind requires that they should declare the causes which impel them to the separation.

> We hold these truths to be self-evident, that all men are created equal, that they are endowed by their creator with inalienable rights, that among these are life, liberty, and the pursuit of happiness — that to secure these rights, governments are instituted among men, deriving their just powers from the consent of the governed, that whenever any form of government becomes destructive of these ends, it is the right of the people to alter or to abolish it, and to institute new government, laying its foundation on such principles, and organizing its powers in such form, as to them shall seem most likely to effect their safety and happiness.

Jefferson drew from the philosophers he had read all his life — John Locke, Montesquieu, and Montaigne. He even went back to the Scottish Enlightenment, where he had been inspired by the moral philosophy of Francis Hutcheson. Hutcheson had emphasized the "moral sense" inherent in all people that no government could violate. This did not mean extreme individualism where one could do anything one wanted, it was more a communal idea, a belief that a community could depend on its inhabitants, if allowed to be free, to behave ethically. His vision predicted that outside governmental coercion was unnecessary because an independent people would happily do the right thing.

When he was in doubt, Thomas discussed difficult issues with the country's contemporary intellectuals — primarily Benjamin Franklin and John Adams. Debate on his draft began on July 1, 1776. The room in the State House was relatively small, with an unimposing desk at the front of the room and pew-like seating with a central aisle. The delegates could walk forward to make a point from the front of the room or stand in place while speaking, so intimate was the space. Thomas was glad to leave the public speaking to the better orators, John Adams and Patrick Henry, and to have only the responsibility of drafting the document.

As Congress tore apart his language, Thomas suffered both humiliation and indignation. His harshest words about England were struck out so as not to offend King George III, just as his denunciation of slavery was crossed out to protect the sentiments of Georgia and South Carolina. What would be more difficult, he wondered — to separate from the mother country? Or, to achieve a union of the disparate colonies?

On July 2, 1776, Thomas witnessed the adoption of his resolution for independence by the delegates, and on July 4, they formally ratified the Declaration. "God bless the free states of North America!" was the cheer and by necessity, the call to arms. Thomas felt it to be an auspicious moment in the burgeoning history of the country, but for some reason, he felt more pride about his contribution to the new Virginia constitution, which he had been working on as well. There, he had emphasized in the text the separation of powers, a bicameral legislature, an independent judiciary, and a less powerful executive branch. Thomas also wrote into the constitutional manuscript a provision for religious freedom and a property qualification for all voters — though he recommended giving fifty acres to every resident of the state in order to make the stipulation more fair. Many believed the state constitutions to be the most important order of the day.

He couldn't wait to leave Philadelphia, mostly because he longed for his family and the privacy of Monticello, but also because he hated the changes the Congress had made to his Declaration, and he felt besieged by contrary opinions. With great relief, he headed home with Jupiter in his handsome phaeton.

1778

The Revolutionary War reached a boiling point quickly and held it almost without reprieve. The Patriots forced the British out of Boston in 1776, but subsequently, the redcoats captured and held New York City for the duration of the war. England blockaded the ports and captured other cities for brief periods, but were ultimately unable to defeat Washington's forces. A British army was captured by the Americans at the Battle of Saratoga in late 1777, and when the French openly entered the war as allies of the United States in early 1778, it changed what had been a contained fight into an international struggle.

The news from home was not good. Patty had experienced a dangerous miscarriage. Thomas learned she had bled profusely and feared the worst when he received no letters from her. Aching to be with her and his daughter, he deliberated daily how he could stay in Philadelphia with his crushing worries. But he could not tear himself away either, feeling his contributions were critical to the war effort.

One of the problems plaguing the colonies and keeping him in Philadelphia during this turbulent time was that of the Indians. Although Thomas believed them to be a noble race, he agreed with other white landholders that eventually the whites should take over Indian lands. He believed the whites' culture to be superior and thought the Indians should be taught the ways of their betters. However, unlike some of his compatriots, he believed the Indians were intelligent and could learn. But would they agree to adopting the white man's culture, he wondered?

Finally, in early autumn of 1778, Thomas took the road back to Monticello. At last he would be with Patty and Patsy, who had just turned six in September. He decided he would work henceforth in Williamsburg, helping to establish the new government of Virginia, and somehow find a way to have his family with him. No longer were they a colony, but a state in the newly declared Union. He clearly understood he was a better writer than speaker and determined to make his contributions with his pen.

When Thomas's former law teacher and friend, George Wythe, offered the Jeffersons his house on the town green in Williamsburg, the state capital. Thomas accepted with alacrity. It would be the perfect solution to his need for serving his country and his heart's demand to be near his wife and child.

Patsy

1777-1778

PATSY COULDN'T IMAGINE LIVING anywhere but Monticello. She knew nowhere else would be as nice — a cozy home, fields and gardens to play in, and horses to ride. But when she heard they would be with their father if they moved — just for a while, he said — she decided not to put up a fuss. And she noticed that her mother was making no complaints about moving house, so relieved was she to have her husband back.

Patsy had grown used to the necessity of her father being away when he was serving in the Continental Congress, but she sensed the best times for her family were when he and her mother played music together — Patty on the pianoforte and he on his violin — in the sitting room at Monticello. She also loved the days when he perched her on a pony and allowed her to ride in the ring next to his tall horse. And though she always loved being read to, it was somehow best when her Papa spoke the words in his quiet voice.

She listened as Patty and Thomas carefully chose which servants would accompany them to Williamsburg. They would leave the majority at Monticello to tend the fields and keep up the family supplies of beer, pork, and vegetables. The plantation went a long way in feeding all of the inhabitants of the big house and the slave quarters. It was a small industry on top of the mountain, and Thomas viewed it as a little utopia, a humming contented lot living together. The Jeffersons decided to take most of the Hemings family with them, including Sally, who was Betty's sixth child fathered by John Wayles, Patsy's maternal grandfather. Sally had been born a few months after Patsy, when the Hemings family had first moved to Monticello upon Wayles's death. It didn't dawn on Patsy that this meant Sally was her aunt, and no one ever mentioned it.

"She will help keep Patsy entertained," she heard her mother say to Thomas.

Patsy was very glad to hear this because she and Sally enjoyed playing together. Patty fussed at them about being tomboys when they would come in from the garden, dirty and even with torn dresses on occasion. Well, why shouldn't they be able to climb a tree when they saw the other children on the plantation doing so? Patty knew she couldn't blame Sally, who was the quieter of the two girls; it was her daughter who was the ruffian and the ringleader.

Not long after their arrival in Williamsburg, Patsy stood behind Betty Hemings when she opened the door to a messenger. Hearing the commotion, Thomas came into the foyer and opened the envelope. Patty, curious about the noise in the hall, arrived in time to see her husband's face contort. He nearly threw the letter upon the floor, but regained his composure. "My dear," he said to his wife, "John Hancock, the new governor of Massachusetts, informs me that President Washington implores me to be our country's representative to France."

"Oh, not now. Please, not now!" Patty's voice shook.

Thomas well understood the importance of this European ally in the colony's struggle against Britain. Without the support of France, America had little chance of success. Weren't the French helping them in the Revolutionary War? Yet how could he ask his family to do without him again? And he could not bear to leave Patty either. They were meant to be together, and he did not see how he could take her with him, given her health problems. Not wanting to alarm Patsy, who was carefully watching the scene, he only said, "We'll discuss all this later. Now let us have some lunch on the terrace and enjoy the autumn sunshine."

Patsy felt a new tension in the household as her father dithered for days, making the messenger wait for his response. She heard her parents speaking softly to one another out of her hearing range, but she did overhear him explain that Benjamin Franklin and Silas Deane of Connecticut also had been invited to serve in this capacity. She could not imagine what her father was being asked to do, but imagined it must be dangerous, since her mother was so nervous.

Thomas's heart was torn, but he finally sent back a "no" to John Hancock, saying, . . . *Circumstances very peculiar in the situation of my family, such as neither permit me to leave nor to carry it, compel me to decline a service so honorable and at the same time so important to the American cause.* He told himself he could offer valuable and important service to the new government of Virginia instead. But it did feel as though he was badly letting down his closest colleagues.

Patsy liked many of her father's friends who served in the Virginia legislature, especially James Madison. He came to their house frequently, simply to sit in the library with Thomas and discuss matters of state or philosophy, or he would join them for dinner. Jefferson was eight years older than his new friend, but he never patronized him, for they quickly grew to trust and admire one another's intelligence. Thomas was much taller than James, who remarkably didn't seem to mind his diminutive appearance. Rather, Madison towered over most everyone else with his astute and broad intellect.

Of course, Patsy couldn't understand most of what the gentlemen discussed for hours and hours, but the pair never said they minded her playing with her dolls at their feet. One of their favorite subjects was religion and freedom of conscience, and so she heard words like "enforced baptism," "dissenters," and "religious observance" float around her head. Sally also was allowed to play quietly with Patsy, sprawled on the carpet near the fireplace, sometimes giggling at the funny words they heard. They thought it odd that adults liked to talk so much.

Patty proudly announced she was pregnant again, and so Thomas moved his little family back to Monticello in May. He teased her because when she was pregnant, she liked to eat johnnycakes, an unleavened cornmeal pancake that the slaves took to the fields for lunch, lathering them with molasses. Back at home, Patty gave birth to a son, who lived only seventeen days. The parents were stunned. They had now lost two children. Patsy had been very excited about having a little brother, and was shocked that he could be gone so quickly. The mood in the house became very somber, and she wished she could do something to make it different.

The incident left her mother weak and despondent, which Patsy found particularly worrisome. But Patty was soon pregnant again, and regained her sweet and cheerful character. Patsy knew all was well when she listened to her parents playing music side by side in the evenings after dinner. Only ten months later, on August 1, 1778, to everyone's relief, Patty gave birth to Mary, whom Thomas decreed should be called Polly.

"Ah, my dear wife, this little one clearly resembles you. Lucky girl!"

Patsy developed the habit of carefully watching her mother to be sure she was all right. She gradually began to relax as Patty Jefferson, despite illnesses and numerous pregnancies, remained resilient. Patty would laugh and say, "I'm delicate like my flowers, but I always bounce back like they do in the spring." Indeed, she was extremely graceful and an accomplished conversationalist as well. Patsy loved to listen to her mother chatter away with family and guests, and imagined herself one day doing the same.

Patsy also enjoyed watching her mother dress for the evening. Mother and daughter put their heads together over fashion plates, and Patty explained to Patsy which garments were considered fashionable and pretty. Since she had just been pregnant, it was difficult for Patty to wear the tight stomacher and long-waisted pointed bodices, but she still could make a fashionable appearance with a low-necked gown and three-quarter sleeves. Powdering the hair was quite in style, but Thomas said he preferred his wife's natural color, and Patsy agreed, finding powder silly and messy. Patty laughed and told them she could always count on an admiration society of her husband, daughter, Betty, and Sally after dressing for one of their social gatherings.

WILLIAMSBURG AND RICHMOND

GOVERNOR

1779-1881

. . . experience hath shewn, [sic] that even under the best forms, those entrusted with power have, in time, and by slow operations, perverted it into tyranny; and it is believed that the most effectual means of preventing this would be, to illuminate, as far as practicable, the minds of the people at large . . .

Extract from Thomas Jefferson's "Bill for the More General Diffusion of Knowledge," December 1778

THOMAS

1779-1780

THOMAS SMILED ABOUT HOW EXCITED Patsy became when he was elected governor of Virginia. She remarked how much everyone admired him and sought his company, but he counseled her it was meaningless attention. Patsy was devastated, however, when she learned this honor meant he now must move back to Williamsburg — but this time, without them. He explained to her that British soldiers were too close for him to risk their presence in the capital. He and Patty had largely been able to keep the Revolutionary War mostly out of sight from the children, but now this was becoming impossible.

By the summer, however, he changed his mind about bringing his wife and girls and decided they should be with him. He missed them terribly and decided the Governor's Palace in Williamsburg would be a fine place for his family. He sent word that not only should his wife and children come, but a number of the servants as well, especially Betty for Patty and Sally for Patsy.

The palace was a commanding building of red brick with a double cupola. More brick buildings, like the Bruton Church and the Exchange, where men talked business the whole day through, made the town a pleasant place. Thomas enjoyed frequenting The Coffee House and the printing office of the *Virginia Gazette,* where he could buy books and music. When the Assembly was in session, the population of the town doubled from 2,000 to 4,000 and the crushed oyster shell streets became crowded with horses and wagons. The Duke of Gloucester Street was considered especially fashionable, and Patty, once somewhat settled, liked riding down the thoroughfare with Patsy so they could observe their fellow inhabitants.

To make everyone feel at home at the palace, Patty made her special Mexican black bean soup, which simmered slowly for five hours. She started with browning the meat with a small amount of butter, then added roots, herbs, and water. Before serving, she skimmed off the fat and added a sprinkling of chopped cilantro. "Now we are all together again," she happily said with her first spoonful.

At first, the palace seemed too big to the Jeffersons and they all longed for the more intimate Monticello. The huge space worried the parents as they often lost Patsy, who ran freely from room to room with Sally. The girls played hide and seek for hours, and Patty complained that her daughter was becoming a feral cat.

Threatened on two fronts — there were British soldiers to the east and the west — Thomas became consumed with the menace of a British invasion. The English had already seized Georgia and were nearing Virginia, forcing him to consider his own personal protection, as well as that of the country. He determined he ought to do something important and symbolic to boost a feeling of unity among the colonies, as well as make a show of their consolidation in the face of the enemy. He aimed to "arouse our people from the lethargy into which they had fallen, as to passing events . . ." Therefore, upon being prompted by the Continental Congress, Jefferson issued a proclamation to set aside a day of "public and solemn thanksgiving and prayer," to commemorate recent military successes, and to seek the "continuance of {God's} favour and protection to these United States."

It became apparent that Williamsburg was indeed threatened by the British, and a quick decision was made in the spring of 1780 to move the capital to Richmond, on the beautiful James River. The river widened as it meandered through the center of town and provided many pleasant vistas. But Richmond was a rustic village compared to Williamsburg and their house provided little comfort or elegance compared to the fine palace in Virginia's first capital. The war continued to creep even closer and tidings abounded from the front of debilitating cold and of troops, horses, and wagons being mired in mud. Thomas's mood became more fearful with the news of the fall of Charleston, South Carolina to the British on May 10. What should he do? And to make it worse, another baby was due in a few months.

Patty needed to be brave again in November when, amidst all the chaos, she gave birth to a baby girl whom they named Lucy Elizabeth. Thomas tried to hide his worst worries from Patty, hoping to keep the new mother calm, but he had less luck with his alert daughter.

"What is a traitor, Papa?" Patsy asked one day in late December after Mr. Madison had left and she had been listening to their conversation.

"A traitor is someone who betrays his country or a friend. We were speaking of General Benedict Arnold, my dear — the American, who lied to his country, sold himself to the British, and now is threatening to lead an invasion of Virginia." It was useless, he realized, to withhold information from Patsy, who appeared to understand so much. She had been able to read since age five, and Thomas had begun to teach her French early. He even enjoyed sharing figures with her about running a plantation. Her aptitude with arithmetic made this a pleasant occupation for the two of them.

"Oh," Patsy replied, clearly thinking about what this betrayal might mean for her family.

There is no existing image of Sally Hemings

SALLY

1780-1781

SALLY LOOKED OUT the window of the coach in awe as it brought her and her mother to the Governor's palace in Williamsburg. Betty explained to her that their master had been elected Governor of the entire state and now needed to live in a place called the capital. Sally would be expected to help keep Patsy entertained and to behave exceptionally well. This didn't sound particularly alarming, because she thought she always conducted herself properly. In fact, she always watched Patsy carefully to know how she should act too.

She had even felt a bit proud when Patsy had hugged her and said, "You're coming with us!" She didn't want to admit she was anxious about traveling so far from Monticello, especially with rumors of British troops turning up in unexpected places. But it was tremendously exciting to be riding in a Jefferson carriage that followed the Jefferson family.

Monticello had always seemed like a mansion to her, but the imposing building in Williamsburg was beyond anything she had imagined. There were five dormer windows peeking out from a tall steeply pitched roof, crowned with a double cupola. She wondered if she and Patsy might climb up to the top and view the countryside.

Betty had more ladylike pursuits in mind and suggested to Sally that she and Patsy do some sewing together. Sally usually enjoyed this activity and had become amazingly proficient with her embroidery needle for an eight year old. They would settle down with this for a short while every day, but mostly, they preferred to explore the big palace and would entice Isaac Granger, if he weren't busy, to join them in a game of hide-and-seek. He was a bit older than they, but that made it especially fun.

Sally liked watching Mr. Jefferson at work, bent over his desk or talking with visiting officials. He was so tall — it often seemed daunting to have to look up so far to talk to him. Sometimes, he kindly knelt down to her and Patsy's level, and she realized she never feared him. But these days, with continuing word of the nearness of the British troops, and seeing Mrs. Jefferson abed after the birth of the new baby, both she and Patsy often whispered together, trying to allay one another's worries. What would they do if the British attacked Richmond? They wouldn't dare harm the Governor, would they?

PATSY

1781

PATSY WATCHED HER FATHER pace the floor. She could see he was extremely agitated. When he finally stopped, he said to her mother, "I believe, my dear, that the British are too near for comfort. I think it wise for you and the children to flee to Tuckahoe." This was the nearby home of his childhood friend Thomas Mann Randolph. Jefferson's mother was a Randolph, and so they were cousins as well.

"Oh, Thomas," Patty wailed. Patsy literally shook with terror. She couldn't leave her father behind. Hadn't he just told them it was dangerous? She sat down in the foyer and refused to go. "I'll stay here with Papa," she firmly announced. When Patty tried to comfort her, she kept asking, "But when is Papa coming? And what about Sally?"

Thomas called for Robert and James Hemings and commanded them to ready the carriage to drive his family. "I think you are right, little one. I will send Betty and Sally with you and your mother. They can help take care of you. I think everyone else here will be safe." He then asked his secretary William Short to accompany them to the Randolph plantation in his stead. William was related to the Jeffersons through the Wayles in-laws, and like Jefferson, he had graduated from the College of William and Mary and had studied law with the same mentor, George Wythe.

Patsy immediately liked the idea of Mr. Short coming along. Encouraged that she was somewhat consoled, Thomas continued, "Worry not, my precious. The mountains and darkness will delay the British." He appeared serene while giving his advice, but the advice became more frightening when he continued, "Do not admit who you are to any strangers. Make up anything, but do not let anyone who stops you know you are connected with me."

Patsy looked up at her father. "But that would be a lie," she whimpered in confusion

"Unfortunately, telling a lie is sometimes necessary," he said, clenching his jaw. What vile lessons children learned in wartime.

Thomas

THOMAS CONTINUED TO DRAG his feet regarding intelligence about the danger of General Arnold or the proximity of the British troops. Two days passed, and he still hadn't called for protection. Regrettably, not wanting to alarm the populace any more than necessary, he waited too long to call up the local militia. As troops moved closer to Richmond, realizing he'd made a dreadful mistake, he sent a note to Robert and James Hemings, via Jupiter, to drive Patty and the girls even farther away to a piece of Jefferson property called Fine Creek, west of the new capital. Thomas now understood he, too, must flee in order to avoid capture and immediately departed, leaving George Granger at the governor's mansion with the keys.

When the British arrived, the approaching racket of the mass of troops and musketry sounded like an earthquake to the poor man standing before the empty home. When asked for the master and the keys, George handed over the keys, but managed to sputter, "The Master, he's gone and the silver, it's been taken up the mountain." Actually it was hidden right under a bed in the kitchen. Bravely standing his ground, George saved the master and the silver but felt his courage waning when the British forced him to come with them.

Thomas cringed when the Virginia Burgesses instantly censured him for not calling out the militia in a timely manner. And he had endangered George! Perhaps he had been unwisely worried, he thought, about demanding too much of a public that wasn't yet invested in the war. He had been foolish not to call for help. He was shocked that the British also had captured Jupiter, who had attended Thomas since college days. Why had he been so careless with his servants' safety? They had also carried off other servants who had been left behind: Sukey, the cook; Ursula; Mary, a seamstress; and children, including Isaac Granger. Thomas assumed George and Ursula had been forced to go with the British. It was too hard — unseemly even — to think they would have chosen to leave.

Thomas constantly thought about the issue of slavery. He had inherited all of his slaves and rarely sold any. He told Patty he had not freed any of them either, because as far as he could judge "from the experiment, to give liberty to, or rather, to abandon persons whose habits have been formed in slavery, is like abandoning children." Yet it bothered him that he relied heavily on those he called "children."

British troops continued to harass Richmond, and Thomas, trying to stay a step ahead, kept moving his family from one planation to another, finally coming full-circle back to Richmond. In the middle of an already upsetting situation, on April 15, at 10 a.m., Lucy Elizabeth died, not quite six months old. It was a staggering blow and Patty's hysteria seriously alarmed him. She was so devastated and heartsick, he chose to stay behind with her the next day instead of attending the General Assembly. But when the British advanced inland toward Charlottesville on May 28, he reassembled his family back at Monticello, thinking he might then be able to rejoin the government.

Fortunately, a burly Virginia militiaman — he was six feet, four inches — by the name of Jack Jouett, took it upon himself to ride forty miles through the night, reaching Monticello in time to warn Thomas that the British were nearby and coming to capture him. Once again, Thomas summoned a carriage for his family to ride to safety at a nearby plantation. Too weak to object, Patty allowed herself to be packed into the conveyance. Thomas quickly realized that, as his state's leader, he must protect himself too.

He asked Thomas Martin Hemings, called "Martin," one of Betty's children before John Wayles bedded her, and who Thomas had made butler at Monticello, to remain on the mountain for a short while. Thomas jumped on his best horse, Caractacus, and fled after Patty and his children, who finally had come to rest at Poplar Forest, one of Patty's family's plantations. Along the way, in his agitation and probably not paying proper attention, he took a bad spill from Caractacus, falling on his arm. The horse stood over his master quietly until he was able to pull himself up into the saddle. Thomas surprised himself with the stream of curses pouring from his lips. When he reached his family, the shock had worn off, and he unhappily perceived how badly hurt he was;

his arm was broken. So worried had he been about his loved-ones, he claimed not to have even felt the pain.

Heeding his master's orders, Martin had bravely remained at Monticello to guard the home, though he couldn't stop shaking like a pecan tree in a storm when the redcoats arrived and held him at gunpoint. He and a fellow slave, Caesar, were frantically hiding the family silver under the porch when the soldiers arrived, and Caesar was trapped below the floorboards. Martin dropped the last piece of silver practically on Caesar's head when he heard them coming, and steadfastly refused to say where his master had gone. One of the redcoats cocked a pistol and held it to Martin's chest. Martin later told his family that they said, "Tell us where Jefferson is, or I'll fire."

"Fire away then," Martin bravely stated. Caesar, who heard the remarks, later told the story. Remarkably, the soldier didn't shoot, and after consuming much of Jefferson's best wine and wrecking his wine cellar, the British spared Monticello. But they were not so generous at nearby Elk Hill, Patty's family's plantation, where they looted and burned buildings. The British also carried off about thirty slaves, most likely offering them liberty as enticement to leave. Poor Caesar remained trapped overnight under the porch until the soldiers finally took leave and Martin freed him.

Though safely sheltered at Poplar Forest, Thomas, Patty, and the children were all showing signs of the trauma of war. Patsy began to have trouble sleeping and often refused to leave her father's side, while Thomas literally staggered and reeled with a dizzying headache. The censure for failing to call the Virginia militia in time caused him intense shame, and he told his brother-in-law Francis Carr that it had "inflicted a wound on my spirit which will only be cured by the all-healing grave." He also had heard stories that General Washington, Senator Burr, and Alexander Hamilton had criticized him for not serving in the military. They felt he hadn't done enough to serve his country. His throbbing arm didn't help his mood either.

One evening a horse's hooves sounded near their hiding place at Poplar Forest. Thomas was appalled to feel himself literally quaking, but mercifully, the rider revealed himself to be Mr. Short, appearing quite dirty — a stark contrast to his usual debonair presentation. They all soon forgot his appearance when he told them his news: "The British general, Tarleton, has turned back to join up with Cornwallis, who is being harassed by the French General, Lafayette. Thanks to Lafayette, the British are retreating!"

Patsy began crying with relief, hiccupping uncontrollably. Might they come out of hiding now?

"But it is not all good news, Mr. Jefferson," Short continued with a grim expression. "We were able to convene a session of the legislature, and Patrick Henry spoke against you. There will be an investigation into your conduct for failing to call up the militia."

Thomas took the blow silently, but Patsy caught his look of humiliation.

By the fall of 1781, most of the escaped or captured slaves had made their way back to Monticello amidst the turmoil, and all of the Hemingses had returned. In September Thomas again was asked to be America's envoy to France and again he turned it down. When Patty said, "No more, Thomas, no more," he heeded her wish. They had lost three children, and he felt he could ask no more of her. He remained out of office, tending to Monticello for about a year and a half, licking his wounds of disgrace, caring for his mountain idyll, Patty, and the girls. Patty was pregnant once more, and he dared not leave her. The country would have to wait.

In fact, Patty was very busy helping him run the plantation. Her favorite task was the making of cloth and sewing clothes from the fabrics they produced. They raised sheep for wool and grew cotton for muslin. Even though Patsy was still young, Patty began to tutor her, from cotton field to spinning, from shearing to the loom. She taught many of the slaves, as well as her daughter, how to make clothing that they could wear and enjoy. Patsy often requested that Sally be there to share these lessons with her. Thomas loved watching his wife's tiny frame busily going about the plantation chores and proudly boasted of her skills to neighbors and family. He sometimes thought she insisted on having her way too much, but for the sake of peace, he didn't argue. He began to relax with her apparent resilience.

Patty often made him smile with some of her household remedies, and he laughed out loud one day when he found one of his favorites in her recipe book — "To cut fresh bread, heat the blade of your bread knife." This was followed by, "A rusty knife can be cleaned by running it through an onion, then allow it to stand for several hours. Later a rubbing in sand will polish it." "You should write a book, my dear," he advised her. He loved her boiled eels, which involved cleaning them thoroughly, cutting off their heads, and drying them before boiling in salt water. She served the fish with a tasty parsley sauce.

A victory in October 1781 at Yorktown, led by General Washington with help from the French, led by the Marquis de Lafayette, would be the pivotal and nearly final battle of America's revolution. Isaac Granger had remained a captive of the British, and witnessed the fiery end. Upon returning to Monticello, he recounted to all about hearing the screams of the wounded men. "I can never forget," he said, shaking his head.

MONTICELLO

1782

. . . I think a change already perceptible, since the origin of the present revolution. The spirit of the master is abating, that of the slave rising from the dust, his condition mollifying, the way I hope preparing, under the auspices of heaven, for a total emancipation, and that this is disposed, in the order of events, to be with the consent of the masters, rather than by their extirpation.

Extract from Thomas Jefferson's *Notes on the State of Virginia*, [Query XVIII, "Manners"] 1782

THOMAS

1782

ALTHOUGH AMERICA WAS VICTORIOUS, Thomas came away from the war feeling a failure. He was mortified at the disaster stemming from his poor choice not to call the militia in time, and the ignominy of rejection from the cuts to his original draft of the Declaration still stung. The end of the war and the birth of another child should have restored his spirits, but he continued to be melancholy.

In May 1782, Patty bore him another daughter they called Lucy Elizabeth, named after the baby who had died. But Patty appeared to be at the end of her strength, though gentle and courageous as ever. Sick with worry, he wrote to his friend Madison after the birth, "She has been ever since, and still continues, very dangerously ill."

Patty had endured six pregnancies in ten years, the move to Williamsburg, another move to Richmond, and the escape to Poplar Forest after the death of her baby. She had a terrible cough, as well as being depleted from the most recent birth. Neither chewing cinnamon nor doses of tar-water morning and night seemed to do any good. Her body simply was unable to recoup.

Ursula and Betty, the servants who had tended her for her entire life, nursed her now. For months she lay in bed, with Thomas often appearing at her bedside, apprehending her needs and administering her medicine. He slept in a small room near her and as the end drew near, he could rarely be persuaded to get some sleep. His widowed sister, Martha Carr, and Auntie Elizabeth Eppes, were there to help with the nursing, but they found Thomas unable to talk, so distressed was he.

With Thomas perched on her bed, Patty recalled some lines from Sterne's *Tristram Shandy,* and wrote them down.

> *Time wastes too fast; every letter I trace*
> *tells me with what rapidity Life follows my pen;*
> *the days and hours of it . . . are flying over our heads*
> *like light clouds of a windy day never to return more*
> *Every thing presses on —*

Exhausted, she handed him the pen, and he finished the verse,

> *. . . And every time I kiss thy hand to bid adieu,*
> *and every absence which follows it, are preludes to that*
> *eternal separation which we are shortly to make!*

Close to noon, on September 6, it was clear Patty was near death. The house servants were by her side as well as the family. Betty Hemings, who had been somewhat of a proxy mother to Patty, and Betty's own daughter Sally, were there to witness her last words. Patty wept when she looked upon her children — Patsy, Polly, and Lucy — and holding up her hand, said to Thomas, "I can not die happy if I think my children would ever have a stepmother brought in over them."

Some by her bedside gasped, for Thomas was still, at age thirty-nine, a young, virile man and had children to be cared for. Thomas knelt by her side and holding her hand, promised his wife he would never marry again. He could not imagine Monticello without Patty as its mistress. Nor could he imagine being without her for the rest of his life. He felt as if he could not breathe.

Patsy, age ten, Polly, four, and Sally Hemings, nine and a half, witnessed the tragic scene. Patsy clasped Sally's hand. Who else could she turn to as her father appeared out of his senses?

When Betty pushed Sally forward to say goodbye to her half-sister, Patty picked up a silver hand bell from her bedside table. "This is a memento for you," Patty weakly whispered. It was the bell that had often called Sally to some little service to be done for her, yet it was, at the same time, a parting gift for her half-sister. Sally accepted the little bell and drew back, now holding on to Patsy again.

Thomas collapsed over Patty's body when she expired her last breath at 11:45 a.m. She was thirty-four. Thomas's sister had to pull the delirious man from his wife and lead him to the library, where he fainted. Patsy was frightened to death that she might lose her father too as he lay on the carpet, insensible for quite a long while. Betty tried to draw Patsy away but she wouldn't leave her Papa. He appeared incoherent upon regaining consciousness and stumbled out of doors, screaming with grief and rage. Betty finally pulled the young girl away.

During the night when he repaired to his room at last, Patsy crept in to cling to him. She had lost siblings, and now her mother; she was terrified about what was to come. Father and daughter, through the days that followed Patty's death, continued to cleave to one another. For three weeks Patsy refused to leave his side, and he depended on her sweetness. She told Betty, "He walks almost incessantly night and day, only lying down occasionally, completely exhausted, on the pallet that you brought in during his long fainting fit."

Thomas chose the epitaph for Patty's tombstone from Homer's *Iliad*:

If, in the melancholy shades below,
The flames of friends and lovers cease to glow,
Yet mine shall sacred last; mine undecay'd,
Burn on through death, and animate my shade,

He could not stop his weeping, feeling his life had ended with Patty's death. He had planned Monticello to be the idyllic place where they and their children would abide forever. He refused an invitation from Patty's sister Elizabeth Eppes to come with his children to Eppington, and tried to explain. "I can not come until my countenance can hide my melancholy," he wrote. He depended solely on Patsy for company as they wandered over his mountain on horseback together. What would he do without this dear daughter, who held him by a fine thread to life?

PHILADELPHIA

1783

The whole commerce between master and slave is a perpetual exercise of the most boisterous passions, the most unremitting despotism on the one part, and degrading submissions on the other. Our children see this, and learn to imitate it. . . .

Query XVIII, "Manners" " Notes on the State of Virginia," 1782

Patsy

1783

PATSY COULDN'T CONTAIN her excitement, rushing around the house like a red squirrel, burying books in one trunk and a silk scarf in another valise.

"I wish you were coming too," she told her sister Polly, noticing that Polly looked rather morose, perched on her bed next to Patsy's.

"I don't even want to go!" Polly grumbled.

"Well then, perhaps you will visit."

The plan was for Jefferson and Patsy to proceed by coach to Philadelphia and wait there for a ship to France. Patsy wasn't afraid of travel. Indeed, it was the southern custom for gentry to move around the country from one relation to another and to stay for an extended period. And after all, she had moved from Monticello to Williamsburg when her father served as Governor of Virginia in 1779. When the capital moved to Richmond the family had moved there too, accompanied by many of their domestic servants. Now she wouldn't have her mother or any of the servants' friendly faces around her, but she would have her father.

Patsy recalled how the war had breathed down their necks last year when the British attacked nearby. Her Papa had quickly scuttled his family off again, that time to Tuckahoe to stay with his friend and relative, Thomas Mann Randolph, who had five daughters and three sons. Over a period of five weeks the Jeffersons had moved six times, but her father's calm had kept panic at bay. Finally, by the spring, the family had moved safely back to Monticello, but the war had taken a toll — on the family and on the house. She remembered how the familiar sight of the redbud trees, with their blossoms arising directly from the branches, and sweet-smelling dogwoods had helped allay her feelings of malaise. The greatest shock had been seeing the damage to their home and to her mother's ancestral estate nearby. She had remarked to her Papa, "I hate what the British did to our home. And it really made me angry when they blamed you for not calling the militia out earlier."

"They may have had a point," he responded.

While they waited to leave for France, Patsy followed him around the plantation, as he buried himself in rebuilding and redecorating. With her reddish-gold hair and gangly body, many commented that she looked like his shadow. She stood by his side as he described to her all the new fruit trees he would plant and the architectural changes he would make upon their return. She reveled in these activities, but now she felt ready to follow her father to Europe or wherever he was going. As long as he was by his side, she would be content.

The morning of December 19 dawned cold and gray. A dense fog hung over Monticello, chilling their bones and resolve. Patsy hadn't expected that leaving her four-year-old sister Polly and toddler Lucy Elizabeth would be so difficult. She tried not to cry but failed to staunch her tears and an alarming quivering in her stomach. They had celebrated an early Christmas at a family dinner last night, exchanging a few gifts, and singing Christmas carols, but why on earth had they decided to leave before the 25th, causing this additional and unnecessary pain?

When Polly began to whimper and refused to release her hand, Patsy had to look to her father for help. She still couldn't get used to the fact that her mother wasn't here to see them off, and knew that Polly must feel this even more than she. It was also upsetting and difficult to leave Betty and Sally. Patsy hugged them both very hard and whispered to Sally to look after Polly. Now she understood a little bit what her father must have felt, leaving his family to go to Philadelphia or Richmond. But this was so much farther!

Jefferson's valet, Robert Hemings, traveled on horseback behind their two-horse phaeton piled high with baggage. Robert, now twenty-one, and training to be a barber, essentially moved about the country like a free man, but Patsy was aware that he was always at her father's beck and call. She knew her Papa depended on Bob (as Thomas had taken to calling him) for many things, for he had made sure that all the Hemings boys were literate. Indeed, perhaps because of their literacy, all the Hemings men developed lives off the mountain, but always kept in touch with the master so he could reach them when need be. He trusted them to do this, and they repaid him with their loyalty. It was a rather unusual arrangement for a slave, but it's what worked for her father.

The trip to Philadelphia took a full eight days, and Patsy often was glad to have Bob's familiar face and strong arms along for assistance. After three days over the hilly, stony roads of northern Virginia, they were relieved to reach the wider thoroughfare between Baltimore and Philadelphia. But sometimes, when there were too many ruts and holes, they had to get out and walk. Crossing the Potomac, Patapsco, Susquehanna, and Schuylkill rivers required the assistance of ferrymen, who helped carry them across. Again, Patsy appreciated the presence of Bob at their side when she looked down at the rivers' swirling waters.

Along the way, Jefferson explained that they would lodge the first night in Philadelphia at the Indian Queen on Fourth Street, a large tavern cum hotel of sixteen rooms with slave quarters on a top floor garret for Bob. When the noise and strange people frightened her, Jefferson realized this arrangement was too bawdy for his young daughter, and moved them on the second day to a private boarding house on Fifth and Market. This turned out to be a felicitous decision, because they were informed they must wait a full month for the next ship to France.

Jefferson was acquainted with the owner, Mary House, from the days when he and his friend James Madison served in the Continental Congress and stayed in Philadelphia. Apprehensive and lonely during her early days in the city, Patsy welcomed the friendly approaches of Mary's daughter, Eliza. Eliza was a warm and sociable acquaintance of her father's, and her fiancé Nicholas Trist was setting up a home for them in western Florida. Patsy and the thirty-one-year-old lady became good friends, and Jefferson found himself relying on this kind woman's stewardship of his child. Patsy realized he had not thought ahead about traveling with a young girl, and it made her miss her mother even more.

Travel plans became even more fraught, and they hastened to Baltimore for a departing ship. But upon learning that British naval vessels along the American coast threatened their safety, they finally gave up and, much dispirited, returned to Philadelphia. The war was over, but the British continued to harass American shipping. Patsy tried to hide her frustration from her father, because it was clear he was as downhearted as she. Eliza attempted to keep Patsy busy with visits to the milliner's and shoe shop, but the days dragged on. She found the neat three- and four-story brick homes lined in a regular pattern on every street monotonous, standing as straight and strict as toy soldiers. She missed being outdoors where she spent so much of her time at home, and she longed for Sally and Betty. But she didn't complain.

Finally, in April 1783 the Continental Congress, which was governing under the Articles of Confederation until a proper constitution could be prepared, notified Jefferson he need not go to Paris yet. He and Patsy climbed into their carriage once more for a discouraging return trip to Monticello. The happy sight of Polly and Sally quickly banished Patsy's disappointment, and three peaceful months sped by at home before the state legislature asked him to return to the Congress, this time meeting in Annapolis. Once again, Jefferson elected to bring along his daughter and leave her in Philadelphia. "You will receive a better education in the city," he told her, "and I like having you with me." These last words were the sweetest.

This time he brought along James Hemings, Robert's younger brother. Aware that Eliza House Trist would leave soon to join her husband in Florida, Jefferson searched for a private home where Patsy would be secure and could continue her schooling in Philadelphia, the so-called "Athens of America." He settled on the home of Mary Johnson Hopkinson. Mary Hopkinson was a widow with seven children, whose husband had been the President of the American Philosophical Society and Benjamin Franklin's collaborator in his experiments on electricity. Mrs. Hopkinson was a well-educated liberal, but Patsy missed Eliza and failed to warm to Mary. However, she didn't want to burden her father by making too much of a fuss as she sensed he missed her mother as much as she did. When Jefferson shortly left for Annapolis, where the

Congress was convened, she had no idea it would be six months before she would see her father again.

Upon leaving, he hired a dancing master from Paris as well as music, art, and French tutors. Still, Patsy discovered she had many idle hours without a mother, friends, or cousins to divert her. Nor did she have the expansive outdoors of Monticello to play or ride. She wrote a letter to Polly and Sally, pretending to be content, but she also told them she missed them very much.

Thomas wrote to his daughter, meaning to comfort her, but he couldn't restrain from counseling her as well:

Annapolis, 28 November 1783

The conviction that you'd be improved in the situation I've placed you solaces me in parting with you, which my love for you has rendered a difficult thing. Consider the good lady who has taken you under her roof as your mother, as the only person to whom, since the loss with which heaven has been pleased to afflict you, you can now look up.

The acquirements I hope you'll make under the tutors I've provided will render you more worthy of my love, and if they cannot increase it they'll prevent its diminution. I've placed my happiness on seeing you good and accomplished, and no distress this world can now bring on me could equal that of your disappointing my hopes.

Jefferson received a letter from Mrs. Hopkinson soon after his departure, saying that Patsy often was careless about her clothing. He immediately wrote to his daughter with detailed instructions: "Let your clothes be clean, whole and properly put on." He strongly believed that a female's dress was a direct statement of her moral worth and proper behavior. He went on to tutor his eleven-year-old, "Nothing is so disgusting to our sex as a want of cleanliness and delicacy in yours." Patsy blushed at her father's reprimand and chafed a bit at his further caution regarding her relations with Mrs. Hopkinson, "to be obedient and respectful to her in every circumstance" and "to consider her. . . as your mother." Never!

Patsy bridled even more at his enforced absence and at the detailed schedule Thomas stipulated for her to follow. He wrote,

from 8 to 10 o'clock: Practice music.
from 10 to 1: Dance one day and draw another.
from 1 to 2: Draw on the day you dance, and write a letter the next day.
from 3 to 4: Read French.
from 4 to : Exercise yourself in music.
from 5 till bedtime: Read English, write, & . . .

She pushed the list into a desk drawer in her room. When was she supposed to eat and socialize, she wondered? But of course she would heed his directions because he explained that he would feel more pride and affection for her as a result of her achievements. Excellence in these subjects would "render you more worthy of my love."

He also instructed that he required her to spell properly in her letters to him and to her relations. Sometimes he expected too much of her, she thought, and treated her as though she were much older. So, when he chided her for not writing to him more frequently, she quietly rebelled, delaying a few more days before sending a return letter.

SALLY

1783

WHEN PATSY DEPARTED, Sally felt strangely bereft. She knew it was foolish to think she could go with her — but hadn't they taken her to Williamsburg and Richmond with them? She had grown accustomed to having Patsy as a playmate and now she had been left behind. Sally mentioned it to her mother, and Betty looked at her in consternation, "Silly girl, your place is here on the plantation with your own family."

Life felt bleak for a while without her friend to run around with but she soon began spending more time at work with her mother, and her sister, Critta. There was always a lot to do, and she realized she had been given a lot of slack due to the expectation for her to help amuse Patsy. Critta was three years older than she, and Critta already knew how to do a lot to help around Monticello. One of her first lessons for Sally was how to make bayberry candles.

Tallow, often used for candle making, was a fatty substance made from rendered animal fat, but it was smoky and smelly. Bayberries (or wax myrtle), however, which grew in the maritime climate of Virginia, produced a waxy substance used for making aromatic candles for special occasions like Christmas. Since candles were so important for lighting each and every evening, it seemed they never could have enough.

Critta showed her how to make a double boiler by using a kettle with an inner container for the wax. They would pour water into the kettle so that it came halfway up the side of the wax pot. When the water came to a simmer over a fire, they would add bayberry and beeswax to the pot to melt it. Critta then showed her how to make the length of taper candle she wanted by cutting a wick spun from cotton to be a few inches more than twice the length she wanted. When the wax was fully melted, she would dip the wick into the wax over and over, until the desired thickness was achieved. Usually they would tie several wicks to one stick so they could dip several candles at once. Once the candles were thick enough, they would remove them, press the bottom so it was flat, and then hang the candles out to dry.

Sally was happy doing this with Critta but enjoyed spinning and sewing more. She suspected it was because she could just let her imagination run free while her needle did its job. She liked daydreaming about the happy days running through the governor's mansion. Even more, she liked visiting Patsy's old room where she found lots of books she enjoyed reading. Patsy used to tell her about what she was studying and sometimes would share her books with Sally. When her mother found her there, she would shake her head and say, "Miss Sally, I think you better get back to work."

"Just two more pages, Mama, and I'll be there." But she knew she could get away with at least a half an hour more.

ANNAPOLIS

1784

The General assembly shall not have power . . . to permit the introduction of any more slaves to reside in this state, or the continuance of slavery beyond the generation which shall be living on the 31st. day of December 1800; all persons born after that day being hereby declared free.

Extract from Thomas Jefferson's Draft of a Constitution for Virginia [before 17 June 1783]

THOMAS

1784

THOMAS FRETTED OVER LEAVING Patsy behind in Philadelphia, but he couldn't figure out any other option. The Congress was the only national governing body, and he very much wanted to be a part of leading the new country he had helped create. He was somewhat surprised when he soon learned firsthand that Congress had very little real power because the states remained in control of taxation, trade, and other major issues. How would the country move forward as a sovereign power? He believed in more central control. Otherwise, there would be anarchy. And what should be the distribution of power, he pondered? The young government was obviously in the throes of defining itself.

Meanwhile, he agonized constantly about the wellbeing of his motherless children and realized he must deal immediately with specific arrangements for Patsy. He consulted Eliza House Trist about schooling. But on New Year's Day, as he lay sick in bed in Annapolis, he felt he was getting nowhere with his many problems. The Congress hadn't even managed to obtain a quorum of states to ratify the Treaty of Paris, which would formally end the Revolutionary War and grant the United States recognition as an independent nation.

His friend James Madison was even more morose than Thomas, as his fiancée had just broken their engagement. James depended on his friend, who had recently lost his wife, to guide him through this difficult, albeit less serious, disappointment. The two bereft bachelors kept one another company throughout the gloomy holiday period with no close family to warm their spirits. They reminded one another that they were performing an important duty in Annapolis.

Finally, Connecticut and New Jersey arrived at the table, the treaty was ratified by the nine states necessary, and they forwarded the document to Paris. It would take a long while for the messenger to take it by ship, and the terms of the treaty demanded ratification within six months of its signing, which had occurred on Wednesday, September 3, 1783, in Paris at the Hotel de York in the rue Jacob.

Feeling profoundly lonely, Thomas began imagining and making plans for his friends to live near him in Virginia. He wrote to James Madison that their friend James Monroe had already bought a parcel of land near Monticello, and he urged Madison to do the same. He revealed that William Short, the young lawyer, whom he had just invited to be his private secretary, planned to do this as well. He wrote, "Life is of no value but as it brings us gratifications. Among the most valuable of these is rational society. It informs the mind, sweetens the temper, cheers our spirits, and promotes health." Of course, his daughter must be feeling lonely too, he thought.

Thomas felt more overwhelmed than he could ever remember. One of the problems dogging the Congress was a shortage of funds. The governing body was unable to pay the Continental Army and the legislators, and the British were still demanding unpaid prewar debts. The states continued to bicker about boundaries between them, and many prickly issues having to do with the settlement of the great American West needled him. So many problems with unanswered solutions! In this low moment, he was stricken by one of his migraine headaches and could only lie abed in a dark room for several days.

During this time the Virginia legislature decided to formally cede to the United States its claims to the Northwestern Territory. Being a stickler for detail, Thomas amused himself in bed, dreaming up names of states for the uncharted territory in the West. He came up with: Sylvania, Cherronesus, Assenisipia, Metropotamia, Illinoia, Michigania, etc. More importantly, he wrote into this Ordinance of 1784 that slavery would be banned in the new territory by 1800. Because one delegate failed to arrive due to illness, the ordinance failed to pass by only one vote. Dispirited, he decided he must abandon the cause of emancipation of the slaves for the time being. He wrote, "the fate of millions unborn was hanging on the tongue of one man, and Heaven was silent in that awful moment!"

On May 7, an invitation arrived to lift his spirits. The Continental Congress again asked him to join Franklin and Adams in Europe with the mission of establishing alliances for their new nation. Even more enthusiastically than before, he welcomed the opportunity for foreign travel and a meaningful goal. With renewed energy, he also asked James Hemings, now eighteen years old, to come along as their cook, promising to have him trained in traditional French cuisine. And the best part of the solution would be to take Patsy with him! She would benefit from a French education, he felt sure, and they could be together. There was still a huge hole in his heart, but these plans became a welcome distraction.

He needed to bring James, who was still at Monticello, to Philadelphia and instructed Short to make this happen. Short was the right man for the job because through his family, he also had Hemings connections. His cousins were married to John Wayles's daughters, Tabitha and Anne Wayles. In the Wayles/Hemings/Jefferson tangle, these women were James Hemings's half-sisters.

Luckily, James now owned his own horse, which Thomas had given him, as well as a pass for when he was out and about. But Thomas knew it still would be dangerous for a black man to travel across the country alone. Since 1680 in Virginia, slaves who traveled without supervision of a master were required to carry a pass. And, even though James was a "bright mulatto," a nineteen-year-old black man could easily be apprehended for just about anything. He hoped the young man would arrive without problems.

PARIS, FRANCE

AMBASSADOR TO THE COURT OF LOUIS XVI

1784-89

. . . societies exist under three forms sufficiently distinguishable: 1. without government, as among our Indians; 2. under governments wherein the will of every one has a just influence, as is the case in England in a slight degree, and in our states in a great one;. 3. under governments of force, as is the case in all other monarchies and in most of the other republics. To have an idea of the curse of existence under these last, they must be seen.

Extract from Thomas Jefferson to James Madison, Paris, January. 30. 1787

PATSY

1784

HER FATHER WAS TRULY taking her to Paris! Patsy could barely breathe, she was so excited. She tried to contain herself but couldn't stop dashing around the house. Her feet just jiggled unbidden. When would they leave? Thomas returned to Philadelphia in mid-May, in time to take her to an exhibition of hot-air balloons. He explained that just one year earlier, Pilatre De Rozier, a French scientist, had launched the first hot air balloon. A sheep, a duck, and a rooster were the chosen passengers, and the balloon had stayed afloat for a grand total of 15 minutes before crashing back to the ground. He recounted the story he'd heard of many hysterical, bewigged French men and women, running beneath the little flying basket, hilarious with the show. "We will be able to see more of this extraordinary sight when we are in Paris! Now, we must buckle down and prepare for the trip," he instructed her.

James arrived from Virginia just in time for their departure on May 26, and the threesome set out two days later. The first leg of the trip involved a ferry across the Delaware River to New Jersey, which was not easy because of all their traveling trunks. The entire arrangement atop their carriage looked extremely precarious to Patsy but she tried to hide her fears. They reached New York on the last day of May and remained there for six days before taking up the journey in earnest. She didn't dare complain, but the twenty-one days it took to cover the 270 miles to Boston from Philadelphia often left her feeling tired and grumpy. She was constantly grateful for the presence of James who helped with such necessities as carriage repair or shoeing the horses.

Upon arriving in Boston, they were disappointed to learn that the next ship departing for Europe would not embark until early July. To Patsy's chagrin, Thomas immediately left her with John Lowell, a Boston judge and his family, having decided he should tour the ports of New England to better his understanding of eastern commerce. She couldn't help but worry that he would be gone longer than he promised, recalling their last delayed trip.

Once again, Patsy had to cope with living amongst strangers. Judge Lowell had a large family, and so at least she felt fairly comfortable with a number of other children around. But she cringed sometimes at the dinner table conversation, as she listened to a serious condemnation of slavery for the first time. Indeed, John Lowell had been a part of the movement to end slavery in Massachusetts in 1780. She frequently found herself turning crimson in the face and staring into her dinner plate.

The long-awaited departure aboard the ship *Ceres* was scheduled for July 3, but they were told it would be delayed again. Then only one day later it finally did leave — with six passengers, including Abigail Adams, who was traveling to join her husband in Europe, and Thomas, Patsy, William Short, and James. Patsy helped tend to Mrs. Adams, who was seasick most of the trip, but wrote home announcing that "they had a fine sun shine all the way, with the sea which was as calm as a river." Indeed, they accomplished the crossing in the almost record time of three weeks.

Things were not so agreeable upon landing at West Cowes on the Isle of Wight. Patsy was embarrassed she had to slow their party down, but she felt too sick to leave her bed. Thomas tried to calm her, assuring her she had done nothing wrong. He called a physician in Portsmouth because her florid color and hot skin indicated she had a fever, which alarmed him. She gradually began to improve, but Thomas insisted she rest for four days before crossing the English Channel to France.

Both Patsy and James were given tiny, airless quarters in the small ship, and stormy rough seas made the thirteen-hour trip miserable. At least it was not only she who was ill this time. On the last day of July, upon landing in Le Havre, Patsy and Thomas immediately felt the disadvantage of not speaking French well. Patsy clung to him, as beggars frequently accosted their carriage during the ride to Paris. She grabbed her father's arm in fear when one particular toothless, haggard face banged with a stick on the carriage door.

Thomas sent James ahead to secure lodging in Rouen, even though James spoke or understood less French than they did. He knew he could count on the young man's courage. Patsy was glad she had studied the language a bit throughout her young life, and Thomas also had studied French at school. Taking in the sights all along the way, Patsy wrote to Eliza Trist that the church of Notre Dame in Mantes, "had as many steps to go to the top as there are days in the year. There are many pretty statues in it. The architectures is [sic] beautiful. All the winders are died [sic] glass of the most beautiful colours that form all kinds of figures." She also raved about the cathedral in Rouen and the lovely French countryside as they drove up the Seine Valley.

Thomas encouraged her enthusiasm. "I think it wonderful also, my sweet girl. This may be the most agreeable country on earth."

When the trio finally reached Paris on August 6, 1784, they crossed into the city at the Pont de Neuilly, and for the time being, they domiciled at the Hôtel d'Orléans facing the rue Richlieu and extending back to the rue de Montpensier, which bordered the gardens of the new Palais Royal. Thomas suddenly realized how much needed to be done to set up house. He had been so caught up in the excitement of departure, he had failed to sufficiently plan ahead. And, he admitted to himself, he was accustomed to having his slaves make life easy for him.

Patsy wrote immediately to Eliza Trist, saying, *I am sure you would have laughfed, [sic] for we were obliged to send immediately for the stay maker, the mantua maker, the milliner, and even a shoe maker, before I could go out.* Fashionable Paris would be a challenge for a Virginia country girl, she warned her Papa. While she was busy outfitting herself, she observed her father purchasing lace ruffles, a sword, belt, and shaving apparatus. And of course, he needed books and a map right away. The arcades of the Palais Royale were always tempting — a startling assemblage of delights to tempt the imagination and the palate. There were theaters, cafés, and shops for everything: furniture, jewels, textiles, books, clocks — whatever ones heart desired and more.

Patsy felt overwhelmed and dizzy with so much happening. She was twelve years old and had never seen such a large vibrant place as Paris. She held her father's hand like a young child, as they made their way through the crowded streets. The attention to fashion was particularly striking; it looked like many people's daywear would be proper for going to a ball in Virginia. And the poor wore such rags that one could often see skin through the tatters. The slaves in Virginia were much better taken care of than these people, she observed. She also found the background noise of the incomprehensible language nerve-wracking. She laughed and told her father, "I'm too young for this kind of life!"

Patsy was relieved when Abigail Adams offered to take her in hand at the dressmaker's. She couldn't make herself understood in French yet, and felt shy about deciding on choices of fabric and color. Together, they settled on a blue silk with a lighter blue petticoat beneath and splurged on vertical blue bows down the center to decorate the bodice. They would need to come back, of course, because they couldn't do it all in one day. Abigail also insisted that she have a bonnet with flowers, shoes with buckles, and a side-hooped petticoat, which was in fashion. Never had Patsy felt so spoiled, but her father seemed to think it appropriate. She threw her arms around him, overcome with her bounty.

Thomas and Patsy were invited to dine with John and Abigail at their Paris home on August 15. Patsy proudly donned her new finery to go out, and was especially glad that English would be the language of the evening. Nabby, the Adamses' daughter, came up and hugged her immediately. It was the first time the two girls had met, and Patsy was very grateful to have a girlfriend. Nabby took her by the hand to show the visitor her room and tell her all about living in Paris. Patsy sensed herself truly relaxing for the first time abroad, and smiled at this generous, friendly girl. She admitted to Nabby that her mother, Abigail, had been a tremendous comfort to her. Later, she was proud when she heard Nabby telling her parents that Patsy was a "sweet girl with amiable and lovely manners." Her Papa would be proud of her.

Thomas

1784-85

THOMAS WAS ESPECIALLY GLAD the Adams family resided in Paris because Patsy had warmed to Nabby so much. It became an expected occasion for the Adamses *en famille* to dine at the Jeffersons' on Thursday evenings. Thomas could see that their presence greatly helped his daughter feel at home in the foreign country. Patsy, being without a mother, obviously found Abigail, as starchy as she was, extremely soothing.

After only two months in temporary housing, Thomas understood he needed to look for something more comfortable and was drawn to the Chaussée d'Antin and the Boulevards, an area which recently had become popular with the elite. He found a relatively small town house without grounds or a view in the rue et cul-de-sac Taitbout and signed a lease, agreeing to pay 1,500 *livres* each quarter. As it was unfurnished, he happily threw himself into purchasing furniture, carpets, and all one needed to be at ease and properly presentable. He felt he couldn't do without his music and rented a pianoforte for 12 *livres* a month. He did complain to his friend James Monroe that "my expenses should be paid [by Congress} in a stile [sic] equal to that of those with whom I am classed." He grumbled about having to take money out of his own pocket to buy what he needed and asked Monroe to present his case to Congress.

The chill and gloom of the Paris climate was a shock to both Thomas and Patsy, who were accustomed to the crisp Indian summer days of Virginia. They missed the golden glow of the trees on their mountain and shivered when early darkness brought down the curtain between day and night. Thomas, being a man of detail and schedule, put in place a routine for fires to be laid in every fireplace throughout the house in the mornings, so they could be lit as soon as the light disappeared outside. The glowing hearths helped to raise their spirits immensely.

But a warm fire couldn't assuage the blow from the tragic news the Marquis de Lafayette brought to their door in January 1785. Little Lucy, age 2, had died from a whooping cough infection at Eppington. When they saw Lafayette's dashing figure in a powdered wig and martial blue jacket with gold buttons at their door, they gladly received their friend, but immediately his grim face told them he must bring bad tidings. "Your little Polly survived," he said. "But Lucy is gone."

Gone. Patsy could not fathom what he meant. How could she be gone? Her father's grief caused him to shudder and shake before the sobbing broke free, and Patsy, realizing finally what it meant, joined in with wails of her own. What cruel news! She felt as if she would faint and grabbed a chair to steady herself. Her father clasped her to him to soothe them both.

Patsy already was fond of the Marquis and was confused that this kind man could be the bearer of such dreadful tidings. Lafayette was a big man, with dark curly hair, a straight nose and wide mobile mouth. A bulbous prominent chin stood in the way of his being called handsome, but his warm demeanor caused everyone to find him attractive. His direct and honest mien made him seem more American than French, she decided.

When they received the news that baby Lucy had died, Thomas's first thought was that he must quickly rescue Polly. Lucy was the daughter who was born shortly before his wife died, and so it felt like a double blow. Lafayette also told them that one of the Eppeses' daughters had perished too from the virulent infection.

"Oh, Papa, poor Polly must be even more upset than we are," Patsy sobbed. "She must be very frightened!"

"Yes, my sweet girl. I'm sure you are right. She is feeling even more despair and fear from this unexpected loss than we, because we have one another."

Nabby noted that Mr. Jefferson and Patsy were "greatly affected," and to show her sympathy, invited Patsy over to her house to go sliding on the ice. Patsy felt this was a lovely gesture and accepted with alacrity. Nabby confided to Patsy during their outing that she was very unhappy because her father had insisted she reject a dashing suitor. Patsy felt quite proud that Nabby had shared her sentiments.

The Lafayettes often invited the Jeffersons to dinner at their townhouse in the rue de Bourbon to help alleviate their mourning. Thomas and Patsy had met Adrienne, the Marquis's wife, while in England, as the Marquise had become a good friend of Abigail Adams. The Lafayette children even entertained them, with Anastasie and George Washington Lafayette singing, and Kayenlaha, a twelve-year-old Iroquois boy, brought back to France by the Marquis, dancing in a scant costume. Patsy was extremely grateful that she could now say she had a few friends in Paris. But it worried her greatly to have been absent when her little sister had died.

Thomas was invited to the estate of the duc de La Rochefoucauld, a member of the aristocracy and a famed author of memoirs and maxims, and then to the home of the Marquis de Condorcet, an illustrious mathematician. He became immensely excited about their ideas and was delighted to be included in their circle. Of course, he already knew the Marquis de Lafayette, whose friendship and support during the American Revolution had been so important.

As ambassador, Thomas wished to advance America's security and economy by attending to this relationship with France. And at the same time, there was so much stimulating intellect here to enjoy! He was relieved that no one seemed to mind his southern accent and wondered if they even noticed. His poise and supremely good manners seemed to win over the French immediately, and he sensed his aristocratic bearing impressed the court.

He enjoyed answering questions for his new French friends about America and was astonished at how often they asked about the American Indians. The French, as explorers in the New World, had encountered tribes but hadn't enjoined with them as a people as extensively as the Americans had done. The Marquis de Chastellux, another member of the peerage, was curious about American treaties with the indigenous Americans, but inquired especially about their way of life. Thomas answered him, "I believe the Indian . . . to be in body & mind equal to the whiteman [sic]. I have supposed the black man, in his present state, might not be so, but it would be hazardous to affirm that, equally cultivated for a few generations, he would not become so." When they pressed him about slavery, he assured them he thought the unfortunate institution would die out soon in America, and they appeared appeased.

Like most Americans, Jefferson's idea of France was that it was a country ruled by tyranny and dominated by the Catholic religion. Britain's culture was immediately more accessible and understood by their former colony, and Thomas knew he would need to find a way to convince his countrymen to welcome French culture and partnership. He had a tough job on both sides. His first duties would be to assist Benjamin Franklin, who had been America's ambassador to France since 1776, and John Adams in negotiating treaties for agricultural products crucial to the American economy: tobacco, rice, wheat, and whale oil. He planned to stay for two years as an ambassador to bring about these changes. Yet, always in the back of his mind was the desire to soak up all the European culture he possibly could and to bring ideas back to his new country. America, he believed, needed art and architecture to call its own, as well as trade goods.

His primary challenge for the present, however, was to find a proper school for Patsy. It had been two years since Patty had died and in these moments of responsibility for his daughter, he missed her sorely. Abigail alarmed him with her stories of the morals of French women, and so he was drawn to the idea of a convent school. Yet many Americans, most of whom were Protestant, looked down upon the idea of a Catholic education. However, the Marquis de Chastellux, whom he was growing to trust, recommended a prestigious convent school at the Abbaye Royale de Panthémont. Thomas approved of the curriculum there, as it included manners, music, and drawing, as well as geography, arithmetic, history, Latin, and modern languages. Thomas prayed his naïve daughter would be safe among the nuns at the corner of the rue de Grenelle.

When interviewing the head Abbesse, he made a point to make it clear to her that he strongly believed in freedom of religious choice for every individual. She, in turn, assured him that fifteen of the fifty-five girls residing there at present were Protestant. She was firm but compassionate, and he decided this place would be a happy solution. He was relieved also to learn that Patsy would not be required to study catechism, but agreed it would be appropriate for her to attend Catholic religious services with the other girls.

On the first day Thomas drove Patsy in their private phaeton (they had brought this beautiful Monticello-built carriage to Paris on their ship for their use while abroad) to the school at 39, rue de Bellechasse. Patsy held his hand tightly as they looked upon the rhythmical arches forming the façade of the respected institution. She wouldn't let go as she was introduced to a line of girls of all ages wearing crimson uniforms, with hooked-on white cuffs and tuckers. Then one of them took her by the hand to lead her away from her father, pointing out the bed and little writing desk that would be hers in one of the large rooms arranged for sleeping, called a *dortoir*. Her fellow students were mostly daughters of aristocrats, both French and English. Indeed, Josephine de Beauharnais, the future empress of France, attended the school in the 1780s.

"Papa," Patsy complained. "I am the only American girl. I can't stay here alone." She felt like she was going to cry but didn't want to be a baby. She must not be a burden to him. But this felt like too much for him to ask of her. Thomas could understand why — so many new faces and routines were overwhelming, but he suspected her fear largely came from her inability to speak the language of the nuns and her fellow students. Realizing what a difficult beginning it was for her, he knelt down on one knee to her height.

"I promise, dear girl, I promise to come to the school every evening to visit for as long as you need me to do so." Bravely, she shook her head in agreement.

PATSY

1785-86

PATSY'S FACE WAS LONG and thin like her father's but her tresses were curlier and more cinnamon than his ginger. She had a rather wild streak, preferring to run rather than walk, and a somewhat unladylike laugh. She liked to joke, and her intelligence shone through the first shy demeanor. Soon, the other girls warmed to her. Nevertheless, she was terribly lonely the first few weeks.

Patsy suffered another blow when she heard the Adams family would be leaving Paris for London, as Mr. Adams would take an assignment in England. She had enjoyed Nabby greatly, even feeling she was like an older sister, and Thomas, though often irritated with John's stubborn personality, treasured their friendship. Upon their parting, Nabby told her that Abigail greatly regretted leaving Mr. Jefferson. She quoted her mother's words to Patsy: "He is one of the choice ones of the earth."

"You shall come and visit me in London," Nabby added, also sorry to be separating from her new, younger friend.

Gradually, Marie de Botidoux became a close French friend, and she endowed Patsy with a nickname — everyone began calling her "Jeffy," which Patsy especially liked when Marie said it in her French accent. The two shared sleeping quarters in one of the four large dormitory rooms. She would be fine there, Thomas told himself. He still was exasperated, however, at her continuing tendency to let her clothing become disheveled. Patsy blushed as she read yet another straightforward warning to her about this in a letter. She must try and do better.

The only other American girl, Kitty Church, seemed determined to torment her. One day with several other girls in a sewing class, Kitty addressed Patsy, "Is it true your father owns African slaves?"

Patsy was speechless. As the other girls joined in, Patsy's face turned more and more crimson, making her freckles bloom.

Her tormentor continued, "I'll bet you didn't know that by French law any slave who reaches the shores of France will be freed." Patsy just hung her head over her embroidery, too stunned to reply and tried not to cry. She must ask her father if this were true. These girls just didn't understand that their slaves were like part of her family, and that no one would ever mistreat them at Monticello.

On May 24, 1785, Thomas arrived at the Abbaye to escort Patsy on a special excursion to watch the ceremonial procession of Queen Marie-Antoinette to Notre Dame, where she would kneel to thank God for the birth of a son.

"I do not admire this queen," he informed Patsy when the royal procession neared. "She is too extravagant. I want you to remember the American values of simplicity and hard work," he added. Indeed, Patsy had never seen such a sight as that of the bejeweled queen with her court assembled around her. Even while moving ahead, the courtiers managed to bow and scrape to their monarch whenever the opportunity arose.

"Yes, Papa. Mrs. Adams tells me the same thing."

"We share values with them, and so I was so glad for you to spend time with her and Nabby." He continued speaking but didn't look at her. He appeared to be watching the sky instead. "And I know you heard of the scandal recently when someone, posing as the queen, fooled the Cardinal de Rohan into secretly purchasing a diamond necklace for her. It turned out to be a false accusation, but everyone believed it because of the queen's selfish character."

Patsy listened, fascinated by this extraordinary tale. But her father wasn't finished. "You may take a lesson from this, Patsy." Now he looked down at her. "*Reputation* is everything. A soiled reputation in an ordinary person may reduce them to impoverishment, but a soiled reputation in someone like the queen may take down a government."

She wasn't sure she understood what he was trying to tell her, but she sensed his serious tone. "I think I have a good reputation," she murmured.

"Of course you do! I never thought you didn't." Sometimes it seemed like her father spoke in riddles.

He exploited another occasion for more fatherly advice when he escorted her to a ballooning exhibition — after all, ballooning had begun here. "The more you learn the more I love you, and I rest the happiness of my life on seeing you beloved by all the world, which you will be sure to be if to a good heart you join those accomplishments so peculiarly pleasing in your sex."

"I understand, Papa," Patsy said. Although she wasn't at all sure she did. "But look, look! Another balloon is taking off into the clouds," she exclaimed. His moment for preaching was over. They strolled home, stopping at bookstalls and a café for a *chocolat chaud avec chantilly,* and she thought she had never tasted anything so delicious.

As the winter closed in, James proved to be having an especially tough time adapting to the damp air and unwholesome water in the city. He also complained about the dirty streets, the beggars, and petty theft. When he fell ill in December, they had to postpone his training to become a chef. The entire household began to rely more and more on William Short, Thomas's secretary, for errands and organizing. Mr. Short simply moved into the Hôtel de Taitbout to make life simpler, and Patsy found she enjoyed his presence more and more each day. He often made a point to speak to her specifically in a conversation, making her feel more grownup. Much of everyone's chatter included complaints about the weather, and Patsy, too, grumbled daily over the freezing temperature in the convent. She told her father the nuns wouldn't even allow a fire in the room unless there was ice in the water basins.

Thomas frantically began to look for a larger house, telling his daughter he wanted space to have both his girls with him, and only a few months later, he signed a lease for the neoclassical Hôtel de Langeac. He would be paying 3,500 *livres* quarterly, which was more than the Taitbout townhouse, but he would have more room, gardens, and the stables particularly excited him. The residence was situated about halfway up the Champs-Elysées at the northeast corner of the rue de Berri. The rue Saint Honoré, at the other end of the street, was the main thoroughfare of the Right Bank and was crowded with elegant boutiques and moving carriages. Without sidewalks, it often presented a challenge to the distracted window-shopper.

Patsy gawked at the splendid mansion when the family moved in on 17 October 1785. Thomas showed the garden to her and James with enthusiasm, "We can even grow some greens and corn for our table! And we will place tables outside for all to dine *en plein air.*" He had already begun to sprinkle his English with French when he wasn't speaking the new language.

He led Patsy and James around the mansion's exterior of creamy stone with sculpted friezes at the roofline. They all admired the high decorative metal gate guarding a spacious courtyard and steps leading up to the front door. Inside, to the left, were a reception hall, a circular room with a skylight, and an oval room leading out to the garden with the ceiling painted to represent the rising sun,. A sweeping pink marble staircase led to the upper floor where there were numerous bedrooms, each with a private bathroom and dressing room. Next, Thomas took them to see the bathing tubs of porcelain and copper standing in each bathroom, and of all the luxuries, he clearly found the *lieux anglais,* or water closets, the most exciting addition. The ceilings were painted with scenes and figures in many rooms, and the walls were covered in silk damask. It took Patsy's breath away, and her father had to speak firmly to her to stop running up and down the pink staircase. "It is not ladylike," he reprimanded.

Of course, so much more space required more servants, and so he hired a gardener, several maids, and acquired horses and carriages, which in turn necessitated a coachman. He explained to Patsy that he must keep up to the stylish standard that Benjamin Franklin had established.

When they moved in, all the neighbors stood in the street to watch the strange Americans. They pushed forward against the metal gate to see better as a hand-painted harpsichord was carried up the steps, and crystal chandeliers were uncrated outside to be carefully hauled inside. When the new harpsichord was carried in, he put his hand on his daughter's shoulder, saying, "So that we may play together, my darling girl, and I have been lucky to find copies of several new Mozart compositions in a stall on the Left Bank."

So much commotion was unusual in this newly developing neighborhood, and the tradesmen were delighted to see all the activity. Patsy watched her father become more and more exasperated as Polly, now six years old, dragged her feet. He had secured the larger house, and she too wished her sister would join them soon. Yet Polly strongly resisted the prospect, claiming to be frightened by the idea of coming to Paris. This irritated Thomas, but with the demands of his new office, he let months go by without the issue being resolved.

Patsy learned that Benjamin Franklin was now leaving the office of ambassador solely to Thomas, and she understood this would demand more of him than his economic negotiations had done. She heard the Comte de Vergennes, when he announced the appointment, say, "You replace Dr. Franklin." Her father modestly replied, "No one can replace him; I am only his successor."

As his job became more time-consuming — his French title was Minister Plenipotentiary to the King of France — she saw her father only about two or three times a month, and he often sent her allowance to the school via William Short. She began to look forward to Mr. Short's visits, and the other girls teased her about the attractive older gentleman who was paying her so much attention. Patsy calculated he must be about thirteen or fourteen years older than she, yet she found it so easy to chat with him.

THOMAS

1786

THOMAS TRAVELED TO ENGLAND in March, leaving Patsy at the Abbaye de Panthémont. She begged him to take her with him so she could see Nabby again. But in a letter to her, he refused:

You have your schooling. The more you learn, the more I love you. Lose no moment in improving your head, nor any opportunity of exercising your heart in benevolence. Your duty is to attend your studies at the convent. My duty takes me to England.

Before he left he had a note from Abigail Adams asking him to bring a few pieces of fabric from fashionable Paris to England and sending love to Patsy. Abigail also said, "I am really surfeited with Europe, and most heartily long for the rural cottage, the purer & honester [sic] manners of my native land." He understood her sentiment well for he had just written to Baron von Geismar from Paris, only a few months earlier, saying, *I am savage enough to prefer the woods, the wilds, & the independence of Monticello, to all the brilliant pleasures of this gay capital . . . for tho' there is less wealth there, there is more freedom, more ease & less misery.*

Indeed, he was baffled by the French in some ways and judged Americans to be a much happier people. He wrote to his friend Mrs. Trist saying,

> *It is difficult to conceive how so good a people, with so good a king, so well-disposed rulers in general, so genial a climate, so fertile a soil, should be rendered so ineffectual for producing human happiness by one single curse —that of a bad form of government. But it is a fact in spite of the mildness of their governors, the people are ground to powder by the vices of the form of government. Of twenty*

millions of people supposed to be in France, I am of opinion there are nineteen millions more wretched, more accursed in every circumstance of human existence, than the most conspicuously wretched individual of the whole United States.

Thomas was taken aback by Patsy's chilly reaction when he told her he was going away again in late summer 1786 — this time, he would depart for Italy with a certain artist friend, Maria Cosway. Patsy looked down and away from him, which was unusual.

"What is the matter, my dear?" he probed.

"*Rien*, Papa," she answered.

He thought she said "nothing," because she couldn't really explain her discomfort. Sometimes it was so difficult to decipher her feelings and wondered how much he should tell her. He did feel a bit squeamish about his plans because he had not socialized much with other women since the death of her mother. He intuited this was most likely the source of the problem.

How difficult it was to raise a daughter in this society — where women of supposedly good name shared their salons with their husbands and lovers. And of course the husbands behaved likewise. Patsy was an observant young woman and would be taking this all in. What should he say to her? He thought he must talk to her about how a righteous American woman values domestic happiness above all other. This tendency of French women to flirt and argue politics was not a proper pastime.

John Trumbull, the American artist and his friend, had introduced him to the Cosways the summer before at an extravagant party hosted by the couple at the Halle aux Blés, the grain market in Paris. The structure, a wood-ribbed dome with twenty-five glass insertions, bestowed a transporting mood of wonder and delight. Maria Cosway's violet-blue eyes carried him further heavenward, and he couldn't resist the desire to hear more of her exotic Italian accent. M. La Rochefoucauld warned him that Maria treated men like dogs, but Thomas was too enchanted to listen. Somewhat sensitive about his awkward, lanky body, Thomas was surprised that this young goddess seemed attracted to him. Perhaps she understood that his outward, sometimes-shambling demeanor belied an incisive and imaginative mind.

Indeed, he wanted to brag a bit about what he had just learned — that the Virginia Assembly had passed an Act for Establishing Religious

Freedom in January 1786. He had been the author of the legislation and believed it to be extremely important. But he doubted if his new French friends would appreciate its value.

PATSY

JEFFERSON LIKED AND ADMIRED John Trumbull tremendously and so, with his usual grand generosity, offered him a room and studio at the Hôtel de Langeac while the artist was painting his portrait. Trumbull often allowed Patsy to sit nearby and watch him work, chatting with her in a friendly manner. M. Trumbull related to her that Mrs. Cosway was an artist too. Thereafter, Patsy carefully studied her Papa's behavior when he visited her at school to see if he talked of Mrs. Cosway or let slip other information. Why would he be traveling with her, she wondered? She was a married woman and his infatuation seemed inappropriate. Patsy had heard rumors from a few of the girls at the Abbaye that this woman was a glamorous socialite, and they revealed to Patsy with giggles that Maria had enticed M. Jefferson into her circle. But, at least he had appeared to be happier lately, she thought.

In early September Thomas invited Patsy to join him at the opera. "It will be a reward because you speak French now as easily as English! While Mr. Short and myself are scarcely better at it than when we arrived. You're nearly fourteen," he continued, "and I will buy you a very special dress for the occasion."

She was ecstatic. She would, at last, see true French society — and on the arm of her father, a minister to Versailles! All of her friends at the Abbaye were envious, but she tried not to be too proud. She knew that was a sin. Her Papa had warned her that pride costs us more than hunger, thirst, and cold. Her good friend, Marie de Botidoux, helped her to dress in the new gown and satin shoes.

"You're beginning to look like a real lady," Marie told her. Patsy was disappointed when Thomas asked William Short to bring her to the opera from the Abbaye instead of escorting her himself. Surely, he would be awaiting her outside le Théâtre Italien, where the performance was being held, but she was again surprised when she must descend from the carriage only with the aid of Mr. Short's helping hand and proceed alone into the reception hall. But there he was, at last! Towering over everyone, wearing a white wig and a slim blue satin jacket. He waved to her to come and join him, and she had to restrain herself not to run. At his side stood a petite beautiful woman, her hair powdered, with flowers and jewels hiding in its waves.

"Allow me to present Maria Cosway. Maria, this is my lovely daughter Patsy. Patsy, Maria is both an artist and a musician."

Patsy gave a proper curtsy and smile to the older lady. "*Enchantée de faire votre connaissance, Madame.*"

So, she wasn't to be the center of his attention after all. She called upon her manners to hide her disappointment and walked on her father's other arm up the grand staircase. The performance that evening, 9 September 1786, included two works: Grétry and Sedaine's light opera *Richard Coeur de Lion,* and a one-act harlequinade in verse, Florian's *Les Deux Billets.* At the interval, Thomas mentioned that he hoped to escort his favorite ladies soon to hear *Idomeneo,* by Mozart, which had debuted in Vienna in 1781 to great acclaim.

The trio shared a box, and although she was enchanted with the opera, Patsy couldn't help but notice that her father was more enchanted with Maria. She found it all the more confusing because she knew Maria was married.

THOMAS

MARIA WAS WEDDED TO THE successful miniaturist, Richard Cosway, but she had subtly made it clear to Thomas that the marriage was unsatisfactory. The couple appeared to follow their separate paths. He inferred from her circumlocutions that Mr. Conway perhaps preferred men. Thomas was completely infatuated with this golden-haired Anglo-Italian. He worried because she was sixteen years younger than he, but she made him feel fresh and vigorous! And he found her accomplishments in art and music especially ravishing. Thomas couldn't understand why she had married Cosway because his face resembled a monkey's, and his manners, though vivacious, were distinctly odd. Perhaps she had been too young to know better, he surmised.

Maria was not only lovely, she was truly a talented artist. She specialized in engravings and small paintings, and exhibited in London salons. She told him her parents were English, but she had been schooled in Florence. He was a bit surprised and embarrassed by how her worldly sophistication and blond beauty so entranced him. During August and September the couple enjoyed an intense flirtation, and he couldn't remember feeling so passionate and alive in a very long time. He felt truly carried away — like one of the hot-air balloons he'd seen floating above Paris recently.

Since she was an artist, he speculated she might enjoy a visit to the Louvre with him to view some of the fine painting going on in Paris. The Louvre hadn't been used as a royal residence for many years and was slowly morphing into a national museum. It already housed much of the royal art collection and some of the country's artists lived in the Cours du Louvre, including the up-and-coming Jacques-Louis David.

Maria agreed to the plan, and he had trouble focusing on David's recently created *Oath of the Horatii,* so enchanted was he with the petite woman standing at his side. He couldn't resist putting his arm around her dainty waist to steer her from painting to painting. They moved on to view a few oils by Madame Vigée-Lebrun, who was becoming quite popular among the elite of Paris. Maria seemed particularly taken with her portrait of Marie-Antoinette and her children. Thomas dared to differ, saying he didn't particularly like her coloring. "I don't think I would choose her to paint any of my friends or family," he asserted. He put his arm around her again to direct her to a bust by Houdon, one of his favorite sculptors.

In October he persuaded Maria to join him for a walk and picnic in the Cours-la-Reine, a park on the Seine. James, acting as their coachman, drove them in the phaeton the short distance to the shaded glade. Thomas had chosen this area, located along the River Seine between the Place de la Concorde and the Place du Canada, as a perfect spot for a leisurely romantic meander. The landscape had been finely manicured with carefully shaped shrubs and alleyways of tall trees, and the golden low light made the lawns shine like a Renaissance painting. He felt like jumping for joy. A low ramshackle fence enticed him, and making a run for it, he dared a clumsy leap over the pickets.

On his back, on the other side, he was filled with embarrassment. Had he been showing off for her? Maria hurried through a break in the slats and his humiliation only increased.

"I'm afraid I have broken my wrist," he said, trying not to moan. For a moment he felt like he was going to be ill as well. She helped him to rise and return to their carriage, where James awaited them.

James took one look and said, "Master, I think we must hurry back to your home and the doctor. It is swelling quickly."

"Ah, Madame, I am afraid we must forego our picnic for today. I apologize for being so foolhardy."

Maria laughed with the engaging sound that so delighted him. "It is of no serious consequence. Let us go immediately to find help for you."

He was crushed. This delightful woman was to leave Paris again in a few days. The excruciating pain in his arm caused him to miss another date with her before she left. What a fool he had been! He was no longer in his twenties, for God's sake! Her beauty had completely chased away his senses.

At her departure on October 12, he composed a dialogue between his head and his heart, clearly exposing the tug of his attraction and sent it off to her.

Heart: I am indeed the most wretched of all earthly beings. Over-whelmed with grief, every fiber of my frame distended beyond its natural powers to bear [sic]. . . .

Head: These are the eternal consequences of your warmth and pre-cipitation. This is one of the scrapes into which you are ever leading us . . .

Heart: . . . I am rent into fragments by the force of my grief! . . .

Head: . . . Harsh therefore as the medicine may be, it is my office to administer it.

Heart: May heaven abandon me if I do! . . .

Head: I wished to make you sensible how imprudent it is to place your affections, without reserve, on objects you must so soon lose, and whose loss when it comes must cost you such severe pangs . . . Everything in this world is a matter of calculation . . . . Do not bite at the bait of pleasure until you know there is no hook beneath it.

Heart: And what more sublime delight than to mingle tears with one whom the hand of heaven hath smitten! . . . We are not immortal ourselves, my friend; how can we expect our enjoyments to be so? We have no rose without its thorn; no pleasure without alloy. It is the law of our existence; and we must acquiesce.

Now, when he thought about it, he was only more embarrassed. She hadn't responded to his letter, and he was afraid he had frightened her away.

He was further humiliated when he had to cancel an appearance at the Hôtel de Ville where he had planned to present the mayor of Paris with a gift from the state of Virginia. It was a handsome bust by Houdon of the Marquis de Lafayette, honoring his role in the American Revolution. The injury to his wrist turned out to be worse than originally thought, and it was clearly too painful for him to attend.

1787

In late February Thomas left Paris to journey alone in the South of France and northern Italy. He decided Patsy would be safe at school and at the Hôtel de Langeac with Mr. Short, James, and the other servants in attendance. He loved architecture and was determined to study the history of this engrossing subject during his sojourn. He made many architectural drawings of the edifices that pleased him — some with the idea of copying them for government buildings in America and a few that gave him inspiration for improvements at Monticello.

Among his favorites was the Maison Carrée at *Nîmes*. He described the building in his personal notes: *Erected at the time of the Caesars and which is allowed without contradiction to be the most perfect and precious remain of antiquity, I determined, therefore, to adopt this model and to have all its proportions justly drewed." [sic]* He was also riveted by the Pont du Gard, in the Languedoc region, which he visited in the spring.

He wrote frequently to Patsy during his travels and couldn't help but chide her when she complained that her Latin translation "put her out of her wits." He responded, "I do not like your saying that you are unable to read the ancient print of your Livy but with the aid of your master . . . We are always equal to what we undertake with resolution." Occasionally, he wondered if he expected too much of her, but he had witnessed her intelligence and he couldn't abide laziness.

While abroad, he corresponded also with Abigail Adams, indicating that even though traveling, his mind was on governing. He wrote on February 22: *The spirit of resistance to government is so valuable on certain occasions, that I wish it to be always kept alive. It will often be exercised when wrong, but better so than not to be exercised at all. I like a little rebellion now and then. It is like a storm in the Atmosphere.*

And from Aix en Provence, on March 28, he wrote again to Patsy, this time to counsel against indolence in any guise:

Of all the cankers of human happiness none corrodes with so silent, yet so baneful an influence as indolence . . . Idleness begets ennui, ennui the hypochondriac, and that a diseased body. No laborious person was ever yet hysterical. Exercise and application produce order in our affairs, health of body and cheerfulness of mind, and these make us precious to our friends.

It is while we are young that the habit of industry is formed. If not then, it never is afterwards.

He smiled upon receiving her reply, which assured him he need not worry about her becoming lazy enough to have hysterics, and put his hand on his heart when she wrote, *You say your expectations for me are high, yet not higher than I can attain. Then be assured, my dear papa, that you shall be satisfied in that, as well as in any thing else that lies in my power; for what I hold most precious is your satisfaction, indeed I should be miserable without it.*

At last, upon returning on June 10 from this extensive journey, after waiting for two years since the original decision to bring Polly to Paris, Thomas and Patsy shared truly happy news — Polly was due to arrive in July! They had been apart for four years, and Patsy told her father she wondered if she would even recognize her sibling, who was six years younger. Now, at age fifteen, Patsy felt quite adult and international, and though she again reminded herself that pride was a sin, she couldn't help but be glad about her accomplishments at the Abbaye de Panthémont. She thought back to how nervous she had been upon her arrival in a foreign country and marveled at how capable and independent she had become.

They discussed whether Polly should have her own room or whether they should share. After all, they would be at school most of the time, and Polly might adapt more quickly if her sister were close night and day.

"Let's share for now," Patsy told her father. "I want her to be happy, and I remember how frightened I was when I first arrived."

"Yes," her father agreed. "Strong family attachments require close physical proximity. Now that we will have our girl here, let's make the most of it!"

SALLY

1787

SALLY TIGHTLY HELD HER mother's hand. She didn't want to leave. The only world she'd ever known was Virginia — Monticello and Eppington — and she'd somehow assumed she would always be here. Now, she'd learned from Mrs. Eppes, Polly's aunt, that she was to serve as Polly's chaperone across the ocean to London and then to Paris. She had met the Adams family in Virginia, and she kept telling herself that at least there would be a few familiar faces. And of course, Mr. Jefferson and Patsy would welcome her in Paris. Paris! She couldn't imagine what that would be like.

Betty, hiding her own distress, tried to comfort her. "The best part, Sally, my sweet girl, is that you will be seeing your brother again. And I know he will be happy to have you with him."

This was true, but nevertheless, she was frightened. She didn't know whether to fear the travel or the new responsibilities more. Aunt Elizabeth Eppes and Betty helped the two girls pack and prepare for the voyage. Sally certainly had no proper clothes and so the seamstresses at both Monticello and Eppington were sewing like whirling dervishes. She kept being told, "Oh, Mr. Jefferson will buy whatever else you need over there." Which was probably best, Sally thought, because she suspected Virginia clothes and Paris styles would not be the same. That was the least of all the worrisome matters.

She did not speak French. She didn't understand what being a chaperone for Polly really meant, and she certainly didn't know what Mr. Jefferson expected of her in Paris. James apparently was doing all right in a foreign country, and so she probably would be fine too, she told herself. She could always ask him a question. Sally had often been told she was pretty, and she instinctively counted on that to help. Polly was pretty too, and the

97

girls might even be taken for sisters, so light was Sally's skin. In fact, her mother, too, was often called a "bright mulatto" woman.

Sally's complicated ancestry had prepared her somewhat for the complex world she would face ahead. Betty had recently decided that age fourteen was the right age for Sally to hear what she wanted her daughter to know — that long ago, a white ship captain named Hemings had bedded an African woman, and those two were Betty's parents. Subsequently, Betty had become a slave belonging to John Wayles of Virginia, although originally she had been owned by his wife, Martha Eppes Wayles. After Martha Wayle's death, and the death of two subsequent wives, John Wayles had taken Betty as a "concubine," which to southerners, meant "substitution for a wife." She had borne him six children: Robert, James, Thenia, Critta, Peter, and herself. So Sally's father was white.

In Virginia, a child born out of wedlock was considered by law and society as a *filius nullius,* "a child of no one." Moreover, since miscegenation was against the law, any child of a white and black was necessarily illegitimate. It was helpful to hear her mother's story again, but Sally had always considered John Wayles to be her father — though he had died the year she was born, and she had no real memory of him. There were many such children in Virginia.

John Wayles, and his "proper" wife Martha Eppes Wayles, had a legitimate daughter, Martha (Patty), who had married Thomas Jefferson. Therefore, since Sally shared a father with Mr. Jefferson's wife, she was Patty Jefferson's half-sister. As a quadroon, however, in the minds of Virginians, she would be a second generation half-Negro. Sally also understood from her mother that her father John Wayles was Patsy and Polly Jefferson's grandfather. Patty, their mother, had been twenty-five years older than Sally, making it easier to ignore this remarkable relationship. No one ever dared mention it and blindly accepted it as a fact of life. But now the generations had caught up. Sally and Patsy were only months apart, yet this heritage meant Sally was Patsy's and Polly's aunt. In that capacity, it made perfect sense for her to be Polly's chaperone, but truly, she was going on the journey to be Polly's servant.

Seeing this voyage as a great adventure, Sally, though nervous, tried to soothe Polly's fears. She put on her most grownup voice. "We will be with your Papa and your sister," she coached, "and we shall see so many wonderful sights."

Polly's large blue eyes became teary and her mouth quivered. "But I don't want to leave Auntie Eppes."

"I understand, dearest. I really do. But your sister and father want to see you and need you."

"Then they can come here," the logical child rejoined.

"No, Polly. Mr. Jefferson has work to do for our country in France." Somehow it made Sally proud to say that.

In truth, Thomas had no idea it would be a fourteen- year-old girl who would accompany Polly across the ocean, and he had no word of it until the two had already set sail. Only a few days after learning this, he heard from Abigail Adams that the girls had safely arrived in London on June 26. Some days after that, he received a delayed letter from Elizabeth Eppes explaining that she had complete confidence in the ship captain, Ramsay, who would watch over the two.

The *Arundel* took two weeks longer than Patsy's ship had taken to make the crossing, but Sally relaxed when Polly settled down and developed an attachment to Captain Ramsay. Actually, Polly was very angry with her Auntie and Uncle Eppes, who had essentially tricked the poor girl. The ship had been moored on the James River, not far from Eppington, the Eppes family home. The family pretended they would go on board to play games, and when she fell asleep, they all disembarked and the ship sailed away with Polly and Sally. After five weeks at sea, the girls arrived in London, and Abigail wrote to Thomas: *The old Nurse whom you expected to have attended her [Polly], was sick and unable to come. She has a Girl about fifteen or sixteen with her, the Sister of the Servant you have with you.*

She continued writing Thomas the next day:

The Girl who is with her is quite a child, and Captain Ramsay is of the opinion she will be of so little Service that he had better carry her back with him. But of this you will be a judge. She seems fond of the child and appears good naturd.[sic]

Abigail kept Thomas up to date:

The Girl she has with her, wants more care than the child, and is wholly incapable of looking properly after her, without some superior to direct her. As both Miss Jefferson and the maid had cloaths [sic] only proper for the sea, I have purchased and made up for them, such things as I should have done had they been my own . . .

In fact, Sally was fourteen and not sixteen, as the Adamses supposed. In any event, Aunt Elizabeth had found her mature enough while in their household to look after Polly. Now, Abigail was struck by the young chaperone's charm and beauty. She had long black hair, large, dark, amber eyes with fleeting flecks of gold, and a warm sienna tint to her skin. It was quite disconcerting that one could see a slight resemblance to her half-sister, the former Mrs. Jefferson.

Sally sensed Mrs. Adams was not comfortable with the idea of her continuing on to Paris with Polly. Her suspicions were confirmed when she was on her way into the sitting room to return a thimble to Mrs. Adams when she heard her speaking to Mr. Adams, "I do not think this young girl is competent to take on the duties necessary to be Polly's chaperone in Paris. Nor do I think it is a wise plan to send such a lovely young girl into the home of a bachelor."

"I can understand your apprehensions, my dear," Mr. Adams said. "However, the Eppeses knew that Polly was comfortable with Sally and attached to her. It might be unnecessarily cruel to separate her now, in a foreign country."

"This might be painful now. But how much more difficult it would become if problems arose in the future. You remember how upset I was last week when we attended the play *Othello*. You yourself expressed the belief that racial intermixture is against the laws of Nature. We do not want to put temptation before our friend."

"I doubt that will be a problem, Abigail. And we also have a duty to protect this young slave girl, who would be traveling alone for weeks on a ship with naught but sailors."

"Heavens, John! I cannot worry about her too! It is Polly and Thomas who are my concern and responsibility."

"But this is a serious matter, my dear. You must realize that if the girl goes to France, she has the opportunity to be free. I know you object to slavery as much as I do, and it would be wrong for us to deny her this opportunity."

Sally knew she should not be listening but she was riveted to the spot. She would escape now if she were sure not to be heard. When Mr. Adams rose to stir the fire in the hearth, she tiptoed quietly backward as the logs made a covering clatter. She must somehow quickly prove her worth.

Sally was rescued from this problematic effort the very next day when Jefferson's servant, Adrien Petit, arrived with passports and passage for him and the two girls back to Paris. Petit had impressed Thomas years earlier by leaving his French homeland to fight in the American Revolution. He had sustained wounds at the Battle of Yorktown and been returned to France on a stretcher.

The Adamses could not fathom why Thomas had not come himself, and Polly burst into tears when she did not see her father. John and Abigail dared not take Sally away from her now or she would never go. Jefferson explained in a letter delivered by M. Petit that he had just returned from southern Europe and was detained by catching up on ministry affairs. Still, they were appalled that the father could so coldly welcome his child.

Sally had never met the stranger who arrived to chaperone her and Polly to France. She was as disappointed as Polly but intuited she ought not reveal this. At least he spoke English. Polly balked at leaving the familiar Adams household and especially sweet Nabby, who had welcomed them so warmly. Nonetheless, Sally held Polly's hand and whispered in her ear that they should go because that is what her father wished. Also, she knew her brother James would be awaiting her in Paris. She had been eleven when she last saw him, but she knew he would embrace her.

"We're near the end of our journey," she told Polly. "Do not worry anymore. We shall see your father and sister very soon."

Thomas

MARIA COSWAY WAS DUE to arrive in Paris at the moment Thomas would need to leave for London to fetch Polly. If only he had known the date of his daughter's arrival earlier, he might have made some accommodation. Maria had been traveling away from Paris for quite a while, and he had missed her terribly. She would still be there when he returned from London, but he could not bear to wait a moment longer. His infatuation with the twenty-seven-year-old won the day.

Besides, he did not want the Adamses to think of him as a slaveholder, and they would definitely be reminded of that if he were in their household in Sally's presence. Moreover, he did not trust the British and did not want to get into serious discussions about international relations on British soil at the moment. He would send Petit, his French *maître d'hôtel*, in his place to chaperone the girls home. Yes, the best plan would be to greet them at Langeac when they were due to arrive and enjoy the next few weeks with Maria before she needed to leave again. Her company was so refreshing.

His heart allowed him to ignore the noise from his head, and he remained in Paris to see Maria instead of going to London to meet Polly. For the moment, temptation allowed him to accept unresolved contradictions.

A letter from Patsy from the convent surprised him. She heard so much at the Abbesse's table, it was difficult to keep anything from her. She had learned of a captured "Virginia ship" with a cargo of "Algerians" who would be sold as slaves. His intelligent and compassionate daughter wrote to him, "Good God, have we not enough? I wish with all my soul that the poor Negroes were all freed. It grieves my heart when I think that these our fellow creatures should be treated so terribly as they are by many of our countrymen."

His daughter's time in France certainly would have an effect on how she viewed life in Virginia and her role as plantation mistress when they returned home. He hated how the evil taint of slavery affected every generation. He had set an immoral example for his children and had no proper answer for it. He shuddered. Another unresolved contradiction!

PATSY

1787-1788

PATSY WAS FURIOUS with her father. She couldn't remember ever being so angry with him. Why had he not gone to London to fetch Polly? She could have gone with him. And she would have enjoyed seeing Nabby again. But then she suspected she knew the reason why when she saw him spending so much time with Maria. Was this flirtatious woman more important to him than they were?

When Polly walked in the door of the Hôtel de Langeac on Sunday, July 15, 1787, Patsy gasped. She was so like their mother — with a delicate prettiness and dark hair. It disappointed her, actually hurt her feelings, that Polly acted shy with her and their father — even appearing afraid of the tall man awaiting her. She kept holding Sally's hand as though she preferred Sally to her own sister. However, Patsy soon learned that Polly, however timid, was sweet and docile. Abigail had written to them about how she had found Polly particularly lovely.

At first, Patsy proudly presented Polly to her friends at the Abbaye and encouraged her to participate in activities. But since Polly did not yet speak French and was seriously homesick, Patsy soon found her to be more of a burden than a pleasure. She thanked heaven Sally was around when they came home for visits to help cope with Polly's moodiness.

Even though Patsy hadn't seen Sally for four years, their childhood friendship made re-acquaintance easy. Moreover, Sally worked at learning French more than Polly did, and she was always eager to go out walking to explore the city. It felt as though she had a friend at home with her again. When Patsy, Polly, and Sally were in their carriage on the way to school, or on shopping expeditions, Patsy often caught people staring at them. She quickly realized they probably saw a resemblance among all of them, but wondered why one had a somewhat different skin tone.

Thomas allowed the girls to go out together, but frequently cautioned them to be alert because opposition to King Louis XVI was becoming more visible and more frequent. Small riots would erupt in the streets, and the king's men would rush to the site to crush the insurrection. "Whenever you hear a commotion, you must run the other way and come home as quickly as you can," he counseled. The girls found this extremely exciting, and often hoped to come across some excitement in the avenues to talk about at the dinner table. It all seemed like a great deal of bluster at the moment — nothing like the war they had lived through in America.

Thomas

1788

WHEN THOMAS RECEIVED news that the American constitution had been ratified by the Congress on December 7, 1787, he was delighted it had finally happened. But he couldn't help but feel some disappointment he had not been there to celebrate with his colleagues over this mammoth achievement. He had had more of a hand with the state constitution of Virginia, and after all, he believed state constitutions were more important than the federal document. He continued to believe the states would remain the *primary* government. While thinking about these issues, he was prompted to write to James Madison on December 20, 1787: *I think our governments will remain virtuous for many centuries; as long as they are chiefly agricultural; and this will be as long as there shall be vacant lands in any part of America, when they get piled upon one another in large cities, as in Europe, they will become corrupt as in Europe.*

World affairs challenged Thomas, keeping him extremely busy. He had witnessed a recent crisis in the United Netherlands, where Britain, France, and Prussia were all exerting pressure on the small nations. He thought it a good lesson for his fledgling country and wrote to John Jay in November: *It conveys to us the important lesson that no circumstances of morality, honor, interest, or engagement are sufficient to authorize a secure reliance on any nation, at all times, and in all positions.* He went on to explain that alliances were always suspect and added, *we are, therefore, never safe till our magazines are filled with arms.*

Thomas desperately wanted to increase trade between America and France and felt he was the right man to make this happen. He wrote numerous memoranda to Versailles, discussing why both countries would benefit from abolishing tariffs — France would receive cheaper raw materials and the United States would buy France's manufactured goods.

Moreover, he would be making life more difficult for his hated enemy, England. But politics and folderol at the French court constantly thwarted his endeavors.

Despite Thomas's heavy work schedule, he often missed his wife, longed for Maria, and wished for female companionship. When John Trumbull suggested he meet an American woman who was visiting Paris in December 1787, he welcomed the opportunity. Trumbull had just finished a portrait of Angelica Church, and because he knew of Thomas's often-difficult relationship with Maria Cosway, he immediately thought of his friend as an appropriate companion for her.

Angelica Shuyler Church was charming, beautiful, and certainly less complicated than Maria. After the introduction, Thomas gladly took it upon himself to give Mrs. Church a tour of the city he loved so much, and for two months the two enjoyed the sights together. Angelica, like Maria, was bored with her marriage. She had already entertained a serious flirtation with Alexander Hamilton, who now was married to her sister. Angelica's daughter Kitty attended the Abbaye de Panthémont, and so the two could chat about their children. When he shared this news with Patsy, she surprised him by erupting with anger.

"Kitty Church is the one who attacked me about owning slaves when I first arrived. You can't socialize with Mrs. Church!"

"But dearest, Kitty did you no harm. You could discuss the subject with her in a calm and reasoned manner," he suggested. His daughter astonished him by stomping out of the room in a temper.

Thomas found himself more relaxed in Angelica's presence than when with Maria, whose total Eurocentric point of view sometimes bothered him. Maria appeared to become irritated when he would try to explain to her why he thought America superior in many ways. Also, her Catholic religiosity worried him when he thought about any kind of permanent relationship.

He happily wrote to Mrs. Church, feeling his ideas would be well received:

Indeed, madam, I know nothing so charming as our own country. The learned say it is a new creation; and I believe them; not for their reasons, but because it is made on an improved plan. Europe is a first idea, a crude production, before the maker knew his trade, or had made up his mind as to what he wanted. Let us go back to it together then. You intend it a visit; so do I. . . .

But as with Maria, there were other complications. Being the daughter of a Revolutionary War hero and the wife of a British aristocrat, Angelica was extremely visible. Yet, he allowed her independent spirit, her sassy wit, and sharp intellect to seduce him. He also admired her American style, which he found less flamboyant than that of French women.

Ironically, Maria grew jealous when she did not hear from Thomas while Angelica was visiting Paris. She wrote to him hinting at her concerns for his affection. Thomas reveled in this social whirlwind at the moment for it helped him to forget Patty, whom he had sworn never to forget. His feelings often seemed to be in such a scramble, and he definitely preferred life to be more settled.

Trumbull was astounded when he received a request for a miniature portrait of Thomas from both women.

Thomas now housed three, young, beautiful girls. He doted on Patsy and Polly, and sincerely believed he should take good care of Sally too. He decided he must have her inoculated against smallpox soon after her arrival. Louis XV had died of the dreaded disease and epidemics continued to occur from time to time. Thomas already had insisted Sally's brothers must receive the treatment, which involved taking a minute amount of secretions from the pustules of a sick individual and placing the inoculum into a small incision on the healthy person. That person was then quarantined with the expectation and hope they would mount an immune reaction to the disease.

In Europe a Dr. Robert Sutton had acquired fame by refining the technique of taking the inoculum from a person who had been inoculated, rather than from a sick person. They found this drastically reduced the mortality of his patients. Thomas decided to call Dr. Sutton and paid him the exorbitant amount of forty *livres* to treat Sally. He asked Patsy to encourage the reluctant Sally and to help convince her the procedure wouldn't be so bad.

"But Papa, Sally witnessed how Polly and I suffered through the experience in Virginia. I can't lie to her about it," Patsy exclaimed.

"But you can remind her that you both survived and are now safer for it," he rejoined.

SALLY

SALLY GAZED AT MR. JEFFERSON in wonder when he told her she must leave Langeac and stay in a house outside of Paris for the smallpox treatment. Both Patsy and James persuaded her, saying they had not suffered too greatly; but hadn't she seen the terrible scars on other people that the disease might inflict if the inoculation went wrong? The thought of permanently damaging her skin and her face was horrifying. Not wanting to be a coward, she finally acquiesced and attempted to hide her fear. Besides, she guessed Mr. Jefferson would not allow her to remain in Paris unless she agreed, and she didn't want to admit she was more apprehensive about being alone at the clinic for such a long time than of the inoculation.

Fortunately, she had no idea she would spend forty days away from her brother and her proxy-family while she convalesced. At least Dr. Sutton was English, and she could understand what he told her to do and not do. The doctor insisted that his patients get fresh air and fresh food, which partially explained the high cost. Sally had little to do while recuperating except walk around the gardens and think about her life. She doubted if many other black people had the opportunity to be inoculated — especially in such a nice place and for so much money. She thought it extremely kind of her master to want to protect her health.

Being young and strong served her well, and in a little more than five weeks she returned to the comforts of the Hôtel de Langeac. She couldn't believe she lived in this mansion, with numerous rooms for guests and a special room on the ground floor for baths. She gawked at the rooms for servants, where she and James had private quarters. Because she was very busy only on the weekends when the girls came home from school, Sally would sometimes help James in the kitchen. He was occasionally instructed to cook for up to thirty persons at dinner, and she marveled at how he stood up to the demands. Presentation of the food was a big part of his training and success as a chef, and so the more hands to help him the better, he told her. Sally especially enjoyed being in the kitchen because it gave her another opportunity to listen to and speak French, and she picked it up very quickly.

Sally's mother had trained her for tasks an adult woman slave would perform at Monticello — sewing, cleaning, and making soap and beer. She found the kitchen's pace and gourmet cooking much more interesting and exciting. She carried herself with poise — the demeanor Abigail Adams had recognized as perhaps too haughty to be proper in the Jefferson household. Indeed, when Marie de Botidoux came to visit Patsy at Langeac, Patsy introduced Sally as "Mademoiselle," and not just "Sally," so leading her friend to believe Sally was higher than a servant in the family.

At times Sally marveled at her good luck. Her world had changed from a rural and isolated mountaintop to a city of 700,000 people. Here, she was expected to speak another language, to know when someone was trying to hoodwink her, and to be able to find her way through unknown streets and passageways. She enjoyed the challenge, and quickly learned the city ways of not speaking to everyone you met, keeping a passive expression, and making no eye contact with people passing by. This felt like she was being rude at first, but then she came to understand the necessity for the behavior with such a throng pressing close in every avenue and street. She appreciated many idle hours when she could wander through the neighborhood, or sit on the balcony at Langeac and view the street scene.

Not long after her inoculation procedure, since the girls weren't at home that much, M. Petit asked her to be Mr. Jefferson's *femme de chambre* in addition to taking care of Patsy and Polly. James tutored her about her duties as a lady's maid, as did M. Perrault, her French teacher. Being a gentleman's maid should not be so different from what she did for the girls, she imagined. In January 1788 she received her first wages from Mr. Jefferson; he counted out twenty-four *livres*, plus an additional twelve as a gift for New Year's into her palm. The money felt like a live creature in her hand, and she covered her mouth with her other hand to keep from laughing out loud. After that, he cut the amount to twelve *livres* per month, which is what he gave to Patsy for her allowance.

James told Sally that her salary was the highest level paid in a French household for this type of service, and that Mr. Jefferson had immediately agreed when James suggested she be paid, just as he was, while in Paris. She was expected to take care of the master's wardrobe and linens, and she was led to believe she would be taking over this position when they returned to Monticello. Even though she was a slave, she knew her family had been, and would be, treated with care by Thomas Jefferson. As a member of the Hemings family, she had never expected to endure the hard life of the other slaves at Monticello. Now, being paid for her work gave her an intoxicating feeling of liberation, and she wanted to please Mr. Jefferson for giving her such an opportunity.

James continued to talk to her about staying on in Paris with him when Mr. Jefferson's term as foreign secretary ended and the family returned to America. They could be free people just by staying in Europe. He told Sally he was angry with their mother because she should have made John Wayles love her enough to free her children. Instead, he had gifted them to Patty in his will.

James must be right, Sally thought. She should take his advice. But then she would miss her mother and other siblings so much. She already did. Her mother probably never had expected to see her again when they said goodbye at Monticello. The Jeffersons had treated her family well, and now he was taking such good care of her in Paris. It was all so confusing.

Sally realized she should be saving some of her new money, but there were many temptations for spending it — on clothing, going to street fairs with her brother, or visiting one of the new lower-class theaters popping up around the city. Or, she could buy gifts to take back home to her family. But then, what if she chose to stay in Paris? She realized she should wait before parting with her money for this purpose. Might she make even more money one day if she worked for someone besides Mr. Jefferson? She began to observe what some of the newly freed slaves were doing in Paris, and saw many opportunities — she might have her own market stall, become an innkeeper with James, have her own dressmaking shop. Her dreams were endless.

PATSY

WHILE SALLY WAS AWAY for her inoculation, Patsy enjoyed taking care of her little sister. She liked helping her choose what to wear, styling her hair, and she even played dolls with her. Soon, Polly was chattering to her in a more natural manner and appeared to have lost her timidity with her older sister. They snuggled together in bed at night, and Patsy described to her what to expect at the Abbaye — which nuns were nice, and which ones were not. She was careful not to mention Mrs. Cosway or Mrs. Church and why their father was away so many evenings. She chafed a bit when she received a letter from her father about how to take care of her sister when she thought she'd been doing such a good job. He wrote to her of the "precious charge on your hands".

> *The difference of your age, and your common loss of a mother, will put that office on you. Teach her above all things to be good, because without that we can neither be valued by others nor set any value on ourselves. Teach her to be always true; no vice is so mean as the want of truth, and at the same time so useless. Teach her never to be angry; anger only serves to torment ourselves, to divert others, and alienate their esteem. And teach her industry, and application to useful pursuits. I will venture to assure you that, if you inculcate this in her mind, you will make her a happy human being in herself, a most inestimable friend to you, and precious to all the world. In teaching her these dispositions of mind, you will be more fixed in them yourself, and render yourself dear to all your acquaintances. . . .*

When Sally returned, Patsy felt like the big sister toward her too, and they had a wonderful afternoon, going through Patsy's wardrobe, choosing a few dresses that Patsy no longer wanted and that Sally might use. Sally appeared overcome with her generosity, and shy about regarding herself in the mirror.

"No, look, look! How nice the blue one looks on you. With your dark hair." She'd started to say "and with the color of your skin" — for it was true. But she sensed that might not be appropriate. Of course, since Patsy was so tall, most of the garments had to be shortened for Sally, but she was so handy with a needle and thread, it was no problem, and Sally seemed thrilled.

One afternoon Mr. Short invited all the girls to go ice-skating. They donned their coats, hats, and gloves, and headed to one of the new venues for this delightful pastime. Louis XVI had introduced the activity in the French capital during his reign, and they were excited to try. Patsy had skated once with Nabby Adams but still felt unsure of herself. Mr. Short, leaving Sally to make do on her own, held Patsy and Polly by the hands, and they began to glide over the smoothed surface. Patsy could feel the warmth of his hand through her glove and dared not look at him.

She found the cold exhilarating and soon, catching the rhythm of the motion, headed off on her own. Perhaps he would catch up with her. She looked back and *voilà*, he had left Polly on the edge and was chasing after her. She sped up but stumbled and tumbled to the hard surface. Mr. Short hurried to her aid, and knelt down beside her.

"Are you hurt, Patsy?" he asked with concern.

"No, no," she declared, laughing. "This is delightful!" But she didn't rise immediately and allowed him to help her to her feet. He clasped her more closely than necessary she imagined, and she let herself lean against him for longer than need be. She felt a little breathless and was having trouble regaining her aplomb. "Perhaps I was a bit stunned. Let's go and join my sister."

He does care more about me than the others, she thought. He truly does.

SALLY

SALLY WAS IN AWE of her brother's success in their foreign surroundings. He had left Virginia as a slave and now, for all intents and purposes, was a free man. He roamed around Paris at will and was the master in the kitchen. He knew how to make exquisite sauces and present them with a flourish on beautiful dishes. Mr. Jefferson provided handsome clothing for his servant, wanting him to make a good impression when outside the Jefferson household, and his strong figure made an impressive sight.

James was a tall, good-looking man with a muscular body and shiny black wavy hair. He often had a touch of melancholy about him, which only increased his romantic aspect. But often enough, the simmering covert anger about being enslaved would be replaced by an enticing smile. When he could, he helped Sally with her French and pressed upon her the need to become capable in the language. "We both have the possibility to become free here," he told her over and over again, as she looked at him, wide-eyed with disbelief.

He explained to her that France adhered to the "Freedom Principle," which held that once an enslaved person arrived, he or she was free. Therefore, unlike in Virginia, she need not carry a pass with her when she left the house. However, all persons of color in France at this time needed to carry identity papers called *cartouches*. Sally didn't see this as a whole lot different from the pass she must carry in Virginia.

For now, she was delirious with excitement — over the beauty of the city, the freedom of her walks, and the nice clothes Mr. Jefferson had given her when he shopped for his girls. If she were going to accompany them on their outings, he had explained, she would need to dress in an appropriate manner as well. Her favorite garment was a soft woolen cloak she could wear when she walked outside. Also, having time on her own to wander around Paris when the girls were at school allowed her to soak in information to share with them when they came home for their bi-monthly visits. And, the best was that because Mr. Jefferson paid her wages, she was able to make private purchases.

"You are a beautiful young woman," James told her, "as I think you know, and you have skills as a seamstress. Maybe one day you could live here in Paris with me and work in the fashion trade."

The transformation from slave girl to "lovely young woman" when she looked in the mirror took her breath away. She began to wear her hair loose under her cap, instead of tied back as she did when working. She suddenly perceived the dusky color of her skin in a different way than she had in Virginia. There were skins of all colors here in Paris, and she realized that some color to the skin could be seen as exotic and attractive.

Sally carefully watched the way French women behaved and studied the modest and graceful behavior being acquired by Patsy and Polly. She had been taught to read at Monticello, by both her mother and Patsy when they were together, and she used some of her free time when the girls were at school to improve her bookish education. Mr. Jefferson already had a big library here, and he was glad to make suggestions for her reading. Indeed, he seemed impressed with her desire to improve in that vein.

She remained alert not to shirk her duties at the Hôtel de Langeac and carefully pressed the girls' clothes, making sure their wardrobes were clean and neat, and straightened their rooms. The luxuries of the Hôtel made her life easier, especially the indoor plumbing. She need not empty chamber pots, and there were other servants who did most of the cleaning. She was essentially a privileged lady's maid. She began to forget the slave quarters she had lived in before coming to Europe.

While she was working, she would plan her afternoon promenade. And what she would buy on the street to eat. She'd developed a taste for the roasted chestnuts one could purchase, and she loved exploring the little *ruelles* with modest shops where tiny bells tinkled above the door when she entered. James might be right about making a plan to stay here forever.

THOMAS

THOMAS REALIZED HE NEEDED to stop and consider how his life was proceeding. The pace was dizzying — with his challenge to serve the new republic of the United States of America by recruiting France as an ally, his liaisons with two married women, trying to raise two daughters without a mother in a foreign country, running a household — the demands felt endless. He decided to use the Hôtel de Langeac as his office as well as his home; it would simply be more convenient than a separate office.

He listed several items for his constant attention: the receipt of whale-oil, salted fish, and salted meats on favorable terms; the admission of American rice on equal terms with that of Piedmont, Egypt, and the Levant; a mitigation of the monopolies of U.S. tobacco by the Farmers-general, and a free admission of our American production into their islands. Equally time-consuming were the many problems brought to him by stranded, or other American citizens with problems overseas.

He'd allowed himself to be distracted from these more serious matters by the titillation of a secret rendezvous in the Bois de Boulogne and sneaking in and out of hired carriages with Maria or Angelica. Always liking new experiences, he had recently taken Angelica to The Grande Taverne de Londres in the rue de Richelieu. Food for the public had previously existed in taverns, inns and cafés, but this was something called a "restaurant," invented by a man named Boulanger in 1782. M. Boulanger served restorative broths, hence the name "restaurant" — a place to relax and restore oneself. He offered a list of dishes on a menu and served them at small individual tables.

That had been an invigorating evening, but he definitely preferred dining at home. He was always captivated with the intellectual stimulation he found with Condorcet, Lafayette, La Rochfoucauld, and others. Evenings at the Hôtel de Langeac, consuming exquisite meals prepared by James with brilliant guests, caused him to feel he had found his true milieu.

Although he enjoyed the thought-provoking discussions at his dinner table, at times it became fraught with opposing viewpoints. Condorcet could be particularly strong about his belief in abolishing slavery. No one accused Thomas outright, but Condorcet, on more than one occasion, made it clear he believed in the equality of black people, advising that they must be prepared to become free citizens. Thomas would listen and evade the issue by explaining that all of his slaves in Virginia had been taught how to read. At the same time, he was afraid to speak clearly against slavery in case word got back to Virginia about what he had said on the subject while in France.

Since his fall last year with Maria, he often had trouble using his right wrist. It pained him much of the time, but he had learned to write almost as well with his left hand as with his right. He always used the clever copy machine he had invented, which moved a second pen over a paper next to the one he was writing on. He needed to invent an automatic writing machine as well!

What a fool he had been to literally chase after Maria. He had not seen her now for quite awhile. Surely she would have written him if she were in Paris. Thomas tried to keep his mind on his work, but he was finding the presence of Sally in the household extremely distracting. He had insisted that she be inoculated against smallpox, and he took care of her personal needs like he did for his daughters. But she was a well-developed, fifteen-year-old, and he could not dismiss her attraction. Surely, she must be sixteen by now.

He found himself looking forward to early morning when he would see her for the first time each day. Of course, she did not sit down with him and his girls, but would come and go in the breakfast room, serving and removing dishes, and he had to exercise restraint not to reach out and touch her. It would be unseemly in any case, but absolutely taboo in front of his daughters. He wished Maria would return to Paris to distract him from the unbidden thoughts crowding out matters of state.

He purposefully kept Sally at Langeac, even when the girls were at school. He didn't want the nuns questioning his daughters about the status of their servant because slavery was forbidden in France. He couldn't ask Patsy and Polly to lie about it, and so it was simply easier to keep the problem hidden. Also, since he hadn't registered Sally or James when they arrived, he wanted to conceal the fact that he was breaking the law. But he wasn't really, he decided, since he was now paying them both. Moreover, he represented the United States in France, and so he, of all people, couldn't risk any embarrassment to the country because of his personal arrangements. Actually, he preferred to keep the conundrum hidden from himself as well. It was more pleasant to think that James and Sally were happy within his family.

In the evenings when he retired to his chamber, he found a quiet, lovely young woman waiting to serve him. She laid out his nightclothes, stoked the fire, and asked if there were anything else he needed for the night. Sometimes he would ask her to button or unbutton an article of clothing because of his sore wrist, which she offered to bathe and massage when it was particularly painful.

This young woman was more like the Virginia women he was accustomed to. Women in France acted so self-assertive and could be emasculating, he felt. And Angelica, though American, had adopted many of the European characteristics of female equality which he found off-putting. Sally's softer touch was definitely more appealing. And she looked so fresh and pretty in the dresses he had given her for her walks with the girls. He liked his servants to make a good appearance.

Often Sally reminded him so much of Patty, he thought he would dismiss her, or send her back to Virginia. He didn't want to be reminded of what he had lost. At other times, he was appalled that he wanted to take her in his arms and crush her to his chest. She was more refined now than the slaves at Monticello, but he also didn't want to be reminded that she was a slave.

To take his mind off of Sally, he sat down at his escritoire, and penned a note to Maria Conway, who, he'd learned on inquiring, was in London, telling her of the Paris scene, and adding, . . . *for assuredly nobody will care for him who cares for nobody. But friendship is precious not only in the shade but in the sunshine of life; and thanks to a benevolent arrangement of things, the greater part of life is sunshine.*

SALLY

1788

SALLY HAD LITTLE EXPERIENCE with men of any age. She realized she had lived an amazingly protected existence for all of her fifteen years, not very different from Patsy or Polly's lives. And besides, she had always had big brothers to protect her when she was in the sphere of Monticello. The first threat she had felt from this quarter had been Captain Ramsey, who had gazed at her with open desire and tried to put his arm around her waist on the ship to Europe. She had spun away and dashed after Polly. The thought of returning on his ship if Abigail had gotten her way had been daunting.

Perhaps she was being overly sensitive, but she thought she had recognized a similar expression on Mr. Jefferson's face several times recently, and she had quickly looked away. She was well aware of her mother's life as John Wayles's concubine, and she'd accepted this arrangement as a way of life in Virginia, as everyone did. No one dared talk about it, but everyone appeared to understand the conventions. She couldn't put the feelings into words but she had always sensed between owner and slave a strange combination of affection and indifference, possessiveness and disinterest, making her feel off-balance. She instinctively knew she could trust James or her mother more than any of the Jeffersons.

Yet, she was accustomed to living with the Jefferson family, and by and large, she believed they would be kind to her. Mr. Jefferson had never been otherwise. But now she found her stomach fluttering when they were alone, and she kept her eyes down, hurrying about her domestic duties. She admired his sapphire-blue eyes and found his pale translucent skin fascinating. She'd even caught herself staring at the reddish-gold hair on his arms when she handed him his shirt, and she'd been shocked she found it so attractive. Should she talk to James about her worries? That would be too embarrassing, she felt. He would only be angry with her. How she wished her mother were here!

It had been nine months since her arrival in Paris. Sally realized she looked forward to her late night duties with Mr. Jefferson. He constantly begged her to tell him of life at Monticello since he had been in Paris. Who had died? Who had married? He wanted to know everything he had missed, but mostly, she suspected he wanted to hear her soft Virginia accent — because he told her so.

Patsy would be aghast to know how she was thinking about her father. It felt strange to keep a secret from Patsy who always had seemed more like a friend than an owner. Now these secret thoughts about Mr. Jefferson brought anxious feelings of guilt. Why had she ever offered to massage his painful wrist? Sally asked herself. She had thought it would be the kind thing to do, but now the touch of his skin began to make her feel overly warm.

"Goodnight, Sally," he said. "Thank you as always for your help."

At least he was going to be away for a short while.

THOMAS

THOMAS ARRIVED BACK IN PARIS from Germany in April to find a letter from Maria. He did not hesitate in writing back, and confessed to dreaming about her recently:

> *At Heidelberg I wished for you . . . In fact I led you by the hand through the whole garden . . . You must now write me a letter teeming with affection; such as I feel for you.*

He also quoted a metaphor from Sterne's *Tristram Shandy* regarding noses and phalluses. After he posted it, he realized he sounded like a schoolboy. He must have been unduly influenced by the French foolish sexual mores, he decided.

Unbidden, he thought of Sally. She was truly lovely, and reminded him of an amazing painting he had recently viewed while in Dusseldorf. It was dated 1699 by the Dutch artist van der Werff, and the subject matter was Abraham, bedding his young servant Hagar. He must not think like this!

He had also received missives in December from James Madison about the writing of the new American constitution. From his observations in Paris, Thomas worried more and more about a tendency toward monarchy in America. He wrote to John Adams specifying some of his likes and dislikes in the document draft. He told John he found it distressing that there was not a *bill of rights to assure freedom of religion, freedom of the press, protection against standing armies, restriction against monopolies, the eternal and unremitting force of the habeas corpus laws, and trials by jury.* But he did think the authors had gotten it right in designing a division of powers into executive, legislative, and judicial branches. It also pleased him that the federal government had been given sufficient autonomy and power to govern *without needing continual recurrence to the state legislatures.* However, it bothered him terribly that he was not there to join in these discussions or to help with drafting the document.

His birds' eye view of the Bourbon monarchy in Paris made him abhor absolutism even more than before and fear some version of this form
of government taking over in America despite the recent revolution. On
July 18, 1788, in a rather pessimistic frame of mind, he wrote to his friend
Edward Rutledge: . . . *we can surely boast of having set the world a beautiful
example of a government reformed by reason alone without bloodshed. But
the world is too far oppressed to profit of the example.*

PATSY

PATSY LIKED DRESSING UP for her father's dinner parties, and she especially enjoyed shopping for fashionable clothes. Polly did too, and the happy evenings at Langeac became a panacea for the entire family. The girls understood they were to excuse themselves when the meal was over, but the conversation at table could be enlightening and stimulating. Patsy especially enjoyed the banter for, as the elder sister, she was expected to participate. She also sensed her father counted on her to give an aura of domesticity and stability to their home. Rumors about him and Maria Cosway were definitely not appropriate for an American statesman, and he relied on her to counter these rumors. He hadn't explained this to her, but having heard the chatter at school, she knew it to be true.

Thomas occasionally would escort his daughters on shopping expeditions, wanting them to be properly dressed for an introduction to society. She noticed that he also purchased a few gowns for Sally, and Patsy discovered it made her feel a little jealous. She chided herself that she was being selfish and feared this feeling bordered on sin — the nuns talked a lot about sin at the Abbaye. They visited the milliner, seamstresses, and shoe salon, but the most exciting gift from her father was a ring — her first real piece of jewelry, allowing her to think he now considered her a grown-up. He allowed her to resume riding in the Bois de Boulogne, bought her a proper riding habit, and hired a dancing master and harpsichord instructor.

She loved the riding coat, cut tightly in the waist with split coat tails in the back. She preened before her mirror, admiring the ruffles on the blouse protruding from the wide lapels and brandished her dashing riding stick. She thought the wide brimmed hat a bit impractical and silly, but she didn't argue. When she asked her father if she could go to one of the more famous salons led by popular women of the day, he made it perfectly clear how he expected her to behave more circumspectly than those French ladies did.

"Absolutely not! French women flirt shamelessly. An American woman conducts herself in a much more virtuous manner. She should be happy with the society of her husband, her fond cares for the children, the arrangements of the house, and the improvements of the garden, which fill every moment with a healthy and useful activity."

Patsy paused, seeming to consider his advice and then offered him one of her more infectious grins. "But, Papa, can I go to the ball next week given by Marie de Botidoux's family?"

He laughed. "Why certainly! I don't see why not. That would be a perfect occasion to practice your skills of dancing and conversation for your introduction back into Virginia society."

She didn't tell him that the real reason she wanted to go to the ball was to have the opportunity to dance with Mr. Short. Even though he lived at Langeac, and she thought he flirted a bit with her, she was aggrieved that they never were able to talk alone. The fact that he was thirteen years older than she gave him a certain urbane and cultured air that she found exciting and attractive. And his gift of easy conversation always made her surprisingly comfortable in his presence. Thomas had made William Short his most trusted staff member, even treating him somewhat like an adopted son. Patsy believed this must mean that her father thought very well of the younger man.

William Short was of small to medium stature, which, given her unusual height for a young woman, made her feel awkward. She often felt herself to be all elbows and knees. She would turn seventeen in September, and at least so far, she wasn't taller than he. Patsy had learned that William had enjoyed an affair with Lilite, the daughter of a couple with whom he boarded for a while in Saint-Germain-en-Laye, in order to immerse himself in the French language. Lilite eventually had married someone else and had two children, and so Patsy wondered why William continued to visit the family. She knew from the conversation at school that such affairs were not unusual in France, but she believed he was spending less time in Saint- Germain-en-Laye for the moment, and more time at Langeac, helping her father.

Sally helped Patsy dress for the ball, arranging her hair in complex curls and clasping a necklace around her neck. Because of her young age, her hair would not be powdered. Patsy complained about her freckles, but honestly, Sally thought she looked lovely tonight in a green embroidered gown and told her so. Polly fussed that she should be allowed to attend too, but Sally only laughed. "Silly girl. You are six years younger than your sister. You will be at home in bed, Cherie."

Patsy couldn't suppress an ardent wish to Polly and Sally. "I wish Maria would spend more time with her husband. She only causes trouble!"

"But she is so beautiful," said Polly.

"And so old!" rejoined Patsy. "I've heard she is already twenty-five!"

The excitement of the evening was making Patsy feel very emotional. Suddenly, she burst out saying, "I wish with all my soul the poor Negroes were all freed. It grieves my heart!" She turned to the surprised Sally, who was buttoning her dress in the back, and embraced her.

The Jeffersons entered the Botidoux's ballroom — Thomas with his daughter on his arm and William Short walking behind them. The dazzling chandeliers, hanging low from a golden ceiling, cast a magical radiance upon the whirling dancers. When William took her gloved hand to lead her to the dance floor, Patsy was afraid he must be able to hear her heart thumping. She silently thanked her father for the dancing lessons as she gradually relaxed, easily gliding with her partner around the floor. The couple then walked together to pay their respects to Marie and her family, and Marie squeezed her good friend's hand. "You look so happy," she whispered in her ear. "I can tell he really likes you."

"Oh, *Merci*, Marie. *Comme tu es belle ce soir!*" Patsy responded with her best French accent.

The couple bowed to their hosts, and William led her back to the dance floor. Patsy hated to let him go when another gentleman requested a dance. Over her partner's shoulder, she spied her father admiring the architecture of the Hôtel Botidoux and its interior ballroom with carefully placed columns around the edge. He loved architecture almost more than anything, she thought. The women's gowns were extraordinary, ballooning more at the hips than their day dresses and the artistry of their hair was a sight to behold. One woman even had a tiny decorative birdcage on her head, a fashion made popular by the queen. Patsy was surprised at the thought of giving up this glamorous way of dressing when she returned to Virginia. The bustles surely would not be convenient for "bustling around" Monticello. She smiled at her own pun. Feeling rather sophisticated, she leaned her head back and swept into the dance with her partner.

The winter of 1788-89 was the coldest on record for the last fifty years, and at the beginning of December, Patsy and Polly both succumbed to typhus. Thomas brought them home from the Abbaye to recuperate. Patsy stayed out of school for five weeks, but Polly, who wasn't as strong, remained at Langeac for two months. Patsy thought the illness made Polly deaf and "stupid" for the duration, and often observed that in some sense, her little sister never recovered her mental faculties completely. The best medicine — primarily gruel and Madeira wine — was prescribed by an English doctor, Richard Gem, whom Thomas admired.

Dr. Gem, knowing the disease to be contagious, suggested to Thomas that Sally should be sent to a rooming house nearby to protect her from contracting the disease. Thomas agreed and sent her to Dupré's, a respectable boarding house, even taking on some of the nursing tasks for Polly himself.

Sometimes Patsy wished for more privacy because Thomas always packed the house with guests. Yet his invitations to his daughters for his formal dinners pleased her enormously, and she prided herself on the manners and conversational skills she was acquiring at these functions. She especially loved it when her Papa nodded at her in approval when she spoke up, displaying her blossoming intellect.

More and more she enjoyed the company of William Short, and found his conversation at dinner scintillating. His experience and sophistication appealed to her, especially the way he smoothly combined these attributes with an unaffected manner. When she returned to the Abbaye after her typhus scare, she confided in her friend Marie how much she enjoyed William's attentions.

"I think he truly likes me. He seeks me out for conversation and compliments my eyes." She blushed a bit at this admission.

"And do you like him?" her friend asked.

Patsy giggled a bit. "I think so. But he is so much *older* than I."

"That does not matter," advised Marie. "I know of many couples with a bigger age difference. And you are quite sophisticated for an American girl."

Patsy let go with one of her guffaws. "Now you let me know what you really think of Americans!"

"Not at all. But there *are* differences in manners, you know."

SALLY

1789

SALLY COULD TELL when her master was in pain or when he was worried or unhappy. She found herself searching his face for signs of his mood and wanting to soothe him if he were distressed. She knew about his liaisons with Mrs. Church and Mrs. Conway from hearing talk from the other staff and from listening to Patsy and Polly discuss their worries about these women. Indeed, she watched these female guests carefully when they visited the Hôtel de Langeac for soirées. Yet she felt special when she was around Mr. Jefferson because he always focused so completely on her. He had a caring look when he asked her questions about Monticello or wondered how she was getting on with her life in Paris. And he often complimented her on her progress with the French language. He seemed as genuinely interested in her as he was in his daughters.

Why couldn't she talk with James about her problems? She sensed she was dealing with treacherous feelings, and yet it was tempting to simply trust her own instincts. James, as a man, wouldn't understand her anyway. She had allowed her eyes to linger on Mr. Jefferson's face for longer than she should have yesterday, and his gaze had locked upon hers. She felt like she would swoon. When she handed him his eyeglasses, their fingers touched. Was she imagining his interest in her?

The next evening when he asked her to bathe his wrist, she looked up again into his sympathetic face. He had taken to addressing her with her name in the French pronunciation — Sah-lee — and it sounded so intimate and sweet. He changed to his nightshirt behind a screen and offered her his hand to dip into the warm water she had prepared. His fingers were long and graceful, and she began to press his palm and his wrist to soothe the painful area. Her belly began its excited flutter, and she tried to wrest her eyes from his, but they held one another intensely.

"Ah, my pretty girl," he murmured. "You are so lovely." All of a sudden the bowl of water was no longer between them, but on the floor and he pulled her tightly to his chest. She reached her arms up around his neck and clasped him as tightly to her. When he led her to his bed, she did not resist, allowing his kisses to transport her to another world. She had known nothing of men, but she trusted he would be kind.

THOMAS

THOMAS AWOKE THE NEXT morning to find the peaceful sleeping face of the sixteen-year-old girl in his bed. Her innocent profile filled his heart with tenderness. But, *Ah, Mon Dieu!* She was the same age as his daughter! Even somewhat younger. And the half-sister of his deceased wife! In Virginia, influenced by English law, it was considered incest for a man to marry the sister of a deceased wife. But this was different, wasn't it? Good Lord! What kind of monster was he? He rose quickly and quietly from the bed and dressed. He must get outside for a walk. What would she think when she awoke? Would she be frightened? Of course, she would.

He walked quickly out of the gates and through the neighborhood, as though he were being chased, trying to quiet his agitated mind. It felt as if a storm raged in his head. He rounded the corner from the rue de Berri and headed along the rue du Faubourg Saint-Honoré, the quarter's main boulevard. Nothing was open yet, except the little rustic inn. No, he wouldn't stop for a café. He must return home and attempt to act normally.

Why could he not resist her? Was it because she reminded him so much of Patty? Had he been afraid of losing her if she stayed in Paris with her brother? No, it had not been that rational. He had simply wanted her and took her. He must take care of her as he had all of his slaves. Why had he not been thinking clearly? He had crossed a forbidden line!

When he returned for breakfast, there she was in the dining room, moving about with the dishes, lovely as ever, as though nothing were amiss. He allowed himself to look directly at her and she bravely met his gaze. Patsy and Polly had been at home for the weekend, which both simplified and complicated the situation. They wore their crimson uniforms in order to return to the Abbaye de Panthémont this morning.

He couldn't help but compare Sally to his girls. She had not had their opportunities but being with them, she had soaked up so much. And he did believe that mixed-race people definitely were superior to a full-blooded black. He saw an improvement in body and mind in these people and believed this phenomenon was accepted by everyone.

"Dear girls," he said, addressing the table, "I must leave tomorrow for six weeks. I will be traveling with Mr. Adams to Amsterdam and the Rhineland. I want you all to study very hard while I am away." He looked up from the table and smiled at Sally. "And you too, Sah-lee. I will expect improvement in your geography and your French."

"Yes, Master," the girl replied.

Indeed, he must come to his senses and tend to a major financial crisis for his country. One of the problems for the Confederate government was that the states attended to their own monies and often failed to raise the cash necessary for payment of federal debts or general expenses of government. Matters had deteriorated to the point where Thomas felt he must race to Amsterdam to meet John Adams, where the two would hopefully obtain a loan from the Dutch that would finance the American government for the years 1788, '89, and '90.

The two responsible statesmen were successful in aborting a financial disaster and managed to secure sufficient credit to keep the government afloat. While he was gone, Thomas took care to write letters to all three girls, which James delivered when they arrived at Langeac. It struck him as somewhat odd that his master had taken to writing Sally too, but then Mr. Jefferson was known for his idiosyncrasies.

SALLY

WHILE MR. JEFFERSON WAS AWAY, Sally tried to remain calm. She spent much of her time with James, either in the kitchen or taking walks. He continued to speak with her about what they might do when the Jeffersons went home. They would both stay in France and both be free, James argued in his intense manner; they must begin to think about what they would do to support themselves — but the most important thing was that they would no longer be slaves!

"Do you think you would prefer to cook with me or become a dressmaker?" he asked her earnestly. "You are talented at both, I think," he told her.

"I just don't know yet, James. I never thought of such a thing for myself."

"But now you can. And you must!"

She knew she wasn't being completely honest with her brother. She loved Patsy and Polly and felt safe with the Jefferson family. Why would she want that to change? And she would miss her mother so much if she did not return to Monticello. She smiled to herself, enjoying the thought of the master's arms around her. At least she didn't need to decide right away.

Occasionally, she went to visit the sisters at the Abbaye. She could walk to the convent in the rue de Bellechasse, where she so much enjoyed their warm girlish chatter. Mr. Jefferson said it was an easy stroll, but he had such long legs, she thought smiling. Nevertheless, she enjoyed the hour-long walk down the Champs Elysées and through Les Tuileries. Sally knew sometimes the master would rent chaises for sitting in the gardens, but she couldn't waste her money on such a luxury. She found the approach to the gardens breathtaking, framed as they were by horseshoe-shaped walks, leading up to grand terraces and flanked by winged horses. Choosing not to spend her money on a ferry across the river, she would walk further and cross to the Left Bank via the Pont Royale, built during the reign of Louis XIV. She liked to stand above for a while to watch the flat boats moving underneath its stone arches. She would then proceed up the rue du Bac and turn northward again onto the rue St. Dominique, where she admired the façades of several townhouses that the master had pointed out to them. Next she turned left into the rue de Bellechasse. A little further along would be the convent at the corner of the rue de Grenelle.

The other girls in the school accepted her company, calling her Mademoiselle, like any other girl. To them, she was not a slave. One day they took off their uniforms and asked Sally to join them in practicing the new Parisian walk, modeled on the queen's walk. It was essentially a skating glide so as to appear to be walking on a cloud. The hoop skirts now in style hid the movement of the legs, which was extremely unnatural from a regular walk. They gave Sally some hoops to wear and they all slid around the highly waxed floors on stocking feet. They laughed as they held their upper torsos immobile and attempted to make their skirts float along the floor in a magical movement. Sally thought they looked like windup toys. It all seemed so silly that they collapsed in a heap upon one another, giggling with delight. Sally could not imagine leaving these girls. They were like her sisters.

When Thomas returned a month and a half later, she laid out his nightclothes but quickly returned to her small bedroom. She would wait for him to call her because she didn't know how he would feel or what he would want. She didn't know what she wanted either and was afraid and confused about their meeting again. She sat on her bed, trembling. What should she do?

He stood in her doorway. "I missed you, my beautiful girl," he said softly, holding out his hand.

She knew she could go to him or refuse. He would respect her, she thought. She rose and walked into his arms.

Every night her lover asked her to stay and every night she melted into him. She had never known life to be so delightful. Nothing could offend her; life was a dream. He told her that her skin felt like velvet; he told her that her lips were like warm plums and he wanted to taste them. She could not believe her good fortune that this fine man said he loved her. And she told him she loved him. But she called him Master.

In the mornings she awoke to the shock of the real world and she had to hide her feelings from everyone.

One day Mr. Jefferson came into the kitchen when Sally was helping her brother.

"James, I'm planning an especially large group for dinner Saturday night. And I want something special. What suggestions might you have for me?"

"Well, Master, I've been wanting to try a *velouté d'aspèrges* because the asparagus are nice and fresh now. We could serve this soup for a first course and a *filet de sole à la sauce moutarde* would be pleasant. Would that be appropriate, do you think?"

"Splendid, James, splendid! And something special for dessert also."

"Certainly, Master. Let me think about it."

"I know I can depend on you."

Thomas could not resist giving Sally's arm a squeeze as he left.

James froze. As soon as the master was out of sight, he turned on his sister. "Why was he touching you like that, Sally?" he asked between his teeth.

Her blush and silence told him everything he feared. "Uh, uh, I don't know," she mumbled.

"Oh, you foolish girl!" he tried to keep his voice low so as not to alert the others in the kitchen. "What have you done? Do you want to make the same mistake as our mother? Oh, Sally!" He felt like crying. It was all he could do not to slam one of the copper pots down on the counter.

"But James, he is so kind. He will not hurt me."

"Do not throw your life away, Sister. Do NOT cast away this once-in-a-lifetime opportunity!"

Sally's eyes began to tear up. She hated to see her brother angry with her and she was so confused. She turned and quickly left the kitchen to seek the privacy of her room. James made her feel ashamed, and she hadn't felt that way with Mr. Jefferson.

PATSY

PATSY COULD NOT SUPRESS her foolish dreams. She fantasized about her father's handsome secretary and about living with him in a small house outside of Paris. How cozy they would be! She knew he loved Europe and wanted to have a career here, and so it was doubtful he would return to Virginia with them. She would be at his side, helping him advance his prestige and position. At Langeac during dinner in the evenings, she often took the place next to him and trembled when she thought his knees were close to hers under the table. She believed that he purposefully slid his hand close to hers on the table and once allowed their fingers to touch.

She was so filled with thoughts of him she couldn't resist asking Sally, who was helping her dress. "Do you not find Mr. Short attractive? And he's so thoughtful."

"That he is, Miss Patsy."

"Do you think he cares for me?" the besotted girl inquired.

"Why, certainly he does. He enjoys spending time with you and Miss Polly."

Patsy didn't like hearing the ". . . and Polly," and immediately ended the conversation, feeling a bit embarrassed at her revelation.

Her dreams came crashing down when the Marquis de Lafayette, a frequent guest at their table and definitely a family man, laughed at Mr. Short one evening, saying, "*Mon bon homme*, I hear you are enamored of the Duchesse de La Rochefoucauld. You need not chase the married women, you know!"

Patsy's ears burned when more chortles and ribald jests followed. She did not want to hear anymore and felt like she would be sick. Perhaps it wasn't true. But everyone seemed to know about it, and the Duchesse was exceptionally lovely and clever. How could she have been so idiotic! To think he might be interested in an awkward school girl like her! Rather clumsily, she rose from the table and excused herself, saying she wasn't feeling well.

Mr. Short continued to accompany the girls on outings — as a chaperone — skating, shopping, or visiting museums. And Patsy now felt more self-conscious with him, realizing his sophistication put him out of her league. She had let her fantasies run amok since the lovely ball where they had whirled around the ballroom floor together. Those were simply delusions.

Patsy began to think seriously of entering the convent. Several of her friends at the Abbaye were doing so, and they seemed ecstatic with their choice. She had been exposed to Catholicism at the chapel services and the nuns were both compassionate and impressive. The way Catholics were passionate about their religion appealed to her as well. And what better way to be true to one's conscience than to lead a monastic life? There was just so much hypocrisy and immorality in the world. She could see it all around her; she would be better off away from such a dissolute society. She was repulsed when she watched Maria Cosway flirting so obviously with her father. She decided she would take her vows.

Patsy read his dismay when she shared her choice with him. She knew he hated to lay down the law to her, but he cleary found her proposal totally unacceptable. He would not allow it to happen! He could take her out of school, but thought that action might be too strong. He told her the reasons he thought it was a bad idea, and then he enticed her with a higher allowance and more glamorous parties. He always preferred using the carrot rather than the stick. Obviously he suspected she would be wooed by the world she would leave behind if she were to enter the convent.

In April, however, he surprised her by suddenly changing course and removed both girls from school, saying it was in preparation for their return to Virginia. Sometimes Patsy went to three balls a week, and Sally went as her chaperone. He told Patsy that Sally also needed to be properly dressed. At Monticello the slaves were expected to make their own clothes, and again, Patsy found herself feeling some envy and discomfort when he bought Sally clothes just as he had for his wife and did for his daughters. Soon, several fashionable gowns hung in Sally's wardrobe. Somehow, it seemed extravagant and inappropriate to Patsy, but she didn't dare challenge her father.

At one of the balls Thomas asked Patsy if by chance she had received a letter from cousin Tom Randolph.

"No, should I have?"

"I wrote and invited him to visit us in Paris this summer. I'm worried not to have had a word from him. I hope he has not befallen some accident."

"I sincerely hope not. He is probably just too busy."

"You are most likely right. But I have great plans for Tom. I think he needs a guiding hand, and I believe it would behoove him to study law in France for a few years before taking on a political career. He comes from a fine family and would be well accepted as a leader in Virginia. He has land and the reputation of the Randolph family."

Patsy suspected her father liked to mentor younger men, first, Mr. Short, and now, cousin Tom. Perhaps because he had no sons, she thought; she wished she could fill that role for her father too.

SALLY

SALLY ENJOYED THE BALLS when she accompanied Patsy and Polly to such lavish events. Her master saw to it that she was properly dressed for these occasions. Even if she did not participate in the dancing, he said she should be formally attired. She stared at the ballrooms of the opulent mansions, at the art and architecture, the food and clothing — amazed that this world could exist. It was difficult now to remember her life in Virginia when she was amidst all this finery.

It seemed extraordinary that her father had been white and was the same father as that of the woman Thomas had married. John Wayles had died the year she was born but she carried his blood. She found it nigh impossible to understand what it meant to be a mixed race person. It made no difference in Virginia; she would be a slave no matter her skin color or who her father was. Her mulatto mother decided her fate. But here in France, one could be a full black and be free. It was confounding to her that there were no absolute laws in every country based on what was right and just. She counseled herself to remember that if she chose to stay here to be free, she wouldn't have a life that included balls and school.

The time had come when she must decide what she was going to do. Should she stay in France, or return to Monticello? She went back and forth a million times a day, feeling pressure from James and the opposite expectations from her master. She knew her mother and grandmother had led their lives as concubines. That life did not seem so strange to her, and she knew these women had been well cared for and contented in a way, even if they had no choice. She also knew she could trust Mr. Jefferson to treat her well. James told her on several occasions he was furious their mother had not been able to secure freedom for herself and for her children from Mr. Wayles. But maybe *she* could get Mr. Jefferson to free her because he loved her!

When James spoke to her of what they might achieve in Paris, she would become momentarily enthralled. "Just think, Sister, we will be free!" But she couldn't really imagine the life he described. It was beyond her experience, and she would miss her mother and sisters so much if she stayed here for the rest of her life. She didn't want to disappoint Mr. Jefferson, or be separated from him. Hadn't he told her that he loved her? And she witnessed his caring for her daily. She didn't dare tell James she suspected she might be pregnant. She longed for her mother. Oh, what should she do?

James startled and upset her with another idea. "Do not expect him to be faithful, Sister! He will soon tire of you and find another mistress!"

The thought of his being with another woman made her go cold with jealousy and fear. She must somehow hold on to him. For wouldn't love make her free? How she wished she were older than her sixteen years! She knew she looked more mature, and in order to gain confidence, she preened a bit in front of the mirror, admiring her slim waist and full breasts. What would she do if he deserted her?

Thomas's approachable manner, which was often confusing to his European friends who valued formality, was part of what made it so easy for her to be with him. He could assume the role of patriarch while not being too overbearing, and his demeanor engendered loyalty and affection from all of his staff. Clearly he believed in his role as protector. She must be brave enough to speak to him of her concerns about returning to Monticello.

It was a hot July night and the family enjoyed a lighter than usual supper in the garden. Grapes, peaches, and plums with an assortment of cheeses still graced the table. Sally helped James serve the family and listened to their desultory conversation. Her heart skipped a beat when she heard her master mention he was awaiting permission from President Washington to return to Virginia.

"I believe my work here is done for the time being. I can return when need be. I also worry now that there may be some danger in remaining in Paris."

"Will Mr. Short be returning with us?" Patsy couldn't resist asking, looking across the table at William's face for his reaction to this question.

"That will depend on what my secretary chooses," Thomas responded, nodding to William. "He knows I would welcome his assistance," he added, smiling at his secretary.

"Thank you, Mr. Jefferson," William inclined his head, but didn't answer him directly. "It has certainly been an interesting time in France!"

That evening when Thomas lay with Sally in his cozy bed, he began talking of his plans for Monticello.

"Ah, my Sah-lee, we will make it the most beautiful place in the world. I will redesign the gardens, plant vineyards with French and German grapes, and bring olive trees to Virginia. I will borrow ideas from the elegant buildings here in Paris."

The dreaded moment had come. Before she could think twice, she blurted out, "Master, my brother wishes for me to stay in France with him."

Thomas sat up. "But no! I want you to always be with me. I suspected this." His face clouded.

Sally began to cry. "I had planned to return with you. But now I cannot. I am *enceinte*," she stumbled. "Pregnant, Master. I want my baby born on French soil. I want him to be born free!" She knew he had promised Patty not to remarry and he had been true to this pledge so far. But perhaps there might be a space in his life for her.

"Oh my dear girl." He held her closer. "Trust me, Sally, trust me. You will have your baby at Monticello. I will take care of you and the babe. Surely you know that."

"Yes," she gulped. She must be strong. "But that is not enough for my children. They must be free."

He paused a moment before answering. "I swear to you. When your children are twenty-one, I will free them. I promise to cherish you. I promise never to desert you. I promise you, your children will be freed."

She didn't want to leave this gentle and intense man. He had been a safe harbor for her entire life.

"And I will take care of you," she promised.

"Of course you will," he echoed, with his arms around her.

She suspected this was as close as they would ever come to marriage vows. She thought, with surprise, being a slave had made her wise beyond her years.

PATSY

PATSY FIRST AND FOREMOST wanted to please her father but she was sometimes puzzled as to what he wished. She knew he liked the repartee between the clever minds at the dinner table, but he would always tell her what he wanted most for her was to master the traditional domestic duties of a good wife. He expected her to know how to sew and cook and carry on an interesting conversation. And he would criticize the acerbic wit of Madame de Stael or the loud laughter of Angelica Church. It was somewhat confusing to her as he also escorted her to the Théatre Français, in the rue de l'Odéon, to see a play by Racine, and on another occasion to laugh with him at Beaumarchais's clever new play, *Le Mariage de Figaro.*

"My dear girl, I want you to appreciate Figaro's daring witticisms. He speaks of the important issues — equality of birth, freedom of the press, and arbitrary imprisonment. These are matters I want you to understand and think about." And he seemed so proud when she could converse at dinner about art and literature.

She noticed how her father's poise and elegant mien blended in with the aristocrats he dealt with daily. And how they leaned in close to him to hear his soft voice. Patsy, called Mademoiselle Martha by guests, carefully observed the scenes at the dining table with French aristocracy, including Charles Maurice de Talleyrand-Périgord, and American diplomats with their wives, often in vibrant wordplay. She witnessed heated arguments, obvious flirtations, and kept up-to-date with the political, national, and international news. She realized it was the best education a girl could get and found she had no regrets about shedding her crimson convent uniform. Ever since her father had removed her from the convent, she had questioned her desires to become a nun. Now she believed that life would have been too restricted. He usually knew what was best for her, she grudgingly admitted.

Still, the social interactions in Paris remained a conundrum. She didn't remember everyone acting so excited and boisterous in Virginia. And she certainly had not observed the play at romance, the overt erotic behavior among married men, and even married women, with partners who were not their spouses. Ribald, suggestive manners appeared to be an accepted form of conduct in French society. Perhaps she had just been too young when she left Virginia to understand this. And perhaps her father's flirtations were to be accepted — with married or unmarried women.

For the final two months before they were to leave, Mr. Short resided full-time at Langeac in order to help Mr. Jefferson prepare for their impending departure to America. Patsy thought he spent an inordinate amount of time exchanging little notes with her, discussing books, and taking walks. Patsy was very happy to hear her father try to persuade him to return with them.

"Finding prosperity in Europe will prove difficult, William," he argued. "You will find many more opportunities in our new country. The only resource for a durable happiness is to return to America, where you might earn enough to support a wife with whom you can enjoy the amusement and comfort of children."

Would her Papa accept Mr. Short as a proper suitor for her, she wondered? She feared he might think the age difference too much of an obstacle, and then decided he might more seriously object to him because he wasn't a landholder. He only had his secretarial salary to support himself and a wife if he chose to marry. She suspected that Papa would find such a financial situation too modest for a Jefferson. An even more outlandish idea popped into her head — actually, it had been a continuing fantasy for months now — perhaps she could stay in Paris and let her father and Polly return to Monticello. She began to consider this more seriously and asked her friend Marie what she thought of the idea.

"Oh, I would love for you to stay, *Jeffy*. Truly. What fun we would have!" Somehow Patsy thought this response sounded less than responsible.

THOMAS

DAILY, THE MOOD IN PARIS became more alarming and anxious, and the monarchy was unable to quiet the unrest. The unusually cold winter made living conditions for the poor ever more wretched, and food shortages sprang up everywhere. People were beating down the doors of bakeries, stealing food wherever they could find it, and attacking the king's men with pitchforks. The situation was deteriorating rapidly. Not only did Thomas fear for the safety of his family — he was also growing weary of the useless splendor of the monarchy and of the blasé removal from reality in which the aristocracy lived. They played silly games, he thought, to fill empty hours and stupidly refused to face the downward spiral of their country.

One hundred people were killed in riots that occurred at the May meeting of the Estates General, a legislative body representing the three estates of the realm. The First Estate was the clergy, the Second Estate the nobility, and the Third Estate effectively comprised the rest of French society. On Wednesday, June 17, the Third Estate, in frustration at not being able to obtain any of its demands from the king, declared the Estates General null and void, and named itself the National Assembly. Thomas understood this to mean there would be no turning back from a full-blown revolution. On the same day he wrote to Thomas Paine: *A more dangerous scene of war I never saw in America, than what Paris has presented for 5 days past.*

A little less than a month went by, and Thomas received a plea from Lafayette: *Please, break every engagement to give us a dinner tomorrow, Wednesday. We shall be some members of the National Assembly — eight of us, whom I want to coalesce as being the only means to prevent a total dissolution and a civil war.*

The very next day, July 11, 1789, the *Declaration of the Rights of Man and of the Citizen* was adopted by the National Assembly. Thomas felt some pride at this because it had been primarily written by Lafayette, who was greatly influenced by America's Declaration of Independence, and he had sought Thomas's counsel while writing the French document.

That night the group pledged to craft a new revolutionary French constitution. When Lafayette left Thomas's house, Thomas told him he had been honored to be a silent witness to such coolness and candor of argument unusual in the conflicts of political opinion. He praised him on his "logical reasoning, and chaste eloquence, disfigured," he claimed, "by no gaudy tinsel of rhetoric or declamation, and truly worthy of being placed in parallel with the finest dialogue of antiquity, as handed to us by Xenophon, by Plato, and Cicero."

"What would we do without friends like you?" Lafayette asked, embracing his American ally.

On the night of Tuesday, July 14, Thomas was dining at the home of his friend Mme de Corny. He had entertained a slight flirtation with her, as he found her witty and intelligent. One of her servants dared to enter the salon after the meal began in order to whisper the news in her ear — the Bastille has been stormed and the king's troops have slaughtered the attackers! Mme de Corny rapped on her crystal goblet and shared the news with her guests. Thomas knew that the Bastille, which held political prisoners in Paris, had become a symbol of the monarchy to the populace. He jumped up from the table.

"I must seek news of my friend Lafayette," he offered to the company. "I beg you to excuse me from this charming gathering, and I will send you more news should I receive it." He dashed off, barely remembering his manners, as the invited guests regarded his departure with some astonishment.

Lafayette was in charge of the safety and security of Louis XVI and Marie Antoinette, and so Thomas assumed he would be in danger, as well as the king and queen. He knew Lafayette supported the grounds for a revolution, but the Marquis also believed it should proceed peacefully. Clearly, things were spinning out of control. Moreover, he regretted he had not been successful in removing French tariff protection from inexpensive American food imports. They would have gone a long way in feeding the desperate hungry masses in France.

Thomas learned the next morning that the Bastille had fallen to the rebellious mob. And he worried even more because Patsy was sick in bed, probably ill from the fright she had taken when, returning from visiting

Lafayette's children, she had witnessed the mob's behavior. She told him she felt like a prisoner in their own house and was too afraid to venture out any more. "Let's go home NOW, Papa," she said.

Matters settled down somewhat for a few weeks, but the unrest continued to be disturbing. Thomas morbidly joked in a letter to Maria Cosway, saying, "Here in the midst of tumult and violence . . . cutting off heads has become so much à la mode, that one is apt to feel of a morning whether their own is on their shoulders."

He worried about what this meant for his family's safety as the Hôtel de Langeac was robbed three times, and one could not walk in the avenues without the possibility of encountering a street battle. On occasion the family could even hear gunshots in the distance. From the vantage point of their balcony, they peered through their telescope to look down the Champs-Elysées, still mostly fields, to the Place Louis XV. There, they saw the king's dragoons in red, white, and yellow uniforms, attempting to maintain peace among a hysterical crowd. From so far away, it resembled a play upon a stage. Patsy and Polly insisted on wearing the revolutionary's tricolored cockade when they went out, worrying their father greatly.

Thomas was against monarchy in principle as a form of government, but in addition, he had a low opinion of Louis XVI. He wrote to Madison, explaining his thoughts:

> *He has not a wish but for the good of the nation, and for that object no personal sacrifice would ever have cost him a moment's regret. But his mind is weakness itself, his constitution timid, his judgment null, and without sufficient firmness even to stand by the faith of his word. His Queen, too, haughty and bearing no contradiction, has an absolute ascendency over him.*

Indeed, he felt that the feckless queen was one of the main reasons the country was heading toward revolution. But he needed to turn to the problems in his own home. Thomas was particularly agitated about the unresolved situation with James. He knew from Sally that her brother

144

wished to stay in France in order to secure his freedom. He also feared that James might still persuade Sally to stay if he did. He greatly respected this young man and understood his ambition. One evening he asked James to come to his study.

"James, you have done a wonderful job here in Paris. I assume and hope you know I greatly appreciate your efforts."

"Yes, Master." James stood before him with a stony face and upright posture. Thomas gave his chef credit for looking strong and unbending. James wore a fine linen shirt with a collar made of a wrap-around tied linen bow, and a silk vest. What a long way this young man had come.

"I strongly suspect you wish to remain in Europe. Although I can appreciate your desire, I urge you to return to Virginia with me."

"But I want to be a free man, Sir." James didn't look him in the eye, which surprised him. He suddenly realized the man probably knew about his liaison with Sally and surely was angry with him for jeopardizing his sister's future as well as wanting his own freedom. He knew James was already twenty-four years old, and he shouldn't think of him as a boy anymore.

"I wonder if we can't find a solution. Your family will miss you if you stay in Europe, and I imagine you will miss them. I think you know that I care greatly about you and your family. What about your returning with us, and I will repay your loyalty by granting your freedom? And I will continue to pay you a salary in Virginia if you train another cook for me."

James looked up in surprise. He had clearly not expected this.

"I will think about it, Master," he said. Now James looked at him as he spoke. "But what about Sally and her baby?"

Thomas tried to hide his shock. Of course, he should have known that James had figured it out. "I have promised her that her children will be free at age twenty-one and so shall she, when I die."

James shook his head in some disbelief and left the room.

Maria and Mr. Cosway left Paris, having decided it had become too dangerous to remain. Thomas expected more of a scene at their *adieus,* but found it less difficult than he had expected. He still thought her agonizingly beautiful, but perhaps the affair had simply run its course. He guessed that she, as well as he, realized there were too many differences in their views to form a permanent partnership. She was thoroughly European, and he was a staunch American, with everything that implied. He looked back now on his dreams of her visit to Monticello as a silly fantasy. What a naïve romantic he could be. She wasn't a family woman and he had ignored that. It somehow helped that the Cosways left before his own departure, and he truly felt no constraints holding him in France for now.

In August, it was with great relief that he read President Washington's letter granting them permission to leave France and return home. "Just in time! Let's begin packing!" he said to his family, smiling.

SALLY

NOW THAT IT WAS TIME to depart, Sally began to question her decision not to stay in France. Even though she was pregnant, might she not have a better life here with James? Her baby would be *free*. It was hard to imagine. She'd been so frightened when she realized she was carrying a child. What would he look like? Would he have even lighter skin than she?

But where would they live? And how would she take care of the baby without her family? Sally understood they had lived in a very comfortable manner while in Paris, in a soft cocoon, and she was afraid to think of being out on the street, unable to secure proper housing. Even if her mother would be disappointed that she had become a concubine, she knew Betty would lovingly help her with the baby. And, she didn't want to say goodbye to Thomas. In fact, she couldn't imagine leaving him. She couldn't discuss it with James because she was too embarrassed, and, to be honest, she didn't want him to convince her otherwise.

That night Sally told her master she would return to Virginia with him, Patsy, and Polly. She watched his face light up with relief and joy and when he clasped her tightly to him, she prayed she had made the right decision.

Sally was happily surprised when, at the last minute, James informed her he, too, would return. He explained that he had told Thomas a few days earlier he would agree to the offer to go back if he could be assured he would be paid at Monticello and would be freed when he trained a replacement chef. He told her what Thomas had offered to do for him and grinned, "Besides, sister, I need to take care of you, don't I?"

She hugged him with tears in her eyes. "Oh, James, thank you, thank you." Everything would be all right.

PATSY

PATSY, POLLY, AND SALLY LOOKED down from the balcony of the Hôtel de Langeac to witness the procession of the king and queen being escorted to the Bastille by her father's colleague and their family friend, the Général de Lafayette. The majestic red and gold coach with the king and queen hidden within led the somber parade, and soldiers followed to prevent any attack upon them. Patsy thought it looked like a strangely decorated beetle on wheels, creeping up the avenue. The people were remarkably silent, but then huge cheers for Lafayette arose from the crowd pressing near. Lafayette noticed Patsy at the balustrade above and bowed his head to her. She pressed her hands to her breast, overcome with gratitude for this recognition, understanding it to be a sign of the common cause of the American and French revolutions. For some odd reason, she wasn't afraid.

What she dreaded most now was leaving Mr. Short. Why had he been so stubborn about coming with them? He had seemed to be such an integral part of their family; she really thought he would. He had promised to write, but if he truly cared about her, he would have behaved differently, she suspected. Patsy had given him several chances to speak to her alone, but he seemed to be avoiding her rather than engaging her warmly. It hurt her feelings, making her moody and even sullen. Thomas, noticing it one day, picked her chin up between his thumb and finger, "Don't despair, *ma fille*, we will come back to Paris soon." They both ignored her earlier inclination to enter the convent and never discussed it. At least he hadn't guessed the real reason for her sadness.

On the last Sunday of September 1789, the Jeffersons closed the door of the Hôtel de Langeac for the final time. Thomas had already bid his close friends *adieu* — Lafayette, Condorcet, and La Rochefoucauld. He would be leaving them with the hope that they would live to old age and enjoy the fruits of their Revolution. He worried that his family's carriage and additional wagons, following with thirty-eight packing boxes and trunks, which included many cases of fine French wines, might be blocked or attacked on the way out of the city, but they managed to reach the port of Le Havre without incident. Patsy noticed his anxiety and put her hand in his. "Papa, this has been the most wonderful experience. I shall never forget it."

He leaned over and kissed her forehead. "That you were here with me made all the difference," he said. "You have learned to be sociable and charming, industrious and active. I am so proud of you. I now hope you will continue this healthy way of living and not resort to Virginia indolence. That is one thing that worries me, for making every minute count in our lives is of utmost importance."

Polly and Sally sat across from them in the large conveyance and James rode behind. Sally began to complain she didn't feel well with the rocking carriage, and Patsy pooh-poohed her weakness. Usually Sally was the hardiest of the three girls. As Sally looked more and more uncomfortable, Thomas suggested they stop for a while to let her rest.

"Sit down a bit, in the fresh air," Patsy suggested. "Perhaps it was the buttermilk at breakfast." When Sally only looked greener at this suggestion, all of a sudden Patsy realized what might be the matter. She looked more carefully at her former playmate and saw the bodice of her dress filled out more tightly. Recognizing the symptoms her mother had often displayed, Patsy tried to hide her shock. Sally was only her age. How and when had this happened?

James stepped down from his horse, inquiring what was wrong.

"Nothing to worry about, my boy," Thomas said. "Let us be on our way again."

They found discontented citizens all along the way, looking at their fine coach with disgust, and were relieved when no one accosted them. They were getting out just in time, Thomas told his travelling companions. Patsy always relied on her father to be calm and composed, and so his nervousness was especially unsettling. It took six days to reach the coast, and they noticed the rioting decreased as they got farther from Paris. However, they were greatly disappointed to find all ships stuck in port due to severe storms. Their party had to wait from October 5 until October 22 to set sail.

They passed the time with surprising enjoyment, exploring the Isle of Wight, often with Nathaniel Cutting, a sea captain from Massachusetts, who was presently living in Le Havre. Mr. Cutting told Thomas that he found Patsy "an amiable Girl, tall and genteel, who though she has been so long resident in a Country remarkable for its Levity and the forward indelicacy of its manners, retains all that winning simplicity, and good humoured reserve that are evident proofs of innate Virtue and an happy disposition."

"You warm my heart with those kind words," rejoined Thomas. The two men agreed that these "characteristicks [sic] eminently distinguish the women of America from those of any other Country."

Patsy sensed her father clearly was comfortable to be back in the company of a fellow American. He chose to spend a lot of the time wandering the hills above the town in search of a Normandy shepherd dog called a Bergère. He dragged Patsy and Polly around the countryside with him, but Sally, excused herself, saying if they didn't need her, she felt too tired. They finally found a pregnant bitch, and "Buzzy," as she came to be called, boarded the *Clermont* with them. Thomas was also taking French furniture and books back to Virginia — not to mention all the fine clothing the family had purchased. But when would they wear such finery in America, Patsy wondered? She somehow sensed it would not be appropriate. Perhaps they could use the elegant materials to remake the garments into American style clothing.

MONTICELLO

1789-90

Agriculture . . . is our wisest pursuit, because it will in the end contribute most to real wealth, good morals and happiness.

Thomas Jefferson to George Washington, 14 August 1787
Library of Congress, Washington DC
Jefferson Letters Collection

THOMAS

1789

THOMAS EXPERIENCED BOTH joy and relief upon his return to Monticello. The jubilation of the slaves upon his homecoming was profoundly moving, and he laughed with them when they literally picked him up and carried him over their heads into the house.

He had been in France for five years, and here, in Virginia, was the life he loved — close to the land, with his family and friends around him. But the return to the rooms, where he and Patty had been so happy and where he had imagined a long life with his wife, was devastating. He felt his old melancholy return like a rocky, muddy tide and he had to literally gasp for air. He must strive to concentrate on his farming projects and his children. It was clear — the beautiful, young, mulatto woman, who had agreed to return to America with him, soothed his spirit.

He was immediately struck by one of the wonders of America — so different from the world of France. The New World was pivoted toward the future and the workingman, whereas France was tethered by the aristocracy and the past. Thomas hoped the revolution in Paris would change that focus, but for now, he would bask in the exciting promise of the United States.

He made contact with all family members upon his return, including his youngest and only surviving brother, Randolph Jefferson. He had already written to him from Paris on January 11, saying, . . . *no society is so precious as that of one's own family.* He was ecstatic to be close to everyone once again. And what a relief to be back in the comfortable clothing he wore around the plantation — heavy cotton knee breeches and loose linen shirts. He happily reverted to his plain, somewhat neglected, style. When he needed to dress for an occasion, he favored a pair of red leather breeches and pointed shoes with bright buckles.

One of his first missions was to find a proper husband for Patsy, who had turned seventeen in September. He was aware of her infatuation with William Short, having witnessed her adulation of his secretary at the dinner table. Although he thought William a fine young man, he very much wanted Patsy to be part of his life in Virginia. He had not been unhappy when Short decided to remain in Europe, but was somewhat surprised when he turned down the offer to come back to America with him. Thomas believed Mr. Short erroneously imagined he could make an important diplomatic career abroad.

Patsy had grown up among the landed gentry, and Thomas was convinced a tie to the land was the future of the country and therefore the best future for his daughter. The New World, he thought, would be a utopia of gentleman farmers and statesmen ruling communities with a benevolent hand. He decided her twenty-one-year-old, third cousin, Tom Randolph, might be just the right man for Patsy. Not only was he distantly related, but he was also the son of Thomas's childhood friend, Tom Randolph, Sr.

Patsy

PATSY CLUNG TO BETTY Hemings almost as long as Sally did. It was so comforting to embrace this woman who had helped raise her and who had been by her mother's bedside when she died. Patsy realized she had been a surrogate mother for her in so many ways. Betty looked older because her hair was gray, but her face remained virtually unlined. She'd always found Betty's dark chestnut eyes with her *café au lait* skin exceptionally lovely. Patsy felt her shoulders drop their tension, just at the sight of this loyal woman. Being back at home also made her realize how much pressure she had felt in Paris to act like an adult. She almost wanted to be a child again, but sensed her father had other immediate plans for her.

Many of the slaves greeted them at the bottom of the mountain and sang and danced their joy as they practically pulled them up the hill. It seemed to her that everyone was laughing and crying at the same time, including her father. The trip home had taken almost a month, and it felt like a miracle now to be welcomed back by so many people. As Ursula and the other house slaves led her into the house, she was shocked and saddened to see how the place had deteriorated while they were abroad. Paint peeled at the window frames and doorposts, the stairs seemed to lean drunkenly askew, and there were leaks in some of the ceilings. It dawned on her that there would not be the indoor plumbing they had enjoyed in Paris. *Quel horreur!* How odd it was that she was thinking in French!

The familiarity of her home helped diminish some of the pain she'd experienced upon leaving William. But she missed him terribly and longed for a letter. She didn't know if he would write; perhaps he knew her Papa had other plans for her. To be honest, she wasn't even sure about William's feelings for her. He hadn't asked her not to leave, and she assumed he was still involved with Mme la Rochefoucauld. Perhaps he preferred these loose liaisons to permanent ties. She shouldn't think about him so much! Sometimes she resented her father's total control of her life, but she also understood he wanted the best for her. And she wanted so much to please him.

"I've invited our friend Tom Randolph for Christmas," Thomas informed Patsy only a few days after their homecoming. "I'm impressed with his performance at the university in Edinburgh. He will be a leader in our community one day. I'm sure of it."

She thought her father not terribly subtle in his praises of Tom and easily guessed his motive. She remembered meeting her cousin at his plantation, Tuckahoe, as a child, and then again in 1781, when they were escaping the British troops. And yes, she now recalled the time in Philadelphia when she and her father had been waiting to go to Paris. She remembered a rather awkward and gangly young man — but it had been a long time since they'd met. Papa informed her he'd also invited her first cousins, the Carr brothers. She imagined he was hoping to make it a merry holiday to push away the memories of past Christmases and happy times with Patty.

Patsy continued to watch the daily mail for a note from William, but there was nothing in the post except letters from Marie de Botidoux and several more of her French girlfriends. How she missed them! For she had no other close friends nearby. Whom would she talk to now that she was back in Virginia? Polly was too young to understand her present concerns, and a definite tension had arisen between her and Sally. Patsy was shocked at Sally's metamorphosis, from slender girl to pregnant young woman. They had been so close, and now an awkward restraint wedged them apart. She found this hurtful, but not as upsetting as the horrific suspicion that her father might be the father of Sally's child. The sight of Betty who had been her grandfather's concubine had sparked this horrific idea.

One morning Patsy saw her father help Sally lift a heavy dish in the breakfast room and touch her hand as he took it from her. The look he gave her was one of blatant affection. Even though she had suspected, a shock went through her body and she turned away. How could Sally have done this? Hadn't she wanted to make a life different from her mother's? Patsy was filled with revulsion and darted out of the room in anger.

For days Patsy avoided Sally and felt embarrassed and mortified at the thought of her father and this girl together. How could it have happened? When she'd heard the banter of extramarital affairs at table in Paris, it had seemed a far remove, but this was in their home! She had worried about Maria Cosway and stupidly ignored what had been happening under her own roof. The thought of being with a man herself was a bit alarming, and she could not — would not — imagine Sally with her father.

Her misgivings grew when she saw him being exceptionally tender toward Sally when she was tired. She pushed away the thought. It couldn't be true! But what other men had Sally been close to? Might William be the guilty party? He had been in their home constantly. No! Absolutely impossible! Sally must have coupled with a friend of her brother's or some other Frenchman. In any event, the girls did not discuss Sally's condition, which was now blazingly apparent, and Sally kept close to her mother. She lived in the slave cabins on Mulberry Row, and rarely crossed paths with Patsy and Polly since their return.

PATSY

PATSY HEARD THE THUNDERING horse's hooves before she saw animal and rider charging up the drive to the front portico of Monticello. She had gone outside to pick some flowers for the evening table as they were expecting many guests, including Tom Randolph, who brought his steed to an abrupt halt before her. The man who jumped down from the saddle was a strong improvement on her recollection of him. He was her third cousin, she'd been told. He was much taller than she — which was saying something — and his black hair and olive complexion were impressive. She would later learn the Randolphs claimed to be descendants of the princess Pocahontas.

"You DO look like a French woman!" he exclaimed. "I'd heard the rumor but now I see what they mean."

"Well, *I* certainly don't know," Patsy huffed. Falling back on her manners, she smiled, and asked, "Would you like to come in? You can give your horse to Isaac." The young slave had emerged from the side of the house to attend to the needs of their guest.

"Yes, ma'am," Tom rejoined. And Patsy almost laughed at the southern way of talking. She had almost forgotten. She'd expected, "*Oui, Mademoiselle.*"

As the afternoon and evening progressed, Patsy warmed to this energetic fellow, who had been well educated and who expressed an ambition to better his position in life. It was clear her father saw him as someone with the talent and connections to make a good mate for her. But why was her father in such a hurry? She was only seventeen and Tom was twenty-one. Then she remembered how she had been attracted to William, who was thirteen years her elder. But Tom could not hold a candle to William's wit and sophistication. How she missed him!

They all sang Christmas carols after dinner and Patsy noticed Tom had a nice bass voice. He smiled at her and she smiled back, but thought she wasn't ready to get involved seriously yet. She lowered her eyes. She just wanted to settle into plantation life — riding, tending to domestic tasks, and talking with her father about spring planting. She also enjoyed chatting with him about the repairs he foresaw as necessary for the house. She needed some time to define her new role at home and relearn American ways.

THOMAS

THOMAS'S RESPITE FROM PUBLIC life didn't last long. The family had arrived in Virginia on November 23, 1789, and in late December, James Madison knocked on his door at Monticello. Both he and George Washington wished him to be secretary of state. Madison assured his friend he would not have to worry about domestic affairs; rather the job entailed advising the president on foreign policy. Thomas's experience in Europe had surely been good preparation for this endeavor. They also suggested he might return to France, but Washington pressed him to serve in New York, close to him.

One issue for Thomas in accepting the post was the salary — quoted to be $3,500 per year. He was already in debt from dipping into his personal wealth to provision his family while in France, when his salary had been severely insufficient for what he needed abroad. Now the plantation was in dire need of repair and refurbishing. He would have hoped for more; yet, to be in the first cabinet of his country was a thrilling opportunity and an honor. He wanted to serve his country and he accepted.

He dragged his feet, however, about leaving for New York. He felt an extreme urgency to settle Patsy's situation before departing. Her attraction to William Short had alarmed him, and he now suspected it would not be a good idea to leave her idle and undirected. Besides, she might become infatuated with someone entirely inappropriate. How he wished his wife were here to help him with this difficult responsibility. He believed Tom's recent visit augured well, and he wrote to his friend, Thomas Mann Randolph and his wife Ann Cary about their sentiments for a union between Patsy and Tom. They responded with enthusiasm — and so, having planted the seed, now he would have to leave it up to Patsy and Tom. He would not force her to do something she didn't want, but he assumed she would follow his advice and wishes.

PATSY

1790

ONLY A WEEK LATER, in mid-January, Thomas and his girls were invited to Tuckahoe to attend the wedding of Tom Randolph's sister, Judith Randolph. She was to marry another Randolph — Richard, of Bizarre Plantation. Great merriment and dancing extended into the evening to celebrate this family affair, and Tom tried to keep Patsy as his constant partner, acting jealous when the Carr brothers and other young men cut in. He finally grabbed her hand and pulled her out the door with him into the cold.

"It's too hot in there," he said as a way of explanation. "Come. We'll be warm enough in the barn." Once inside, he immediately pulled her to him and pressed his lips to hers.

The strength of his arms surprised and thrilled her, as did his tall frame. She began to return the kiss and he only pulled her more tightly to him. "Ah, Patsy. You are ravishing."

"This seems so — so sudden!" she managed to break in. But he only kissed her again and plunged his hands into her hair. This was exciting, indeed, and she leaned into him. He then moved one hand to her breast —

"No, no, Tom. What are you doing?" she gasped.

"Patsy, Patsy. I am not being fresh. I want you for my wife."

"But I am only seventeen!"

Tom held her at arm's length. "Oh, Patsy, that is of no account! I have discussed it with your father. He agrees that we are a good match. Our families have a longstanding bond, and I will inherit my father's fortune." He appeared so adamant and assured.

Patsy was surprised her Papa had talked with Tom about this before saying something to her, but she knew he had been hinting at it for months — even before they left France. She had lost faith in her dream of William

161

turning up at their gate, and this man overwhelmed her. What he said was true — that there was much to say in favor of the match, but she didn't feel ready, only confusion.

Tom fell down on one knee, holding her hand, "I must have you, dear Patsy. You are a delight! You bring the exotic flavor of Paris to Virginia, and yet you are the best our rural corner has ever fashioned. You are beyond my dreams!"

No one had ever spoken to her in this manner and looking into his handsome face, she thought it might be wonderful to spend her life with him.

"I'm so — well, astounded, Tom! But thank you." She paused, trying to collect her thoughts. Sudden emotion clouded her mind and she fumbled for words. "Just give me a little time. We've only been home for three months. And we've known one another such a short while."

He clasped her to him again, "Not really. Since we were children, actually. We'll be happy, Patsy. Truly, we will." He sounded positively convinced.

The next day, back at Monticello, she entered her father's study. She didn't begin with small talk, but said, "Papa, Tom has proposed to me." She wanted to reprimand him for not warning her but couldn't seem to criticize her father.

"Oh, my dearest girl! What wonderful news! And did you give him an answer?"

"I told him I would think about it."

"But what holds you back, Patsy dear?"

She saw anxiety in his face and wondered why. "Is it what you would want, Papa? It just seems rather soon to me."

"Only if you are happy with the idea. It would be a fine union, I believe. The land he would bring to the table would settle some of our debt." He stopped, realizing the implication, then added hastily, "But of course, you are not for sale."

Oh, My Lord! She knew he had recently been forced to sell Elk Hill, his wife's favorite plantation, to cover his debts. Her marriage would remove some of the financial stress. She'd not thought of this. She tried to focus on Tom's positive attributes: he was a neighbor and a friend, a kind, and well educated, good-looking young man. They would share common interests and enjoy intelligent conversation. She smiled. And his kisses were entrancing — and he wanted HER.

If she'd learned anything these past few years, it was that life kept turning up surprises. Now her father was going to New York as secretary of state, and he wouldn't be at Monticello for them to work together as they'd planned. She was no longer a child. She'd rather be mistress of her own house, she thought, than go to Eppington to be with Aunt Elizabeth and Polly.

"If you think it's the right thing for me, I'm glad to consent, Papa," she said, moving into his arms for an embrace.

Patsy wrote to Tom and accepted his proposal. In true Tom style, he immediately leapt on his horse and rode to Monticello to whirl her across the parquet floor in the huge entrance hall. Light streamed in from the columned portico opening to the front lawn and she laughed with delight. She enjoyed his arms around her and floating across the room. His eyes were merry and his smile enticing.

"Let us marry soon! I cannot wait another minute to have you. And your father will be happy to know you are settled before he leaves for New York."

She knew this to be true and agreed to plan the wedding for two weeks hence. This was entirely possible because in Virginia, weddings were usually fairly simple family affairs, with friends and neighbors, and no special dress was expected. The slaves would prepare mounds of food, rum, and beer — and for a Jefferson wedding there would be champagne from France! The rush made it all the more exhilarating.

The next afternoon Tom informed her their fathers had talked, and Mr. Randolph would give him Varina, a plantation near Tuckahoe, on the James River, along with forty slaves. Thomas would gift to Patsy 1000 acres in Bedford County, which had been part of the Poplar Forest Plantation, with twenty-five Negroes, along with all the livestock and utensils. Patsy gasped. She did not want to own slaves. But, in truth, the slaves would be Tom's because in Virginia law, everything in a marriage belonged to the husband. So in truth, the gift became a dowry.

"However, I know you wish to be close to Monticello," he smiled at her. "And so I plan to buy a small farm near Edgehill, here in Albemarle County, also because I don't want lands that need a lot of slaves to be successful. I think slavery is an abomination."

"Oh, Tom. I am so glad to hear that. You have only strengthened my decision to marry you."

On Tuesday, February 23, Patsy chose to wear the bronze silk she had donned for her first ball in Paris. It was a good thing they had packed all the finery for their return after all. The color brought out the shiny molasses tones of her hair, which she asked Polly to help her style in a French manner. She told Sally she didn't need her help and watched her leave the room with a hurt expression. Well, she wasn't to blame for the awkward situation, Patsy told herself.

There wasn't much in bloom yet, but white hyacinths and narcissus had been forced to bloom early by the clever Monticello gardeners. Patsy wanted white flowers to symbolize purity since she wasn't wearing white, and they would look beautiful with her coppery gown and hair. While she was dressing, Thomas appeared with a necklace for her to wear.

"It belonged to your mother, my darling. And she would want you to have it on this special day." As he clasped it around her neck, in the mirror she saw his eyes were wet and she turned to embrace him. It was sometimes difficult to hold on to a clear memory of her mother, and this man had seemed like both father and mother to her for so long.

When her Papa relinquished her hand to Tom's, she felt it was more an end than a beginning, and she struggled to maintain her equanimity. Tom clasped her fingers, forcing her to raise her face to his. The look of tenderness there rescued her, and she warmly returned his gaze. However, when she laid her hand on a Bible that had been her mother's to say her vows, she struggled to hide the wave of sadness that swept over her. It was greatly a sorrow of knowing all she had missed by not having a mother for so long. The kind expression of the Episcopal clergyman, the Reverend James Maury, who was officiating and who had been a family friend forever, comforted her.

The slaves busily carried heavy trays, laden with myriad treats, for the guests and refilled punch cups for hours and hours. But Sally wasn't there, making Patsy feel both angry and sad. She was hidden away on Mulberry

Row, hiding her pregnancy on a dirt street lined with slave shacks, work-shops, and sheds, and no one mentioned her absence. James had made a special wedding cake for Patsy, proud to display his newly acquired pastry skills. He was working hard to fulfill his promise to the master to train someone else so that he would then be free to come and go as he pleased.

The music, performed by a Negro family hired from Charlottesville, lasted into the wee hours as everyone jigged and waltzed to their happy tunes. A few of the slaves who were known for their dancing, including Isaac Granger, were asked to come up to the Big House and perform to the music of several black fiddlers. Patsy asked Tom to pause their dancing so she could watch the quill blowers, whom she had enjoyed since she was a child. The skilled, slave musicians miraculously could coax different notes from a rack of porcupine quills, which essentially resembled a panpipe. But she couldn't pay attention because Tom constantly whispered in her ear that it was time for the bride and groom to retire to the bedroom. She blushed at his clear demands and looked around to see if anyone else heard him.

When they did excuse themselves, it evinced a few catcalls from the Carrs. Tom didn't want to wait for her to change. "I want to undress you as fast as I can," he laughed. "You are all I ever could have imagined!" he crowed as he covered her with kisses and covered her body with his own.

She panicked at first, but after the first discomfort, she welcomed his animal ferocity. Patsy found herself giving in to his rapture and found a rhythm matching his. She hadn't known what to expect or how she would react. Now, she couldn't believe herself but welcomed this passion with something close to ecstasy. She walked around for days intoxicated with this new feeling of bonding with her husband, and began to understand Sally's feelings for the man who had taken her to his bed — probably her father. It sickened her but she realized she must try to forgive Sally if they were going to live side by side.

Elated to see Patsy smiling after her wedding, Thomas was relieved he now could go away, knowing she would be well taken care of.

"It devastates me to be separated from you again, dear one. I think I must call you "Martha" now instead of "Patsy," being as you are a mar-ried woman. And you will be known as Mrs. Randolph to our neighbors. Think of that! So, now remember, Martha, your new marriage will call for an abundance of little sacrifices. But they will be greatly overpaid by the affections they will secure you." He took both of her hands. "The happiness of your life depends now on pleasing a single person. To this, I know all other objects must be secondary, even your love for me."

"Oh, Papa, my love for you will always come first. But I will make it my duty to please Tom."

"And I will be a faithful friend to both you and your husband." He placed a hand on her cheek. "Now, I must make a request of you as well, to watch over Polly — he paused — and the servants," — he paused, "while I am away."

Patsy blanched. She believed he had just confirmed her suspicion. She knew it must be difficult for him to ask because it revealed how much he cared about Sally. He hadn't said her name. Patsy hesitated. Of course, she would keep his secret, for now she understood his tie to his concubine better than before she'd experienced the passion ignited by Tom. Sally was expecting Thomas's child, and she shouldn't turn her back on this girl, who was legally her aunt, and who had been her childhood friend and help-mate. But it also felt a little bit as though he had substituted Sally's love for hers.

"Of course I will, Papa," she replied.

SALLY

IMMEDIATELY AFTER THE WEDDING, Sally continued to feel Patsy's coldness and rejection. She knew she shouldn't be surprised, but wondered how they would continue to live near one another if this strained atmosphere persisted. At least Patsy would be leaving soon for Varina when she returned from her wedding tour. But how would they ever live under the same roof again? Betty advised her to just stay out of everyone's way for a while. After the freedom of France, it felt particularly unjust. Hadn't she proven herself capable of working at several jobs? Hadn't she managed to find her way around a foreign city? She also had learned how to cook some with James, and she had become a better seamstress. Yes, it definitely was not fair. Why should one person have a power like this over another?

Sally had worried a bit when Patsy married, fearing that Thomas might decide to name her to be Patsy's slave as part of the girl's dowry at her marriage. Indeed, she had heard talk to that effect, and it was a natural expectation because the young women had been close since childhood. But he never suggested it, and she hoped it was because he wanted to keep her close by.

The rough log walls of the cabin seemed to close in on her and the dirt floor simply made her angry. She never felt she could get truly clean and dust seemed to be circling everywhere. Mostly, she craved light and stayed outside whenever the temperature allowed. There were a few pretty pieces of crockery Betty had collected, but she longed to have finer things around her. When she went over to the big house to help polish silver or assist James, she found herself dreading the return to the slave habitations. At least in Paris, she imagined, she would be living in a real house, even if a simple one.

Sally didn't have to wait long after Patsy's nuptial festivities for her labor pains to begin, and she thanked God she had both Betty and Ursula at her side. Although she had witnessed other childbirths, she couldn't believe the strength of the contractions, how they took hold of her entire body and held her as a prisoner. It seemed to go on forever and she lost all track of time. When she thought she was totally exhausted, her mother said, "Sally, you need to push one more time," and sure enough, her little boy was born. Betty placed him in her arms and told her how brave she had been. Betty also commanded her, "Get freedom for this babe and for yourself, Child." Sally proudly named him Thomas Jefferson Hemings.

The family parted to make a path to her bed for Mr. Jefferson, who had arrived to congratulate her. He took Sally's hand with tears in his eyes and told her she would be a good mother. Then he told her he must leave the next day for New York. Sally didn't know how she would bear it, but nodded and tried to smile at him.

"Your mother will take good care of you," he said and left. His tall backlit figure in the door made her both proud and desolate. She could live here with her mother and siblings and he would provide for them all. But she hadn't found her footing, and she ardently wanted more than that.

One morning, when little Thomas was only seventeen days old, he wouldn't nurse. She called Betty and in tears, asked what she could do. He was also coughing and felt limp. Betty ran and got a cloth that she dipped in some milk and put to his lips. But he wouldn't suck. Sally began wailing in panic and wasn't even sure when he stopped breathing. Her mother took the dead child from her, and she felt as if it were her own life that had been taken.

Why wasn't Thomas here with her? Had he ruined her? She gulped and howled and howled. James came running and held her so tightly, she began to calm down a bit. What could she do now? At least her little boy would be buried near her, at Monticello. She asked James to please take the news to the master. Perhaps he would bring back a message for her.

Sally felt crushed and abandoned, and sometimes simply numb. When she woke in the mornings, she sensed a gray curtain between herself and the world. She wouldn't have had the strength to take care of the tiny mite anyway. No letter arrived from Thomas.

PATSY

ONLY DAYS AFTER HER wedding, Patsy found a letter addressed to her father from William Short. Apparently, right before leaving for New York, Thomas had left it perched on a salver in the hall for everyone to see. William wrote of news from Paris — especially how Lafayette had calmed an angry mob. She searched in vain for a particular note for her but found only the closing, which said, "Present my compliments to the young ladies." Her first emotion was anger, that he could so casually allude to her. Then she raised her chin with pride and gratitude, for she was now a married woman, and she would have nothing to do with this cocky fellow! Fortunately, she had not flirted too ostentatiously with him. She wanted to tear up the offensive note but managed to control her temper.

The plan was for Patsy and Tom to move immediately to Varina, where Tom would begin farming in earnest. He still wanted to pursue his studies in order to become a better statesman in Albemarle County. But first, as was the custom for newlyweds, they were to make a tour of extended family plantations on both the Randolph and Jefferson sides, leaving young Polly with the Eppeses at Eppington during their sojourn. Because Thomas was in New York, Patsy had essentially taken charge of her sister.

Upon their return, the young couple settled at Varina. The plantation lay near Tuckahoe, and in Virginia, sons generally stayed in the vicinity of their father's estates. However, Tom Jr. apparently had a tense relationship with his father, and Patsy yearned to live close to her own father. She wrote to him, intimating that she preferred to live in Albemarle, and essentially granted him the opportunity to meddle. She explained that without his company, her happiness "can never be compleat" [sic] although she was cognizant of "her commitment to please Tom "in every thing and . . . consider all objects as secondary to that *except* my love for you." She hoped he would contrive a way for them to move there.

Patsy and Tom continued to have many conversations about where they should make a permanent home, and she often brought up the warm

feelings and trust Tom had for Thomas. She knew she was being manip-
ulative but she believed it was in both of their best interests. Soon after
their marriage another factor entered their discussion — she discovered
she was pregnant! So much had been happening so fast, and she didn't feel
at all ready for this change in her life. Moreover, she had no family support
at Varina. She found herself hauling water, cooking, even chopping wood
— and when she stopped to think of herself sipping wine at Paris dinners,
she laughed. Would that have been her life if she'd remained with William?
But he hadn't offered that to her, and she ought not think of him anymore.

Auntie Eppes kept telling Patsy she needed a maid. And Patsy agreed.
"We couldn't get by without our slaves," she told Patsy, "and, don't forget,
they couldn't survive without us."

Patsy felt her high intentions to live without slaves crumbling as she
struggled against nausea in early pregnancy and toiled to get the new plantation up and running. Hot weather in the spring and summer at Varina
turned the tide, for Tom developed a terrible affliction from the heat. His
skin reacted with an allergic rash, and they both pined for the cooler air
atop the mountain at Monticello. The couple easily agreed to spend some
time there in September when Thomas would be visiting from Philadelphia.

NEW YORK

SECRETARY OF STATE

1790

. . . a mind always employed is always happy. this is the true secret, the grand recipe for felicity. the idle are the only wretched. in a world which furnishes so many emploiments [sic] which are useful, & so many which are amusing, it is our own fault if we ever know what ennui is, or if we are ever driven to the miserable resource of gaming, which corrupts our disposition, & teaches us a habit of hostility against all mankind

Extract from Thomas Jefferson to his daughter,
Martha Jefferson Randolph

May 21, 1787

THOMAS

1790

THOMAS WATCHED THE SNOW fall as his carriage made its slow way north to New York. He would be glad to see the Adamses again, now happily ensconced in a house they had named Richmond Hill, in a neighborhood called Greenwich Village by its inhabitants. Thomas thought it wise not to be far away from good friends and found a small house at 57 Maiden Lane, also in lower Manhattan. Feeling extremely lonely, he wished for the cheer of his family around him and for the warmth of the tawny slave girl in his bed.

He wrote to Patsy shortly after his arrival:

New York, April 4, 1790

> *I am anxious to hear from you, of your health, your occupations. . . . Do not neglect your music. It will be a companion which will sweeten many hours of life to you. I assure you mine here is triste enough. Having had yourself and dear Poll to live with me so long, to exercise my affections and cheer me in the intervals of business, I feel heavily the separation from you . . .*

He threw himself into his work, which he perceived as an invigorating challenge and the best medicine for the doldrums. He admired President Washington, and the two met almost daily to discuss foreign affairs and the general progress of the country. For several days soon after his arrival, he kept Washington company while their friend John Trumbull worked on a portrait of the president. Generally Thomas approved of Washington's prudence and strength, yet he shared some reservations about the president with his good friend John Adams: "His mind is great and powerful, without being of the very first order; his penetration strong, though not so acute as that of a Newton, Bacon, or Locke; and as far as I can see, no judgment was ever sounder. It can be slow in operation, being little aided by invention or imagination, but sure in conclusion."

"Ah," Adams replied. "I think you have the measure of the man, Thomas. I fear he also could be tremendous in his wrath if his temper broke its bonds."

The stress of being judged himself by so many great men was taking a toll on his health during the first winter in New York, now a bustling city of 33,000 people. Then, when he received the news from James that Sally had lost her baby, whom she'd named Thomas, he put his head in his hands. How devastating for Sally! And he was helpless to come to her aid. He didn't dare write to her. He felt it would show too much favoritism if he singled her out for a personal note among his slaves. He took to his bed with one of his crushing headaches.

Thomas learned from the president he would not be required to return to Paris and so immediately wrote to Mr. Short, requesting that he and Adrien Petit please pack up the remainder of his possessions at the Hôtel Langeac and send them to America. Eighty-six crates, bursting with sculpture, scientific instruments, books, and more wine would make their way across the ocean to Monticello. Furniture, other decorative items, and kitchenware were also included, for he wanted his French discoveries to be always around him. Petit himself decided to come too, desiring to serve "le Roy des maîtres" once again.

Thomas was in the habit of depending on his close friend James Madison to discuss ideas. At the moment he was greatly consumed with the problem of how the states should communicate with the Senate and House of Representatives and what should be the balance of power between them. Having not been much exposed to him before (with the exception of the original members of the Continental Congress), politicians in New York talked about him as a newcomer. He was aware of this and sensitive to their remarking on his rather casual demeanor and rambling manner of discourse, but was relieved when Madison assured him most were impressed with the amazing combination of imagination and profundity in the ideas he expressed.

Thomas began to resent the strength of the Federalist tilt to politics in the north. He perceived the bowing and scraping around the president as a hint of a predilection for monarchy, which he had grown to abhor in France and began speaking out against the dangers of hereditary power. But he also continued to think about moral and social issues and wrote to a French friend: *To be grateful, to be faithful to all engagements and under all circumstances, to be open and generous, promotes in the long run even the interests of both: and I am sure it promotes their happiness.*

Alexander Hamilton was a rising leader among the Federalists, and Thomas saw himself as the countering spokesman for the group called the Republicans. The differences were clear — Hamilton favored a strong national government and supported a national banking system based on the British model. In general Jefferson was suspicious of those he called the "money men," as he believed they disdained agriculture and placed industrial development above farming. Jefferson also believed Hamilton to be dangerous because he entertained the possibility of a hereditary or lifelong presidency and/or Senate; in Jefferson's mind, Hamilton surely would be a threat to the liberties of the revolution and the broad power of the people.

Yet both men wanted their country to succeed. One evening over a dinner designed to address the logjam, they came to an agreement that would solve the current debt problems threatening the solvency of the new country and proved compromise was a workable *modus vivendi*. Jefferson approved Hamilton's plan to make the federal government the center of the nation's financial system by allowing the federal government to fund the country's debt and to assume all state debts. Then Thomas cajoled Madison, who had strongly objected to Hamilton's plan, into agreeing as well if the Federalists would locate the new capital of the country in the South on the Potomac River. The financial capital of the country was clearly the North, and to place the political center in the South, Jefferson thought, would definitely sweeten the deal for the southern Republicans. The pact saved America from bankruptcy, and Jefferson touted cooperation as the best solution to many problems.

Chafing under the political demands of leadership and longing for his family, he wrote to Patsy, "Continue to me your own love which I feel to be the best solace remaining to me in this world." How he missed them all!

In addition to Hamilton at Treasury, his fellow cabinet members were Edmund Randolph, Attorney General, and Henry Knox, Secretary of War. He was thankful he still had Madison, who was serving in the House of Representatives, and Adams, who was vice president, nearby to discuss matters of import. Washington, knowing of Jefferson's avid interest in science, had included in Jefferson's duties oversight of patent applications. Thomas found the amount of work a burden, but he was thrilled when Eli Whitney applied for a patent, which would separate the seed from a boll of cotton. Whitney called it a cotton gin. News like this kindled his desire to be an inventor himself more often.

The threat of war in the Northwest between Spain and Britain over islands in the Pacific off the coast of America kept him awake at night and agitated him to the point of migraines for months. The conflict occurred in the Nootka Sound. The Spanish had claimed sovereignty over the area deriving from a Papal Bull 300 years prior, and the British said the territory had belonged to them ever since Sir Francis Drake laid claim in the 1500s, as well as dating from Captain Cook's rediscovery of the islands in 1688. In Jefferson's mind, the proximity of the incident clarified how America must be a world player in order to survive as a country. Spain eventually backed down, and the British, represented by George Vancouver, signed a treaty with the Spanish to end the crisis. Thomas perceived the episode as an alert to the fact that calamity could come out of nowhere and that he must be at the ready constantly.

He was barely settled in New York when the decision was made to move the national capital to Philadelphia until the District of Columbia would be ready to house the government. How he longed to visit Monticello and to see everyone there! He had heard nothing from Sally after the news of the death of their child, and he still dared not write to her. He didn't want anyone to learn of their relationship. He wondered if it hadn't been for the best, then felt horrible to have harbored such a thought. He had the idea to write to her in French and insist she burn his letters. She could write to him in the same way and ask a member of her family to be the messenger. But this would be folly. He couldn't wait to hold her in his arms as soon as he saw her again.

MONTICELLO

FATHER AND FARMER

1790-96

Deep rooted prejudices entertained by the whites; ten thousand recollections, by the blacks, of the injuries they have sustained; new provocations; the real distinctions which nature has made . . . will divide us into parties, and produce convulsions which will probably never end but in the extermination of the one or the other race. To these objections, which are political, may be added others, which are physical and moral.

Extract from Thomas Jefferson's *Notes on the State of Virginia*, 1782

Patsy

1791

PATSY PRIDED HERSELF on the new responsibilities she had shouldered but sorely missed the proximity of her father. One of the letters she received from him during the summer made her truly glad, for he reported he was having some relief from his headaches:

Philadelphia, June 23, 1791

> *I wrote to each of you once during my journey, from which I returned four days ago, having enjoyed thro' the whole of it my perfect health. I am in hopes the relaxation it gave me from business has freed me from the almost constant headache with which I had been persecuted thro' the whole winter and spring. Having been entirely clear of it while traveling proves it to have been occasioned by the drudgery of business. . . .*

During the fall Thomas traveled to Tuckahoe to negotiate buying 1600 acres at Edgehill on behalf of Tom and Patsy. Tom's father finally agreed to a price of 1,700 dollars[2], but then out of the blue, said he would only accept 2,000. Patsy was furious, accusing him of being ornery and mean. Tom wrote angry letters to his father, but then apologized, saying his anger had been fueled by "his desire to gratify Patsy."

Patsy longed to have this new parcel of land so near Monticello, feeling she was anxious to start a home they would call their own. More news from Tom, Sr., however, made them wary for their future. Tom, Sr. had just up and married a young widow, Gabriella Harvie, who would certainly bear children — who then would compete with Tom's expected future

2   On July 6, 1785, the Continental Congress of the United States had authorized the issuance of a new currency, the U.S. Dollar.

inheritance. And they had not even been invited to the wedding! Irate, Tom slammed doors and cursed under his breath, but of course, there was nothing he could do about it.

Thomas advised the young couple not to seethe over the matter, writing to Patsy in July,

> ... *my dear child, redouble your assiduities to keep the affections of Col. Randolph and his lady ... in proportion as the difficulties increase. .... If the lady has any thing difficult in her disposition, avoid what is rough, and attach her good qualities to you. Consider what are otherwise as a bad stop in your harpsichord, and do not touch on it, but make yourself happy with the good ones. Every human being, my dear, must thus be viewed, according to what it is good for; for none of us, no not one, is perfect; and were we to love none who had imperfections, this would be a desert for our love. All we can do is to make the best of our friends, love and cherish what is good in them, and keep out of the way of what is bad; but no more thinking of rejecting them for it, than of throwing away a piece of music for a flat passage or two ...*

With great relief Patsy and Tom arrived at Monticello in September for a visit. Patsy used the excuse she was six months pregnant to negotiate staying longer after Thomas returned to Philadelphia in November. She brought her puppy Grizzle, a descendant of Buzzy, who had accompanied them on the ship from France. Everyone agreed the climate at Monticello was the most pleasant in the entire state, and healthier as well. Patsy especially enjoyed sitting out on the back terrace into the evening, delighting in the sunset gold frames around fluffy clouds. But she mustn't ever dally, she reminded herself: she had a plantation to manage — new recipes to learn, a staff to oversee, silver and china to count and care for — the list was endless ...

Thomas instructed his overseer to make certain that "Mr. Randolph and Patsy would be furnished with all the plantation could provide — corn, fodder, wheat, what beeves [sic] there may be, shoats[3], milch [sic] cows, fire-wood to be cut by the plantation Negroes, and brought in by mule-cart or ox-cart." He also stipulated they be given nine house servants, including Ursula, Sally, and her sister Critta, for the time being. Patsy no-

---

3 Young, weaned pigs

ticed her father didn't call her Martha since her marriage as he'd suggested he should — to him, she was still, and forever, Patsy.

By March, Patsy and Tom were ready to move ahead with acquiring the Edgehill property, but Tom again expressed his concerns about owning slaves. The declining price of tobacco made relinquishing slave labor appear more attainable, since they could then plant less slave-dependent crops. But all Patsy could think about was the impending birth of their first child, and she was determined it would be at Monticello.

SALLY

1791-1792

SALLY FELT BEREFT and betrayed. Her master, by becoming Secretary of State, had removed her dream of returning together to Paris out from under her feet. Nor would she have the comfort of being with him at Monticello. She understood as never before that she was but a single blossom on the tree of his life.

When she had lost the baby, Sally wished she too would die. She could not stop crying, whether working, or sitting in the rocking chair. She was too young to feel so defeated, she told herself. After all, hadn't he told her he loved her? She felt his warm affection when he worried about her, and when he counseled her about life, just in the way he advised his daughters, whom he doted on. He *would* come back to Monticello. He *would*! She had pictured herself as the mother of his children and being accepted by the rest of his family. And she had thought her siblings would look up to her as the mother of the master's progeny. What insane fantasies she had allowed herself!

She continued to feel uneasy, unable to settle down to a task, wandering adrift amongst the busy hum of the plantation. Her mother encouraged her to go back to sewing, and she would stitch muslin garments for hours, her head in a blank fog. James worried about her too and asked her to help him sometimes in the kitchen. But with the master gone, there was no reason to prepare anything special. The sparkle had disappeared from anything she wanted to do.

It frightened her that he might meet a white woman in Philadelphia or Washington, whom he would marry, and who would watch over young Polly and their future grandchildren. But hadn't he vowed to Patty never to marry again? She heard people talking, saying he needed a woman in his life. Well, he has one, she thought. Oh, Dear Lord! Might he be sorry he ever took her to his bed and sell her to get her out of his sight? She shouldn't let herself think these things.

Moreover, there was an increasing strain between her and Patsy. Patsy was, without a doubt, the mistress of Monticello, and prided herself in this role. Sally had to defer to her many times a day as to what needed to be done to keep the plantation running smoothly and making choices for beautifying the interior. There was usually such a crowd of people in the house they had little face-to-face interaction and when they did, they both were overly polite. It rankled Sally when Patsy gave her orders because she had become used to essentially making her own agenda with Thomas. Yet she knew she was just as much a burr under Patsy's blanket.

Sally had to admit she was glad when Mrs. Randolph (that's what they were to call her now) and Mr. Tom — well, it should be, Mr. Randolph — returned to Monticello. At first she was angry with Thomas for now naming her as one of the slaves to serve Patsy and Tom. She felt nervous it would be too awkward. Of course they would not say a word about who the father of her baby was, or what she had named him. She shuddered inside, seeing how happy Patsy seemed, expecting a child, when her own loss still felt so fresh. But at least helping Patsy move in gave her something to do, and Patsy seemed to be trying to be friendlier. The two managed to gradually settle into a polite, if not warm, exchange.

Sally had been close to her oldest sibling, Mary, forever, even though Mary was much older than she. Mary told Sally she had requested that Thomas hire her out to a Mr. Bell, who owned a store in town. She confided to Sally that Thomas Bell was sweet on her, and maybe if Sally put the bug in Thomas's ear, he would let her go to Mr. Bell. Indeed, Mary already had two children by Mr. Bell. Thomas agreed with his slave's wish right before his departure, and Sally was sorry to see her sister leave Monticello. At least she would be close by in Charlottesville. Sally knew Mary had already given birth in 1780 to Joe Fossett, fathered by another white man, and Joe was a productive slave at Monticello. If Thomas imagined it comforted Sally to see a similar situation to theirs, he was dead wrong, she thought. Thomas hid their relationship while Mr. Bell did not, living outright with Mary like a common law wife.

PATSY

1791-1793

ON JANUARY 23, 1791, Patsy sensed her first labor pains. She was somewhat alarmed as it was a month earlier than expected. She had worked hard the day before, helping with work in the smokehouse, and had thought she experienced a few twinges then. This only made her work faster to get more done before her confinement. But today, the pains were real, and she called out to Ursula and Betty. The two women, extremely experienced in childbirth, rushed to make her comfortable and called Isaac to search for Mr. Randolph.

Betty placed Anne Cary Randolph in her arms that very evening and Patsy cried with joy and relief. What a glorious moment! She thanked God she had not inherited her mother's weakness in bearing children! Even though little Anne carried Tom's mother's name, Patsy saw the baby had inherited her fair skin. Sally came to the bedside to congratulate her, and Patsy grasped her hand to thank her. She wanted to show compassion to Sally about having lost her baby, but she couldn't think of what to say. The two couldn't seem to shake off a reticence in their behavior toward one another, but at least they were speaking.

Seeing Sally made Patsy remember how her mother's father had taken Betty as his concubine, and Patty apparently had endured it without complaining. Patty must have known. So why did she think she had a right to complain about her own father's relationship with Sally? This was the way of the South. She also understood that it wasn't just black people who were chattel, but women as well. That had become obvious to her when she married and then understood that everything she owned now belonged to her husband. Still, she stubbornly thought of Monticello as hers.

Patsy knew that many southern matrons who were aware of their husband's affairs made a point of making life miserable for slave concubines. It was usually evident by the features of the offspring, who among the slaves was descended from whom. And white women owners had many means to quietly punish the female slaves instead of the roving husband. But it wasn't Patsy's husband who was out-of-line; it was her father, whom she loved and respected so deeply. And she had grown up with Sally as her friend. Sally had lost her baby, and Patsy determined she must be more compassionate and forgiving. Yet, she still felt immense shock and doubted if that would ever change.

Patsy and Tom stayed on at Monticello, but again began to discuss more seriously the need for their own home. Surely, they would have more children, and the time had come to be by themselves. However, it was Tom who dragged his heels this time because of the argument over the price with his father. On January 1, 1792, he finally agreed to pay Thomas Randolph Sr. $2,000 for 1,593 acres of the Edgehill plantation, including the enslaved families already there. Since there was no habitable house as yet on the land, Tom began farming at Edgehill, but Patsy and the baby stayed on at Monticello. Neither wanted to return to hot, buggy Varina.

Polly had moved back home from Eppington and required a good deal of oversight. Patsy found she had her hands full, taking over Polly's education and mothering her. In fact, just keeping up with her family was proving a full-time job. Tom was away quite a lot due to responsibilities at his new farm and also at Tuckahoe, where his father continued to make unreasonable demands on him. Patsy missed him and welcomed his wild and feverish lovemaking when they were together. His tall figure and dark, handsome swagger totally swept her away each time she saw him, and she loved it when he swore he couldn't live without her.

Patsy again gave birth on September 12, 1792 and assured her anxious father that she was doing well at Monticello. This time it was a boy, whom they named Thomas Jefferson Randolph. Tom also wrote to Thomas, saying that the "baby was thriving and the new mother was in good health." Two of Tom's seven sisters, Nancy and Virginia, wanted to help the new mother and even lived at Monticello for a while. Patsy, appreciative of their help, gladly became good friends with both of them and began to call them "Sister." Indeed, a parade of female relatives continued to cycle through the halls of the mansion, providing some help, but sometimes only making more work for Patsy, who immediately became pregnant again. She began to think of it as a permanent condition.

Moreover, some of Tom Sr.'s other children fled to Monticello when they decided they didn't like Tom Sr.'s young wife. The latest mistress of

Tuckahoe gave birth to a son that year, making their fears reality as the new child supplanted Tom as the heir to that plantation. His father had made it clear that his wedding gift would be Tom Jr.'s complete inheritance. Rubbing salt into the wound, the parents named the new baby Thomas Mann Randolph, exactly Tom's name. "It's like my father is trying to obliterate my existence," Tom cried. Patsy couldn't help but agree.

As though the drama over Tom's father wasn't enough, his sister Nancy, with whom Patsy had become quite close, caused a serious scandal of her own. Nancy was suspected of adultery with her brother-in-law, Richard Randolph, and was even accused of murdering the child. Patsy struggled to believe the preposterous tale, and Nancy's brothers, including Tom, blamed Richard totally, trying to quash the story to protect their sister's honor.

Dreadful news from France weighed on Patsy's mind. She'd heard that the queen, whom she had seen on many occasions, had been led to the guillotine in late October to be beheaded. Others, including sisters from the convent whom she had known and cared for deeply, received the same fate. It was too gruesome to think about. She read with supreme relief that her best friend Marie de Botidoux had been spared, and Lafayette, though imprisoned in Austria, was still alive.

Just when they thought there could be no more upheaval, Tom's father died unexpectedly in November 1793, throwing the family into extended haggling over his will. What would Tom and his siblings inherit and what would go to Randolph's widow and their progeny? It soon became clear that Tom would inherit no more land but now inherited, with his siblings, an unpaid debt of 64,000 pounds. On top of this blow, as executor, Tom found himself embroiled in a great deal of unpleasant argument and bickering among the extended family.

"That bastard left me nothing beyond my marriage settlement," he raged to Patsy. "My sisters say if I'd been close by at Varina, this wouldn't have happened. Instead, I wanted Edgehill for you."

"No, no, Tom. That can't be true. Don't blame yourself. Or me! You know it is your step-mother, Gabrielle, who insinuated herself in your stead."

"Why didn't my father love me, Patsy? Why didn't he? Am I so unlovable?"

She cradled his head against her breast, "Tom, Tom. I love you. My father loves you. Your children love you. Your father's behavior is incorrigible." She was so angry at the cold-hearted man, she was shocked at her un-Christian thoughts. Tom sobbed uncontrollably, probably more for the loss of his inheritance, Patsy thought, than for the loss of a father he had fought with for years.

The news that Thomas was to return to Monticello broke the melancholy atmosphere. Thomas had agreed to stay on awhile as Washington's secretary of state for his second term, but now found he couldn't tolerate President Washington's clear favoritism for the policies of the secretary of the treasury, Alexander Hamilton. He threw up his hands in frustration and resigned his post as of December 31, 1793. Patsy decided they would plan a party for family, friends, and neighbors to welcome the statesman home.

THOMAS

1794

THOMAS WAS GLAD to leave the "Monocrats," as he called the Hamilton contingent. For all his political life he had striven to quell any tendency toward monarchy or dictatorship, and he always sensed these inclinations around the Federalists. He couldn't understand why Washington favored this party over his Republicans, but perhaps it was the military bent that pointed him in that direction. Thomas did support a strong central government, but wanted to protect certain rights for the states as well. He described his working relationship with Hamilton as "daily pitted in the Cabinet like two cocks." Now, he found himself tired of the fight.

Life had become especially stressful in the city because of a yellow fever epidemic. He watched thousands dying with symptoms of severe headache and backache accompanied by a high fever. The sick people turned a putrid yellow and vomited dark blood. Even without the tension of the political fracas, he was more than ready to leave this frightening situation.

He would wait no longer to return to his little utopia on the mountain. As had become the custom, the slave rumor mill beat the drums of his return and they welcomed him below to draw him up to the portico at Monticello. There, Patsy awaited him, with Anne, age two, and Thomas, age one. Also present was Tom, ready to receive his father-in-law, on whom he depended a great deal.

Thomas's eyes immediately searched for Sally — and there she stood, in a group of Hemingses, smiling at him. He could not wait to embrace her slender body, but it would be difficult with so many people close about. They would have to wait for darkness to finally entwine themselves tightly together.

He immediately and happily set about the reconstruction of Monticello on a grander scale. His trips across Europe had supplied him with a plethora of ideas for his estate. Not only did he plan a new design for the big house, but he wanted to add new slave cabins on Mulberry Row, expand the smokehouse, create a dairy, carpenter's shop, blacksmith's shop, sawpit, and a wash house. He admitted to all who looked on in wonderment, "Architecture is my delight, and putting up and pulling down one of my favorite amusements."

A small manufacturing business became his special pride — a nailery, where young slave boys produced up to 10,000 nails per day, wrought nails and cut-nails according to Isaac Granger, who was one of his best boys. Thomas couldn't help bragging a bit to William Short when he wrote to him that: *my nailery flourished, and still flourishes greatly, employing sixteen boys at a clear profit of about 4. to 500£ annually.*

Thomas would lope around the property with his long strides, busy every moment of the day, wearing a pedometer on his ankle, as he was always interested in data. Eager to have an English garden, he chose only cultivars that would thrive in Virginia. He chose Persian jasmine, lilacs and gardenia, calling the latter cape jasmine, and managed to interest Polly in helping him with this project.

He sat down to draw an octagonal dome, resembling the one atop the Hôtel de Salm, situated on the Left Bank and his favorite structure in Paris. His pencil hovered over his paper as he recalled many pleasant visits to the private booksellers, called *les bouquinistes,* along the Seine, just across from the Hôtel. How many fascinating volumes he'd found at these quaint wooden-box stores! He turned back to his plan that eliminated the former attic at Monticello in order to make room for this architectural gem, which would provide privacy for the family bedrooms.

He placed his own apartment on the ground floor, where he envisioned a high ceiling with a large skylight. He happily designed a bed alcove between the bedchamber and a study, making it cleverly open to both. Even more ingenious, he congratulated himself, was a private room he designed for Sally, which had immediate access to his room, and which allowed her to approach it from the outside so no one in the house would see her crossing the public hall to reach his rooms.

During this idyllic time, spending hours with the children and grandchildren, hunting, fishing, and building, he struggled with rheumatism, which he claimed kept him "in incessant torment." Yet without the stresses of government, he was grateful to be keeping the raging migraines at bay. He knew that politics still lay in his future, however, for James Madison encouraged him incessantly to seek the presidency. Indeed, after awhile he found himself beginning to long for the clamor of the world and wrote to his daughter Polly,

> *I am convinced our own happiness requires that we should continue to mix with the world, and to keep pace with it as it goes; and that every person who retires from free communication with it is severely punished afterwards by the state of mind into which they get, and which can only be prevented by feeding our sociable principles.*

Upon leaving his friend John Adams, who was serving as vice president to Washington, Thomas told Adams he depended on him to keep him apprised of what was happening in the government. Indeed, he relied more and more on his former colleagues for news. He wrote to James Madison about the ignorance of the people beyond the capital:

> *I could not have supposed, when at Philadelphia, that so little of what was passing there could be known . . . as is the case here. Judging from this . . . it is evident to me that the people are not in a condition either to approve or disapprove of their government, nor consequently to influence it.*

All in all, he was content to be back at home for the time being. He smiled, thinking that his animals — 34 horses (8 were for riding), 5 mules, 390 hogs, 249 head of cattle, three sheep, and 3 dogs — were better company than his compatriots in Philadelphia. Adrien Petit had returned with him and helped wherever needed in the house, and Queenie's mix of Southern cooking and his French recipes suited his palate. Life was good. He wrote to Angelica Church, saying, "I have my house to build, my fields to farm, and to watch for the happiness of those who labor for mine."

He never could forget his responsibility for those who served him, and yet he couldn't imagine giving up their help either. He knew freeing them was the right thing to do, but more and more he made the excuse that it would be impossible. What would happen? He feared black and white could never live together peacefully. They absolutely must solve the intractable problems of deep-rooted prejudice and all the ugly history before thinking of emancipation.

He intuitively didn't want the necessary outbuildings to be part of the main structure and so arranged for them to be out of sight, under long terraces extending from the back of the house. In the passageway to the terrace he built a beer cellar, wine cave, cider room and housewares storage room. Then under the south terrace he planned a kitchen, cook's room, servants' quarters, dairy, and meat-smoking room. He housed stables, a carriage house, laundry and icehouse under the north terrace. Thomas hid from himself and others what he was doing — hiding his slaves from view.

He also invented a clock that never needed winding for the reception hall and even told the day of the week. A weather vane atop the front of the house was attached to an indicator in the hall so that one need not go out to discover which way the wind was blowing. He was overjoyed when, on October 13, 1794, Patsy gave birth to another daughter, Ellen Wayles Randolph, and placed the little girl in his arms. How could he think of leaving this happy place, he asked himself? Yet simultaneously he felt driven to apply the democratic ideas of the constitution he had helped to write for this fledgling nation.

SALLY

1794

WHEN THE MASTER FINALLY came home in early 1794, Sally knew immediately from his smile that he truly had not forgotten her. She had been so uneasy without his presence and realized how much she pictured herself through his vision of her. He had been like a father, then a protector, then a lover. She desperately needed him and wanted him. And he made her feel like the five thousand acres of Monticello belonged, in some way, to her too.

The first time he came to her after their long separation, she felt nervous and hesitant. But when his enormous hands cupped her breasts, she unfolded. He stroked her head and admired this exotic creature, with curly hair and creamed coffee skin. She felt he had created her in a way, teaching her about art and language and love. He told her again and again that he loved her. "I'll not go away again," he promised. Then he smiled. "I can't deny it. You make me feel ten years younger, but that is not the reason I care for you." She was afraid to believe his promise because she had learned how the country counted on him, but it encouraged her to know he felt that way.

The face he showed her was so different from his public face, she realized. She saw his doubts, his worry, and his passion. Would that she could tell others of this miracle — but she knew that would end it. Too many knew already. She was surprised how she liked his graying hair and ruddier face, and was foolishly proud of how his body remained taut and strong, like a younger man's.

In March Sally began to seriously worry about whether he would return to politics. She discovered him one day, in an agitated state over the possibility of war with Britain and he explained to her that it regarded economic issues. He busily wrote letters to Washington and Madison, condemning John Jay's treaty designed to facilitate trade. Jefferson believed

Jay's plan conceded too much to Britain because of a desire to avoid war. Thomas put down his pen and told Sally that he saw the treaty as a codification of close ties to Britain, which his antagonist Hamilton favored. He wandered outdoors and paced the garden until she thought he would wear down the grass he'd so carefully planted.

Despite his consternation, the treaty was narrowly ratified as Washington, and a two-thirds majority of the Senate agreed it was not worth going to war. She could see he was having a very difficult time staying out of the fray. Without even being present, he had become the clear leader of the new Republican Party.

Patsy

1795

PATSY EXCELLED AND REVELLED in her role as mistress of Monticello. Having her father at home and sharing the daily running of the Big House seemed like a perfect existence. She grew especially excited about his plans for reconstruction. At the same time she strove to be supportive of Tom, although he was away much of the time — at Varina or Edgehill. She worried about him working too hard, with his responsibilities at the two plantations, and also trying to fill in with something she or Thomas needed done at Monticello. He not only directed the pulling out of old trees, but picked up an axe and joined the working men. He wasn't afraid of work.

When Tom received an appointment as justice of the peace in April, she felt so proud. Then, to crown this achievement, Tom was successful in his application for a captain's commission in the county militia. He admitted he had no experience in the "military art," but imagined he could learn it. It was significant to them both that he had been recognized as a leader of the gentry in his community. She smiled at him at dinner, when he was at Monticello one evening. "You are a good father, my Tom," she told him, gazing at their happy children. "Look what a fine boy Jeff is becoming, and big sister Anne is a wonderful girl. Little Ellen doesn't have much to say for herself yet, but she will," she laughed as Ellen spat out the cream-of-wheat mash being spooned through her tiny lips.

Patsy's good spirits were short lived, for the summer of 1795 proved to be a disaster for agriculture in the area. Barely anything came up and farmers shook their heads in puzzlement. It was dry, but it shouldn't be this bad. To make things worse, the cruel Federalists had suspended commerce with France, and so the Randolphs and many others lost their prime market for Virginia tobacco. When her father showed her a letter Tom had written to him, she cringed; he had written, "There is a story of an ancient king whose touch turned everything to gold. You will recognize in me the makings of Midas, except that everything I touch turns to dust."

She cried for him and tried to buoy his spirits, telling him that everyone was suffering, some more than they. It wasn't his fault. She suspected he was hiding from her how bad their financial situation really was. "You can sell the tobacco to France next year, Tom, when the embargo is lifted."

"With my luck, it will have rotted by then," he snarled, punching the wall with his fist.

In mid-July she and Tom decided to go to a hot springs in western Virginia in order to revive his spirits. The therapeutic baths were believed to cure melancholia, and the healthy mountain air would be invigorating after the hot, heavy air at Varina. They took nine-month-old Ellen with them, and Patsy enjoyed the scenery and pleasure of travel. They stopped first in the town of Staunton for the night.

How had she been so naïve and placid at their contented family scene only a few months before? For it seemed only the space of a minute and she was holding a dead child in her arms, in a strange room, at an inn. Patsy gasped for air with hysteria when the little girl breathed her last. They asked one another, why? Why had Ellen become so sick, so suddenly? With horror, they watched the life flicker from her eyes. "No, No," Patsy wailed. The baby's thin porcelain skin spoke of the fragility of all life, and Patsy began to fear for all her children.

In total shock, at the suggestion of her father, they sent the baby's tiny body back to Monticello for burial, and continued on to Sweet Springs, desperate to find relief for Tom. He said he was unable to bear the funeral. Patsy was numb, incapable of thinking or feeling, but afterward, Tom claimed to have experienced an "almost perfect recovery." She regarded him in confusion.

Upon returning to Varina, Tom's condition immediately worsened. He began drinking more and passed idle days, morosely wandering around the plantation. The doctor called it a nervous condition, and said he could offer no more cures. Patsy knew how defeated her husband felt — he would not be the master of Tuckahoe; Varina was a sinkhole of debt; and Edgehill looked like it would require more work than humanly possible to make it a thriving enterprise. Moreover, he was continuously fighting with creditors over his father's debt and getting nowhere.

Even though Patsy sympathized with Tom's illness, she was constantly frustrated by his indecision. She had even read in his commonplace book, "Whenever I find myself very strongly compelled to any act, a doubt whether it be right always arises. The voice of reason is low and persuasive, that of passion is loud and imperious." She would point out his constant vacillations that were such a trial to her, but it would do no good.

Patsy wept through the nights for her precious little Ellen, still unable to grasp what had happened. She would pull herself together for the day, somehow accomplishing small tasks in a rote manner. Neither Patsy nor Tom had the strength to help the other, and despair gripped the household in its bleak, bony claws.

SALLY

IN AUGUST THE JEFFERSONS held a ball at Monticello to show off some of their new construction, and Sally, with a kerchief on her head instead of the finery she had worn in Paris, stood on the side watching the whirling dancers. How she missed the world of Paris! She crossed her arms across her chest to hold in the sorrow. She had made her choice to return, and she did not regret it because she loved her master. But how she would like to put on a gown like she'd worn there! How much she would enjoy going once again to the shops with the little bells that rang when you entered. She thought the Virginia gentry looked like a pale, sad attempt at Paris fashions and then laughed at herself for her snobbery.

The party spilled outside into the gardens as the evening began to freshen, and Sally observed some folks walking around the winding path along the wide west lawn. The moonlight shimmered on the freshly scythed grass and softly caressed the flowering borders. What a magical place this could be! She watched Patsy dancing with her handsome husband and admired her courage. She had to admit that Patsy had an extremely agreeable personality, and people were drawn to her graceful and easygoing manner. She moved somewhat awkwardly like her father, but also like him, the intelligence shone through. She could charm a coyote out of taking a chicken, Sally thought. She knew Patsy was already pregnant again, and was bravely trying to smile when she had just lost her baby only a month ago. She must have already known she was pregnant when Ellen died.

Polly, who had recently announced she wanted to be called by her given name Maria, was wooed at the ball by Mr. Giles, a Virginia senator, whom Thomas believed would make a grand son-in-law. But Sally knew it was not to be because Maria had confided in her she had fallen in love during the summer with her cousin Jack, properly called John Wayles Eppes. Sally gently broke Polly's news to Thomas late that night when he persuaded her to remain after she prepared his room for the night. They saw no one watching as to whether she left or not, and the lovers blissfully enjoyed their hideaway.

Happy in his arms, Sally told him her news. "I'm expecting another child, Master. It will be born around Christmas time, I think."

"I had guessed, lovely Sah-lee. There are smart people here who will be counting the months from when I arrived back at Monticello. But you will hold your head up, my darling girl, and not say a word. We don't want a scandal."

"Of course, Master." When would he tell her to call him by another name? But she did take Thomas's advice and hold up her head.

It wasn't Christmas. The little girl arrived early, in late October. Sally called her Harriet, at Thomas's behest, as Harriet was the name of one of his favorite sisters. Sally immediately passed the baby to Suzy, a slave wet nurse. Betty angrily asked her daughter, "Why don't you nurse your own child, Miss Fancy-Girl?"

"Because, Maman (she used the French term when she was irritated with her mother, instead of Mammy), I'm needed in the Big House and can't be tied to the baby's schedule."

"Hrrumph!" said Betty.

For those who tracked such things, Thomas had arrived back at Monticello more than nine months before the baby was born, and Sally was especially careful to keep the new baby out of sight of Patsy who, although pregnant again, had lost little Ellen so recently. She knew Patsy was a Christian woman, but it was always tempting to compare their roles — the daughter and the concubine, and it was the daughter now who had lost her child. Nevertheless, she couldn't help but feel resentment that everything was so much easier for Patsy. She probably didn't realize how much power she had, just being Thomas Jefferson's daughter. If Sally let herself think about it, it made her blood boil to think what the slaves, who didn't work in the house, ate — onions, pokeweed, clabbermilk, and taters — while the family dined on fine fare.

On Christmas Day, Sally, Betty, and James had their private celebration when the master gave James his freedom. Thomas signed a document he called a writ of manumission, which, to the three Hemingses, was beautiful to behold. Betty no longer worried about Sally like she did her sons because she believed the master truly loved her daughter, just as he had loved his wife, Sally's half-sister. James had held to his part of the deal with Jefferson, serving a total of five years in his kitchen while he was secretary of state in Paris, and then training his brother Peter to be the new French chef at Monticello.

198

Sally had watched as Jefferson often had artfully played on James's sense of loyalty, reminding him of the expenses he had incurred in order to train him as a chef. James felt aggrieved about this but for some reason, had never brought the issue to a head. Even now, he seemed to have no particular plan to leave right away and so the women basked in his continuing presence. But James didn't wait too long to be off. In February 1796, Jefferson allowed him to take his horse and what James called a "paltry thirty pounds for his expenses" as he headed to Philadelphia in search of a career as a free man.

James didn't know about the master's debt, Sally realized, and she didn't tell him. Thomas had recently confided in her that he was crushed under the financial obligation left by Tom Randolph Sr. He had been forced to sell slaves at a low price in order to cover some of his obligations, receiving only 40 pounds per slave when earlier he would have gotten 200[4]. Thomas had protected James and given him his freedom. Why was her brother still complaining?

---

4 Currency differed from state to state until the 1860s, e.g., it could be termed New York money or Virginia money, and the units could be dollars or pounds.

PATSY

1796

PATSY PROPOSED TO TOM that they sell Varina. They had come to the plantation in order to be present for litigation regarding the debt from Tom's father's estate. She instantly reacted against the small rooms, the stifling air, and the whir of insects.

"We both heartily dislike the place," she argued. "Although I'm not superstitious, I sense bad luck here, Tom. It's just a sinkhole for more liability."

"You're wrong, Patsy. Land is everything," he informed her in a voice brooking no argument.

Patsy knew that's what her father also believed, but she felt terribly discouraged by the difficulty of making a living from the land. She was amazed when Tom suddenly announced he was going to run for the state legislature. He was a good farmer, but she doubted he had a talent for government. Yet she didn't dare suggest this in his present state. The family often said jokingly, "Well, Tom has the 'Randolph' in him," referring to his irritable personality. But it wasn't a joke to her anymore.

Tom's chest expanded as he propounded his reasons: he had gone to university in Edinburgh to study politics; he admired Jefferson for his commitment to public service; and he would prove that his own father was wrong about him. He would succeed.

But he didn't. Again he surprised her when he chose to take the children for their smallpox inoculations when he should have been campaigning. Patsy surmised he thought the Randolph name was enough to pull him through to victory, but Tom never even visited the town square, nor made speeches, nor passed out pamphlets, as she occasionally suggested. The community passed him over, handing him another blow.

He returned to her at Varina with the children, who had survived the pox procedure, but Tom was whipped over his defeat. Red faced and staggering, he stepped drunkenly down from the wagon as the terrified children ran inside and away from their father. Patsy looked at him in horror and fear. She was furious with him, but so relieved over the children's safety, she abandoned him in the yard and ran after them to console and coddle them.

Let him sleep it off, she thought. But then what?

Tom passionately apologized the next morning and attributed his behavior to "his illness."

"We must find help for you, Tom," she responded. "You ought not worry about me and the children, but you must go to the doctor we have heard about in Boston, or the one in New York. I don't want you to suffer so."

Her father thought maybe Tom had the gout, but she knew that wouldn't cause the terrible fits of temper and depression. Tom took her advice and made several trips without her to seek medical advice, giving them temporary hope.

Patsy had her own worries as she was close to giving birth again. She couldn't abide the idea of it happening at Varina. She hated the place — the heavy air, the stingy house, the climate! Tom, who was ashamed of his recent behavior, readily agreed to move the family to Edgehill for the birth. Ellen Wayles Randolph, named after the sister who had died only a year and a half before, came into the world in October 1796. She thrived from the beginning, and the tense family began to relax. Patsy knew Tom was still ill, but she told herself he showed some sign of improvement. She loved it when he wrapped his strong arms around her and swore to her again she was the only woman in the world for him. Perhaps together they could make him well.

PHILADELPHIA

VICE PRESIDENT

1796-1797

Monticello Apr. 19. 09

It has a great effect on the opinion of our people & the world to have the moral right on our side.

Extract from Thomas Jefferson to James Madison. RC (DLC: Madison Papers). PoC (DLC).

Published in *PTJRS*, 1:154–6.

THOMAS

1796-1797

AS MUCH AS THOMAS was enjoying residency at Monticello — brimming with excitement over his architectural and farming projects — he began to feel the tug of the public arena more and more. He always found pleasure in his refuge, but being at the center of the nation seemed to be an essential need of his existence. When he was out of society, he felt his brain was atrophying. He explained it in a letter to Polly: *the effect of withdrawing from the world has led to an antisocial and misanthropic state of mind, which severely punishes him who gives into it; and it will be a lesson I shall never forget as to myself.*

He also wrote to his friend John Adams, unable to remain out of the fray. On February 28, 1796, he penned, *. . . this I hope will be the age of experiments in government, and that their basis will be founded on principles of honesty, not mere force.* Then, Washington's Farewell Address on Monday, September 19, 1796, became a call-to-arms for Thomas. President Washington urged Americans to avoid excessive political party spirit and geographical distinctions. In foreign affairs, he warned against long-term alliances with other nations, and Jefferson sympathized with this credo. He wrote to another friend saying, "Commerce with all nations, alliance with none, should be our motto."

The country appeared to be split evenly between Adams and Jefferson for their next president. Jeffersonian supporters responded vehemently to an article on the Thursday of the next week in *The Columbian Mirror* and the *Alexandria Gazette*, which accused Jefferson of being too weak to be President as exemplified by his having "fled the wartime governorship at the moment of an invasion of the enemy . . ." Those supporting Jefferson declared that the present election was not about the past but about contrasting visions of the presidency — as a monarchy or as a republican model.

As much as Thomas admired John Adams' mind, he perceived him as a monarchist-in-hiding, and so feared his election. This worry, and his constant distrust of Hamilton, finally prompted him to officially throw his hat into the ring. He wrote to explain: *There is a debt of service due from every man to his country, proportionate to the bounties which nature and fortune have measured to him.*

Thomas agonized alone at Monticello through an unusual cold spell, where the temperature was only 12 degrees, reading the newspapers and awaiting the results of the election. When he wasn't worrying about politics, he was fretting about his crops in the bitter weather. He read slander about himself daily from Adams and Hamilton supporters, who were busy campaigning against him. Thomas had a robust popular following, but it was still a tight race. The constitution had been written to bestow the vice presidency on the candidate who came in second, and Thomas began to think more seriously of the benefits of becoming the vice president. The mail travelled daily back and forth by government or private horse-messenger, and James Madison reminded Thomas of the constitutional rule that the election would be thrown into the House of Representatives if there were a tie.

Despite his criticism of Adams, Thomas wrote back to Madison, authorizing him in this case to:

> *fully solicit on my behalf that Mr. Adams may be preferred. He has always been my senior from the commencement of our public life, and the expression of the public will being equal, this circumstance ought to give him the preference.*

However, Madison, knowing his friend well, suspected that Thomas was only playing the gentleman, and really wanted the top spot. He recently had read a letter Thomas wrote to James Monroe where he rhapsodized upon the power of the presidency: *You will have seen . . . that one man outweighs them all in influence over the people who have supported his judgment against their own and that of their representatives. Republicanism must lie on its oars, resign the vessel to its pilot, and themselves to the course he thinks best for them.* Because of this, Madison feared that if Thomas came in second, he would refuse to serve, and begged him to recognize what a valuable contribution he would make in serving as counsel to the Federalist-leaning Adams if he were to be vice president.

When the results were finally tallied, Adams had won by a margin of only 3 electoral votes, and Thomas came in second. He would be the vice president. Thomas gracefully congratulated Adams, and wrote: *This is certainly not a moment to covet the helm.*

Due to the slow pace of mail and other procedures, it took several months to dismantle the old government and plan for the new. Therefore, the inauguration was scheduled to take place on March 4, 1797, four months hence. Having witnessed Tom's growing dependence on his whisky, and Patsy's fatigue, Thomas agonized over the continuing stormy domestic situation in Virginia and welcomed the additional time to put his affairs in order at Monticello.

Sally was trying to be strong, and he sympathized with her worries over his departure. At least she had her large family nearby. He ached at the prospect of leaving her and put off his leaving until February 20, when he finally set out, driving his phaeton and pair to Alexandria. From there he took the stagecoach, sending Jupiter back home with the horses and carriage. He finally reached Philadelphia on March 2. His first call was to the president-elect, who was currently living at the Francis Hotel on Fourth Street.

Thomas was somewhat surprised to hear Adams's first assignment for him — to return to Paris in order to boost their alliance with France. On second thought — John Adams changed his mind on the spot, and said, "I'm afraid this would actually be inadvisable, because if something were to happen to me, you need to be here to take over immediately."

"I concur, Mr. President. And so, whom do you have in mind?"

"James Madison should be our man."

"I doubt if he would accept the post," Thomas said.

"I still will select him. And if he refuses, it will be your responsibility to make it happen, Thomas."

He'd known Adams could be tough, but he deemed this a bit unreasonable. Still, he didn't want to start on the wrong foot and so nodded his agreement.

Thomas was correct. Madison refused the posting to France, but Adams backed down on holding Thomas accountable. Instead, he appointed Timothy Pickering, a fellow Federalist, as his secretary of state and held over many of Washington's cabinet members to fill the other secretarial positions.

SALLY

1797

SALLY HAD BASKED IN THOMAS' presence for a little over two years, and now she had to let him go again. She had seen it coming for at least three months — the constant letters between Thomas and Madison, his agonizing over the state of the union, and his fretting over not being in Philadelphia to make his case on so many issues. Ever since Washington's farewell address, she realized she could not restrain him any longer. But she mourned about his coming departure. It also hurt that he was so eager to be gone once the election was decided and he clearly saw his new path ahead.

Sally was rather embarrassed about her sense of pride, but she did enjoy having Patsy away at Edgehill; it allowed her to believe she was the mistress of Monticello. Well, in truth, she and her mother together ruled the roost. Betty carried the big ring of keys to all the important storage rooms at her waist. And now that Patsy had a healthy new baby at Edgehill, Sally didn't need to be so careful about hiding Harriet at Monticello. But still, the resemblance of the little girl to Thomas was never something to be showing off.

In February Sally's world and small sense of entitlement came crashing down. Little Harriet died in her arms. As was so often the case, they really couldn't determine the cause. She had had a cold, but had not appeared very sick. What had she done wrong? Should she have listened to her mother and nursed the baby girl herself?

Now, in addition to her grief, she somehow felt she had failed Thomas and was crushed by her inadequacy. How she wanted to feel the warm baby's body in her arms again! In the middle of her sorrow, she remembered how brave Patsy had been when the first little Ellen died and realized she must do the same. That is what her master would expect. And she must make the most of his last days here.

PATSY

PATSY'S ENTIRE UNIVERSE was falling apart. She and Tom had traveled hither and yon to find help for him. Yet his melancholy remained as deep as the dark sky, and he immediately headed for his cups when it got bad. Of course, the whisky only exacerbated his wild or depressed behavior, and she felt at her wit's end to help him. She found comfort daily in her well-planned children's routine, insisting that they have plenty of outdoor exercise, a diet of fresh meat and vegetables, and making sure they were always clean and simply dressed. She home-schooled them with rigorous lessons and was pleased at the dedication they brought to their studies. She often thanked her father for the wonderful education he had given her, saying she wanted her children to benefit from the same opportunity. Teaching her children was the aspect of motherhood she loved best. And since she had slaves at Monticello, Varina, and Edgehill, she could devote many hours to this preferred occupation.

Molly Hemings, the daughter of Sally's sister Mary, was one of Patsy's favorites among the slaves, and she asked Molly, at age fourteen, to become her personal maid. Patsy imagined Molly took gossip back to Sally about her life with Tom, but there was nothing she could do about it. The rumor river on Mulberry Row would spread any interesting news no matter what she did.

In the middle of the year Patsy and Tom moved permanently to Monticello as they found the climate at Varina basically unlivable and were told the house at Edgehill wouldn't be ready until next year. The time spun away like a child running, letting out a kite string, and they ended by spending the spring, summer, and early autumn in Albemarle County.

Thomas returned from Philadelphia in mid-July, believing he could carry on the business of the vice presidency from his mountaintop during the summer. All of the children relished his presence, often pulling him outdoors to play with them. Thomas remarked to Patsy he was a bit worried about little Jeff's "tempests," saying he hoped it were not indicative of his father's family's nature. "Boys are just different from girls," she laughed.

In October Patsy gladly helped Polly plan her wedding to Jack — Patsy couldn't get used to calling her Maria — and on the festive day, both she and Sally attended Polly's dressing for the occasion. Polly wore their mother's white satin wedding gown, and Patsy reminded them of all the fun they had had in Paris together, dressing up and dancing. Polly hugged them both, and said, "You are my dearest friends." Patsy noticed Sally's grateful expression and wished she could be as forgiving as her sister. She and Polly never had discussed Sally's little girl who had looked like their father; after all, what could they say?

Polly showed Patsy a letter from their father written when he heard she was to be married, and they had a little chuckle over his preaching: . . . *harmony in the marriage state is the very first object to be aimed at . . . that a husband finds his affections wearied out by a constant string of little checks & obstacles.*

Polly further confided in Patsy, "I know that Papa is sad we are not going to be living in Albemarle County. But Jack and I prefer to reside at the Bermuda Hundred that Father Eppes gave to us. It's so very pretty, on the south side of the James River, and it is not very far to travel."

"Of course, you must live where you wish, my dear Polly. It is just that we both will miss you so."

Tom's behavior at the wedding was unremarkable, for which Patsy thanked her lucky stars, and she let herself enjoy floating in his arms around the dance floor. When he crushed her to him later that night, they wept in one another's embrace. "I do love you, my Tom, I do," she declared. She swore she would do anything to cure his consuming despair.

SALLY

1797-1798

SALLY DIDN'T NEED to wait long for Thomas's return. He told her he thought he could work from home since there wasn't much work during the summer. He clearly wanted to be away from the city, and she hoped he also wanted to be near her. She observed he tended more to his crops than to state duties.

She found she missed Polly since her move to her own plantation after her marriage. She had served somewhat as a filter between her and Patsy. Somehow Polly had always been easier to get along with than Patsy, who considered herself mistress of Monticello and guardian of her father's welfare.

Sally retired to her stone cottage on Mulberry Row for the birth of William Beverly Hemings on April 1, 1798, exactly thirty-eight weeks after Thomas's return home. She and Thomas decided to call him by his middle name, which was not unusual at the time, thereby effectively erasing the first name, which came from Thomas's family. Thomas told her he had chosen this name because he had recently read about William Beverly, an important man in Virginia history.

As busy as she was and not wanting to totally hand over the reins to Patsy, she handed over her baby to a wet nurse once again on Mulberry Row, much to Betty's chagrin.

"You should be thinking about your own children," she told her daughter.

"I have my duties to attend to," she informed her mother.

THOMAS

1798-1799

DISLIKING CONFRONTATION INTENSELY, Thomas always favored conducting his battles behind the lines. Whether domestic or political, he preferred to dominate with intelligence and cunning rather than temper. One of the reasons for this strategy, he knew, was his thin skin; he resented and feared attacks by his opponents. However, he discovered that by the end of the vice presidential election, he was better able to withstand the blows with a more sanguine frame of mind.

This proved to be essential for his survival in the last two years of the century. He felt constantly at odds with his Federalist foes. The worst for him was the hard-fought fight over the proposed Alien and Sedition Acts, passed by the Federalist Congress in 1798 and signed into law by his colleague, President Adams. He perceived these laws to be a formidable threat to the constitution. It made him extremely angry but felt like a personal blow as well.

The entire country had been at loggerheads over the recent Jay Treaty with Britain and also by what became known as the XYZ Affair with France. The French foreign minister, Talleyrand, had sent three French diplomats, code named X, Y and Z, to negotiate problems with America, that were threatening war between the two nations. X, Y and Z demanded bribes and a loan before negotiations could begin, shocking and offending the American diplomats. M. Talleyrand finally managed to calm tempers and war was avoided. Because of these two incidents, President Adams argued that the Alien and Sedition Acts were a necessary reprisal to any foreign threat.

The alien laws included a new power for the president, which enabled him to deport any resident alien whom he considered dangerous. In this hysterical time, the result was that all foreigners came to be considered as dangerous to American security. The Sedition Act forbade anyone to "write, print, utter, or publish . . . any false, scandalous, and malicious writing or writings against the government of the United States, or either House of the Congress of the United States . . ." In other words, there could be no public opposition to the government. Under these broad terms, over twenty Republican newspaper editors were arrested and some were quickly imprisoned. Jefferson and the Republicans interpreted the Acts as a greater jeopardy to the constitution's Bill of Rights than the imagined foreign dangers.

Thomas cursed his weakness as he took to his bed with a throbbing migraine. He had to be well to confront this abominable attack on essential personal liberty! He even began to fear his mail was being watched, and complained by letter to Patsy: *Politics and party hatreds destroy the happiness of every being here . . . They seem, like salamanders, to consider fire as their element.*

He was truly anguished by all of this and wrote to his daughter again to lament not being with his family. He mused,

> *Indeed, I find myself detaching very fast, perhaps too fast, from every thing but yourself, your sister, and those who are identified with you. These form the last hold the world will have on me, the cords which will be cut only when I am loosened from this state of being. I am looking forward to the spring with all the fondness of desire to meet you all once more, . . .*

He worried constantly about everyone in the family, and they all teased him a bit about being a mother hen. He wrote to Patsy about his grandson, whom they all called "Jeff," on May 31,

> *I am sorry to hear of Jefferson's indisposition, but I am glad you do not physic him. This leaves nature free and unembarrassed in her own tendencies to repair what is wrong. I hope to hear or find that he is recovered. Kiss them all for me.*

A letter from Patsy on July 1, 1798 soothed his spirits greatly:

> *. . . The heart swellings with which I address you when absent and look forward to your return convince me of the folly or want of feeling of those who dare to think that any new ties can weaken*

the first and best of nature. The first sensations of my life were af-
fection and respect for you and none others in the course of it have
weakened or surpassed that. The children all send their love to grand
Papa and count the days with infinite anxiety. Yours with the ten-
derest love and reverence,

MRandolph

He read it over and over before making himself turn to other knotty problems. Especially frightening was the danger he perceived to the viability of the democracy stemming from the practice of "judicial review," which he had helped to write into the constitution. He believed this practice, which allowed the Supreme Court to consider the constitutionality of laws, had not been sufficiently developed. Therefore, since he couldn't depend on the Supreme Court and since all of the justices were strong Federalists, Jefferson, with his friend Madison, turned to the state legislatures to overturn these new laws.

Equally daunting was the state of his personal finances. Due to Tom's debt inherited from his father, Thomas was largely covering the household expenses of Patsy and Tom; tobacco prices were low; and he hated selling his slaves to raise cash. He was land rich and cash poor. He turned to leasing several of his good slaves in order to raise revenue.

Campaigning and talk of the next election for president were already becoming part of the national conversation. The differences between Federalists and Republicans were clearly drawn, and Thomas — thin skinned, debt-ridden, and weakened by headaches — decided to seek the top office once again. The threat by the Federalists to the fledgling democracy was more than he could or would abide. He felt it to be a personal responsibility.

George Washington died at Mount Vernon in December 1799. The end of the century was closing with the death of America's first leader, and Thomas wondered what to make of this symbol. He had admired Washington in so many ways, but had always feared he was leading the country toward monarchy instead of upholding the first principles of the American Revolution. He would not attend the funeral. He did not think it wise for the country to link him too closely to Washington's policies going forward.

PATSY

1799-1800

PATSY WAS WITH CHILD AGAIN and chastised herself over how tired she always felt these days. At least Tom was momentarily happy with the idea of another baby, ever hoping for another boy. Relieved that prices were higher for tobacco, he threw himself into work on their house at Edgehill. In the meantime, she could enjoy the luxury of Monticello, especially all the help from the slaves with the children — Anne, who was already eight years old; Jeff, age seven, her consummate ragamuffin, always running around, inside or out, in any weather, without shoes (they'd given up trying to make him wear them); and Ellen, almost three.

In mid-July Patsy gave birth to Cornelia. She chose the name after the Roman mother of two famous reformer brothers in the second century BC. "You and your literature," Tom grumbled. But she knew he was secretly proud of her unusual education. Having just gone through childbirth, she began to worry about Polly, who was also expecting, and mentioned to Tom that she would like to go to Eppington to be with her sister.

"Over my dead body," he shouted. Patsy cringed from his vehemence. "She hasn't come to visit us here for the two years since she's been married, and her husband is a deadbeat. Everybody loves him because he's so 'nice,' but Jack is just a simpering phony."

Patsy thought he might have a point, but she continued to argue. "Polly has our mother's frame and I am worried for her. It is my duty as her sister to be there."

"You can't go, Wife, I need you here," he flung at her. When he slammed the door as he left, Patsy held Cornelia closer to her pounding heart to try and staunch her anger. A few weeks later, they received the grim news that Polly had lost the baby.

Tom appeared at dinner, looking somewhat chastened. "I know you are angry I didn't allow you to go to Polly," he admitted. "I will take you now if you still want to go." His voice didn't sound contrite, but she would ignore that.

She looked up. "Of *course*, I do, Tom. She must be sick with grief over the loss of her child."

"We'll leave for Eppington in the morning," he promised.

Patsy was shocked when she saw her sister. It was worse than she'd even imagined. She still lay abed, frail and thin, her usually luxuriant hair stringy and pasted to her cheeks with perspiration. The family doctor had been purging her daily with castor oil, and she was too weak to get up. Patsy was furious and spoke to Jack that evening in private.

"Jack, Polly is — I'm sorry — I should say, Maria, is not made for bearing children! She is like our mother. I'm going to say it plain and true." She raised her voice. "If you want your wife to remain alive! And happy! And healthy! You have to stay AWAY FROM HER!"

Jack looked startled. "But it's my right," he stammered. "She is my wife."

"I understand. But you see how she is. She won't survive another childbirth!" Patsy had chosen to deliver the message herself instead of giving the job to Tom because she knew the two men disliked one another. They would end up throwing punches. Better that he think her crude and impolite. She had to say it.

The Grim Reaper seemed to be swinging his scythe over the plantation all winter long. Patsy thought she was crying more often than smiling and tried in vain to forestall feelings of total helplessness. An unknown illness first struck Mammy Ursula's husband and son, both called George. A man who called himself a doctor, whom Patsy came to call "the witch doctor," gave them both a potion, which probably killed them faster than they would have died as a result of the illness. Then Jupiter was struck down too, and the slaves called on the same doctor, who administered a brew to the poor man. Immediately upon drinking the mixture, Jupiter fell to the muddy ground, writhing in a convulsion. Unfortunately, the children were with her when this happened and sobbed uncontrollably at the bitter sight. Patsy screamed to someone, anyone, to go after this murderous quack. But they were too late on both counts, the "doctor" got away, and Jupiter died nine days later.

Patsy noticed that Sally pretty much stayed away from her these days as she too was expecting again. Her little Beverly resembled Thomas all too much and neither young woman could talk about it. Patsy hesitated to share her problems with her father, but she was feeling so anxious about Tom, her sister, and their economic situation. Who else could she turn to? She finally broke down and wrote to him:

> *I feel every day more strongly the impossibility of becoming habituated to your absence. Separated in my infancy from every other friend, and accustomed to look up to you alone, every sentiment of tenderness my nature was susceptible of was for many years centered in you, and no connexion [sic] formed since that could weaken a sentiment interwoven with my very existence.*

SALLY

SALLY STOOD WITH PATSY over Jupiter's deathbed. Jupiter was the same age as Thomas, and she knew Thomas would be devastated. She watched Patsy kneel down next to him to come close so she could stroke his withered face. "Uncle Jupiter, the master is counting on you to join him at the President's House. I do believe he is going to be President. He needs you, so you get well. And who else can drive those bay horses like you do?"

"Thank you, Miss Patsy," he said, calling her by her childhood name. She couldn't stop the tears. This man had cared for her like a father and was a patriarch of the slave population at Monticello. Sally offered her hand to Patsy to help her up and continued to hold her hand. "I wish to God we could keep him with us," Patsy said. "He is one of the finest men I've known."

Sally looked at her in surprise but knew she meant it.

James arrived back from Paris for a visit, and they hoped to keep him there for the rest of the summer. He looked so handsome, but they wondered why he still had no wife. He brought news from France, which Sally lapped up. She would tell Patsy later if she hadn't already heard: Lafayette was in prison; Mme de Corny was a widow; and Mrs. Cosway had gone into a convent in Genoa; M. de Condorcet had barely escaped being hung; and the duc de La Rochefoucauld had been ripped to pieces by a mob in front of his mother and wife. She looked at her brother in shock. Had they all just barely escaped such horrible fates themselves?

"My Lord! I'm glad we're safely here," she replied.

"Hah!" exclaimed James harshly. "I wouldn't say the slaves here are any better off than they were before the Revolution. We aren't any better off under a president than we were under the British governor. We should follow the French example and take up our pitchforks against our masters."

Betty jumped in. "Don't you talk like that, James! You know our master takes good care of us. He is good to us. You're going to get us all in trouble!"

In fact, there had recently been serious slave uprisings, and everyone was extremely nervous as to whether the landowners would be able to keep a revolt at bay.

"I've come back, Sister, to give you another chance to get away," James said. "Come with me and you'll be free. We'll get jobs in Europe like we talked about."

Sally looked at him in disbelief. She was pregnant with another child and Beverly was not yet two. Two of her children were buried nearby. "What do you think I would do with my children?"

"Our mammy will watch over them," he said, as though it were the perfect, obvious solution.

"I'm glad I came back," she threw in his face. "I want to be with Mr. Jefferson and our children for the rest of my life!"

"Well, you're a fool to stand there with that big stomach and no daddy to claim him. Don't say I didn't try and save you!" he flung back, and left the two women distraught and upset.

"I wish he'd keep his opinions to himself," said Betty.

"He's become a snob," Sally said.

Sally didn't have much longer to wait for the baby, who appeared in December. She and Thomas didn't even have time to decide on a name, because she lived for such a short time. When Sally placed the tiny body in the ground next to her other children in the Monticello graveyard, she mourned alone, for Thomas was away in Philadelphia. She knew Patsy would have stood beside her, but she didn't want that. And so she had kept it a secret from the big house. Of course, there were no secrets on the plantation, and the next day Patsy came to her on Mulberry Row with a plate of sausages and cheese. "I know this won't really help, but I also know how you are feeling, and want to extend my sympathy."

Sally's lip started to tremble as she looked into Patsy's compassionate face. The two women, who understood what it was to lose a child, embraced awkwardly. After all, Sally thought after Patsy left, Patsy was the baby's cousin. And she was grateful that Patsy had come.

THOMAS

1800

THOMAS DIDN'T HAVE the stomach for this presidential campaign. He was running on the Republican ticket and John Adams stood as the Federalist's candidate. Thomas believed the election would hinge on the issue of the Alien and Sedition Acts and trusted in the good sense of the populace to understand the right thing to do. He strongly held that a good education was the road to an informed majority that would elect the right man. He wrote to Patsy: *Our opponents perceive the decay of their power. Still they are pressing it, and trying to pass laws to keep themselves in power.*

This wasn't an overstatement, for the Federalists were resorting to phony news and exaggeration. When the Baltimore *American* published rumors that Jefferson had died at Monticello after "an indisposition of 48 hours," his family was in shock, frantically trying to find out what could have happened. It took several days for the truth to finally emerge that he was alive and well, and the opposition had leaked the false information.

In the fall Thomas was further shaken by information of slave conspiracies and insurrections in Richmond, Norfolk, and Petersburg. Whites responded viciously with counterattacks, hanging twenty-six of the organizers. Of course, the Federalists used the incident to attack Jefferson as a slave owner, and he responded simply by keeping his head down. The race only became nastier. The Federalists called Jefferson "a swindler begot by a mulatto upon a half-breed Indian squaw," and in return, Adams was dubbed a "hermaphrodite" by Jefferson supporters. Thomas's heart ached when he thought about how the cruelty of politics was placing a strain on the friendship he and the Adamses had honored for so long. Could they all rise above this insanity?

Feeling that the world had truly gone mad, Thomas retired to Monticello to wait out the results. He celebrated when he heard he'd won New York, definitive Hamilton country. Also, news that so far, the Republicans were holding the South and Pennsylvania was encouraging. He wrote to Patsy, saying, *I have sometimes asked myself whether my country is the better for my having lived at all. I do not know that it is. I have been the instrument of doing the following things, but they would have been done by others; some of them perhaps a little later.* His list included the Declaration of Independence and the introduction of olive trees to the United States.

Thomas became worried as he watched the Federalists striving to execute various malignant strategies, including backing Senator Aaron Burr, his running mate and a Republican, but one whom the Federalists felt they could manipulate. This was aimed specifically at keeping him out of office, since the vice presidency went to the second place winner.

Thomas understood Burr would be a serious contender, having been educated at the College of New Jersey (later Princeton), where his father was President. Moreover, Burr was extremely articulate, charming, and ambitious. He had proven to be a successful politician, from state assemblyman to state attorney general, and had been elected U.S. senator for the state of New York in 1791. Alexander Hamilton, the secretary of the treasury, wielded a clever pen, and Hamilton's backing of Burr over himself certainly intensified the threat.

On the last Sunday of 1800, all the electoral votes had been counted. Jefferson had defeated Adams, 73 to 65, but there was a tie between Jefferson and Burr, who also had amassed 73 votes. Now, under the terms of the constitution, the election must be turned over to the House of Representatives.

PATSY

1800

PATSY WAS AFRAID FOR her father's life. The Federalists' behavior could not be trusted, and the stories became more violent and extreme every day. Tom claimed she was overexcited, but he hadn't witnessed the French revolution as she had — where the mob had thrown a respected man like General Lafayette into a dungeon. Nothing or no one was respected. She knew that when the tide turned, the waves wiped everything up in their wake and churned the debris into a sea of public hysteria. She began to fear for the children, too, and wondered where they could all go to feel safe. She recalled the days of the American Revolution, when they had fled from plantation to plantation to avoid the British soldiers. And the false news that her father had died had been truly shocking.

By throwing the ultimate choice into the House of Representatives, the tie between Burr and Jefferson gave the Federalists a chance to keep Thomas out of office. Hadn't she counseled him against choosing Aaron Burr as his running mate, and now the scoundrel was more than willing to play the pawn of the Federalists in order to become President himself. Patsy had never trusted him, and now he was proving himself to be the viper she had always suspected. Let him be president, she thought. Just let her father be safe from the raving populace! But she knew he wished to win the office, and she shouldn't foster such disloyal thoughts.

Tom tried to soothe her. He could be as gentle on occasion as he was brutal on others, and she prayed he would throw off the darkness that so often consumed him. "Your father won't allow violence, and the people respect his temperament and reputation. You need not worry for him," he reasoned.

But she did worry. All day, every day. Now there were rumors that the House of Representatives might choose John Marshall or Burr instead of Jefferson. Let them have it, and bring her Papa back home, she chanted.

THOMAS

1801

WASHINGTON CITY WAS A MUDDY mess, a perfect metaphor, Thomas thought, when he returned to the capital for the election decision. The architect and engineer Pierre Charles l'Enfant, French born but now American, had been engaged to design the capital plan, and the organizers were determined to swear in the new president in March 1801 in the new buildings. Now it appeared that nothing would be finished in time.

A tense state of affairs persisted because of the tie, causing extreme machinations from both sides. Republican partisans, suspecting unfair maneuvers by the Federalists, threatened to march on Washington, and the Federalists did whatever they could to subvert the election. John Adams performed a clever coup by naming John Marshall, presently secretary of state, as chief justice of the United States. Marshall was a longtime foe of Jefferson's, and Adams knew he would be putting a Federalist at the head of one of the three prongs of the American government. The Federalists continued to secretly support Aaron Burr, and Burr, still pretending to be a Jefferson ally, began to more openly cooperate with them to prevent Jefferson from winning.

On February 11, the House of Representatives met to decide between Burr and Jefferson for president. The weather was cold and snowy. Ballot after ballot, the tie prevailed. One representative from Maryland was carried into the legislature on a stretcher, up the slippery, icy, House stairs in order to cast his vote. Finally, on February 17, 1801, at 1:00 pm, the thirty-sixth ballot named Jefferson president of the United States.

Thomas had maintained his composure throughout the ordeal only with difficulty, and now experienced great exultation and relief. Throughout Virginia, canons, fireworks, and general revelry announced his victory in cities and towns. Their former member of the House of Burgesses had ultimately prevailed! Thomas wished Patsy and Sally were here with him to celebrate. They would probably hear before his letter arrived; nevertheless, he went to his desk at Conrad's to write to Patsy.

He had maintained a civil relationship with the Adamses throughout the circus of the election, and Abigail quietly invited him to tea at the President's House to congratulate him. She would depart for Braintree almost immediately, but her husband would stay on until power was turned over to Thomas on March 4. All government officers had moved several months earlier from Philadelphia to the six or seven boarding houses open for service in the new capital.

John and Abigail had been living in the President's House, which had been readied for habitation in time, but Jefferson was lodged at Conrad and McMunn's. Conrad's boarding house, on the south side of Capitol Hill, commanded a lovely panoramic view of the wild and woody hill, with the Potomac River winding through the plain below. Thomas was glad he had insisted on this site for the country's capitol; he believed it was an important symbol that the capitol be situated on the border between North and South.

Now that the mantle of responsibility for the country was on his shoulders, he experienced sudden humility and doubt. Would he be able to rule for the good of the people and lead America to a free and prosperous future? It suddenly appeared to be a daunting, almost impossible task.

SALLY

NOW, TO MAKE EVERYTHING WORSE, Thomas was due to leave soon. When he held her tightly in his arms on the night he received news of the tie, she finally broke down, calling his name in the French pronunciation, "Tho-mah, Tho-mah, I cannot bear it." She'd called him by his Christian name. Would he be angry?

"My sweet love, please, dearest, always call me that!" He stroked her cheek, and she gradually fell asleep.

A restless dream dragged her into a fantastic vision where Tho-mah continues to talk to her, suggesting, "Why don't you travel with me for the inauguration? I will simply tell everyone I need your services. I am taking Jupiter, Burwell, and Davey, so why not you too?" Gazing at him in wonder, she is too amazed to answer at the moment, but embraces the idea immediately. Goodness! Where will the inauguration be? Is it Philadelphia or Washington City? She thinks Philadelphia. She searches his face to see if he is joking, but he clearly is not.

Her miraculous dream races on. How wonderful! She won't have to say goodbye right away! She runs to try on one of her Paris gowns. It fits perfectly! Surely no one in Philadelphia will know they are now out of style. Happily, in her dream, Jupiter is still alive and she knows he and her nephew Burwell will take care of her. Oh, how much she longs to go!

Looking out of the coach windows, Sally is frightened by the crowds. The mob recognizes the Jefferson lilac and yellow carriage, pulled by six prancing Monticello bays, and the Monticello coachmen recoil as a roar from the mob assaults them. She clutches Thomas's arm when the noise and close, white faces loom next to their conveyance. An image of the mob in Paris flashes before her — but surely she is safe inside the carriage with the president-elect.

Upon their arrival, Burwell, looking handsome in a golden velvet jacket, guides her at the elbow while accompanying her on a walk through the narrow streets of the town. All the red brick, little townhouses look rather drab, but so many free Negroes — both men and women, dressed in elegant clothing and wearing colorful hats and gloves, stroll down the street as though they own it. Many smile and curtsy to her. She must have seen free blacks in Paris, but the number here is striking beyond belief.

She shivers with excitement when Thomas tells her he wants her in the room to witness the magical moment of his inauguration. With Jefferson's other slaves, she doesn't think she will stand out, but she does. People are looking at her, pointing at her, and asking one another questions. "Who is she? Who could she be?" She can't escape the stares and the threatening, unfriendly faces. She senses that Patsy, who is standing next to her father, is offended at her coming, believing she is overstepping her station. Patsy actually frowns at her, and she wants to run. Instead she surprises herself by holding her chin higher. Her To-mah wants her here!

A very changed figure of Mr. Adams floats into her dream. She smiles at how much weight he has gained. Abigail doesn't seem to be present and Sally can't imagine why she would stay away. She would always be grateful to Mr. Adams, who had transformed her life by insisting she go on to Paris with Polly and M. Petit. Mr. Adams probably doesn't remember her, but when he comes over to confer with Jefferson, he gives her a smile and a nod. Does everyone know who she is? She blushes and suddenly fearful, moves closer to Jupiter. Jupiter senses her discomfort and moves a little in front of her for the remainder of the reception. She hates having to hide!

Jupiter stays behind in Washington to serve their master, and Burwell and Davey help her into the carriage for the ride back to Monticello. She feels like a queen, traveling in the handsome Jefferson coach. This almost seems better than Paris. She sits up straight against the cushions. This was the way her half-sister Patty had traveled when she had been married to Thomas. As the carriage bumps along, she relives her few days in Philadelphia. She had been so embarrassed with all the hostile stares she received at the inauguration. She pushes these haunting faces away as she begins to awaken. Her consciousness alerts her that of course, everyone suspected she was his concubine. But why should she care? He makes her happy and takes care of her.

Sally tried to remain within her fantasy, but reality asserted itself all too quickly. Finally, opening her eyes, she found Tho-mah still next to her, peacefully sleeping. She must have faith he will always be with her. It was tempting to tell him of her dream, but she decides he might think she was begging to go to the inauguration. Better to keep it to herself.

WASHINGTON CITY

PRESIDENT

1802-09

Philadelphia Apr. 8. 1800

I will never believe that man [. . .] is incapable of self-government; that he has no resources but in a master, who is but a man like himself, and generally a worse man, inasmuch as power tends to deprave him.

Extract from letter by Thomas Jefferson to Everard Meade

THOMAS

1801

THOMAS STRODE FROM Conrad and McMunn's to the capitol for the inauguration ceremony. He carried his inaugural address, written in his distinctive careful script in his jacket pocket. He didn't think it necessary, but the District of Columbia Artillery Corps insisted on accompanying him the distance immediately after he exited the boarding house. A small group of congressmen, including two members of the outgoing cabinet, joined the parade along the way. As he entered the capitol doors, a canon's boom sounded across the hill. Since none of his family was there to celebrate this moment with him, he was particularly sorry his friend John Adams had left the day before for Massachusetts. John said he just couldn't wait any longer to join Abigail at their home. Political differences had strained the two men's relationship for ten years now, but Thomas hoped, like himself, that John still harbored feelings of friendship.

Jefferson's swearing in, conducted by the president *pro tempore* of the Senate, was a quiet affair, conducted in the second floor Senate chamber. The room was small, and there was no foldcrol — only getting the business done right. The Senate chamber was crammed with Congressmen and guests, hardly allowing any breathing room. Jefferson walked to the room's dais where John Marshall administered the oath of office. Jefferson then stepped forward to deliver his address in his soft, uncommanding voice:

> *All . . . will bear in mind this sacred principle, that though the will of the majority is in all cases to prevail, that will to be rightful must be reasonable; that the minority possess their equal rights, which equal law must protect, and to violate would be oppression. . . .*

The speech was a political masterpiece of conciliation and inclusion and went a long way to unifying the divided country. Thomas wrote that he wanted to spend his presidency *pursuing steadily my object of proving that a people, easy in their circumstances as ours are, are capable of conducting themselves under a government founded not in the fears and follies of man, but on his reason. . . . This is the object now nearest to my heart.*

He planned to lessen the yoke of government imposed by the Federalists and to do away with what he considered their monarchical trappings, like wearing a ceremonial sword at the inauguration, which he eschewed. Knowing the crowd probably would not be able to hear his soft voice, he had printed copies and passed them out to the attendees. He wanted them to clearly understand his purpose.

That first night he dined alone back at his humble boarding house. He mused that perhaps the most important thing about the day's event had been the peaceful transfer of power from the Federalists to the Republicans. The democratic constitution had successfully effected its work.

When he did finally move into the President's House, he called it "a great stone house, big enough for two emperors, one pope and the grand lama in the bargain." He imagined how wonderful it would have been to have Patty by his side at this moment. She would have made a beautiful First Lady, and they could have planned musical evenings together. He couldn't believe it had already been nineteen years since Patty's death. But he mustn't let himself dwell on what might have been.

As at Monticello, he possessed particular ideas about his comforts. He immediately ordered "water closets" like those he had installed at the Hôtel de Langeac, and when Patsy thoughtfully sent him several mockingbirds to keep him company, he hung their birdcages in various places around the house to comfort him with their singing. When they weren't singing, he sang to himself. He offered the room Adams had used as an "audience room" to his secretary, Meriwether Lewis, and chose for his own office a room on the first floor with a view of the Potomac. Lewis, also a bachelor, agreed to live in the mansion with him, and Thomas remarked they were like two church mice. He also wanted his friend James Madison close by and immediately appointed him secretary of state.

Although Jefferson didn't want pomp and circumstance at his inauguration, or a fancy place to live, he did ask his son-in-law Jack Eppes to buy him four full-blooded bay horses to pull his official coach. The outlay for these gorgeous steeds was $1,600.

Rattling around in the grand government mansion, Thomas found he was lonely and wrote to his daughters, inviting them to come and live with him. However, they were busy with their own households, and Patsy, as usual, was expecting. In order to alleviate his solitary state, he fell into his old Parisian habit of inviting many to sup with him, hoping for the same free exchange of ideas he had found in France. He soon learned he must invite only Federalists one evening and Republicans another night in order to maintain a consensual and harmonious tone at the table. Some commented on the odd wording in his invitations, always saying, "Mr. Jefferson Invites . . ." instead of "The President Invites . . ." but he was adamant about not giving any hint of royalty to the office.

Patsy

HER FATHER HAD FINALLY won! And "the friends of Liberty," as she called the Republicans, would be installed at the top of government. Patsy even felt a little giddy. Perhaps she could put away some of her fears about his bodily harm, but she still didn't trust the Federalists to allow him to govern freely. This past year had been difficult with him away so much, embroiled in electioneering, and therefore unable to oversee plans for the plantation. Projects had been put on hold, and she could see that things were beginning to show unusual wear and tear without her father in charge.

She and Tom moved back to Edgehill at the end of February, and Patsy was severely disappointed in the house, which looked so small compared to Monticello. It was about forty feet wide and two stories tall; the windows let in the drafts, and a damp wind seeped up from the basement. She was becoming a drudge, she thought, as she had to join the help, sweeping and cleaning constantly to keep out the mud and rain. So much for her father's high position, she grimaced to herself.

One day, since the children were obviously feeling cabin fever as well as she, she let them go outside to play despite the bad weather. Jeff got too rough and knocked Anne down in the mud. Anne came running in the door, accusing her brother of hurting her, and before Patsy could say a word, Tom grabbed the boy vehemently by the arm and struck him hard. Jeff managed to wriggle away from Tom and ran to his mother's arms. Anne stood there rigidly, shocked at what her father had done.

"Don't you dare strike a child like that!" Patsy screamed at him. She didn't know she could sound like such a shrew. "Don't you ever! I will take the children away." No one made a move, until Tom turned and thundered out the door.

That night after the children went to bed, Tom attempted to apologize. "I am sorry, dear Wife. Believe me. I have just been so distraught over my finances. I cannot seem to make ends meet. I've just heard from your father that he will pay off my debts at Varina. It will save me from ruin. I am so grateful. I cannot tell you how grateful I am." He put his head in his hands.

Patsy's first thought was that he didn't deserve it, but she kept it to herself. She couldn't think of what to say. It must have been humiliating for him to accept funds from his father-in-law, and she knew he had been trying. She must do all she could to support him.

SALLY

SOMETIMES SALLY COULDN'T believe the life she was living. The man who was president of the country belonged to her. When he looked lovingly into her eyes and she looked back into his, the rest of the world would fade away and they were happily floating in their private cocoon. After they made love, his bony face looked positively beatific to her.

She had a horrible thought. Would being president compel him to leave her? Oh, God! Why hadn't she thought of this before? She trusted him so much. And she was pregnant again. The wound from the loss of the last baby still felt raw, but this new evidence of their passion for one another lessened the pain considerably.

Before he left for Washington, he had told her he couldn't have her with him in the President's House. Although she comprehended his reasons, it stung. She missed him so much when he was gone. She had half-believed in her dream, and sometimes let the fantasy play over and over in her mind. But the reality was what he explained to her, "You know, dearest, we can not have our babies, who look like me, running around the President's House. People at Monticello understand — well, somewhat. But not there. And if folks saw the way I treat you, in a special way, without your being my wife, it would be unacceptable."

Sally couldn't help the tears. "I know. Of course, I understand." She managed to gain her composure and tried to smile as he embraced her.

He was thirty years older than she, but even among whites, it was not unusual for an older man to have a young wife or mistress. Also, many slave husbands were much older than their wives. She knew it was simply a fact of life that they could not marry. That was a fairytale. But, she kept telling herself, he could free her children one day and maybe even herself.

While he was away, Sally, Betty, and the other slaves worked hard to ready the mansion for the homecoming of the president at Easter. All the handsome furniture he had purchased in France was placed where he had assigned it. The beautiful leather-covered books, fine china, and Persian rugs were dispersed to their proper locations. The façade with Doric columns and balustrades, looking out over wide lawns and gardens into the valley, were surely stately and elegant enough to welcome a president.

It did look like the Garden of Eden. Better even, Sally thought, when he came home during the religious holiday for the first time as the leader of the country. But he only stayed a week. Even though she begged him to stay for the birth of their baby, he said he needed to be back in Washington to run the nation.

Their child was born the eighth of May. She tickled the tummy of the little girl she had wished for and decided she would name her Harriet — after the baby they had lost. Thomas had agreed to that before leaving, but Betty was superstitious.

"Daughter, Martha Randolph named her daughter Lucy after the one that died, and the second one died too."

"Never mind, Mammy. I'm not Martha, and I'm naming her Harriet."

Betty wasn't finished bossing her daughter. "Well, you'd better nurse this one, Sally. There is no reason to pass her off this time around."

"Just because Mrs. Randolph nurses hers, doesn't mean I need to nurse mine." Sally shot back.

"Sally, it isn't right. I don't understand you. It won't ruin your bosom if that's what you're worried about!"

Sally began to cry and Betty hugged her daughter with the baby clasped between them. "It's going to be all right, Honey. It's going to be just fine."

Betty still held the keys to Monticello, but Sally knew her mother was sixty-six. Would Betty soon be passing them to her, she wondered?

THOMAS

THE DAY AFTER THE INAUGURATION, Thomas confided in his friend Madison, "I feel a great load of public favor and public expectation. More confidence is placed in me than my qualifications merit, and I dread the disappointment of my friends." But somehow, after his early case of nerves, he began to feel assured of the direction he wanted to take the country: he was confident in the people he would ask to serve in his cabinet, he was confident in the populace, and he experienced a sudden assurance he could do the job.

He worked ten to thirteen hours a day, taking about a four-hour break at midday for lunch, riding, "and a little unbending." He insisted on his privacy, but he was social so many evenings no one commented on it. He invited James and Dolley Madison to join him and Meriwether Lewis at the President's House until their own homes were ready. He and Madison were such long-term comrades, it was like having a brother with him, and he liked Dolley immensely. She was affable, enjoyed playing cards, and gambling. But she had the good sense to wait until she had her own home for that. Dolley had been a widow when James married her in 1794, and Thomas was glad she made his friend so happy.

He appointed Madison as his secretary of state immediately and now hurried to choose ministers for treasury, war, and navy. For treasury he named Albert Gallatin who, like Jefferson, had fought constantly with Hamilton. Gallatin was a brilliant financier, born to an aristocratic Swiss family, and Thomas felt he could trust him. He put Henry Dearborn at war, Robert Smith at navy, and chose Levi Lincoln as attorney general. He was ready.

He disliked full cabinet meetings, preferring to do business primarily by writing to each of his cabinet heads daily. He would send policy statements to all and expect their comments back in writing. He favored a consensual style of management and often enlisted Madison to maneuver behind the scenes to achieve unanimous outcomes.

Many people were shocked at Jefferson's manner of dress when they called upon the president — especially the Europeans who were accustomed to more proper attire. He would even greet them at the front door, refusing to stand on formality by having a servant open the door first. He would laugh at the look on their faces and quip that Virginians liked to dress like farmers. But any visitor quickly would be drawn in by the force of his mind and innate, proper, and genteel manners.

Thomas had his chance in mid-May to exhibit his strength to the world. Barbary Pirates had been harassing American shipping in the Mediterranean for years. He perceived an opportunity to stop their piracy and make a statement about American power. He also aimed to make the points that it was the president who controlled foreign affairs, and the ability to authorize a naval attack was in the hands of the executive — not the legislative branch of government.

The Americans were victorious on August 1, 1801 when the *Enterprise,* under the command of Andrew Sterett, defeated the *Tripoli* near Malta. Jefferson told Sterett, *Too long . . . have those barbarians been suffered to trample on the sacred faith of treaties, on the rights and laws of human nature. . . . You have shown to your countrymen that the enemy cannot meet bravery and skill united.* The Treaty of Tripoli, which had been signed June 10, 1797 by the U.S. Senate, stated in Article 11 that:

> *As the Government of the United States of America is not, in any sense, founded on the Christian religion; as it has in itself no character of enmity against the laws, religion, or tranquility, of Mussulmen (Muslims); and as the said States never entered into any war or act of hostility against any Mahometan (Mohammedan) nation, it is declared by the parties that no pretext arising from religious opinions shall ever produce an interruption of the harmony existing between the two countries.*

Now, beyond stopping the pirates from attacking American ships, Sterett finally had enforced the rules of the treaty.

In December, in his first annual message to Congress, Jefferson outlined some of his most important policies: to reduce federal taxes and spending; to give states the lead in managing domestic affairs; to reduce the national debt; and to suppress the new courts that Adams had added before leaving office. There was immediate criticism from Hamilton, but surprisingly, John Quincy Adams, John and Abigail Adams' son, was more agreeable, saying, "The measures recommended by the President are all popular in all parts of the nation."

PATSY

1801-02

IRRITATED WITH HER FATHER, Patsy paced around the house, turning everything over in her mind. Didn't he realize she had four children at home, between the ages of ten and two? Didn't he see she was pregnant with another child? How could he expect her to come to Washington and play the role of first lady? It was asking too much! Besides, she knew he disliked women to be active and serious about politics and believed it was a man's occupation. Well, she had her occupation here at home! Tom didn't make it easier as their financial worries continued unabated.

Patsy and Tom's child was born in the month of May, soon after Sally's Harriet came into the world. Despite her warning to Jack Eppes not to ever make her sister pregnant again, Polly also had given birth in September. As expected, the delivery had proceeded with much difficulty. They named the little tyke Francis. All three women — Patsy, Polly, and Sally — were now at Monticello, nursing their healthy babies and relying on the help of Betty and her staff. It was a jolly congenial maternity ward, Patsy thought, but she couldn't suppress her anger with Jack when her eyes fell on her fragile sister, or her irritation with her father and Sally when she saw baby Harriet's bright blue eyes.

Tom wanted to name the new baby Virginia. "Let's call her Genny for short," he suggested. Patsy knew he was disappointed not to have a boy and so easily granted him his wishes.

The multitude of people attracted to the president descended on Monticello like irritating horse flies. Thomas didn't discourage them but invited everyone to his home, whether he was there or not, and bore the expense for entertaining them. Believing the president should be accessible to the people, he counted on Patsy to be hostess and his staff of slaves to cater to their needs.

In the autumn, Sally's children started to cough. Polly recognized the sound from the horrible whooping cough she had survived at Eppington before going to France. But she feared the worst. Hadn't baby Lucy died from it, and one of Aunt Elizabeth's children too? Patsy didn't have time to allay Polly's fears as one by one, all of the children fell ill with the dread disease. First Ellen, then Cornelia, and the newborn baby. The symptoms were grave and frightening — coughing fits, fever, and even vomiting blood. Delirious with fatigue, Patsy went from child to child, administering food and water. She prayed out loud as she wandered day and night among the sick. She was numb with fatigue, which perhaps was a good thing, she thought, since it kept her from knowing the full danger. Of course, Sally and Polly helped with the nursing, but for some reason, she always felt she was at the helm.

Tom wore her down even more, wringing his hands and predicting they were all going to die. He swore he could see their little coffins all lined up in the Monticello graveyard. She snapped at him, amazed she didn't strike him. "Don't ever say such a thing! Just leave if you can't help!"

Miraculously, all the children survived, and the three young mothers cried together in their relief, thanking God over and over, and wondering at their salvation. After the children's recovery, Thomas's constant invitations to join him in the capital finally weakened her resolve, and Patsy agreed to come and be his hostess at his dining table. She admitted to herself that one of the reasons she had acquiesced was to get away from the difficulties of her marriage and domestic responsibilities at home.

By May 1802, they had decided on a date for her visit, but this time, measles at Albemarle forestalled the plan and instead, she played nurse and mother for the entire spring season.

SALLY

1801

SALLY HAD ENJOYED THE SPRING at Monticello before all the births. It was a glorious time, with her master's white family's children playing out of doors with all the slave children, including hers. Patsy's Anne and Ellen were taken especially with her blue-eyed Beverly as they all frolicked among the jasmine, honeysuckle, and peach blossoms. The thick aroma of such fertility was dizzying.

Sally thought Patsy appeared unusually tired and even looked as though middle age had eclipsed her youthful beauty. No matter how robust she was, it was no wonder her face looked haggard with what she had to endure with that husband of hers. He appeared more morose than ever, and Sally noticed he drank too much in the evenings.

When Thomas arrived in the summer for the second time since his presidency, everyone vied for his attention. He was the pivot around which this black and white circle whirled. She saw immediately how exhausted he was. He complained of having constant dysentery since taking office and though he didn't mention it when he came home, she knew it was the nineteenth anniversary of Patty Jefferson's death. The death of Jupiter two years earlier had also taken its toll on him. Jupiter had been a steady presence in his life forever, and now he no longer welcomed them in the mornings with his deep voice. She held her lover's body closer to her, stroking his throbbing head on many nights.

Thomas worked in his study during the day except when he went out for a ride or walk. But without fail, he would join the entire family for a companionable, noisy dinner with all the children — sometimes outside, enjoying the late sunlight. One evening he told her he had news of James's return from Europe. She had received letters from him from various capitals, all with entreaties for her to join him. He would never give up on that idea.

The whooping cough siege had scared them all, and Sally was glad to say goodbye to Patsy and Polly, who finally were returning to their own plantations for the fall. Polly took Sally's sister, Critta, along to serve her. Some of the slave boys had been fighting over her, and Betty deemed it wise to separate everyone before real trouble broke out.

Sally and Betty began making preparations for Christmas. They wanted to start early as there was so much to do before everyone arrived at Monticello for the holidays. Bleaching the sheets, twining wreaths, dipping more candles, baking fruitcakes — the list went on and on . . .

Davey, one of the Jefferson slaves who had been a close friend of James's, rode up to Mulberry Row on the fourth of December. He jumped from his horse to impart horrific news. James had been found dead in Philadelphia. Shot. No one knew for sure if it was suicide or murder. Davey told them he had been buried immediately, in unconsecrated ground up North.

Sally started howling and couldn't stop. Davey handed her the few belongings that had been found at his bedside — Trumbull's portrait of Sally in a silver frame and a small silver dagger. She swore at that moment to hold Thomas to his promise to free her children. Davey told her people said James had been crazy with drink during his last days. That drink had killed him. But she knew it was slavery that had killed her brother. He'd had no place to go. Nowhere he would be recognized as a full human being.

THOMAS

1802

THOMAS WAS NOT AFRAID to roil the waters, and enjoined the conversation in the government in early 1802, making a strong statement about freedom of religion:

> *Believing with you (the Federalists) that religion is a matter which lies solely between Man and his God, that he owes account to none other for his faith or his worship, that the legitimate powers of government reach actions only, and not opinions, I contemplate with sovereign reverence that act of the whole American people which declared that their legislature should 'make no law respecting an establishment of religion, or prohibiting the free exercise thereof,' thus building a wall of separation between Church and State.*

George Cabot of Massachusetts and other Federalists criticized him harshly, Cabot saying he feared the "terrible evils of democracy" being put in place by this irresponsible president. They were angry, too, at Jefferson's repeal of the Judiciary Act of 1801, which had created additional courts and judgeships before Adams left office. They began their work to unseat this seemingly reckless leader.

Thomas was angry but even more upset when on September 1, a salacious scandal involving him hit the front pages of the newspapers. The Federalist-leaning *Richmond Recorder* published an allegation against Jefferson:

> *It is well known that the man, whom it delighteth the people to honor, keeps, and for many years has kept, as his concubine, one of his slaves. Her name is SALLY . . . By this wench Sally, our president has several children . . . The AFRICAN VENUS is said to officiate, as housekeeper at Monticello.*

Details, often incorrect, continued to appear in the news through mid-November. James Callender was the author of the pieces, and he had been chasing this story ever since 1789 when Jefferson returned from Paris with Sally, who had been pregnant at the time. Thomas made a point of not responding to any of it and resolved not to allow this brute to shame him. Rather he focused on how to derail his attack and decided that the presence of his upright and dutiful daughters at the capitol, as well as his appearance at church, might help calm some of the vendetta.

He wrote again to Polly and Patsy, requesting that they come to Washington City. Without talking to them about it, he depended on their affection for him to allow them to accept his love and need for Sally. He told himself they surely knew it was common behavior in the south. And of course, they knew their mother had asked him to never marry again. They certainly could not expect him to remain celibate. And he had kept his promise to their mother. Surely he had a right to his relationship with Sally.

But how was poor Sally coping with this situation? He wished he could write to her but he still didn't dare. Especially now! He might send a note to her through Burwell Colbert, his body servant. Burwell was Sally's nephew and had always been a close friend of James's. But what if Burwell were stopped or searched? He sometimes wondered what the other slaves thought about his relationship with Sally, but like his daughters, he expected they understood and accepted it. It just wasn't possible to write; she simply would have to be strong, knowing he loved her and missed her.

PATSY

1802

IN MID-NOVEMBER, DESPITE the cold temperatures and fears about the children, Patsy and Polly finally set out for Washington. There were no childhood diseases keeping them at home for the moment. Polly's husband, Jack, accompanied them part of the way, and Patsy brought Jeff and Ellen with her. She decided to leave Anne, her oldest, and Cornelia, the youngest, with Tom and the servants in Albemarle. She wanted all the children with her but was afraid to leave Jeff with Tom, given Tom's temper and Jeff's occasional boisterous outbursts. She was relieved to have some time away from her husband. Their finances had only worsened, and Tom's self-loathing and anger was a phantom presence in the house. It was nigh impossible to be around him. The trip took five days, although Thomas told them he usually pushed his horse and made the distance in three, making everyone roll their eyes.

Dolley Madison had made extraordinary preparations for the sisters' arrival, including purchasing some of the latest fashions from milliners and dressmakers for them to wear while in the capital. Dolley believed the president's daughters ought to make a good impression. After all, one reason she knew they were invited was to convince the political world that Jefferson was a righteous gentleman. She was relieved to see that Patsy still looked young and cared about her appearance, and Polly's natural beauty always drew admiration. Patsy had sent Dolley a cutting of her hair with the request of two wigs close to her natural color. After they arrived, the two ladies enjoyed styling her hair with ringlets framing her face and hanging shoulder length at the back. Patsy laughed and remarked, "I never have the time at Monticello to take such care with my appearance."

When the young women were introduced, Polly groused a bit that all anyone had to comment about her was her looks, while they admired Patsy's intelligence and patience. Patsy knew her sister was sensitive on this point and that Polly even felt their father loved Patsy best. But Patsy and Thomas both often assured her that this wasn't true. Their father had not mentioned the Callender reports to Patsy or Polly, but of course they knew of it and clearly understood their mission — to banish any credence to the ugly rumors. The President must be seen as an upright family man, who honored women and took care of them.

Patsy largely blamed Sally. Why did the woman insist on continuing her affair with Thomas? Didn't she understand he was so important to the nation that he mustn't be compromised in any way? Why was she so selfish that she must threaten his career and wellbeing? It was so unnecessary! Now she must help cover up the mess Sally had caused. Why, oh why, did he insist on continuing the impossible relationship? And now there were three children further complicating the picture. She tried to brush away her cowardice over speaking to her father about it.

The President's House was still a work-in-progress with many rooms unfinished or simply roughed in. Patsy and the children stayed in rooms on the second floor that hadn't been plastered yet, but the downstairs was already a grand space for the visitor's eye. The dining room had received particular attention from Jefferson, for as usual, he prided himself on the food he served. To that end, he had brought three of his slaves from Monticello: Ursula Hughes, Edith Fossett (wife of Joseph Fossett, Monticello's chief blacksmith) and Fanny Hern (Edith's sister) — all who worked as apprentices to his French chef, Honoré Julien.

Patsy couldn't help but puff up a bit when Thomas led them, one on each arm, into dinner and presented them to several statesmen and their wives. She was reminded of the evenings in Paris where she had participated in conversations with philosophers and aristocrats. She learned the next day, reading copy by the Republican newspaper editor, Samuel Harrison Smith, that his wife thought Patsy to be "one of the most lovely women I have ever met with." Mrs. Smith admired her "intelligence, benevolence, and sensibility" and her "interesting conversation." How gratifying!

Patsy knew she had passed the test, and her father would be proud of her. She felt surprise and relief as she easily slipped into the manners of the group of statesmen around Jefferson's table. She loved the high level of conversation and entered the fray with intelligence and social agility. The fore-planned two weeks extended to six, as she delighted in the attention and respect paid to her and Polly. They attended religious services with their father and went to teas in the homes of women in Washington society, all of which alleviated any outright maligning of President Jefferson's family life. She was pleased to see her father so happy with them at his side.

On December 28, Tom arrived in Washington to accompany Patsy, Polly, and the children back home. She hated for this lovely interim to be over. The return trip was a long slog with restless children, and tempers were short when they finally arrived at Edgehill. Patsy feared Washington life would become a dream of the past, like Paris. She had allowed dangerous reminiscences about William Short to play in her mind while in Washington and couldn't help but wonder what her life would have been like with him in Europe. Like her father, she realized, she enjoyed the world of society and governing.

SALLY

SALLY CRINGED WHEN she heard of the article in the Richmond paper. How could this man be so cruel? Callender could ruin her life and he didn't care one bit. All he wanted to do was to damage Thomas Jefferson. He clearly had informants from Monticello because he knew many details — although he got some things wrong. He claimed she had five children, but failed to mention that some of them had died. He intimated the affair had gone on a long time, which made it sound as though she was something like a wife to him. The clever writer knew this would be an insult to white women.

Now twenty-nine years old, first and foremost Sally thought of protecting her children from slander. She could handle it somewhat better because she was older, but it still cut to the quick. Truth was, she really did want to be his wife, and this man made her relationship sound sordid. Betty tried to hide the newspapers from her, but other slaves, who were jealous of her special treatment, made sure she saw the articles. She felt physically assaulted when Callender called her a "slut as common as the pavement."

Sally blamed Thomas for having gotten mixed up with this snake in the first place. Callender was a Republican, who had offered to work for Jefferson many years earlier. Now, without compunction, he was glad to turn on Thomas for the hope of fame and money. Moreover, he had a profound hatred of Negroes and considered Jefferson a traitor to the white race because of his relationship with Sally. He began making both Jefferson and Sally his targets.

By this time, Sally largely believed both her "white family" and her "black family" accepted her and were willing to live with the situation between her and Thomas. She'd been envious when Patsy left to help Thomas in Washington, but she had to admit her presence would only have reinforced the slander. She began to have nightmares that this public exposure might be more than the president could or would endure. Would he end the relationship, pay her off, and ask her and the children to leave Monticello? All she could do was wait and see and depend on his kindness and love for her. Betty didn't make it any easier, saying every day, "I told you to get your freedom, Sally. I told you so."

THOMAS

1802

THOMAS WAS FASCINATED both by the West and by science and seized the opportunity to merge these two interests. In the summer of 1802, he enjoyed reading Alexander Mackenzie's book *Voyages from Montreal.* The author was a fur trader who described traveling across Canada to the Pacific. Mackenzie had suggested that the British should secure the vast western swathe of North America to add to their empire, but Jefferson had other ideas. He would send an exploratory expedition under the Union's auspices and secure the lands for America. He felt a tremendous urgency to make this happen.

What better person to lead this enterprise than his own private secretary, Meriwether Lewis? Lewis had been discovered by George Washington when Lewis was a lieutenant in the U.S. Army, where he had proven his knowledge of the West and leadership skills. Lieutenant Lewis, in turn, invited William Clark, a fellow Virginian and explorer, to be his second in this Corps of Volunteers for Northwest Discovery. Congress willingly granted $2,500 to fund the expedition, and the two men excitedly began to chart their course across the wide country, from shore to shore.

Jefferson turned to other projects with the same energy. He was blessed with a Republican majority in both houses of Congress and so managed to banish the addition of circuit judgeships that Adams had finagled, simply by repealing Adams' Judiciary Act of 1801. The Federalists were aghast. John Marshall, an ardent Federalist and Chief Justice of the Supreme Court, was also Thomas's cousin, but the two fought like Cain and Abel. They had disliked one another since their youth, and now carried their divisiveness onto the national scene.

Their enmity came to a head in the case of Marbury vs. Madison, a complicated question brought to the Supreme Court, involving James Madison's (acting as Secretary of State) failure to deliver a commission for justice of the peace to one of Adams's last-minute appointees. In his decision, Marshall struck out against Jefferson, who was not pleased with the lecture given him by the Chief Justice, nor with Marshall's affirmation of the Court's power to review acts of Congress. Jefferson strongly opposed Judicial Review as interpreted by Marshall because he thought it violated the principle of separation of powers. Jefferson proposed that each branch of government should decide constitutional questions for itself and only be held responsible for their decisions to the voters.

For practical strategic reasons, Marshall did not say the Court was the only interpreter of the Constitution (though he hoped it would be), and he did not say how the Court would enforce its decisions if Congress or the Executive branch opposed them. But by Marshall's timely assertion of judicial review, the Court began its ascent as an equal branch of government — an equal in power to the Congress and the president.

With all of this weighing upon him, Thomas was overjoyed when his family joined him in Washington in November and their stay extended through Christmas. He, too, read Margaret Bayard Smith's article and smiled with pride and pleasure when she said she found Polly Eppes beautiful, simple, and timid in company, but "when alone with you of communicative and winning manners." And he thought her characterization of Patsy was generally apropos, when she reported Mrs. Randolph to be "rather homely, a delicate likeness of her father, but still more interesting than Mrs. Eppes. She is really one of the most lovely women I have ever met with, her countenance beaming with intelligence, benevolence and sensibility, and her conversation fulfills all her countenance promises. Her manners, so frank and affectionate, that you know her at once, and feel perfectly at your ease with her." He didn't see her as "homely" at all, but Mrs. Smith had certainly discovered her character.

Thomas longed to have Patsy and the children with him more often and began to look for ways to make this happen. When both John (Jack) Wayles Eppes and Thomas Mann Randolph, Jr. voiced an interest in seeking congressional seats, he suggested they might live with him in the President's House if this came to pass. Indeed, they were both elected and had no need to look further for housing in the capital.

PATSY

1802-1803

PATSY SETTLED INTO A ROUTINE after Tom was elected to Congress — if both her husband and father were back in Virginia, the Randolphs and the Eppeses all moved to Monticello; but, whenever Congress was in session and Tom was in Washington, Patsy stayed at Edgehill with their children. She knew her father liked her visits to Washington, and enjoyed her playing hostess at his table, but at the same time, he continued to criticize overly-political women and praise domestic pursuits for American females. On several occasions he expressed his opinion that American women were "too wise to wrinkle their foreheads with politics." She didn't bother to argue with him.

When Tom was away, Patsy took over as overseer and supervisor of the Edgehill plantation as well as keeping up with her duties as mother and running the household. She didn't have time to think about it much, but she sometimes felt she had not fulfilled her purpose in life. But then if she tried to define what that purpose might be, she thought she probably agreed with her father about the role of a woman — to take responsibility for the care and education of the children and to be a helpmate to her spouse.

Their continuing financial straits eroded her generally optimistic outlook, and she realized this burden was also fraying her relationship with Tom. They had a son and four daughters, were saddled with debt, and the tobacco crop had failed again. She couldn't rely on her husband. The only person she could rely on was herself, and so she was going to have to pull herself together. After all, she was Thomas Jefferson's daughter, and he would expect no less of her.

She and the children moved to Monticello for the summer, and the month of August brought some relief and excitement. Thomas invited William Short, who was visiting the United States under the auspices of American diplomat to France, to spend some time at Monticello. Patsy couldn't staunch an excited internal ruffle at the thought of seeing him again. But he must be old and paunchy, she decided. Not nearly as handsome as her Tom. She couldn't believe it had been thirteen years since she had bid him goodbye in Paris. She remembered him chasing her in the snow during their skating party and his helping her from the ice when she fell. The memory still delighted her.

When his magnificent carriage rolled up to Monticello's portico, she held her breath, as a finely dressed, perfectly respectable looking, middle-aged man bent down to kiss her hand in the French manner. "Madame Randolph, what a perfect delight to see you again. And what beautiful children surround you. I would expect no less."

Patsy found herself genuinely smiling back at him, her manners and happiness overcoming her nervousness.

"Mr. Short, it is our pleasure to have you with us. I hope you will make yourself at home in the southern manner."

She saw his eyes alight on Sally and her blue-eyed children. There was a flicker of surprise and then he recovered his aplomb. He didn't take Sally's hand as he had Patsy's, but bowed in a polite greeting of recognition. "And Mademoiselle Sally, what a grand time we all had in Paris, n'est-ce pas?"

"Indeed, Monsieur," Sally bowed her head as well to him. "We are honored to see you in Virginia."

Patsy drew herself up, somewhat taken aback at Sally's tone of ownership. But then the girl had most always been with them in Paris, and it would have been impolite for William to ignore her.

The days of William's sojourn with them flew by, with happy times in the garden and at table. Somehow they were able to find their former ease with one another, and Patsy made sure other people were always around. She mentioned to him her relief that their friend Lafayette had been let out of prison. "I understand you had a hand in securing his release," Patsy said, with obvious admiration.

"I might have offered some help. But the primary effort was made by Messieurs Madison and Monroe."

Patsy saw Tom carefully watching her and listening to their conversation. She could see his impatience grow with things he knew nothing about, and a hint of jealousy in his eyes. She would need to be careful over the next few days not to favor Mr. Short's company exceedingly.

William spoke kindly of each of her children, finding something special in each one. "Cornelia resembles you, I think, and I see Jeff has your kindness as well."

"I sometimes think none of my children has any interest in accomplishments," she confessed. "But my father wisely counsels me that every person has his own special talents and should be appreciated in those terms. I'll always remember what he told me, 'Every human being must be viewed according to what it is good for. For not one of us, no, not one, is perfect.'"

"Ah, he was always the generous and wise man, Mr. Jefferson."

One day at lunch under umbrellas outside, Thomas addressed William, "So, young man, what do you plan to do with your land in Albemarle County?"

Patsy had heard nothing of this and looked at both men in surprise.

"It was more than generous of you, kind sir, to give me this land, but I honestly do not know what to do with it. I do not have slaves to work it, and I will not own slaves. And so it presents a conundrum for me."

Thomas looked somewhat flustered but quickly recovered. "Yes, Yes. I appreciate your feelings, certainly. It is an abhorrent institution, slavery. But at the present time, we landowners could not survive without it. One day, we shall be done with it, and perhaps in my old age, I can look forward to correcting the problem. We shall talk more of this later."

Patsy wondered if they ever did, but heard nothing more of Mr. Short's land, nor of his moving to Virginia. She was also curious about his ongoing relationship with the Duchesse de La Rochefoucauld. She knew of the gruesome death of the Duchess's husband and wondered if she and Mr. Short were still lovers. Of course, she didn't dare ask, and he said nothing of the beautiful widow. She could only imagine that he still preferred loose liaisons to family life, and wondered if she could have ever changed that predilection. A hint of intimacy remained between them, and she detected admiration in his eyes when he looked at her. But she mustn't dwell on lost opportunities and empty hopes.

SALLY

1803

CALLENDER'S SLANDER BURNED in her heart and mind from dawn until dusk and kept her from sleeping many nights. The *Virginia Gazette* had recently asked the question of the President on the front page: *Why have you not married some woman of your own complexion?* Might Thomas do this to stop the vile accusations and defamation of the two of them? What would this mean for their children, Beverly and Harriet? She had even heard that his friend Madison had suggested he send her away from Monticello with her children to go and live with a relative elsewhere. Of course, that made perfect sense to everyone else.

She had to wait until March for Thomas's return to Monticello, and she could see that Callender's personal attacks had taken their toll. He looked thin and his face was pinched with anxiety. There were the usual accolades from the crowd of people welcoming him home — with ninety-five slaves on the plantation and nineteen members of his white family — making it impossible to even draw close to him for hours. She would have to wait until after the evening meal to find the outside access to his living quarters and slip into his room.

He was waiting for her, and she should have had more faith. The fact that their love had been publicly announced seemed not to matter to him. He wrapped his arms around her and whispered in her ear. "They can not separate us, my dear girl. They will not."

He so rarely spoke of their relationship, these were precious words indeed. She could not help her tears as she melted close to him. He was sixty years old now, and she worried more about his health. But to her he was still the strong loving man she had fallen in love with sixteen years ago in France.

THOMAS

1803

THOMAS RETURNED TO HIS MOUNTAIN again in the summer, brimming with excitement that his plan to acquire the Louisiana Territory might be within reach. France had acquired ownership of this territory from Spain at the beginning of his presidency, and it had been at the forefront of his mind from the moment the treaty had been signed in Madrid. He believed it was unacceptable for the great Napoleon to own land in North America. Bonaparte seemed to be a more formidable opponent than Spain, and Thomas deemed this ground should belong to America. He further understood that New Orleans represented a port America could and should not do without.

He brought to bear his deep knowledge of France, its history, and its culture to the problem, and decided to send James Monroe to Paris as his special envoy. Then fortuitously, the incumbent American minister to France, Robert R. Livingston, overheard a conversation in a drawing room party hosted by Joséphine Bonaparte. He was savvy enough to understand that France would declare war on Britain if Britain did not evacuate Malta. Realizing that the French might be convinced to simplify their situation in North America in order to concentrate on their European empire, Livingston cleverly gleaned that this threat might tempt France to part with the Louisiana Territory. America couldn't trade France land in exchange, but it could offer cash.

Knowing the recent defeat in St. Domingue by a motley slave force had threatened Napoleon's power and wounded his ego, Jefferson understood it was challenging for France to rule over such a distant colony as Louisiana. Moreover, the emperor's soldiers were dying of yellow fever and malaria in the Caribbean, and such a distant, fractious colony as Louisiana probably no longer appeared as important as before. Immediately after the drawing room incident, the emperor dispatched his foreign minister Charles Maurice de Talleyrand to sound out whether the United States might be interested in the entire Louisiana Territory and not just the port of New Orleans; Livingston now was sure of his game. He quickly extended this feeler to James Madison, who had arrived in Paris to help Monroe with negotiations, and these two, on behalf of Jefferson, negotiated a treaty to buy the Louisiana Territory for close to $15 million, about three cents an acre. No one could believe how easily and quickly the deal had come together. And without one drop of blood being shed!

When Thomas heard the news on July 3, he was as astonished at their success as he was delighted. Not only did it double America's land mass, it also removed a huge threat to the country's security. The purchase was beyond anything he could have expected. He knew he should seek a constitutional amendment in order to acquire foreign lands and expand the country's borders, but was afraid Napoleon might change his mind if he took the time to do so. He rushed the treaty through and didn't look back. He had a large Republican majority in Congress and they ratified it. Spain still occupied Florida and lands southwest of New Orleans, but he would deal with that problem when the possibility presented itself.

To cap off his elation, he bade farewell in a letter to Meriwether Lewis and William Clark, for they would set out soon to discover the "course and source of the Mississippi, and of the most convenient water communication for thence to the Pacific." Their enterprise had grown to forty explorers and scientists, and Thomas only wished he could join them on this fascinating expedition. How thrilling it would be to venture into unmapped territory! Thomas also knew he must deal more clearly with the Indians and wondered if the explorers would discover new tribes. The majority of their continent remained a vast and mysterious unknown. Of course, he would wait until he had more information when Lewis and Clark returned, but for now, doing nothing was best, he decided. He expected the Indians eventually would abandon their nomadic way of life and adopt agriculture and other American traditions.

1804

THOMAS WAS SHOCKED as never before. On Wednesday, July 11, 1804, Aaron Burr, the vice president of the United States, shot Alexander Hamilton, Secretary of the Treasury, in a duel in Weehawken, New Jersey. Burr shot him not once, but twice. Thomas knew the two men had long hated one another and had run head-to-head in a bruising governor's election in New York. However, the ultimate reason for the duel, reported in *The New York Evening Post,* a newspaper founded by Hamilton, was supposedly disparaging remarks Hamilton had made against Burr. The public responded to Hamilton's death with an outpouring of adulation for the fallen secretary, and Thomas decided the best response was to maintain silence in order to let emotions simmer down.

His astonishment only increased when he learned Burr had gotten away, fleeing westward, after being indicted for murder in New York and New Jersey. The vice president was nowhere to be found. Only a month later, Thomas heard Burr wanted to "effect a separation of the western part of the United States from that which lies between the Atlantic and the mountains, in its whole extent." What was this mad man doing? In any event, Thomas took the threat extremely seriously, for he could easily imagine Burr making a power grab.

He held his head in his hands. He had believed his union of states to be a country of laws. And now, two of its most respected statesmen had dueled. He distrusted Burr, but although disagreeing over policy with Hamilton, had regarded him as a reasonable, worthy opponent. Now George Clinton would become the new Republican candidate for vice president in the 1804 election in place of Aaron Burr. Clinton descended from an Irish immigrant family and Thomas welcomed him to the ticket. He believed — and he was right — that the popularity of the Louisiana Purchase would sweep them to victory in the presidential election.

As he often did when upset, Thomas sat down and wrote to his daughter:

Worn down here with pursuits in which I take no delight, surrounded by enemies & spies, catching & perverting every word which falls from my lips, or flows from my pen, & inventing, where facts fail them, I pant for that society, where all is peace & harmony, where we love & are beloved by every object we see. . . . I long to see the time approach when I can be returning to you, tho' it be for a short time only — these are the only times existence is of any value to me, continue then to love me my ever dear daughter, & to be assured, that to yourself, your sister & those dear to you every thing in my life is devoted, ambition has no hold upon me but through you — my personal affections would fix me forever with you.

Patsy

1804

PATSY BROUGHT ANOTHER healthy baby girl into the world in October 1803, and the Randolphs named her Mary Jefferson Randolph, after Patsy's sister Polly. They never had been able to get used to calling her Maria. Both Betty and Sally came to Edgehill to help at the birth. Patsy had been so angry at Sally during the entire Callender affair, she still couldn't bring herself to look at her father's mistress. She had purposefully avoided Sally for months, repulsed by what the papers implied about her father and his slave mistress. But she knew this strain could not go on between them; they lived under the same roof, and her father clearly cared about Sally. In deference to him, she must be more kind.

Now, when Sally placed the baby in her arms, Patsy looked up into the young woman's face. Sally must have been frightened and hurt by the calumny, she realized. Holding her newborn, Patsy thought of the pain Sally also must have endured upon losing her baby boy, shortly after her return from France. The newspapers had led people to believe the boy had lived and made it appear as though a black boy named Thomas Jefferson was capering around the Monticello plantation. What humiliation the poor girl had suffered — still suffered — and Patsy suddenly was ashamed at her recent rejections of her.

"Thank you, Sally," Patsy met the young woman's eyes for the first time in a long while. "How are Beverly and Harriet getting along?"

"Fine, thank you, Mrs. Randolph," Sally replied formally.

Oh, Dear! Should she ask her to still call her Patsy? Or Martha? It was all so complicated.

In February 1804, Polly, also pregnant, came to Edgehill to be close to her sister since both Tom and Jack were in Congress in Washington City. During their visit, her older son Francis Eppes was struck with what they feared were epileptic fits and Polly, already weak, cried with fear. Through the coming months Patsy attempted to comfort her sister, but grew more alarmed about Polly than Francis, who soon enough threw off his illness. In April, Polly began having early contractions, and appeared to have no strength. Patsy asked Isaac to ride quickly to Washington to tell Jack and Thomas to ride as fast as they could to come to them.

Polly tried to be brave but the premature birth was brutal. There was a great deal of blood, and Patsy fought back tears with dread and frustration. What more could she do? They could hear a cold wind banging at the windows, and she imagined evil spirits were lashing around the house. She must get a grip on herself! She didn't believe in evil spirits! She could and would muster herself to the task. Thank God, Betty and Sally were there to help, and the three women did all they could to calm the poor young mother. Polly's baby girl emerged pale and scrawny, and Polly was too feeble to hold her to her breast. Since Patsy had given birth only four months before, she quickly pressed the new babe to her own breast and tried to soothe the mewling, premature infant.

Polly constantly cried out for Jack, and they reassured her again and again he was on his way. When he finally arrived, he thundered and tripped up the stairs to kneel by his wife's bed. His presence definitely improved Polly's state. Watching them, Patsy could see that the two genuinely loved one another. The next day Polly kept asking to be taken to Monticello where she believed their Papa would come. It was clear she had a severe infection of the breast and was in great pain, but she would not hear that she was too weak to travel the two and a half miles. They finally gave in and built a litter for the slaves to carry her.

Patsy thought what a strange band of refugees they made — women, children, horses, slaves and Jack — walking the distance to the mansion atop the mountain. At least it wasn't too cold and their patient was well bundled up in the litter. Patsy's fatigue rendered her nearly delirious, and she fussed at the children to hurry along the path. No one dared complain, and somehow the group made it to Monticello. Sally, having gone ahead the day before, was the one who rushed toward them as they came into sight. One of the field slaves probably had spied them and heralded their arrival.

Sally took charge and hustled everyone to baths and bedrooms, and efficiently got Polly tucked away in a clean bed. "Your father is on his way," she assured the poor frail woman, now only twenty-five years old. It was clear to Patsy and Sally that Polly — even sick she asked to be called Maria — had childbed fever and might not survive. When she begged for more and more laudanum, their fears increased.

Thomas arrived only in time to take his younger daughter in his arms and rock her like a child. The scene appeared to be a replayed nightmare of their mother's death twenty-two years earlier. "Come now, Maria, you must be strong and . . ." Tears stifled further speech, and he passed the weak girl to her husband's arms. As before, there were Jeffersons and Hemingses around the deathbed, and Thomas stumbled away, wailing uncontrollably.

More than grief, Patsy first felt anger toward Polly's husband. He had refused to hear her warning and so had caused her sister's death. She wanted to beat him with her fists but instead she could only hand over the baby girl as he held out his arms for her, weeping dreadfully. Thomas retired to his study to write in the family register: MARY JEFFERSON, born Aug. 1, 1778, 1h.30 A.M. Died April 17, 1804, between 8 and 9 A.M.

Patsy and Sally insisted they should be the ones to prepare Polly for burial and took care in dressing her, as if she were going to another ball in Paris. The two young mothers guessed one another's needs and sweetly, quietly, made their sister and niece ready for Heaven. Patsy then went in search for her father and cleaved to him as she had when her mother died. When she left the room, she was sobbing so hard she was retching. She sought out her husband, who was waiting for her in their room, and as she collapsed on her bed, she felt great relief that her father had Sally to console him.

THOMAS

1805

NOT LONG AFTER THAT turbulent time, Thomas found himself dealing with untoward actions from his past that were revisiting with serious consequences. He reluctantly sat down at his desk to write a letter to the United States Secretary of the Navy, Robert Smith. He scratched the date — 1 July 1805 — and let the pen continue to hover over the paper. Why had he been such a young fool?

Long ago, he had made unwanted advances to a married woman before he had married Patty, and now her husband, Mr. Walker, having discovered the affair, wanted a duel with the president. Thomas knew he was guilty of the folly, but luckily, the young woman had refused his advances. What should he do?

Patsy, having gotten wind of the allegations, came to his rescue. She rushed to Monticello to beg him not to even consider the duel. It would be, by far, a worse folly than what he had done so many years ago. All he needed to do, she suggested, was to admit his guilt to Walker and assure him his wife was innocent. The fault completely belonged to him.

"Only last summer we witnessed the death of the secretary of the treasury due to such rash and foolhardy actions," she reminded him. She only agreed to leave when he promised to follow her advice.

He finally began to write:

> You will perceive that I plead guilty to one of their charges, that when young and single I offered love to a handsome lady. I acknowledge its incorrectness; it is the only truth among all their allegations against me.

263

There. It was done. But he must never let Sally find out about this embarrassing letter. She would be crushed that he would not/could not admit loving her to anyone else, but he had been forced to admit to fancying another man's wife.

Patsy

1806

PATSY HAD BEEN PHYSICALLY ill since Polly's death, and she knew it was worrying everyone. She couldn't seem to control her hysterical fits, and she would have difficulty breathing, then experience cramps, and an upset stomach. Polly's death felt as if it threatened her very existence. She always tried to be the person everyone depended on but now she was disintegrating before their eyes. She experienced tremendous relief when finally, she began to regain control and recover.

Having seen her father recently in such confusion and despair over the Walker scandal, Patsy gladly turned her worries from her own health to coming to her father's aid. She saw his enemies attempting to stir up disgrace, and so when he beseeched her to come to the President's House again, she gladly accepted the invitation. She wouldn't let the ancient history of that long-ago *faux pas* damage his presidency, and it would probably help her recovery as well, she thought. Therefore, when Congress convened on December 2, 1805, she decided to accompany Tom to Washington City.

Tom begged his wife not to come. "I need you to stay at Edgehill, Patsy. Without you on the plantation to direct and hold things together while I am away, I fear total ruin!" And indeed, he did. He still refused to sell Varina and remained dangerously in debt. The Hessian fly had devastated their wheat crop, and Tom's salary for serving in Congress was only $6 per day. One of the problems at Edgehill, like at Monticello, was that there simply wasn't enough land under cultivation with so much of the property being forest, and the arable land they owned just was not very fertile.

Patsy regarded her husband with sympathy but ignored his pleas.

Tom hadn't counted on Thomas's weapons to persuade Patsy to come and help him. Thomas offered to pay all expenses to bring the children, too, and to pay for their clothing and any new apparel she needed. Patsy admitted to herself that she wanted to go for her own wellbeing, not just to help her father. Oh, Fiddle! She obviously would need more special finery to sit at the President's table again. She wrote to her father, *I do not hesitate to declare if my other duties could possibly interfere with my devotion to you I should not feel a scruple in sacrificing them . . . It is truly the happiness of my life to think that I can dedicate the remainder of it to promote yours.*

As soon as Thomas heard this, he penned a letter to his good friend, Dolley Madison:

> *Thomas Jefferson presents his affectionate salutations to Mrs. Madison & thinks the care she showed him the other day (with earrings & a pin) will answer Mrs. Randolph's views. he begs leave to remind her of the request for such a comb exactly as she sent before. he solicits her on his own account, whenever she shall happen to be shopping to get a garment for him to present to Virginia, another to Anne, and one for Ellen & Cornelia. the two last may be of one piece. Mrs. Madison knows best how to please the respective parties than ThJ does. what she got for Anne on a former occasion was particularly gratifying to her. Mrs. Madison will be so good as to direct the shop managers to send their bills to ThJ for payment.*

Indeed, Dolley wrote she had purchased these items and awaited his daughter in Washington with choices of hats, dresses, and wigs. Patsy, who still missed having a mother, sometimes felt she should call the sweet woman Aunt Dolley, but since her father still addressed this good friend as Mrs. Madison, she did the same. All of this, of course, only made Tom feel more inadequate for not being able to dress his wife properly, and he sourly continued to argue against her going.

When Patsy was dressed for her first night as hostess in Washington again, she looked at herself in the mirror and laughed. No one had counted on her six-month pregnant figure, but for once, she gave thanks for her unusual height, which helped mask her advanced stage of pregnancy. She would just have to concentrate on her headwear and forget the sashes for now.

As with everything she did, Patsy set to her task of First Lady with attention to detail and perfection, and the President's House began to hum like Monticello. She knew the cooks in the kitchen from Virginia and had an easy way with them, greatly enjoying the planning of the evening meals for senators, representatives, and foreign diplomats. Seating arrangements, floral design, conversation, music — she felt at home with it all. The best part of everything, without a doubt, was watching her father in this milieu and his total command of every gathering.

Likewise, she happily watched him with her children and appreciated their seeing him at work. She wanted them to understand how much he was revered by the people and dignitaries alike. Baby Mary was just beginning to talk and was kept in the nursery, but the others would certainly benefit from this remarkable opportunity. Cornelia was six, Ellen, obviously the most intellectual of her brood, was already learning Latin from her grandfather, and Jeff, still with a tendency to be rambunctious, captivated everyone with his decency and good humor. She often gazed with wonder at her lovely Anne, now fourteen, which meant it would soon be time to introduce her to Virginia society.

As during her previous stay at the President's House, the days coasted by, and on January 17, 1806, Patsy, with her usual ease, gave birth to the first child ever born in the president's mansion. Tom was ecstatic to finally welcome a boy and to see his wife in such a happy state of mind. He agreed with her to name the little fellow after Thomas's friend and secretary of state — he would be called James Madison Randolph. The couple agreed Thomas should be the one to alert his friend of the name choice.

SALLY

1806

SALLY ERUPTED WITH ANGER and surprise when she heard Patsy and Tom had named their son James Madison Randolph. She and Thomas had selected that very name for *their* child the year before, and he was a beautiful gray-eyed lad with light hair. And now, the fancy Randolphs wanted to use it too. But she wanted her child to be the only one with that name! Of course, Thomas was in Washington City when Patsy gave birth in the President's House.

Mr. Madison had always been more than decent to her, and she had thought it would please Thomas to name a child after his friend. If it had been a girl, however, she would never have named her Dolley. She found Mrs. Madison snobbish and even rude at times. She wondered if perhaps it was because she was unhappy she hadn't been able to have children. Sally decided she could do what she wanted. If Tho-mah objected a great deal, she would have to change it. But when he returned to Monticello, he only laughed, and hugged her, telling her what beautiful children she had. Still, she thought it insensitive of Patsy to take the name too.

A neighbor had been murdered! The shock echoed through Virginia's valleys. The victim was Thomas's law teacher and friend, Judge George Wythe. A well mannered, mixed-race boy, whom the judge had educated, called Michael Brown, lived with the judge and his manumitted housekeeper, Lydia Broadnax. Sally and Lydia had been friends forever, and many in the community believed Michael was Lydia and Wythe's child. Of course, no one knew for sure, and because the Judge was such an upright individual, no one talked about it — like no one talked about Sally's offspring. Sally deeply understood Lydia's situation.

Wythe's jealous white nephew, George Sweeney, who also lived under the judge's roof, understanding that Wythe planned to leave equal benefits

268

from his estate in his will to him and Michael, poisoned the judge, Lydia, and Michael by putting arsenic in the morning coffee. Sweeney had been known for a long time as a bad seed in the town, gambling and passing forged checks. Brown and Wythe died after several weeks of terrible suffering, but Lydia survived, although blinded in one eye.

Sally was horrified and chastened. Her master was right. She must remain in the shadows. It felt like a double blow, because the murderer was acquitted. Of course, she reasoned, it was because black witnesses weren't permitted to testify. The court would not hear Lydia's testimony that she had seen Sweeney empty odd pharmacy wrapping papers in the trash the day of the murder. Why hadn't Thomas objected to this unjust law, which forbade Negroes to testify at a trial? Thomas seemed even more upset than she over the loss of his friend, and Betty was sickened, but she had a hard time forgiving this sin of omission on Thomas's part.

Sally's mother began to fail after the tragic incident, worrying her a great deal. When Betty handed the keys for Monticello to her and asked her to be sure everything ran according to the master's wishes, she found she didn't want the keys so much after all. She'd much rather have her mother with her. Who else would stand by her as Betty had? Betty held on throughout the year, sitting in front of her cabin, watching her many grandchildren and great grandchildren run around the plantation. Sally had always suspected Betty was particularly partial to her and Thomas's progeny. She wondered if she was especially proud of them, or did she simply love Sally the most of all her children? She couldn't imagine life without this strong woman.

THOMAS

1807

"AARON BURR MUST be a mad man!" Thomas confided to his secretary of state. "I never trusted him — he was always too ambitious. But now he seems out of his mind. Supposedly he is recruiting soldiers, gathering ammunition, and building boats. It's said he has plans to march on Washington, and take over the country. It is too bizarre to be believed."

"Yes, but the stories are true." Madison grimly replied. "We've received alarms now from an American general, by the name of Wilkinson, who formerly was a Burr man, but who now wants to save himself from this particular conspiracy."

In November, Jefferson issued a formal warning to law enforcement about Burr's treasonous plot to take over Spanish holdings and to attack New Orleans. He declared that his former vice president's "guilt is placed beyond question," and by late March 1807, Burr was finally apprehended and arrested. He would be tried for treason in Richmond in the courtroom of John Marshall, Jefferson's longtime foe. Marshall issued a subpoena to Jefferson to bear witness at the trial, but Jefferson responded by refusing, saying he would not be governed by the judicial branch. He agreed to send any necessary papers but would not appear in person. The executive branch, he believed, *could not be commanded to abandon superior duties and attend on them, at whatever distance. I am unwilling by any notice of the subpoena to set a precedent which might sanction a proceeding so preposterous.*

Thomas remembered a letter he had written to Abigail Adams several years ago during the election when he took the occasion to clarify his thoughts about judicial review. He pulled it out from his papers to read again:

Nothing in the Constitution has given them [the federal judges] a right to decide for the Executive, more than to the Executive, to decide for them . . . The opinion which gives to the judges the right to decide what laws are constitutional and what not, not only for themselves, in their own sphere of action, but for the Legislature and Executive also in their spheres, would make the Judiciary a despotic branch.

Yes, he was convinced that he was right about not giving too much power to the judiciary.

After a long and contentious trial, Burr was eventually acquitted, enraging Jefferson even more. He suspected the evidence in the treason charge was weak, but he interpreted the trial as a personal shot at him from his old foe Marshall. Throughout it all, Thomas endured periodic headaches. To make things worse, Tom Randolph made an embarrassing and unpleasant scene, claiming that Thomas loved his other son-in-law, Jack Eppes, more than him and moved out of the President's House, taking residence at Frost's and Quinn's Boarding House near the Capitol. Thomas begged Tom to cease his childish behavior and return, but the depressed, sullen young man would have nothing to do with his father-in-law for the moment. Thomas didn't address Patsy about it because he suspected there was nothing she could do.

Thomas longed for peaceful nights with Sally bathing his wrist before bed and sleeping with his arms around her. She made no demands on him, but his conscience often plagued him for not allowing her to come to Washington with him, for not recognizing their children, and for not admitting his love for her to outsiders, or even his family. But surely Sally understood it would be impossible.

Foreign affairs dominated the rest of the year's agenda. On Monday, June 22, a British ship, the *HMS Leopard* attacked the *USS Chesapeake*, demanding the right to search the American vessel for deserters. When the commanding officer of the Chesapeake refused, the *Leopard* opened fire and struck the *Chesapeake* twenty-two times. The *Chesapeake* finally managed to fire back, but not before three men had been killed and seventeen wounded. Britain refused to apologize and Jefferson determined it an act of war. He assembled his cabinet for an emergency meeting. A proclamation followed, banning armed British ships in U.S. waters, along with a call to arms for one hundred thousand militiamen.

War fever followed for weeks, but Jefferson let the fire simmer down and called the Congress for a special session in October. Surprising many, he left for the summer months at Monticello, but dutifully increased the mail service between his home and Washington City in order to keep apprised of events. He was eventually willing to go to war, but rightfully suspected the Congress would prefer to begin negotiations with a punishing embargo. An unpopular Embargo Act prohibiting the export of American goods was passed on December 22, 1807, and Jefferson decided time was on his side; he would wait out the embargo and allow the threat of war to pass.

There were many on both sides of the Atlantic who resented the cessation of trade, and some were economically ruined by this decision. Yet Jefferson held to his policy, knowing he could not possibly build up a navy to counteract the strength of the British Empire's navy in such a short time. Others asked when the Americans would build up a defense, if not now.

The arguments over the embargo stretched into the presidential election of 1808, becoming a referendum over Jefferson's policies in general. Demonstrating the country's continuing love for the president, James Madison, Thomas's closest ally, won handily, and Thomas, suffering from a massive toothache at the time of the inauguration, gladly handed over the reins of power to his friend. He was proud to have served as president, but at last, after two terms he could go home to Monticello — and Sally.

PATSY

1807-08

WHEN PATSY RETURNED to Albemarle after the exhilarating days in Washington City, she applied herself more seriously to her children's education. She intended to continue teaching them herself, primarily because of her superior education, which made her more qualified than anyone else she knew, but also because of cost. The numerous academies cropping up throughout Virginia and elsewhere were decent institutions but expensive, and she had access to Monticello's fine library, rich kitchens, and who better to teach the young girls manners and life's lessons than herself? Equally important, she loved doing it.

Patsy didn't shirk practical lessons for her children either. The plantation served as a laboratory for artisanal skills, and she called on various slaves to teach them how to sew, weave, make beer, dip candles, and grow crops. There wasn't enough time in a day to cram in all she wanted to share with them. She argued with her father over Jeff's direction; she saw him becoming a planter since he never had liked book-learning, but Thomas wouldn't give up on the boy's intellectual pursuits, insisting he should go to Philadelphia to study law.

For the last few years Betty had moved away from Mulberry Row where the workaday slaves lived, and because of her age, was more comfortably housed in a tiny cottage at some distance away on the plantation. Her little home measured only about 170 square feet, but it had a little window and looked upon a garden. After all, not much space was deemed necessary because most slaves spent most of their life in their master's house, or in the fields, and used their own abode only for sleeping. The plantation had been designed with several roundabouts, each delineating a neighborhood, and the one where Betty lived was a long walk from the Big House. Betty tended her garden and some chickens, and babysat for

Sally, who often would send her children there while she was working at the mansion.

During the summer Patsy realized she hadn't seen the good woman for some time and decided to walk over to the farther roundabout. Asking her daughters Cornelia and Genny to accompany her, they tried to find some rare shade for their stroll. They found Betty sitting outside, dozing in the hot sun. Betty had always been in such a flurry of activity, it was strange to see her so immobile. How much this family owed to this lady! Patsy thought, gazing fondly at Sally's mother. She touched Betty's hand.

"Ah, Miss Patsy," she smiled. "What are you and your girls doing in these parts?"

"We just came over to visit you," she said. "I thought you might like to see how big my children are getting."

"I do see. They're fine looking girls, too."

It was so awkward. Patsy found it hard to mention Sally's children sired by her own father, but made herself do it. "And your grandchildren, too, are getting big and strong. I believe Beverly and Harriet are about the same age as these two." She nodded toward her girls.

"Yes Ma'am."

Patsy failed to mention the two babies recently born, hers and Sally's, and both named James Madison. Her throat just closed up. They chatted a bit more about Betty's extended family, shaking their heads over the teenagers and drying their eyes about James. She took Betty's hand again and squeezed it. What a tragic shock his death still was.

They talked a bit about Betty's garden and then Patsy said, "We miss seeing you up at the house, Betty. Get one of the boys to bring you up for a visit sometime soon."

"I'll do that." Betty smiled. "But the 'thritis makes moving around more difficult nowadays."

"I'm sure it does," Patsy said, leaning down to give the old lady a gentle hug. "Girls, say goodbye to Betty."

Cornelia and Genny managed little bobs, and the trio turned for their return walk. Patsy's heart ached when she left. Betty had been by her mother's side when she died and helped deliver most of her own children. Betty had nursed her in sickness and celebrated with the family in the good times. She was a member of her family. As was Sally. She must accept it. Slavery created such hypocrisy, lies, and unfairness, it made her squirm.

Betty died only a month later, in August.[5] Patsy regarded Sally standing by the grave, holding the hands of her fair, light-eyed children and felt a suffocating mix of affection and consternation. She went over and embraced Sally, "She was a wonderful lady. We'll all miss her," she said.

Sally held her arms across her ribs, as though to hold in her emotions. But her tears broke their bounds, and she pressed her handkerchief to her face. "Yes, we will," she whispered. Patsy let her go, wishing she could do more, but knew they both had to find their own way to deal with the sadness.

1808

At the beginning of the year it was clear to Patsy she was with child yet again, and it was also evident that Sally was expecting too. It appeared they would probably give birth around the same time, and she couldn't help but count back to when her father had last been at Monticello. She wanted to deny the evidence staring in her face, but she could not. She only hoped the rest of the world didn't see it as clearly as she did.

It was to be a year of family milestones as Patsy and Tom's daughter Anne, age seventeen, married Charles Lewis Bankhead at Monticello, and Patsy gave birth at Edgehill to her ninth child. She laughed and compared herself to the successful nailery at Monticello. They turned out nails at a rapid rate and she, just as successfully, turned out babies at a remarkable pace.

She and Tom decided to name the newcomer Benjamin Franklin after their father's good friend and the country's first secretary of state. Everyone talked about him as one of the finest minds who ever lived, and Patsy hoped it wouldn't be too much of a burden for their little tyke to carry.

---

5 There is a slave cemetery at Monticello, but the graves are unmarked. It is not known where Betty Hemings is buried.

SALLY

1808

IN MAY, ONLY DAYS AFTER Patsy's lying-in, Sally gave birth to Thomas Eston Hemings. The baby was named after Thomas's brother-in-law, who had married his sister Jane. "Oh, he looks like Thomas!" Sally exclaimed upon seeing her baby for the first time, and indeed, the pale skin and light reddish hair mirrored his father's. Betty had died nine months earlier and for the first time, wasn't present to help with the birth. Thomas wasn't at Monticello either, and it made Sally acknowledge once again how much she had depended on her mother to be her helpmate. Betty's absence created a painful vacuum, and she wept over and over, missing her with a sharp pain. Her sister Critta had come to help with the birth.

Patsy was still at Edgehill recuperating from bringing Benjamin Franklin Randolph into the world, but she was dutiful in sending over some cake and ale with a kind note as a celebratory gift. Sally appreciated the gesture and suspected it had been sent because Patsy missed Betty too and genuinely shared her sorrow.

Sally thought back to the beginning of the year when, on January 1, the African slave trade had been abolished. There were said to be still over 4 million slaves in the South, but some southern congressmen finally had joined the North in the effort to abolish the despicable practice. This historic effort had happened under Thomas's watch, and she was grateful. Eston was the first of their children to be born after that momentous act. She doubted whether it would make any difference in her life, but she prayed it would sway attitudes in the country and improve the future for her children.

She put the baby to her breast and knew that her mother, watching from Heaven, would be happy. She would nurse this child herself, as Betty always wished. Beverly came and stood by her side, and she put her arm around his small waist. He was growing so fast — almost ten now.

"Mama," he asked, "who is my daddy?"

Oh my Lord! Why shouldn't the boy know? Everyone else on the plantation did, but no one admitted it. Perhaps this new baby who resembled Thomas had prompted the question.

"I think you're old enough now to know the truth, but you have to promise your mama you will never tell a soul. It is to be our special secret."

"Okay. But why can't I tell?"

"Because some people don't want to know," she said. "Your daddy is Thomas Jefferson."

He stared open-mouthed at her. He had known she went to the Big House some nights to sleep, when one of the older slave girls came and slept with him and the other children. "Does the master know he's my daddy?"

"Yes, dear boy, he does. But you're not to talk to him about it." The poor child looked mystified. "Now, I have to get up soon and go to the Big House. She looked down at the keys to Monticello at her waist. Her mother had given them to her only a few years ago, and she laughed at her desire to wrest them from her earlier. All it really meant was more work and responsibility. But when Patsy was away, at Edgehill, she really could feel like she was the mistress of Monticello. After all, it had been her home for most of her life.

When would she tell Beverly that he and his siblings would be freed? It was hard not to do it now, but she knew she couldn't trust the children not to talk. She probably shouldn't have told him who his father was, but she just couldn't keep it in any longer.

MONTICELLO

GENTLEMAN FARMER

1809-1824

Nothing is more certainly written in the book of fate, than that these people are to be free; nor is it less certain that the two races, equally free, cannot live in the same government. Nature, habit, opinion have drawn indelible lines of distinction between them.

Autobiography of Thomas Jefferson, 1821 until death 1826,
Capricorn Books, NY, 1959. This quote is on one panel
of the Jefferson Monument

THOMAS

1809

IT WAS TIME TO LEAVE Washington City. So, this would be the end of his career in public service! Now 66 years old, he felt the age — in his walking and memory acuity. His hips ached every morning on rising. But when he thought of Monticello and his daughters and his grandchildren, he still felt eager for life. In a reflective mood, he wrote his friend, Pierre du Pont, on March 2, 1809:

> *Nature intended me for the tranquil pursuits of science by rendering them my supreme delight. But the enormities of the times in which I have lived have forced me to take a part in resisting them, and to commit myself on the boisterous ocean of political passions . . . I leave everything in the hands of men so able to take care of them, that if we are destined to meet misfortunes, it will be because no human wisdom could avert them.*

In addition to slavery, the primary conundrum he left unattended upon his departure was war versus embargo, a problem ever since the attack on the *Chesapeake*. He couldn't stop turning the issue over in his mind. But he must now walk away from it. He remained in the capital to watch the inauguration of James Madison two days later, glad to witness his friend assume the office of president. He wrote to Patsy, suggesting that his sister Anna Jefferson Marks come and act as mistress of Monticello upon his return, but Patsy heartily rebuffed the idea, saying the servants had no respect for Anna and that she was a terrible manager. Patsy added, *I shall devote myself to it and with feeling, which I never could have in my own affairs, and with what tenderness of affection we will wait upon*

281

and cherish you My Dearest Father. He smiled. He should have known she would let no one else be mistress of his mansion. Including Sally. And that could be a problem.

He looked forward to his bed, snugged between his study with his books nearby and a cozy chamber with a fireplace. How had he amassed so many volumes? He estimated there must be about 7,000 in many languages on his shelves. And he had his garden seeds in vials properly organized and labeled in the cabinets of his room.

He carefully brought his mockingbirds back with him from Washington City in order that their songs soothe his spirit. Indeed, shortly after his arrival on Wednesday, March 15, he noticed that his torturous, tedious headaches began to wane. He could easily stay busy, he thought, in this eleven-thousand-square-foot house, with thirty-three rooms and special spots chosen for all of his art and artifacts, collected throughout his life. He saw his collection as "memorials of those worthies whose remembrance I feel a pride and comfort in consecrating there." To others wandering through the house, it sometimes looked like too much clutter, but he would argue that each piece had its value. He carefully placed his wife's walnut dressing table in his bedchamber.

Thomas immediately threw himself into plans for his gardens. His vision was that of an ornamental farm — a kind of combination working plantation and fanciful park. He had ideas for the orchards, the flower gardens, the vegetable gardens, and especially for a vineyard. For the northeast plot, he decided to plant several European grape varieties grafted onto hardy, pest-resistant, native rootstock. He then designed an espaliered structure to accommodate the growing vines. He generally preferred French wines but in the southwest vineyard, he planted a sangiovese grape, the principal ingredient of Chianti. After all of these varieties had been planted by his slaves, according to his detailed directions, he eagerly awaited his crops.

Indeed, all this attention to his land forced him to face the issue of labor. Slavery was a moral burden, and he could not ignore it. But there seemed no way to avoid it if he were to remain solvent. One of the shocking facts was that about half of his slave force consisted of children under the age of fourteen and twenty out of the 200 were over fifty years old, essentially too old to perform heavy agricultural duties. Tobacco and cotton required rigorous labor, and the south was tethered to these crops for subsistence. All he could see to do was to make the life of his "black family" as comfortable as possible. In a letter to a friend he revealed how many facets of the issue were constantly on his mind.

Feb. 25, 1809: Letter to the Abbé Henri Gregoire:

Be assured that no person living wishes more sincerely than I do, to see a complete refutation of the doubts I have myself entertained and expressed on the grade of understanding allotted to them (blacks) by nature, and to find that in this respect they are on a par with ourselves. My doubts were the result of personal observation on the limited sphere of my own State, where the opportunities for the development of their genius were not favorable, and those of exercising it still less so. I expressed them therefore with great hesitation; but whatever be their degree of talent it is no measure of their rights . . . On this subject they are gaining daily in the opinions of nations, and hopeful advances are making towards their re-establishment on an equal footing with the other colors of the human family.

PATSY

1809-1810

WHEN HER FATHER RETURNED to Monticello, Patsy noticed how white his hair had become. But his strength and enthusiasm — and especially his energy when playing with the grandchildren — allayed any fears she had about his advancing age. One forgot the passing of the years when his eyes flashed with excitement and his intelligence shone as brightly as a torch.

She knew, however, that some Virginians harbored anger toward him. He had his enemies. The trade embargo enacted by Thomas's administration had hurt Patsy and Tom's already unstable finances considerably because it had meant losing the European market. They were not the only ones — some of Tom's siblings had been forced to sell land and turn to running boarding houses in order to make a living. Patsy and Tom finally had tried to sell Varina, but in the present economic climate, they couldn't find a buyer. Reluctantly, they decided to let go of some Bedford county land and pocketed $8,400 for the sale. This sum helped with their debts but would not cover continuing expenses.

Patsy proudly observed Tom's success with his scientific farming techniques. Many of their neighbors were copying his discovery that planting crops horizontally instead of straight downhill reduced erosion, and he invented a special plow to create the furrows in this manner. They had a couple of good years, but Patsy clearly understood they needed to find other means of raising cash. They both quailed at the idea of selling slaves and steered clear of that resource. Separating families was an anathema.

Tom began a cloth-making effort at Edgehill, and Patsy, who had learned spinning as a child from her mother, managed the effort. The invention of the spinning jenny in 1764 in England had transformed the speed of making cloth, and Patsy applied herself to the task of supplying material for the entire population at Edgehill and Monticello.

When she found herself pregnant again early in the year, she begged Tom to allow her to spend most of her time at Monticello. Tom would still need to farm Edgehill, but it would be easier on the whole family, she argued, to operate from Monticello, where she could care for her father, manage a larger spinning operation, and care for the children — all in one place. It would also be a cheaper way to feed the entire family (she knew Thomas had expanded the vegetable gardens at Monticello, which would help feed her family, but that project primarily fed the crowds coming to the plantation to see their former and beloved president), but she dared not say this to her sensitive husband. Begrudgingly, Tom agreed, but not without commenting that she always chose her father over him.

"That's not true, Tom. I'm just looking out for all of us."

Neither of them mentioned another reason it was a good idea. It would protect her father and the family from further scandal. If he were left alone with Sally as his managing housekeeper, tongues would fly.

She also didn't admit she wished Tom would stay away from her bedroom for a while. She always welcomed his lovemaking — that was the backbone of their marriage, but she ardently hoped this would be her last baby. She nursed each one as long as possible, believing it would inhibit conception, but smiled to herself — she was as fertile as the rabbits on her lawn. She thought of poor Dolley Madison, who had been unable to conceive, and told herself not to complain. Her sturdy health and her healthy children were infinite blessings!

In July, Margaret Bayard Smith and her husband were among the visitors at Monticello, and Patsy was glad for the sympathetic company. Mrs. Smith praised her children and said of her father, "His life is the best refutation of the calumnies that have been heaped upon him and it seems impossible, for any one personally to know him and remain his enemy." It heartened Patsy greatly to hear this praise for the man she loved and admired more than any other.

As time went on, Patsy realized it would be better for both her and Sally if Sally had a separate place to work away from the mansion. Sally had become a fine seamstress from her time in France and now was a great spinner as well. Patsy asked her father if they couldn't co-opt a small building on the plantation for the spinning operation and put Sally in charge of it. It would give her a private office in a sense, and Thomas thought it a fine idea. Patsy didn't mention that it would also keep Sally from meddling in the running of the Big House, but she suspected he guessed that was part of her motive.

Meriwether Lewis Randolph was born in January of the New Year, and more exhausted by the birth than usual, Patsy nestled among the pillows, allowing the servants to help her. Comfortable and happy, she was especially glad when her father came to admire his new grandson.

Anne and her new husband, Charles Bankhead moved in as well. Anne loved plants and planned to help her father with his gardening endeavors. It would be wonderful to have the entire family together at long last!

SALLY

1809

IN MARCH, WHEN THOMAS came home after Madison's inauguration, it was snowing. But that didn't stop everyone from flying down the mountain to meet the master — family and slaves as one. They all loved him, but no one as much as she. Sally had been pushing the staff to work hard to ready the house, inside and outside. How she missed her mother in these tasks! The gardeners feverishly planted new trees — mostly peach and pecan; hogs were slaughtered to make sausage, and bacon, and of course, candles and soap were made from the hog fat; floors were polished, and the silver shone. She was determined the house would be perfect for this special homecoming. Surely, he would not be returning to government again.

Patsy and Tom and all their children were there to welcome him too, but Sally noticed he picked up their new baby, Eston, who was crawling toward him, first among all the children. She thought she would burst with pride and happiness and felt his smile was especially for her. But she knew they must be careful about spending time together — with so much of the family now living at Monticello.

At the usual hour of 4:00 pm, the family sat down in the dining room for a festive homecoming dinner. How she longed to sit down with them. Would she ever be invited to do so? The children all played together. Why would it be so difficult to welcome her at their table? She helped today with the service because it was a special meal, and she had even helped a bit in the kitchen, employing some of the skills James had taught her. They offered *carré* of lamb, which Thomas especially liked, and promised rabbit with mustard sauce for tomorrow. Everyone stayed at table for after-dinner conversation as was Thomas's custom and delight.

Even though he was extremely tired from the trip, he asked for a glass of sauterne so he could savor these homecoming moments with those he loved most. She would have him to herself tonight, but a sharp anger burned in her heart. She especially worried more these days about Beverly, whom she saw watching his father and his white grandchildren closely. She guessed he was wondering why he wasn't treated the same as Patsy's offspring.

THOMAS

1809-1812

THOMAS COULDN'T GET ENOUGH of riding around his property atop Caractacus. He had named his Arabian steed after a first century British tribesman, who had resisted a Roman invasion. A Roman historian reported that after being captured and imprisoned, the brave man made such a stirring speech to the Roman senate that he was pardoned and allowed to live the rest of his life as a free man in Rome. When Caractacus was led out from the stable, Thomas would run a white cambric handkerchief across the horse's shoulders. If there were any dust on it, back the animal would go to the stables. But that rarely happened because his stable boys were well trained and diligent.

For riding, Thomas liked to don a pair of overalls over his cotton breeches, which buttoned at the knee, and light woolen knee hose. Because of his fair skin, he often wore a wide-brimmed hat to ward off the strong Virginia sun. What better place on earth could there be than Monticello? He wrote to his friend Benjamin Rush, *From breakfast, or noon at latest, to dinner, I am mostly on horseback, attending to my farms or other concerns, which I find healthful to my body, mind, and affairs.* Indeed, riding made him feel closer to his land. With the horses' hooves planted solidly beneath him and his head now the height of the tree branches, he experienced a mystical tie with nature as the animal moved beneath him, and the aromatic vegetation of the forest delighted his senses. Each season offered different perfumes to distinguish and enjoy.

He managed to follow scientific and educational news, even receiving biological specimens — for instance, he laughed with pleasure when Madison sent the skin of a bighorn sheep from the Rocky Mountains to Monticello. There weren't enough hours in the day for him to follow all of his interests, fueled by his voracious curiosity. But he realized what made him smile most often was the sound of the children's laughter as they ran around on the great lawn outside his study. Sometimes he witnessed Beverly, now eleven, or Madison, just four, joining the fracas, just as he and Jupiter had played together.

He was afraid to show as much fondness for Sally's children as for his white grandchildren. He found them sometimes watching him for signs of affection, and yet he tried to keep them at some remove. It would cause too much talk and criticism among his peers if he openly acknowledged them as equals. He knew it hurt Sally, but he didn't feel he had a choice in the matter. The cruel death of Judge Wythe attested to the culture toward slaves and miscegenation in Virginia. Occasionally, he would notice visitors realize, with shock, the resemblance to their host when they looked upon a Hemings child. But no one spoke of it. For their safety, he rationalized, he must keep them separate.

In October 1809, word of Meriweather Lewis's suicide in Tennessee reached him, and he could not fathom it. His former secretary had been exhibiting odd behavior for a while but to shoot himself, first through the head and then the heart, was an unimaginable horror. They had learned he had been heartbroken when Aaron Burr's daughter Theodosia rejected him and married Joseph Alston. He heard Lewis had taken his life at an inn and the innkeeper's wife had heard the shots. How fragile human life could be, Thomas mused. But having observed Tom Randolph's deep melancholia for so many years, he recognized the frighteningly thin line between sanity and madness.

He was gladdened in 1811 when their common friend Benjamin Rush put him in touch once again with John Adams. Brutal politics had eroded the friendship, but both welcomed the opportunity to correspond. When Thomas heard through Rush that Adams had said, "I always loved Jefferson and still love him," Thomas responded: "I only needed this knowledge to revive towards him all the affections of the most cordial moments of our lives."

Since his departure from government, Thomas had carefully watched the pressure of the British on American shipping and trade. He hoped the two countries could avoid war, but now it seemed to be pressing at their backs. Madison forewarned Thomas he was going to put America's independence to the test, and on November 5, 1811, President Madison sent a preparation of war message to Congress. They could not wait any longer to secure their borders, and what would become known as the War of 1812 began.

Thomas admitted relief that Madison was controlling the tiller instead of himself. He was content managing his small ship here in Virginia. Diligently, he sat down to write a note to Cornelia about some of his ideas for conducting oneself throughout life. He wanted his children and grandchildren to have proper guidance and strict tenets to uphold:

Thomas Jefferson to Cornelia J. Randolph: *"a dozen Canons of conduct in life"*

1. *never put off to tomorrow what you can do to-day.*
2. *never trouble another with what you can do yourself*
3. *never spend your money before you have it*
4. *never buy a thing you do not want, because it is cheap, it will be dear to you.*
5. *take care of your cents: Dollars will take care of themselves!*
6. *pride costs us more than hunger, thirst and cold.*
7. *we never repent of having eaten too little.*
8. *nothing is troublesome that one does willingly.*
9. *how much pain have cost us the evils which have never happened*
10. *take things always by their smooth handle.*
11. *think as you please, & so let others, & you will have no disputes.*
12. *when angry, count 10 before you speak; if very angry, 100.*

PATSY

1810-1814

PATSY WATCHED AS HER FATHER showered the grandchildren with whatever their hearts desired. She warned him he would spoil them, but he couldn't be stopped. He loved to buy gifts for everyone to show them his love. What alarmed her even more was the extravagance when she knew the coffers were bare. Both the Randolphs and Thomas were seriously in arrears.

She enjoyed her routine now at Monticello, whether it was just for their family of twelve, which included her eldest daughter, Anne, and her husband Charles, or quite often, many guests in addition. One night she counted fifty additional people eating and sleeping under Monticello's roof. Breakfast was always at 8:00 am and then Thomas retired to his study. Afterward, she and the children would begin their daily study sessions in the small, square, south room. She had chosen blue for the wall color of this haven and furnished it with several pieces made in the plantation joinery, including a sewing table she loved, constructed by John Hemings. She requested the fireplace be altered to burn wood instead of coal to help with the air quality for the children during their studies. She expected to interrupt her activities five or six times a day to confer with Edmund Bacon, the overseer, who was the general on the front lines of the plantation operation. When Bacon couldn't find Thomas, he came to her.

Patsy trusted Bacon implicitly. Bacon's father and Thomas Jefferson had been raised together and had attended the same school during their youth. Bacon's older brother William had been in charge of Monticello during the four years Jefferson was overseas as Minister to France. When William let it be known he was no longer interested in the job, Jefferson gladly offered the overseer's job to his son Edmund, so keeping it all in the family.

Patsy took her job as Mistress of Monticello very seriously. She wrote in her diary:

> *The government of a family bears a Lilliputian resemblance to the government of a nation. The contents of the treasury must be known and great care taken to keep the expenditures from being equal to the receipts. . . . Let everything be done at the proper time, keep everything in its proper place and put everything to its proper use. . . . Early rising is also essential to the good government of a family. A late breakfast deranges the whole business of the day and throws a portion of it on the next which opens the door for confusion to enter.*

Everything appeared serene to the outsider, but a constant hum of worry about Tom echoed in her mind. The fact he was contributing practically nothing for the family's upkeep made him resentful and antagonistic. She sensed her husband was happiest when the family returned to Edgehill at harvest time and he was master of his world. He regularly rebelled against his father-in-law's authority at Monticello, and he often vociferously blamed Patsy for preferring Thomas to him. "You even chose names for our children after his friends, and not mine," he complained on one occasion.

"But you agreed, Tom. Why did you not complain at the time?"

"Because I wanted to please you," he answered honestly. Patsy understood and was grateful for his kind heart, but she couldn't abide his occasional belligerence. After suffering a miscarriage at four months in 1811, she felt poorly for much of the year. She was finding it harder and harder to assume her usual pleasant personality and demeanor.

Patsy recognized it was crazy to welcome a war, but the War of 1812 felt like the perfect chance for Tom to prove himself. Tom agreed with Thomas that they needed to stop Britain's preying on American shipping, and he proudly sought and succeeded in retaining the rank of militia colonel in Albemarle County. Despite no previous military experience, in March 1813 President Madison nominated Tom for a military commission and confirmed his command of the Twentieth Regiment of Infantry. Many of the officers came from upper society but had not served since the Revolutionary War. Like Tom, they were older and rusty in military affairs.

Patsy ultimately begged her husband to stay at home, especially when she realized she was pregnant again, but he clearly wanted to be away from the daily grind and be recognized as a military hero. He drew up a will before his departure, recommending that Patsy try to sell Varina if need be and left the disposition of his property in her able and trusted hands, "to distribute among her children and certain for her own use as she many think fit after paying all my debts."

Tom's imminent departure reminded the couple of their mutual regard and friendship, and Tom promised her he "would do anything rather than continue to live separately from [you] for any length of time" after returning from the war. When he finally left in August, he led his troops to Sackets Harbor on Lake Ontario. The plan was to invade British Canada and fight the British on several fronts. Tom wrote home his regiment had aided in the seizure of Fort Matilda, but the U.S. forces had been defeated in a more important battle.

There was nothing to do but retreat to a winter encampment, where he quickly became frustrated. Becoming impatient, Tom asked for and secured permission for a leave, arriving home just in time for the birth of another daughter, Septimia Anne Randolph, on January 3, 1814. Patsy failed to bounce back as she usually did after a birth and was happy to have Tom at home to help her. Her father fussed over her as well, and she allowed herself a little time to enjoy the comfort her family offered. But it would be a short respite.

SALLY

1812

THOMAS HAD PROMISED HER there would never be a white mistress of Monticello, but he had broken that promise. When she finally found the courage to speak to him about it, he looked amazed. "But Sally, she isn't a white mistress! She's my own daughter — and your niece, I might add."

She knew he would never admit he had betrayed her. But she was glad she'd said it. She still held the keys, but Patsy ran the show. She did feel a bit sorry for the mistress because she labored almost as much as Sally did. Thomas always allowed any guest to stay over night, and Sally, Patsy, and the staff, at enormous cost, had to cook and clean until they were bone tired. Why did he not stop this extraordinary hospitality? Relations, artists, biographers, friends, foreigners — they all had excuses to come and must be made to feel welcome at Monticello. Especially in the summer.

Sally's feelings about Patsy were a strange a blend of admiration and resentment. She raised an eyebrow when Patsy called all of them "family," but was glad she distinguished the Hemingses as servants instead of slaves. Patsy still insisted on supervising the spinning and acted as counsel to anyone who had a problem, white or black. And she did it well. But Sally always hoped her mistress would turn the spinning completely over to her and allow her to be "official counsel" sometimes. Wasn't she an equally good mother and spinner?

Beverly was already thirteen and a half. He was tall and bony like his father, and she laughed because they walked so much alike; it looked as though Beverly were trying to mimic his dad. He had become a good rider too, and Thomas sometimes allowed Beverly to ride with him. Thomas's hair was now almost all white, but Beverly's was a dark blond with reddish highlights. Sally rejoiced when they rode together, and she suspected Beverly pestered him for knowledge about the plantation. She knew this because Thomas remarked that her son asked very astute questions.

"Might he go to the school with the Randolph boys, in Charlottesville?" she dared to ask.

"No, Sally. That would not be a good idea." Probably because Beverly looked too much like Thomas and there would be unwelcome talk. When he saw her disappointment, he continued, "But perhaps I can work out for him to be tutored after school by one of the instructors there."

Thomas proved good on his word and soon engineered private study for Beverly, as well as allowing him access to his library. But when Sally pressed him for their other children to learn biology, literature, and science, he demurred. It wasn't fair, she raged inside. He said he loved her, but she was still a slave, and their children were not yet free. Her children profited somewhat from his being their father, but there was much they had to endure because of it also. It seemed to her he could easily do more to help smooth it over. He gave violin lessons to Madison (whom she called Maddy; at only seven-years-old he had picked up his daddy's violin and asked to play) and Eston asked for them now too. But he wouldn't agree to send them to school. When they saw how his white children were educated, she knew it made them feel inferior.

To be honest, she thought Patsy should do more for her children also. Admittedly, the poor woman had twelve children and worried constantly about her father and husband. Maybe she didn't have any more room in her heart to worry about the Hemingses too.

Sally and her children sometimes lived under one of the terraces at the Big House, instead of in one of the cabins on Mulberry Row. Still, it made Sally's blood boil, the way they were all stacked up upon one another like logs, cramped in one room. At least it wasn't as hot in summer or as frigid in winter as it was out in the cabins.

Thomas

1814-1818

THOMAS FOLLOWED THE WAR carefully and wrote to his friend Thomas Cooper on September 10, 1814, desirous of furthering their discussion of a comparison of conditions in Britain and the United States. He clearly was mulling over the subject of oppression in a large sense and opined,

> *I am not advocating slavery. I am not justifying the wrongs we have committed on a foreign people, by the example of another nation committing equal wrongs on their own subjects. On the contrary there is nothing I would not sacrifice to a practicable plan of abolishing every vestige of this moral and political depravity.*

But as yet, he couldn't figure out how to emancipate all the slaves unless all the slave owners democratically agreed to do so. Instead, he was watching the *hideous blot* become more entrenched. Indeed, he had written to Edward Coles a month earlier expressing his frustration over how to deal with ending slavery. He admitted he believed the blacks to be racially inferior in general and "as incapable as children." Because they were understandably resentful of their owners, he believed their removal from the United States would be necessary for everyone's safety if they were all to be emancipated. He also truly feared for the viability of the country if the South were to lose its economic clout through the loss of its slaves.

The beginning of the War of 1812 had not been encouraging for the United States. Had he not continuously warned everyone of the perfidy of England? The British torched Washington City, and it was the indefatigable Dolley Madison who salvaged many documents, including a portrait of George Washington by Gilbert Stuart. She removed it from its frame and placed it in the hands of two New Yorkers to safeguard. The energetic Dolley then managed to flee from the President's House with her treasures just before the enemy's arrival.

The battle at Baltimore on September 13, 1814, was the fight that began to turn the tide, and the sight of the harbor and the "bombs bursting in air," inspired Francis Scott Key to write the poem that would become the national anthem. Key was a lawyer and amateur poet, who had helped negotiate the release of American prisoners aboard a British ship immediately before the war in Baltimore. The Treaty of Ghent finally brought peace between Britain and America in 1815, and Thomas felt that one of his long-sought goals had finally been secured. At last, America's shores were free of the overreaching British.

His anger over the burning of the government library of 3,000 books in Washington City during the war prompted him to sell his personal library to begin a new Library of Congress. He wasn't quite ready to part with his precious books, but he was content to know they would serve knowledge for the future. The sale would also settle some of his debts. He asked Beverly to help him start packing up the books and gave his son the ones he wanted. "Don't tell anyone else though, my boy," he said. Beverly noted that he hadn't said "my son."

He told Beverly the President's House had finally been repaired from the destruction of the War of 1812. The charred exterior walls were painted such a bright white, folks started calling it The White House. Beverly wondered if that meant it was only for white people but was afraid to ask.

Thomas considered himself the *pater familias* of his entire brood — white and black. He couldn't help but watch over everyone, and more and more, he feared for his granddaughter Anne's wellbeing. Her husband Charles Bankhead could be vicious; he was a ne'er-do-well, an even worse drunkard than Tom, and had assaulted Anne on numerous occasions. Anne needed to call the overseer Bacon on occasion to come to her aid, and Bacon had the wherewithal and strength on occasion to refuse Bankhead access to the liquor cabinet. Bankhead's father was a physician, and Thomas pleaded with him to treat his son, but so far, if the doctor did anything, it wasn't working.

Thomas refused to admit his hearing was failing somewhat, and he always needed spectacles to read. Sally was usually at hand to give him his glasses. But in general, he ploughed through his days like a younger man.

Rust-colored, bushy brows made his face more forbidding than when he was younger, but the weatherworn skin and alert eyes revealed an intense life within.

It was always with shock that he learned of the passing of a friend — unable to face the fact that time was stealing life from his contemporaries. Abigail Adams died in early 1818 and he wrote to his friend John Adams with true affection:

> . . . *mingling sincerely my tears with yours, it is of some comfort to us both that the term is not very distant, at which we are to deposit in the same cerement, our sorrows and suffering bodies, and to ascend in essence to an ecstatic meeting with the friends we have loved and lost, and whom we shall still love and never lose again.*

PATSY

1814-1818

IT HAD BEEN DREADFUL to see her husband set out for battle, but it was unbearable when twenty-two-year-old Jeff also enlisted with the county's militia to defend Virginia. Jeff told her not to worry — after all, his grandfather had conditioned him at a young age to withstand hardship. Indeed, at age twelve he had walked four miles alone to hunt turkeys in a dense pine forest. About the same age, he had once walked through an icy river, then made it home, going barefoot through the snow for seven miles, arriving cheery and full of his adventure.

Shortly after the British had burned Washington, military activity in the Chesapeake area threatened Richmond, and more Virginians rushed to defend their state. Terrified of losing her son, Patsy had trouble retaining her equanimity. Her father had just turned seventy, and the dark thrum of death haunted her day and night. Although she considered herself an Episcopalian and had taught her children some of the scriptures, she never had turned to ritual except for weddings and funerals. Now, the current stress and anxiety tempted her to seek the balm of faith, though she declared the evangelical tide sweeping through the Virginia populace to be dangerous.

She also became more patriotic, doing all she could to support the soldiers and the war. She even promoted a war effort for weaving and spinning at their local looms. Feeling emotionally spent, she primarily dedicated herself to her immediate family — to her children's coming out in society and helping Tom to repay their debts. Tom had been forced to take out another loan from the Richmond branch of the Bank of the United States, knowing full well he would be unable to pay it back. But what else could they do? The Jefferson name would see them through to better times, she prayed.

Despite the war, Patsy and Tom decided they would bring Ellen out into Richmond society, accompanied primarily by her aunt Randolph. Ellen was eighteen and they didn't want her to be passed over because of the momentary single-minded concentration on military issues. Thomas, always the proud grandfather, purchased her a new dress, and Ellen apologized by letter for buying other fancies she claimed to need for her debut. Patsy thanked her father, at the same time being angered by his inconsistencies. He talked about being careful with money, but continued to spend lavishly on luxuries. How could he overlook his own hypocritical behavior, she often wondered?

Even with the expense and effort, Ellen failed to meet a serious suitor, but Patsy, when pestered by her aunts and in-laws, claimed not to be particularly worried or saddened by this outcome. She was convinced Ellen would know what was right for herself.

Patsy tried to focus on the one encouraging bright spot during this gloomy period — the success Jeff was having as a businessman and plantation manager upon his return from the war. His disappointing attempts in academia had frustrated his grandfather, but Patsy and Tom fully supported Jeff's desire to take charge of the gristmill at Monticello. He proved himself extremely capable in the role, and so when Thomas admitted his energy was declining, Jeff willingly began to take over more of Monticello's projects and business.

Patsy knew her son had already fallen in love with Jane Nicholas, a quiet, dark-haired girl who came from an important Virginia family. In fact, Jane's father, Wilson Cary Nicholas, was the current governor. It was clear to Patsy that the Nicholases didn't consider Jeff a worthy enough suitor for their daughter because of the difficult financial straits of the Randolphs. Anne heard and reported to her family that Mr. Nicholas had complained that Jeff only had "a small tract of land and five Negroes — two of them worse than nothing." Jeff argued he didn't care what everyone said!

Good for him, Patsy thought. She wished she could be so confident and above criticism. For instance, she recalled with some shame one day when Eston appeared in the hall the moment the Nicholases arrived; she'd been so nervous they would see the resemblance between the boy and her father, she rudely shooed him away. She'd told Sally's children to stay out of the way, but they kept turning up here and there. She would prefer to forget they were around.

Patsy was also proud and moved when Jeff brought out a letter he had saved from his grandfather to show her. He has taught me so much, Jeff said, pointing to a few of the lines that meant so much to him:

> I never yet saw an instance of one of two disputants convincing the other by argument. . . . It was one of the rules which, above all others, made Doctor Franklin the most amiable of men in society, never to contradict anybody. If he was urged to announce an opinion, he did it rather by asking questions, as if for information, or by suggesting doubts. When I hear another express an opinion which is not mine, I say to myself, he has a right to his opinion, as I to mine; why should I question it? His error does me no injury . . . It is his affair, not mine, if he prefers error.

"It makes perfect sense," he told his mother.

Governor Nicholas was ultimately impressed with Jeff's dedication, personal presentation, and aspirations. Jeff, with total honesty, wrote to the governor and explained he could only offer Jane "a bare competency and a most enthusiastic and devoted attachment," but he promised to dedicate his "industry and perseverance to improve his station." The fact that Thomas offered Jeff a job and a place to live at Monticello won the day, and the Randolphs welcomed Jane "as a member of our family with very great pleasure and cordiality."

Planning the wedding for the happy couple uplifted Patsy and the spirit at the mansion. Patsy loved the beautiful dining room Thomas had designed. The bright yellow walls, divided horizontally by a carved chair rail, made it always a cheery spot, and the skylight (one of thirteeen in the house) and large paned windows assured good light. A fireplace made it cozy in the winter, as did two sets of window sashes to insulate the room. Wine dumb-waiters on both sides of the fireplace served to bring up wine quickly from the cellar, and a remarkable invention of a revolving door with shelves helped the slaves move dishes in and out of the room easily without intruding on the diners. Generous French doors on one side of the room led to an adjoining tearoom, often chilly because its glass walls looked out upon the charming gardens. In any event, the house made a perfect venue for a family wedding, and Patsy happily got to work with the planning at her little desk next to the fireplace in the blue room.

She was especially glad when, after the wedding, Jane and Jeff moved into Monticello in March 1815. Jane was only seventeen, thus very close in age to Genny and Mary Randolph. These two girls offered Jane warm friendship, and for a while everyone basked in the good cheer. It was a good thing the dining room table could be expanded as so many crowded around it every evening. Patsy noticed that her daughter Ellen always wanted to sit next to her grandfather and would watch to be sure he ate well.

It helped her frame of mind that Tom was feeling better about himself at the moment, having earned some success in his role as a commander. His men let him know they liked him and felt safe with him. Then, in a surprise move, when he was asked to do recruiting for the militia, he decided to give up the military and come home. Patsy was relieved to have him out of harm's way, and Thomas agreed that with such a large family depending on him, Tom did the right thing in resigning his commission. Collecting taxes for the war effort was considered an important mission, and when Madison appointed him tax collector, it appeared to be the perfect solution. Yet Tom suspected that Patsy had applied to the Madisons to give him the job, and he felt humiliated by his in-laws once again. Patsy tried to reassure him this was not the case, but he sulked about it for a good while.

When she was forty-six years old, Patsy headed once again to her bedroom in March 1818 to give birth and named the child George Wythe Randolph. Please, God, let this be my last, she prayed. She was so weak and ill after the delivery, she could not leave her bed. Since she had always been so resilient, it hurt her pride to be knocked down like this. Worse, she had to rely on Sally to organize the housekeeping. Her daughters helped, but it was Sally who picked up the pieces and held things together, with guests upstairs and downstairs, and managed all that needed to be done.

Her father's health occupied Patsy considerably in the summer when his rheumatism aggravated him greatly and threatened to get in the way of his riding regimen. He decided upon a course of baths at Warm Springs, Virginia, but was sorely disappointed with the company at the spa. He wrote to Patsy of the dull time he was having, though he reported he was enjoying the venison. Then the cure led to further problems and he wrote to her,

I do not know what may be the effect of this course of bathing, on my constitution; but I am under great threats that it will work its

effect thro' a system of boils. a large swelling on my seat, increasing for several days past in size and hardness, disable me from sitting but on the corner of a chair. another swelling begins to manifest itself today on the other seat, . . .

Patsy didn't know whether to worry or laugh, but he would be home soon enough.

SALLY

1818-1822

SALLY OFTEN COUNTED the years until her children would turn twenty-one and would be free. Beverly would be the first to "stroll" — as was the colloquial term for leaving home — in 1819, and Harriet would follow in 1822. Harriet was the lightest skinned of all her children, and Sally imagined she would elect to pass for white. She knew it made Madison angry, for he was darker than all of his siblings. He claimed Harriet would be deserting them. It was heartbreaking to think she might never see her children again when they left the plantation for a free life, but she wouldn't hold them back.

Harriet was beautiful. There was no doubt about it, and surely she would find a good, white husband. She had Thomas's fair skin, without the freckles, and her eyes were an amazing combination of Sally's amber and his blue — an original and stunning color to all who saw her. She had been trained to spin and weave in the Monticello small textile shop, primarily under the tutelage of her mother. Spinning was considered to be a less arduous task than most slaves endured; nor did it signal servitude. Moreover, growing up, she'd had Patsy and her mother as role models in manners and grace. Yes, Sally surmised, Harriet would succeed as a wife in the white world.

Thomas had steered the boys in a similar direction, apprenticing them to their literate and talented uncle, John Hemings, who was one of Betty's sons, and who was a master carpenter. John served as surrogate father in many ways to Sally's boys, and she would do anything for John because of that. She knew Thomas respected the artisanal life, and thought he was doing a good thing, making sure that Beverly, Madison, and Eston received this training.

The master had helped their brilliant Beverly acquire a good education too, but it constantly angered her that Thomas would never recognize these children as his own. Everyone knew it, but no one could say it out loud, and Thomas continued to pretend there was no problem with this. Sally suspected Thomas felt it would somehow make Martha's children seem less important if he recognized the Hemings children as his own. Sally grimaced, realizing she often thought of Patsy now as Martha. But she didn't like calling her Mrs. Randolph either. Thomas would never do anything to hurt Martha, and so they were all living a lie.

Sally also worried they would all be at Martha's mercy when he died. She was the white mistress of Monticello and could put them all on the slave block if she wished to. Maybe James had been right — she should have left with him. But she knew she would always make the same decision — to stay by the side of the man she loved. What she hadn't foreseen, or appreciated, was how her choice would affect all of their children.

The time was rushing by so quickly and Sally suddenly felt more pressure from Beverly that his time was coming to stroll. Was there a way for him to leave and still be able to stay in Virginia? She wanted him nearby where she could still protect him — where Thomas could still protect him. But he was nearing twenty-one and there was nothing she could do to stop him or to change the law. Even if he walked away and Thomas ignored his departure, which she was sure he would do, Beverly could still be stalked as a runaway slave under Virginia law. And the only way to ensure that couldn't happen was for Thomas to recognize him as his own.

The irony was that Beverly was more like him in so many ways than Jeff. Beverly was extremely intelligent, and musical, and obviously Thomas was aware of these similarities. Still, he wouldn't admit paternity because of the scandal that would ensue. It would be even harder to let Harriet go. Who would look after her girl? It galled her and broke her heart.

Thomas

1818-1824

AS THOMAS WATCHED the trees waving about in the wind like playful children capering on the hills between Monticello and Charlottesville, he experienced a near-religious vision about what he must do to improve the lives of young people. He would establish a new university in Virginia! And it would be one of the great institutions of the country! He perceived his state's population as equal to that of Massachusetts in its intellectual curiosity and its contribution to education. He wrote: *In a republican nation, whose citizens are to be led by reason and persuasion and not by force, the art of reasoning becomes of first importance.* The project encompassed so many of his interests — education, politics, and architecture. He couldn't wait to get started!

He became a constant storm of activity to forward the plan, and installed a telescope in Monticello's dome to oversee the progress of the construction in Charlottesville, about 4 miles away. When he looked through the lens, he would see a variety of evergreen trees in the foreground and then gentle hills rolling toward the growing town. He composed his thoughts:

> *I know of no safe depository of the ultimate powers of the society, but the people themselves: and if we think them not enlightened enough to exercise their control with a wholesome discretion, the remedy is not to take it from them, but to inform their discretion by education. This is the true corrective of abuses of constitutional power.*

As much as he wanted to bury himself in this enlightening distraction, he dared not turn away from worrisome conditions at home. Tom con-

307

tinued to drink excessively and to complain about Jefferson's authority at Monticello. Thomas could see there was no room at home for his son-in-law to excel and it caused constant, but understandable, friction. Although Tom had achieved some success in the military and with his agricultural ideas, he obviously felt unloved and unappreciated. Thomas's first concern was always Patsy, and he couldn't stop himself from stepping in to protect her from Tom's abuse.

Even more serious, however, was the present situation with his grand-daughter Anne Randolph Bankhead, whose husband Charles's drinking problem only seemed to be worsening. They, too, lived under Monticello's roof, and Edmund Bacon would frequently report to Thomas of Charles's aggressive and abusive behavior. Bacon had witnessed Anne running from her husband to hide on more than one occasion, and there were signs of bruising on the unfortunate young woman. Bacon related that Bankhead, on one of his crazy junkets, was reported to have ridden his horse straight into a barroom in Charlottesville to get a drink.

Tall and good looking, Bankhead could be completely unmanageable. Indeed, Thomas had witnessed this violence on occasion himself. Tom re-counted to him how one night, hearing sounds of a fight, he rushed into the room and saw Bankhead attacking Anne. Tom seized a hot poker from the fireplace and struck his son-in-law in the head, severely injuring him. On another occasion Bankhead got into a fight in Charlottesville with Jeff, Thomas's favorite grandson, who had grown to be an imposing man, even bigger than his great grandfather, Peter Jefferson, had been. It was a vi-cious confrontation, where Jeff horsewhipped Bankhead, and Bankhead responded by stabbing Jeff twice. Thomas, hearing of the struggle, jumped on his horse and rode as fast as he could to the square in town, where he found a bloodied Jeff on the ground. After tending to Jeff, he could not stop shaking himself. He had never been a fighter and he would not abide this violent behavior in his own family. He was appalled they could behave in this manner. And poor Patsy — her son-in-law had stabbed her son.

Jeff survived his wounds, but Thomas could not figure out what re-course he had to rein in the wild Bankhead and tempestuous Tom. In Oc-tober 1819, Thomas lay in his bed with what the doctor called "a painful stricture of the ilium," alarming everyone. He was seventy-six years old. Might this be the end for him? He primarily asked for Sally to nurse him but of course, Patsy hovered as well. He smiled at his daughter; how could he let her know how much she helped him sustain his idyllic vision of

Monticello? He wanted to tell the two women he loved them both, and they needn't compete for his affection, but he couldn't say it, and they wouldn't hear it, he suspected.

As he began to recover, Thomas became aware of an important debate going on in Congress over a statute to admit Missouri to the Union. The House and the Senate were split — the House would only allow the admission of Missouri if antislavery provisions were part of the agreement and the Senate, where slave states dominated, refused this condition. Thomas had been torn over this issue for his whole life but still would not agree to emancipation. Knowing full-well slavery was immoral, he kept telling himself it would eventually happen when the southern economy could bear it. Missouri, he wrote, was "like a fire bell in the night . . . the knell of the Union." Indeed he saw slavery as the greatest threat to the survival of the new American nation. He'd discouraged Virginians from cultivating slave-dependent crops, suggesting they plant rice, wheat, and olive trees instead. This had happened to some extent, and helped. But most southern farmers argued that the need would simply go away on its own accord in time.

Congress finally resolved the Missouri issue with a compromise in March of 1820: slavery would be allowed below the 36th parallel, but with the exception of Missouri, it would be forbidden any further north. Fugitive slaves must be returned to their owners if they escaped into the free regions. Thomas hoped this would evolve to mean that federal regulation of slavery within the states would eventually lead to abolition. Tom pressed him at dinner one evening, accusing his father-in-law.

"I think you are simply refusing to admit you are rejecting what you know is right because it would end your comfortable way of life. You have written on several occasions that slavery is wrong, and we all know it."

Sally stood against the wall in the dining room, holding her breath. She admired Mr. Tom's bravery to speak up.

"Yes, we all know it, but it would just be too hard to achieve at the moment, Tom. And too dangerous. But I pray it will happen in your lifetime," Thomas nodded toward Tom and Patsy. He didn't look in Sally's direction.

When he wasn't fretting about Tom or Bankhead or Missouri and slavery, he worried about his personal debt situation. However, as with the slavery conundrum, he had a tendency to put off for another day any real solution to his problems. As he got older, he found he had less will to put up a fight. And it was always easier to sign another bank note rather than figure out how to curtail the steady stream of expenses. The Jefferson name prevented a lot of problems from coming to light. His daily life bespoke power and luxury, and financial ruin hovered like an unreal specter.

Thomas's aching body signaled he was aging considerably, but he stubbornly refused to give up his independence. He still plunged his feet into cold water when he first arose each morning, insisting it made him stronger. He obstinately took his solitary horseback rides, often to the University of Virginia, to survey how the construction was moving along. Nowadays, he rode his favorite mount called Eagle. Even after falling into a muddy, fast moving stream and reinjuring his arm, he rebuffed any offer of accompaniment on these daily excursions.

"You could have drowned or been more seriously injured!" Patsy hotly argued, but he would not be coddled. In the evenings, he did allow Sally to bathe his aching wrist and arm, just as she had at the beginning of their intense affair.

"Ah, my dear one, what would I do without you?" he asked her most every night. Her quiet presence and loving arms would allow him to rest through the night.

PATSY

1819-1823

TOM HAD RECEIVED PUBLIC recognition from his active role in the Albemarle Agricultural Society, such that he was chosen to be Virginia's next governor in 1819. Many in the state were suffering from financial hardship, primarily due to the ever-continuing embargo, and Tom could personally speak to that constituency. He won three consecutive one-year terms, and would have been happy, except that his wife stayed at Monticello instead of going to Richmond with him. Patsy begged off, citing the need to be close to the children. Tom countered he suspected it was because she wanted to help her father more than him.

He tried to make her see how unhappy he was, being away from his family, and to prove it, he rode his horse hard after supper on Saturday, arriving at daybreak, so he could spend all day at Monticello with them. Patsy found this behavior touching and hard to resist. He grinned, pulling her close, "I've really come home for a taste of your okra and tomato soup." But then he spoiled the moment by complaining. "Without you in Richmond to support me with the social duties, people will ignore me. I'll lose the little popularity I have. Besides," he added, "I've supported your father's insistence to make the new university a totally secular institution. You know, my dear, this is difficult to accept for the religious population of Virginia."

He had her cornered with that argument and feeling guilty, she agreed to come in December 1820, to help with his re-election. She found she enjoyed dressing up again and attending cultural events in the capital, but she smarted at some of the citizens' reviews of her. One former army mate of Tom's accused her of being "vain and sarcastic." Stinging from his assessment, she hurried home. She ardently supported Tom's politics and her desire had been to soften Tom's sometimes abrupt manner. When she was accused of similar behavior, she was shocked and resentful. Fortunately, both Ellen and Cornelia, found more success in Richmond while their father was governor, greatly enjoying the social whirl. They commiserated with each other when neither found a serious beau while residing with him.

Patsy was especially proud of Tom when, during rumors of a slave rebellion, he had the courage to step up, and propose a plan to incrementally abolish the slave system. Tom intended to do this by manumitting slaves when they reached age twenty-one. A condition of manumission would be that they must leave the state. When Thomas refused to support his proposal, she tried to make excuses for her father. And when Tom largely blamed his father-in-law's lack of backing for its failure to pass, she did not say he was wrong, nor did she admit to Tom how much her father's inconsistencies bothered her — about their debts, about slavery, and she had to admit —about Sally.

1824-1825

Tom came home early in 1824, flush with his fame as a three-term Virginia governor, bringing tales of a mummy being on exhibit in Richmond and other such hilarious news. It was Septimia's tenth birthday, and Patsy relaxed with the family, enjoying everyone laughing together. On this glorious day, even Charles and Tom were not at loggerheads, and she gazed with pride and hope upon her son Jeff, who was doing such a good job of helping her manage Monticello. Jeff's sweet face, with the long Jefferson nose, softened by dark soulful eyes, bow-shaped lips, and a soft crown of wavy black hair, always cheered her. And Jane seemed to make him happy.

She loved the portrait Charles Wilson Peale had painted of her son when Jeff stayed with the Peale family in Philadelphia while taking some courses. But she was dismayed when her son reported his grandfather had told him he'd relegated the painting to the second tier in the portrait gallery because he explained, "had you been educated you would have been entitled to a place in the first row. You will always occupy the second." Patsy was incensed. First, she knew it must have hurt Jeff's feelings. Moreover, she knew Jeff's help on the plantation was invaluable and that his talents were just as important as a learned man's. Hadn't her father said that one must appreciate every person for their special talents?

Patsy had been especially worried about Ellen, who was now twenty-eight and still unmarried. Richmond's social season had not netted a beau, yet Ellen seemed undisturbed with her single state. She continued to enjoy her special intellectual relationship with her grandfather and chose to spend time philosophizing with him, rather than be bored with dull suitors.

Ellen needn't have looked so far afield, for upon her return to Monticello from Richmond, she met the one she'd been searching for. Joseph Coolidge was a Harvard alumnus, who had recently returned from a tour of Europe. Wanting to meet the great Jefferson, he came to pay his respects at Monticello. Patsy watched the two young people talking endlessly and slowly falling in love. Joseph brought out the whimsical intelligence of Ellen that had so delighted her family, and they watched her flower before their eyes. Patsy wasn't surprised when the couple brought her the glorious news that they planned to marry the next year, and she tried to cover her disappointment over their plan to move to Boston.

The family would celebrate another happy occasion when their fourth daughter Virginia married Nicolas Philip Trist in 1824 at Monticello. The couple had been devoted to one another for quite a while, and although Nicholas was only a law student, he was serving as Thomas's secretary. Patsy already loved him like a son, and she suggested the two could save money by living at Monticello.

Her father's gradual decline was becoming more of a constant concern, but he, too, appeared relaxed and happy. She felt a bit of unease that Sally and her children remained on the fringe of these family affairs, always a shadow, serving the food and cleaning up afterward, but she still felt it would not be appropriate for them to fully participate.

In April, when it became clear how great Tom's debts were — $33,000, to be exact — Thomas and Patsy told Tom that Jeff, henceforth, would assume his father's obligations in exchange for a deed of trust for Edgehill, Varina, and the slaves on these two properties. Tom admitted to Patsy he saw the sense in this because it would assuage his creditor's anxiety, but he raged at Jeff's control of his property. And at how Patsy and Thomas had come up with this plan behind his back.

"If you take all my land, you know I won't even be able to vote!" he screamed at his wife. "I have to own fifty acres to vote or hold political office. You seem determined to emasculate me. You never gave me a fair chance, and you always choose your father over me!"

She didn't know what to say to him, because she knew it to be true. And every time she chose her father, she realized it diminished her husband. She loved him, but she simply couldn't tolerate the violent temper. He was well educated, handsome, and could be kind. It was such a shame he never had been able to make a go of his scientific agriculture. Jeff, on the other hand, was not bookish, but he was focused and determined to support his family. Patsy felt she couldn't sacrifice the family's well being to humor her weak husband. They managed, just barely, to present a good face to visitors, but she sensed her husband would not stay with her much longer. She was then surprised when, in a short, bright hiatus, he served on the planning committee for the arrival of the Marquis de Lafayette, who was making a tour of the United States and planned to stop at Monticello.

How honored she felt to be standing at the portico steps when Jeff drove the Jefferson landau with the French general and his fellow travellers seated behind him. One hundred twenty mounted Frenchmen followed the carriage. Lafayette, permanently lamed by his years in the Olmutz dungeon, walked without aid also. He chose to greet her first, bending to kiss her hand, saying, "Ah, Madame Randolph, I remember you as a schoolgirl, and then at the table of your father in the rue de Berri."

Thomas then came forward, insisting, though feeble and unsteady with age, that he walk down the steps alone. In honor of the general's visit, he had unpacked and donned a blue jacket he had brought back from France. It was trimmed with gold lace and large buttons made of blue silk and shining with gold trim and still fit him. Some two hundred people — family, slaves, neighbors, and guests — gathered that day to witness the two aged revolutionaries fall into one another's arms, tears in their eyes. What glorious days they fondly remembered, forgetting for the moment their age.

Thomas had purposefully designed the portico at Monticello so that those standing on the steps would have a perfect view to the summit of Carter's Mountain and the Blue Ridge range beyond. He pointed out the panoramic view to his guest, telling him he called the highest peak Montalto and all stood spellbound for a moment before this majestic scene.

Patsy then led the esteemed Frenchman into their home for a formal luncheon. She placed the Marquis and Jefferson at one end of the table, extended to its maximum length, and the Marquis's son, George Washington Lafayette, at the other end between herself and Ellen. All relaxed in mahogany Hepplewhite chairs in this handsome room painted a bright yellow. The mantel frieze, made from rice paste, flour, and plaster, represented some of Thomas's favorite figures from Greek mythology, and light from the garden windows sparkled on the crystal and silver brought out for the occasion. James Madison came over from his house, Montpelier, in time for dessert to join in the reminiscing until the sun began to set behind the Blue Ridge Mountains. How contented her father looked, gazing around the table of family and friends and then outside to the magnificent copper beech and tulip poplars in the garden.

Thomas bragged to his guests that the fish served today came from the pond in the front garden, which they kept stocked for use at their table. The butlers brought wine bottle after wine bottle up from the cellar below, stoking the bright conversation. Thomas remarked more than once, "Good wine is a necessity of life for me." The general laughed and said, "D'accord, mon ami!" On this warm day, they replenished their water glasses with ice, brought to the icehouse from the river by oxen. Later, Patsy suspected he would lead everyone on a slow walk after luncheon, beyond the lawn, where Scottish broom and honeysuckle crowded the forest floor for dominance.

Lafayette and his son stayed at the Jefferson home for eleven days, giving the elderly gentlemen time to cover all their memories of the revolutionary days. At one point, sauntering together along the front garden flowerbeds, Lafayette stopped his labored pace, "My friend, I see your country has not progressed much with the issue of slavery. I must say, I am surprised since you assured us in France, so long ago, that you believed emancipation was near."

Thomas winced. Yes, he had always chosen to model his message to suit the attitudes of those with whom he was conversing. He hated disagreement so much — especially now with a respected friend. Being polite was always a better path than argument. But he should not dissemble with such a loyal friend.

"You are right, mon ami. When I was younger I tried several times to end the abhorrence. Now, I am afraid I must pass the problem on to the next generation. It is morally wrong. That I do not argue. But maintaining slavery is like holding a wolf by the ear, and we can neither hold him, nor safely let him go."

"I still believe it must change," the old general said.

Thomas had no more answers.

Since James Monroe's estate was also nearby, he rode over several times during the week to join the conversations. Thomas told Lafayette again and again how much his country owed to him in the achievement of their goals. The two toasted their friendship and accomplishments and vowed continuing affection. The Marquis promised to return the next year, so moving had been their rendezvous.

By the time Lafayette came back in August 1825, the break between Patsy and Tom was final. Tom agreed that Jeff could sell Varina, but he balked at the sale of Edgehill. "They have no right to sell my property," he shouted. "You are only trying to save yourselves at my expense."

Yes, Patsy, thought. Maybe so, but it was the only way the family could stay afloat. Jeff cringed when his father accused him of "cold blooded avarice," but he held to his belief it was the best choice at this point.

Tom broke down crying before her, claiming it was insane to part with his property. "It has the best climate of any place on earth, the purest water, gorgeous forests of oak, hickory, walnut, and ash." He bragged about his slave workforce, which was the best of any in the state. "Martha, it is our home," he lamented. "How can you let our greedy son sell it?" He only called her Martha when he was especially vexed with her.

Cold shock engulfed Patsy when Tom actually packed and walked out of Monticello to live in the nearby town of Milton, where he owned a small house. He continued to visit and Patsy found these evenings tense and uncomfortable. But she stuck by Jeff's decision to sell Edgehill, and didn't ask Tom to return. Lying in bed at night, alone, she heard the wolves howling in the woods abutting their land. Strange, they had not bothered her so much in the past.

Tom's departure didn't solve their financial worries. The worst part for her was the selling of slaves. She wrote to Ellen, now residing in Boston,

"The discomforts of slavery I have borne all my life, but its sorrows in all their bitterness I never before conceived." The sale of a particular woman slave, Susan, prompted these words, and at least Patsy enabled Susan to choose her new owner, a planter from Mississippi, rather than a local buyer who offered more money. She also stopped the sale of three older women and eight little girls, three of whom were the daughters of Burwell Colbert, whose wife, Critta, had been a nursemaid for several of Patsy's own children. What an ugly business it was, and she despised herself for it. But what else could they do in their present financial straits?

Jeff told her she didn't have the money to offset the sale of these slaves, but she said she would give up her dower rights in her husband's holdings to keep them. She forgot that this made her a slave-owner personally for the first time in her life. Jeff reminded her what the slaves meant personally to him too.

"Not having an older brother or companions when I was young on the plantation, I associated, when out, entirely with the slaves and formed for them the earliest and warmest attachment. For me, Negro association in the county was less corrupting than immoral whites. They would invite me, even when I was too young to withstand the walk, to go on a tramp or coon hunt, or to take a bee tree in the forest. When they thought I was getting tired, they would carry me on their backs by turns. You taught us to treat them with as much courtesy and kindness as if they had been free. I always looked to them as my protectors and they would run any risk for my protection."

Patsy regarded her eldest son with pride and affection, understanding exactly what he meant.

Patsy felt as slow as the old slaves after a hard day in the fields but made herself arise and tend to the duties imposed by running a large plantation. The morning post was often the one bright spot in her day. On August 28, a letter arrived from John Hemings to Septimia, now age eleven. The two were quite attached and Septimia actually called him Daddy Hemings as all the young Hemings did. Septimia read it out loud to her;

Dear miss Septima

Poplar Forest August 28th 1825

> *your Letter came to me on the 23th and hapey was I to embreas it to see you take it upon you self to writ to me and Let me know how your grand Pare was Glad am i to hear that he is no worst dear I hope you ar well and all the famely giv my Love to all your brothars Gorg with Randolph speculy i shoul gite don the house on Tusday that is tining it we have all the Tarrst to do yet wich is one hundred feet Long and 22 feet 8 inchs wide yesterday we just hade one Lode of the stuff brought home fore the gutters and that is 25. mils off whare it came from I am in hops I Shol be able to Com home by the 25 of November Ef Life Last*

John hemmings
I am your obediant sirvent

Patsy smiled with Septimia. "He is such a kind man, is he not?" she asked.

"Yes, and I miss him."

In her despair Patsy took a moment in her busy schedule to write to her older daughter:

Monticello September 1st 1825

> *I must write to you, My dear Ellen, when I can, and not wait for tim[e] to do it quietly and rationally. I have literally not one quiet hour from 5 in the morning my usual hour of rising, till 10 at night, when we generally retire. . . . we have had more company this summer than usual, and I have had more to say to them in consequence of My dear father's indisposition, and I certainly have saved him a great deal . . . but to have a house constantly filled with visiters to be entertained in the day, and accomodated at night, too often "wears out welcome." I am very fond of society but . . . in every situation, dear Ellen, life is a checkered scene of light and shade, that clouds will sometimes arise in Boston as they did at Monticello to obscure the brightness of your day is certain, but let the experience of your past life remind you always,*

that it is but a passing evil, that a few hours perhaps and the scene will be restored to its pristine beauty. You know in the abstract that nothing is perman[ent] neither joy nor sorrow, but you often forget to apply that knowledge in practice— . . . for we always retain enough to enjoy the good in store for us, and it is no loss to have less for the cares incident to every situation in life.

She lay down her pen. She must be careful not to complain overly about any of her life for she disliked herself when she whined.

SALLY

1821-1824

SALLY'S CHILDREN FUMED when Thomas failed to back Tom Randolph's proposal to end slavery in Virginia. Eston and Madison couldn't stop talking about his refusing to finally take action. It felt as if their father was ignoring them yet again. Sally wanted to defend him but she was as angry as they. How could he pass up this moment to finally end the scourge which was punishing their country, and furthermore, how could he ignore the perfect opportunity to support his sorry son-in-law? She didn't have the courage though to even bring it up. She had lived forever with his inconsistencies and wouldn't be able to argue with her master.

She wished she'd had the gumption in the past to raise the issue of slavery in general with him, but he never did, and so she'd kept quiet too. He did say sometimes he wanted to ameliorate the conditions of the slaves, so why didn't she push him further? She just couldn't bring herself to object to anything he did. She wanted to tell him she was afraid that if it were "improved," it would only make it harder to abolish.

With this simmering in her heart, she couldn't help but feel bitter the day the Marquis de Lafayette arrived. He didn't speak to her at first, but finally after luncheon when she was removing dishes, he came over to her. "Mademoiselle Hemings," he said, "I well remember you too. I hope you have pleasant memories of your days in Paris."

"*Oui, monsieur le Marquis. Certainement.*" She answered him in her best French and was proud she could show off a bit. Here was a fine and generous man, she believed, who had struggled for the French Revolution. She could heartily acknowledge his fame and fair mindedness. Where had the United States lost its way, she wondered?

Sally understood the law protected Jefferson. He was doing nothing illegal in Virginia by his ownership of slaves. But it gave him the power of a tyrant. She also understood that he attempted daily to lessen his tyranny by treating them all well. He rationalized that he offered them room and board and his protection. In return, she knew he felt he deserved their loyalty and service. She would never leave him, but sometimes her anger poisoned her soul.

When Beverly and Harriet had both strolled two years earlier, Thomas had let them go. Everyone in the neighborhood knew he had purposefully allowed the two to leave. She missed them acutely and doubted she would ever lay eyes on them again. This was inhumane, she thought. She couldn't help crying whenever she remembered waving goodbye to Harriet as she left on a stagecoach with fifty dollars in her pocket. She had given her daughter the little stiletto James had given to her so many years ago to take with her. Sally had to assume that Beverly, who had left earlier, would watch over his sister when Harriet reached Philadelphia.

Madison, age twenty, really a man now, and Eston, seventeen, still remained with her on the plantation. They both worked in the joinery and both resembled their father, though Madison less so, primarily because of his dark skin. Eston was already almost as tall as Thomas, and Madison was stockier, at about five foot ten. As Thomas became more fragile, she feared more and more for all the slaves at Monticello. She trusted him to never sell them, but she didn't know what would happen after he was gone. Patsy wouldn't want to sell them, but the run-down look of Monticello told her she might have to. Sally better make sure her sons strolled before the master was gone, although he had promised to grant them and others their freedom at age twenty-one, or after he died, whichever came first.

When Ellen married Joseph Coolidge in June of 1825 in the drawing room of Monticello, Sally felt like she was seeing off her own daughter. Ellen had always been affectionate with her, and she had known the girl all her life. She fussed over Ellen's dressing and made a particular effort so that everything would go smoothly for Patsy and the family. When the couple left for Boston, she suddenly and quickly put her arm around Patsy's shoulder to show she knew how it felt to see a child leave. Patsy reached up to touch Sally's hand in gratitude.

MONTICELLO

DEATH IS NIGH

1826

May it [American independence] be to the world, what I believe it will be (to some parts sooner, to others later, but finally to all), the signal of arousing men to burst the chains under which monkish ignorance and superstition had persuaded them to bind themselves, and to assume the blessings and security of self-government. That form which we have substituted, restores the free right to the unbounded exercise of reason and freedom of opinion. All eyes are opened, or opening, to the rights of man. The general spread of the light of science has already laid open to every view the palpable truth, that the mass of mankind has not been born with saddles on their backs, nor a favored few booted and spurred, ready to ride them legitimately . . . These are grounds of hope for others. For ourselves, let the annual return of this day forever refresh our recollections of these rights, and an undiminished devotion to them.

Letter to Roger C. Weightman on the anniversary of the signing of the Declaration of Independence in 1776, This was Jefferson's last letter, written 24 June 1826.

THOMAS

1826

THOMAS KNEW HE WAS SERIOUSLY ill but did not want to alarm his family. He tried to hide and reduce the horrendous pain from continuing prostate problems by taking laudanum daily, but it was impossible to obscure the debilitating diarrhea. Doctors claimed to know a great deal about urinary tract and prostate disease, and he trusted their judgment. He felt more comfortable leaning on Sally and Burwell to care for his failing body than asking for help from Patsy. When he decided to prepare his will on April 13, he could see they all feared the worst.

He listed five members of the Hemings family to be given their freedom: Burwell Colbert would receive $300; John Hemings and Joe Fossett would be freed a year after his death and take with them the tools of their trade to set up their own shops. He also provided for these three men to inherit houses and one acre of land, promising them they would be near their wives and the University of Virginia, where Thomas assumed they could find employment. A codicil continued:

> I give also to John Hemings the service of his two apprentices, Madison and Eston Hemings, until their respective ages of twenty-one years, at which period, respectively, I give them their freedom; and I humbly and earnestly request of the Legislature of Virginia a confirmation of the bequest of freedom to these servants, with permission to remain in this State, where their families and connections are, as an additional instance of the favor, of which I have received so many other manifestations, in the course of my life, and for which I now give them my last solemn, and dutiful thanks.

He had stipulated that he wanted the central focus of his University of Virginia to be a library and not a chapel when he founded the institution in 1819. This hindered his fund-raising among the religious landed gentry, but he continued to hold to this idea. The university had formally opened just a year earlier, in 1825, to great fanfare, but its solvency was not at all guaranteed. He urged Patsy and Jeff to see that his wishes would be followed, and they both nodded numbly.

Worse, still, was the state of his personal finances. Lying in bed, he formulated the idea to ask the Virginia legislature to pass a bill for a lottery to deal with his estate. He told his daughter and son he had requested that his home be left out of the offer. After all, he had been in public service for his country since 1764, and had never taken any public monies — rather, he had paid for many things with his own funds. At first the legislature balked at the plan, but then voted for it, insisting, however, that Monticello be included. But they would allow Patsy to remain there for two years after his death. Thomas cringed at the idea of handing over his prime creation to the state, but realized he might not have a choice if Jeff and Patsy could not come up with the funds any other way.

Extremely tired after attending to these matters, he asked for some time to rest alone. How had he failed so miserably with regard to ending slavery? He believed it was immoral; he believed with all his heart that all men were created equal and should have equal rights. He had said so in the Declaration of Independence; during the American Revolution he had drafted legislation that he and the founders believed would abolish the despicable practice; he had drafted a Virginia law prohibiting the importation of African slaves; he had proposed an ordinance banning slavery in the Northwest territories. But the blight continued. Why had he not been able to finish the job?

He regarded his beloved Sally, who had tiptoed in to sit next to his bed. Their children had suffered because of his sin of omission. He had failed as a father to them. He had been too cowardly. He had been afraid that there would be a race war like the slave revolt in Haiti in 1791. He had feared there would be a civil war because one part of the country favored abolition and the other was dependent on slaves for their livelihood. But in his heart, he knew it was inherently wrong and these chances should be taken. Now he had left the problem in the hands of his descendants, and all he had done was free a few on his own plantation. Would history forgive him this grave error? Would his Hemings children forgive him?

PATSY

1826

PATSY ONCE AGAIN TOOK up her quill to write to Nancy, her favorite sister-in-law, despite Nancy's tempestuous past. Recently, she had chosen not to write because she had only bad news to impart, and she didn't like to be seen as a complainer. But she knew her relations would worry more if they didn't hear from her.

Monticello Jan. 22. 1826

> *I have not written for a long time My dear Sister because in truth I had nothing but painful subjects to communicate. . . . the unfortunate event of the sale I have long anticipated not altogether, however, to the extent it has gone. The property has fallen very far short of the payment of the debt. . . . My life of late years has been such a tissue of privations and disappointments that it is impossible for me to believe that any of my wishes will be gratified, or if they are, not to fear some hidden mischief flowing even from their success. adieu dear sister.*

Patsy also was desperate with concern about her father and first-born child, Anne Randolph Bankhead. All she could do was to wander from sickbed to sickbed. She could not assimilate the specter of the diminished figure of her father, bedridden most of the time, with the vibrant bright man she always depended on. Her daughter's situation was equally dire.

Anne had given birth at age thirty-five to a premature little boy in mid-January and had lain in bed at Monticello with complications from childbirth ever since. Anne already had four live children from twelve pregnancies in seventeen years of marriage. She was exhausted, sad to leave her children and to disappoint her mother, but being very religious, did not appear to fear death. It was a losing battle, and Anne's body was placed in the Monticello graveyard alongside her aunt, Polly Jefferson Eppes. Patsy could not stop crying.

All the Randolph siblings were greatly upset and partially blamed Charles's constant abuse of their sister for her death. Jeff, especially, felt like raising a poker again to the man's head to punish him, but instead, swallowed his anger and moved to Monticello to help his mother. She was so devastated over losing Anne, he feared for her sanity. Jeff and his wife, Jane, agreed to take on Anne's children, as they wouldn't be safe with her drunkard of a husband.

Patsy knew in mid-June that Thomas's final days had begun. She wanted to hold on to him as long as she could. She couldn't bear the thought of losing him. It hurt too much. Still reeling from the loss of Anne, she struggled against this additional punishment. It also stung that he would only allow his servants to care for him, especially Sally and Burwell Colbert, at night. And he wanted them sleeping beside him on pallets near his bed day and night, always ready to care for any needs he might have. He insisted on sparing his white family any discomfort or unpleasantness and didn't seem to understand this dismissal was hurtful.

He did permit Patsy and Jeff to be with him for short visits during the day, and he also asked his granddaughters Virginia and Mary to approach his bedside occasionally. It was a tragedy for them all, Patsy admitted, as she witnessed Sally's tear-stained face at the door.

On Sunday, July 2, Thomas reached over to his bedside table and picked up "a little casket" of personal souvenirs. Included was a handwritten verse he had written, which he titled his "death-bed Adieu." Patsy couldn't restrain her sobs as she read it:

Life's visions are vanished, its dreams are no more.
Dear friends of my bosom, why bathed in tears?
I go to my fathers; I welcome the shore,
Which crowns all my hopes, or which buries my cares.
Then farewell my dear, lov'd daughter, Adieu!
The last pang of life is in parting from you!
Two Seraphs await me, long shrouded in death:
I will bear them your love on my last parting breath.

Thomas and all of the family wished he could hold out until the anniversary of the Declaration of Independence. It would be the fiftieth and they heard that John Adams also lay dying, hanging to life by pure will in order to hear the triumphant bells of July Fourth. And last he did. By mid-morning on the Fourth, with all of his white family members, Burwell, and Sally in the room, Thomas asked Burwell to plump his pillows. He then closed his eyes and slept, falling unconscious about an hour later. Near noon he breathed his last.

Patsy was stunned. She thought her own breath had stopped and she groped for a chair, instead falling over his body. She could not imagine life without him. He had raised her, molded her, accepted and praised her in every role. In her shock, she wondered what possible purpose she would have in the world now? The world could not do without him either. The family learned a few days later that John Adams had died the same day, late in the afternoon in Quincy, Massachusetts.

John Hemings built the master's coffin out of a special wood he had been saving for that purpose. Patsy had to accept that the slave women would prepare his body, most likely Sally and Critta; and Wormley Hughes would dig the grave. *The Richmond Enquirer* posted that:

> *Mr. Jefferson expressly desired that there should be no pomp or parade at his burial. As you may well suppose the fall of so great a man has produced a deep impression on all around him. The Professors and Students of the University, the Citizens of Charlottesville, the inhabitants of the adjacent country, strangers in the vicinity - all will repair to the Family Burial Ground to witness the interment at 5 o'clock this Evening (the 5th).*

His wishes were followed and the only ceremony was held on a rainy day in the Monticello graveyard with family, slaves, students, and friends from Charlottesville attending. The Reverend Mr. Frederick Hatch, rector of the Episcopal Church in Charlottesville, conducted the service without pomp or ceremony. Neither James Madison, nor Cornelia and Ellen Randolph, who were in Boston, could make it there in time for the funeral. The ghostly threat of bankruptcy hovered over the solemn gathering as all wondered what would happen next.

Tom was present, trying to elbow out Jeff over funeral arrangements, and making a scene at the graveside. Other family members were finally able to calm him and persuade him to withdraw a letter making him a co-executor of the estate with Jeff. By late afternoon, Tom glumly announced he would not return to Monticello and no longer considered himself "a member of the family at all."

Patsy was additionally upset by this but did not try to restrain Tom from returning to his small home in Milton, Virginia, only a few miles away. When she thought she couldn't bear another blow, Patsy learned from Jeff that Thomas owed $100,000 at his death. And of course, his descendants were responsible for his debts. She had known the financial situation was serious but the actual amount stupefied her.

"He was always too generous and kind," she wept before her children. As she faced the loss of Monticello, she wondered where she and her children would live. Now she must prepare for the auctioneers. Putting cherished objects from a life up for sale seemed to demean that life. It was too cruel! In going through his papers, she came across a copy of a letter he had sent to her in 1787, and managed to smile over the irony of its lesson.

Paris, June 14, 1787

> *I send you, my dear Patsy, the 15 livres you desired. . . . do you not see my dear how imprudent it is to lay out in one moment what should accommodate you for five weeks? That this is a departure from that rule which I wish to see you governed by, thro' your whole life, of never buying any thing which you have not money in your pocket to pay for? be assured that it gives much more pain to the mind to be in debt, than to do without any article whatever which we may seem to want . . . Th. Jefferson*

SALLY

1826

HE WAS DYING. She could feel it in the weakness of his palsied hands and see it in the sagging of his body. It broke her heart. Without him she would have no center, no touchstone, and she was losing her children one by one. Monticello was her home, but she had fooled herself; it never had been really hers. But Thomas had been hers! And they both knew it.

But why hadn't he been able to give their children his unqualified love like he did his white offspring? He, of all people, should have been above any fear of how people would judge him. But he wasn't. Despite that, all the boys had loved him to some extent, but despised him too. How could they feel otherwise with his half-love, half-rejection?

She sensed Madison and Eston were less angry than Beverly had been. After all, Thomas had given Polly's pianoforte to Eston, paid for his lessons, and supported his love for music. Madison, too, was musically gifted and had become a fine fiddler, always performing for family celebrations. Both would be able to support themselves with the houses Thomas had bequeathed them and the money they would earn as free men. But they had experienced too many denials from their father not to feel inadequate; they couldn't attend the university as students, they could only help build it with their carpentry skills; they couldn't join in the music as equal family, they could only play as servants.

Sally cringed at the thought of turning her fate over to Patsy. She really thought of her as Martha now. Patsy had been her girlhood friend. Yet Thomas hadn't mentioned Sally in his will. Would he renege on his promise? Martha's face showed the passing of years more than her own — Patsy had her father's delicate skin, she had endured the loss of children and her sister, and her husband was no longer living with her. But the one who had

331

always mattered the most to Martha, Sally knew, was her father. And the thought of losing him was devastating to her.

Sally sat hour after hour by his side, holding his hand. She was fifty-three years old and had no idea where she would live after he died. She asked him if she could keep his eyeglasses and inkwell.

"Of course, my dearest one," he whispered. "I only wish I could give you more." She cried softly. He had given her a life she could not have experienced with anyone else. From Paris to Monticello, she had been a part of history and she was proud of that. And she would miss him every day. After he closed his eyes for the last time, she also tucked a shoe buckle of his in her pocket. She only wanted the things he had used every day that had been truly a part of him.

In the last hour before he died, she had to step back from his bedside to let his white family be close. The resentment was almost as punishing as his passing.

PATSY

TWO DAYS AFTER JEFFERSON'S DEATH, Patsy invited Sally to join her in the sitting room. She politely asked Sally to take a seat. Patsy had not remembered doing this before. How strange that she felt so estranged from this woman. They both had suffered. They both had loved the same man, one as a father, one as a lover. She didn't know at this moment whether she felt mostly compassion for this slave woman, or anger that Sally had shared her father's love. Clearly Sally was worried she would be put on the slave block as Thomas had not clarified her fate in his will, but had left it in her hands to do his bidding. She could be cruel or kind.

"Ah, Sally, this is a bitter day. Neither you nor I asked to be here." She paused but didn't wait to tell Sally what she needed to know. "I can tell you that my father asked me to give you your freedom within two years of his death. He was waiting until Eston came of age in order that Eston could act as head of the family. He will be twenty-one in two months, but unfortunately the auction will fall before that — at the beginning of the year."

Sally looked shocked and grew pale. "So soon . . . ?" she gasped, with a harsh intake of air.

"Yes. You are listed as worth $50 on the block. He could not list you in his will because it would draw too much public attention to your relationship with him. That has already done enough damage to the family and we shall not ask for more. Therefore, we cannot wait another minute for me to give you your time and your papers. Papa begged me to free you, and I shall do his bidding. You understand that giving you your time ensures that you would still be legally enslaved but assured of your freedom to move about, live where you choose, and keep any earned wages."

Sally remained speechless. She would not thank her, Patsy realized. Let her be proud. She continued to speak to the mute woman. "Virginia law requires that slaves who receive their freedom must leave the state within a year. I don't know where you will live, but because I am giving you your time instead of freeing you, you can remain in the state. I will make your freedom official in my will and direct my children to give you your freedom if I predecease you."

"I will go and live with my sons in Charlottesville," Sally said. She knew not where this idea had come from but it made some sense. She mostly wanted to remain in control in front of this woman who owned her. The ugliness of slavery had quashed their previous affection for one another and for that, both women were sorry. Patsy rose to leave the room and the two women did not embrace.

Patsy felt shame, anger, and despair upon leaving Sally alone in the room. Anger at her father for having gotten into this mess, shame for not being able to stand up with her convictions against slavery, and despair that she would never again see better days. How had she been brought so low? She had let slavery, in all its ugly guises, corrode her relations with Sally, Betty, and so many others.

She practically bumped into Cornelia in her blind race to her bedroom. Her daughter caught her mother in her arms, and helped her to her bed.

"Mother, Mother, we will all be well. Truly, we will. Ellen wants you to come to her in Boston, and Genny and I think that is a good idea." No one spoke of Tom coming back, or of her going to him, and for that she was relieved. His odd behavior at the funeral had chased away what warm feelings she still harbored, and she hadn't the strength to face him again.

Patsy allowed her children to persuade her that Boston was the best place for the time being, and by mid-October, she was on her way to stay with the Coolidges. Ellen and Joseph both assured her they were more than happy to have her and her youngest children, Septimia, now twelve, and George, only seven. Jeff wanted his mother out of the way when the auctioneers gavel swung down on Monticello, its slaves, and its contents. Her unmarried girls rented a house in Albemarle near a school they planned to begin. Patsy was grateful, for she knew she could not face the scene at the auction block, though Jeff assured her he would not separate families in the sale of their slaves.

SALLY

SALLY CHOSE TO VISIT HIS GRAVE at night, when she usually had shared her time with him. It was less likely she would come across any of the white family in those hours too. She placed some flowers from the garden close to his heart, and waited for him to speak to her. What should she do? Where could she go?

All of the Jeffersons had been her family, not just Thomas, Patsy, and Polly. But also the younger girls and boys, whom she had helped bring into the world. She had bandaged their wounds; they had held her hand. They had called to her when they were happy or sad. The voices of her own children echoed across the fields, the ones she had loved so much and made sure they learned how to read, learned a trade, and stayed healthy.

Now she wanted to stay nearby, to be close to Madison and Eston, who had been granted their freedom and the right to stay in the state, thanks to Jefferson's request to Congress. She imagined Beverly and Harriet would also take their chances and stay in Virginia. Where else would she go? And she wanted to stay close to To-mah, here in Albemarle County. Her eyes searched the horizon for the line of mountains she knew so well, and she felt he was near. They had been together for thirty-eight years, and that would provide many memories on lonely evenings.

1827

On January 15, 1827, Sally held Joe Fossett's hand as he watched his family be taken away at the executor's sale at Monticello. The master had given Joe his freedom but his wife, Edith, and their eight children were led away when the gavel fell, some for prices 70 percent over estimate. She could not reconcile the cruelty of what had just happened with the kindness of her master. He had called them all "family," but now her world made no sense.

Patsy

1828-1835

PATSY EXTENDED WHAT SHE EXPECTED to be a short visit to Boston into eighteen months. During that time Jeff and her son-in-law, Joseph Coolidge, explored various avenues of support for her future. As useless and insolvent as Tom was, they advised her she could not get a divorce — even in Massachusetts, where the only statutory grounds for divorce were consanguinity, bigamy, impotence, and adultery. Nor did she dare leave Massachusetts right away because children were considered the husband's chattel in most states, and the father would win custody if contested in court. She understood she needed to keep Septimia and George with her in Boston.

Yet Tom continued to write to the children, claiming his continuing love for their mother and his hope they would all be together again. He still blamed his own father for losing Tuckahoe, blamed Thomas for their financial problems, and he claimed Jeff was responsible for mismanagement of his property. He included Patsy in his diatribe, saying she always aligned herself with her father instead of her husband. She heard he was still drinking excessively but was showing signs of trying to improve himself. He even had been elected president of the Agricultural Society of Albemarle. Heaven knows what people said about them in town!

The rest of her family was still living at Monticello, which had not yet sold. Obviously feeling some warmth toward Tom, and some guilt as well, they offered their pitiful father the north wing, which he accepted, remaining isolated there most days. He soon became ill, and Patsy, upon hearing of his deteriorating condition, stepped up her plans to return from Boston by May 1.

Her joy at seeing Jeff and his family was sorely tempered when she saw the haggard figure Tom had become. His broad cheeks sagged and his eyes were constantly red. Saddened and shocked at his state, she began spending much of the day and evenings at her husband's bedside. He held on for about six weeks, and actually she thought he seemed happier than he had in many years. He especially enjoyed reminiscing about the good times.

When Tom expressed a desire to reunite with his son, saying "he would not die for the world without making friends with him," she smiled at him. Patsy finally managed to persuade Jeff to visit his father two days before he died on June 20, 1828. Tom breathed his last breath with all the resident Randolphs around him, and she was happy he would be buried at Monticello, close to other family members. However, she admitted to Ellen soon after that becoming a widow simplified her life in many ways, because she could envision no way forward with Tom's jealousies and passions.

Again, she had to face where she would live. All her children were willing to welcome her, but she didn't want to be a burden on any of them. When her son-in-law, Nicholas Trist, obtained a government position with Secretary of State Henry Clay, she agreed to follow the Trists to the capital. Still, money problems delayed her for about a year in Albemarle as Jeff struggled to find a buyer for Monticello and tried to sell published volumes of Jefferson's papers. While waiting for all of this to be settled, Patsy and the three still unmarried Randolph daughters moved in with him and Jane at Edgehill. They had eight children by this time, and poor Jane was exhausted by the inundation of Randolphs on top of their own. Cornelia faced the situation more clearly than her siblings when she wrote, "The truth is, we have been people of consideration in the world, and now are poor and neglected."

In mid-October Patsy packed up the last of her belongings at Monticello and experienced terrible stomach pains after visiting her father's former rooms. Nicholas rented an urban house in the Virginia capital for the entire Trist/Randolph brood, and they all crammed into the smaller abode. Nicholas insisted that Patsy occupy a large room in the front of the house on the second floor. She decorated the space with her father's old coverlet from Monticello and a few chosen antiques — a sewing table and a dressing table that had been her mother's — and three portraits of her father. As she gazed at his portrait, she couldn't stop the thought that her life had been cruel in many ways. But how could she think this when she'd had such a devoted father and her time on earth had been blessed with loving children?

With her journalist friend Margaret Smith, she attended the mob scene of the inauguration of Andrew Jackson. Smith painted it as a sad dismissal of elite society, but Patsy was taken with the new president's talk of the "Age of the Common Man." She saw in his ideas echoes of her father's belief in the people. Martin Van Buren, his secretary of state, had been a former acquaintance of the Randolphs, and both Jackson and Van Buren courted her as a friend of the incoming administration. Ever a mother first, she accepted their friendly social attentions, believing that they might help forward the career of her son-in-law Nicholas. In turn, she bestowed on their raucous dinners, an air of respectability and gentility, just as she had done for her father.

She asked to be called Mrs. Randolph now and had somewhat of a regal carriage at this point, with strands of auburn relieving the gray, and a willowy figure. Her education and impeccable manners served her well, and her grown children in Washington began to be included in the social scene. Her youngest, George, was helped in securing a naval appointment, and President Jackson chose Nicholas to fill the post as his private secretary.

In September 1831 Patsy returned to Edgehill. It was her fifty-ninth birthday, and she knew she was fortunate that eleven of the twelve children she had borne had survived to adulthood, and only Anne had died. The actual sale of Monticello gave her severe stomach distress again, but she was happy to at least retain ownership of the graveyard. She sold the estate to a Charlottesville druggist for what she thought was an unfair sum. A few years later, due to a tip from the Marquis de La Fayette, another more acceptable buyer stepped forward. It was Uriah Levy, a Jewish neighbor, who greatly admired Thomas and who promised to keep Monticello as a monument to the great Jefferson. He paid $7,500 and set to work refurbishing the home.

Patsy again moved to Boston in September and wrote to her sister-in-law Nancy that she was eager to leave New York after a visit because it was full of cholera. Hence, she hastened to Boston where she hoped to help her daughter Ellen, whose husband, Joseph, was in China on business for at least a year and a half. She had more bad news to share with Nancy two years later. She had prided herself on the loss of only one child, but in 1834 she unexpectedly lost another.

Edgehill Feb. 16. 1834

The mournful subject of this letter dear Nancy will excuse the delay in answering your last. I have had the affliction of again losing one of my dear and excellent children. My poor James who no doubt you remember, whose quiet gentle manly manners you remarked as a boy and whose manhood fulfilled all the promises of childhood, was taken from me after a short & rapid illness, during the last 5 days only of which he was confined to his room . . . I ought not to grieve, for it is a selfish wish that would have kept a being so pure, so gentle; to so disinterested a world that he was not formed to struggle with. . . . The little farm which he had cultivated rent free since his grand father's death was obliged to be sold, and his humble establishment broken up without the means of resettling another. He had just come to spend the winter with his family previous to taking such measures as he should determine upon for a future maintenance, when he was taken with what we thought was dyspepsia, and he him self attributed it to the change from very plain living and rather a laborious life to freer living and no exercise at all. The disease progressed so rap . . .

She put down the quill, unable to write any more for the moment.

SALLY

1835

SALLY FOUND A HOME with her sons, Eston and Madison, in a rented house on Main Street in Charlottesville. Her sister Mary lived nearby and she spent her days in her little garden, or cooking for the family. When the rumor of her separation from the plantation echoed around the town, she held her head higher and refused to talk about her past. The census taker came to call and she told him that she and her sons were white. He marked it down just so. Surely he knew who they were, but no one was going to argue with this beautiful, proud lady.

Only a few years later, in 1833, a new census counted them as freed blacks, but she didn't make a fuss over it. It made no real difference in her life anymore since her children were free. Beverly and Harriet counted as white and frequently came to call on their mother. She had worried she would never see them again when they left Monticello, and so she counted every sight of them a blessing. Burwell Colbert also dropped by often to help her clean the house and keep up the yard. Burwell lived at Shadwell, below Monticello, and worked as a painter and glazer, mostly at the University of Virginia or within the former Jefferson community.

She doubted if Patsy would ever come to visit, but heard about her frequently since the family was so nearby at Edgehill. She followed the stories of Patsy being in Washington City, being close to the Jackson administration and all, but didn't envy her that. She was glad for Thomas's sake that his daughter had a large family who would care for her — just as she did.

In 1835, Sally knew her health was declining. She was surprised she wouldn't live as long as her mother had, but she could tell some signs of weakness meant she wouldn't last much longer. She would try to bury her pride and ask Patsy to bury her in the Monticello graveyard, not too far from Thomas, near an old maple tree. In the fall, when she saw the flaming color and inverted heart-shape of the red maple tree, like Cupid's arrow, reaching toward the heavens, she perceived it as a symbol of their love. Whatever happened, they would be together again soon.

PATSY

1835-1836

PATSY RICOCHETED AMONG THE homes of the Trists in Washington, the Coolidges in Boston, and Jeff's family at Edgehill for the next five years. In April 1835, while in Washington, she suffered a mysterious illness, and was so sick she was prompted to pen her will. She had few possessions to disperse among her large family, but she still held a few slaves. She parceled out a few but emancipated two Colbert sisters. She then directed her children to give Sally Hemings, her niece Betsy, and Wormley Hughes "their time." All of them had lived as free individuals since her father's death, but she wanted to be sure their status was clear. If she freed them outright, they would have to leave the state. She counseled Jeff to always protect her father's reputation and deny that any mulatto children had been born to Thomas and Sally. She had kept the slate clean of insinuation during his life and since his death, and she meant for it to remain so.

Fortunately, this will turned out to be unnecessary for another year as Patsy continued to live among her children, travelling between the cities like a much younger woman. She was becoming slightly bent over which angered her. She even sat for a portrait by Thomas Sully, and she thanked the artist for portraying her as much younger, though in a sedate and respectable manner. She was especially pleased the way he captured her resemblance to her father.

In October 1836, she was back at Edgehill with the Trist family when she was felled by a terrible headache. As she sought her bed, she remembered how her Papa had suffered so much from this debilitating pain. She smiled, knowing she had been a good and loving daughter. Suddenly she

342

experienced an intense spasm and fell forward, turning a blue shade according to Virginia and Jeff, who were present. She then died immediately in Jeff's arms. The family buried Martha (Patsy) Randolph in the Monticello graveyard close to her husband and her father, Thomas Jefferson. Both Jeff and Ellen wrote epitaphs for their mother, and they all, feeling unmoored without her, assured one another that at least, they still had each other.

AFTERWORD

When I began to think about what might have been the relationship between Patsy Jefferson and Sally Hemings, I had no idea how fraught and fascinating it would turn out to be. From girlhood to their deaths, it was a bond they couldn't escape and a tie that brought both rewards and unhappiness. The relationship was complicated and thwarted by racial prejudice, jealousy, and family ties, and was held together by Southern manners and mores, economic necessity, and ironically by family ties. In the middle of it all stood Thomas Jefferson — larger than life — statesman, philosopher, father, lover, and genius. It is an American embarrassment that this great advocate for freedom was a large slaveholder, and the inconsistency of his position remains a conundrum for many people.

I have tried to stay as close to facts as possible, only inventing daily conversation and incidental activity, while imagining, given the facts, what their feelings might have been. The many letters among Thomas, Patsy, Polly, and Tom Randolph, mostly preserved by Jefferson himself, provided much of the dialogue. These people left a clear footprint for historians to follow, and it seems a travesty, if not hubris, to invent ideas Jefferson didn't invent himself. The Morgan Library, the Jefferson Foundation and the International Center for Jefferson Studies, the Library of Congress, and the New York Historical Society are a treasure trove of their world. Unfortunately, there are no letters extant between Thomas and Sally because they were afraid to write to one another, lest their bond be brought to light.

Three outstanding books served as the backbone for my story: Jon Meacham's *Thomas Jefferson, The Art of Power*; Cynthia A. Kierner's *Martha Jefferson Randolph, Daughter of Monticello*; and Annette Gordon-Reed's *The Hemingses of Monticello, An American Family*. Each of these books is a scholarly reference work where I could check the facts. A more recent

(2017) and fine Jefferson biography by John Boles, entitled *Jefferson, Architect of American Liberty,* reflects the latest historical research.

Other historical novels and movies make outlandish claims — for instance, about Patsy having a real ongoing affair with William Short, or Patsy telling Maria Cosway about Thomas's relationship with Sally. Making up things, for which there is no evidence, is inappropriate and futile in the effort to understand a time and its people.

Of course, the outstanding unsettling question about Thomas Jefferson is his unresolved attitude toward slavery. The words "paradox," "conundrum," "hypocrisy," and "inconsistency" have all been used to describe the mystery regarding Jefferson's thinking on the subject. In his early writings he clearly stated that he believed slavery was wrong and must be abolished. Indeed, one of the inscriptions from his writings on the Jefferson Memorial in Washington D.C. attests to this:

> *God who gave us life gave us liberty. Can the liberties of a nation be secure when we have removed a conviction that these liberties are the gift of God? Indeed I tremble for my country when I reflect that God is just, that his justice cannot sleep forever. Commerce between master and slave is despotism. Nothing is more certainly written in the book of fate than that these people are to be free. Establish a law for educating the common people. This is the business of the state and on a general plan.*

Yet, on one occasion after another, Jefferson failed to stand up to the challenge. Even when his son-in-law Tom Randolph made an attempt to legislate emancipation when he was Governor of Virginia, Jefferson refused to back him. Why was he unable to do what he knew was right? As he himself wrote, none of us is perfect, but that such a giant as he didn't stand up for what he believed is disheartening, to say the least.

Jon Meacham included in *Thomas Jefferson, The Art of Power,* a fascinating quote by Josiah Quincy Jr. of Massachusetts, written after a visit to the Carolinas,

> *The enjoyment of a negro or mulatto woman is spoken of as quite a common thing; no reluctance, delicacy or shame is made about the matter. It is far from being uncommon to see a gentleman at dinner, and his reputed offspring a slave to the master of the table.*

Throughout his life, Jefferson refused to betray the slightest recognition of any personal resemblance to his mulatto progeny and lived with a code of denial that all around him accepted.

I wasn't sure when I began writing, but after following the events and the characters, I came to believe Thomas genuinely cared about Sally and decided they had a loving, close relationship. He gave evidence of this by loyally remaining by her side for so many years, as well as the way he kept his promise to her, granting their children freedom and ensuring dependable livelihoods for them. Nor did he allow the threats by the journalist Callender to scare him away from her. However, it is shocking that he left it to Patsy after his death to grant Sally her freedom. Even at his death, he refused to reveal the truth about his relationship with her. Yet I think he believed he loved her and through his tenderness and affection through the years, she understood this to be true.

After his grandfather's death, Jeff Randolph introduced a bill for the gradual emancipation of Virginia's slaves, to be followed by their colonization outside U.S. borders. However, the bill failed to pass because of fears stoked by Nat Turner's slave insurrection in 1831. More shocking is the length of time it took for the State of Virginia to finally be brought to justice over its racial laws. It wasn't until 1967 that the U.S. Supreme Court ruled in Loving vs. the State of Virginia, a landmark civil rights case, against Virginia's anti-miscegenation laws, which prohibited interracial marriage.

Chief Justice Earl Warren wrote: "the freedom to marry, or not marry, a person of another race resides with the individual, and cannot be infringed by the *State*." After the ruling, Mildred, a black woman, and Richard Loving, a white bricklayer, who had been jailed in Virginia and then forced to live out of state, away from their families, because of Virginia's harsh miscegenation laws, were allowed to return to Virginia with their four mulatto children. The case was brought to the Supreme Court and funded by the American Civil Liberties Union.

A short walk on a path through the woods close to the back lawn of Monticello brings one to a graveyard enclosed by a tall iron fence. It is both solemn and inspiring to stand before this modest memorial. A gray obelisk at the north end marks the resting place of Thomas Jefferson, with his wife Martha (Patty) and younger daughter Maria on either side. Patsy lies at his head. Other extended family members are buried in this enclosure and the slave graveyard is placed some distance down the mountain. However, Sally's name won't be found there. It is not yet known where she is buried. Jefferson himself wrote the inscription on the simple monument he designed for his grave:

Here was buried Thomas Jefferson,
Author of the Declaration of Independence,
of the Statute of Virginia for Religious Freedom,
and Father of the University of Virginia.
Born April 2, 1743 O.S., Died July 4, 1826.

BIBLIOGRAPY

Adams, William Howard, *The Paris Years of Thomas Jefferson*, Yale University Press, New Haven and London, 1997.

Appleby, Joyce, *Thomas Jefferson, The American Presidents*, Arthur M. Schlesinger, Jr., General Editor, Times Books, Henry Holt and Co., NY, 2003.

Eds. Edwin Morris Betts and James Adam Bear, Jr., *The Family Letters of Thomas Jefferson*, University Press of Virginia, 1966.

R. B. Bernstein, *Thomas Jefferson*, Oxford University Press, NY, 2005.

Boles, John B., *Jefferson, Architect of American Liberty*, Hachette, Basic Books, 2017.

Bramen, Lisa, *When Food Changed History: The French Revolution*, Smithsonian.com, July 2010.

Campbell, Charles, *Memoirs of a Monticello Slave, As Dictated to Charles Campbell in the 1840s by Isaac, one of Thomas Jeffferson's Slaves*, University of Virginia Press, Charlottesville, VA, 1951.

Chase-Riboud, Barbara, *Sally Hemings, A Novel*, Chicago Review Press, Chicago, 2009.

Corsair Catalogue at the Morgan Library, Collection of Autographed Letters Signed: Philadelphia, Washington, etc. to his daughter Martha. Two boxes, unbound, Purchased by J.P. Morgan, Jr., 1925.

Covey, Herbert C., Eisnach, Dwight, *What the Slaves Ate: recollections of African American foods and foodways from the slave narratives*, ebook, 2009. Through Thomas Jefferson Portal at International Center for Jefferson Studies, Charlottesville, VA.

Ellis, Joseph J., *American Sphinx, The Character of Thomas Jefferson*, Vintage Books, Random House, NY, 1998.

Fox News: *Tour Guide Shari Segal, Walking in Jefferson's Footsteps in Paris*. July 19, 2013.

Gordon-Reed, Annette, *The Hemingses of Monticello, An American Family*, W.W. Norton & Co., NY, 2008.

Jefferson, Thomas, *A Summary View of the Rights of British America*. Monticello, May, 1774.

Jefferson, Thomas, *The Autobiography of Thomas Jefferson*, Editors: Susan L. Rattiner, Terri Ann Geus, Capricorn Books, New York, NY, 1959. First published in 1821.

Jefferson, Thomas, *The Declaration of Independence*, Philadelphia, July 4, 1776.

Hall, Gordon Langley, *Mr. Jefferson's Ladies*, Beacon Press, Boston, 1966.

Kennedy, Roger G., *Burr, Hamilton, and Jefferson, A Study in Character*, Oxford University Press, New York, 2000.

Ketcham, Diana and Photographs by Michael Kenna, *Thomas Jefferson's Paris Walks*, Arion Press, San Francisco, June 2012.

Kierner, Cynthia A., *Martha Jefferson Randolph, Daughter of Monticello, her life and times*, The University of North Carolina Press, Chapel Hill, 2012.

Langhorne, Elizabeth, Monticello, *A Family Story, An Intimate Portrait-In-Depth of Thomas Jefferson and His Family*, Algonquin Books of Chapel Hill, 1987.

Ledgin, L. M. Sally of Monticello, *Founding Mother, A Novel*, NM. Ledgin, KS, 2012.

Levin, Phyllis Lee, *Abigail Adams, A Biography*, Ballantine Books, New York, 1988.

Library of Congress, Washington DC, Collection of Thomas Jefferson Letters and Resource material.

Looney, J. Jefferson, Editor, *The Papers of Thomas Jefferson, Retirement Series*, Volumes 1-3, Princeton University Press, 2014.

Meacham, Jon, *Thomas Jefferson, The Art of Power*, Random House, NY, 2012.

Monticello Foundation Website: Monticello.org, Thomas Jefferson Papers, 1606-1827.

Monticello.org/site/plantation-and slavery: Christa Diesrksheide, 2008.

Morgan Library: Collection of Thomas Jefferson Letters.

New York Historical Society: Collection of Thomas Jefferson Letters.

PBS: Video of Interview between Jeffrey Brown and Annette Gordon-Reed, 2008 re: The Hemingses of Monticello.

Randolph, Sarah N., *The Domestic Life of Thomas Jefferson*, Compiled from Family Letters and Reminiscences, by his Great-Granddaughter, published for the Thomas Jefferson Memorial Foundation by the University Press of Virginia, Charlottesville, 1978.

Rice, Howard C. Jr., *Thomas Jefferson's Paris*, Princeton University Press, Princeton, NJ, 1976.

Scharff, Virginia, *The Women Jefferson Loved*, Harper, NY, 2010.

Schama, Simon, *Citizens: A Chronicle of the French Revolution*, Knopf, New York, 1989.

Sobel, Mechal, *The World They Made Together: Black and White Values in Eighteenth Century Virginia*, Princeton University Press, 1989.

Stanton, Lucia, *"Those Who Labor for My Happiness" Slavery at Thomas Jefferson's Monticello*, University of Virginia Press, Charlottesville and London, 2004, 2014, 2015, 2016.

Stanton, Lucia, *Slavery at Monticello*, Preface by Julian Bond, Thomas Jefferson Memorial Foundation, Monticello Monograph Series, 1996.

Tannenbaum, Rebecca, *Health and Wellness in Colonial America*, ebook, 2012. Through Thomas Jefferson portal at International Center for Jefferson Studies, Charlottesville, VA.

Wallace, Anthony F.C., *Jefferson and the Indians, The Tragic Fate of the First Americans*, The Belknap Press of Harvard University Press, Cambridge, MA 1999.

Wayson, Billy L., *Martha Jefferson Randolph, Republican Daughter & Plantation Mistress*, Sherwood Press, Palmyra VA, 2013.

William & Mary College, Earl Gregg Swem Library, Special Collections Database, Thomas Jefferson Papers; William Short letters.

WNYC, National Icons Series: Monticello, Podcast.

ACKNOWLEDGMENTS

First and foremost, I shower continuing appreciation on my husband, David, who laughs about living with a graduate student. He often asks, "When are you going to graduate?" as I plunge into one book after another, or take him on another "walk-in-the-footsteps" marathon tour to further understand one of my characters. As an early reader of American Triangle, he was tremendously insightful and encouraging.

Thank you also to another first reader, travel agency owner, and friend, Neil Kantrow, who has helped me with the travel for all of my research trips. I have depended on him to find transportation and lodging in many unusual places throughout the years.

Librarians are a special and superior breed of people, who always offer invaluable help. I owe a special thanks to Endrina Tay, Anna Berkes, and Jack Robertson at the International Center for Jefferson Studies at Monticello. They helped me find essential study materials and directed me through the labyrinth of extensive data troves when I was a Fellow at the Center for Jefferson Studies. The librarians at the Morgan Library, New York, and the New York Historical Society also gave me their scholarly time and effort.

I am especially indebted to Andrew Jackson O'Schaughnessy, a superb American history scholar and author, and vice president at the Jefferson Foundation, who facilitated my becoming a fellow at the ICJS at Monticello. And a thank you to the history scholar and Pultizer-prize winning author, Anne Applebaum, and my friend, Betsy Applebaum, who introduced me to Dr. O'Schaughnessy.

I highly recommend a trip to Monticello to all who haven't visited this beautiful place, so resonant of our country's past and so splendidly organized and managed by well-informed guides. It is an inspiring and informative experience.

Thank you to Connie Casey, who led me to a beautiful book by Diane Ketchum with photos from Jefferson's walks in Paris. Many thanks also to Mary Copeland, Cindy Williams, Gale Kunkel, and Jeremy Wang-Iverson.

As always, I depend on my Book Designer Nick Pirog, and on my outstanding editor, Andy Nelkin, who is also a closet historian. Writing can be an isolated experience, and all of these friends and professionals helped me to not get lost or become discouraged along the way.

AMERICAN TRIANGLE is Nelda Hirsh's third historical novel. She has also written a biography/art history book about M. Evelyn McCormick, a California Impressionist painter around the turn of the last century. She and her husband live in New York and Boulder, Colorado. Hirsh's illustrated history of American dance, *CATCH THE BEAT*, will appear in 2019.

Made in the USA
Middletown, DE
19 July 2022